W9-AHA-984

YA HUS
Husseym Charmian.
The valley of secrets

THE VALLEY OF
SECRETS

THE VALLEY OF SECRETS

Charmian Hussey

Illustrated by
Christopher Crump

SIMON & SCHUSTER BOOKS FOR YOUNG READERS

NEW YORK   LONDON   TORONTO   SYDNEY

1-7911

SIMON & SCHUSTER BOOKS FOR YOUNG READERS
An imprint of Simon & Schuster Children's Publishing Division
1230 Avenue of the Americas, New York, New York 10020
With the exception of references to H. W. Bates, I. K. Brunel, W. De Morgan, S. S. Hellyer,
W. Morris, A. W. N. Pugin, J. Shanks, A. Spruce, T. W. Twyford, A. R. Wallace, and N. H. Witt,
all characters in this publication are fictitious, and any resemblance to real persons,
living or dead, is purely coincidental.

Book design by Jo King and James Gray
The text for this book is set in Book Antiqua.
Manufactured in the United States of America
2 4 6 8 10 9 7 5 3 1
Library of Congress Cataloging-in-Publication Data
Hussey, Charmian.
The valley of secrets / Charmian Hussey ; illustrated by Christopher Crump.
—1st U.S. ed.   p. cm.
Summary: When strange events occur in his newly inherited manor house in Cornwall, England,
Stephen, a teenager who was abandoned at birth, investigates the mystery and his family history using
clues found in a travel journal kept by his great-uncle Theo
during his trip to the Amazon River region.
ISBN 0-689-87862-1
[1. Inheritance and succession—Fiction. 2. Orphans—Fiction. 3. Family—Fiction. 4. Adventure and
adventurers—Fiction. 5. Cornwall (England : County)—Fiction. 6. England—Fiction. 7. Amazon River
Region—Fiction.] I. Crump, Christopher, ill. II. Title.
PZ7.H9578 Va
[Fic]—dc22
2004013829

This book is dedicated to the peoples, the creatures, and the trees and the plants of the forests of the Amazon Basin and to my favorite county—Cornwall.

—C. H.

Contents

Acknowledgments   xi

Part One

1. Old Fernley's Round   3
2. The Copper-Brown Face   5
3. The Mysterious Letter   9
4. An Old-Fashioned Kind of Boy   14
5. Through the Archway   18
6. The One and Only Mr. Postlethwaite   22
7. The Will   26
8. The Moonflower   30
9. Fish and Chips   34
10. Cornwall, Here We Come   37
11. Toward the Unknown   40
12. A Warning   44
13. Enchanted Cornwall   48
14. Gateway to Mystery   54
15. The Face in the Mirror   59
16. The Throne Room   63
17. A Weird New Species?   67
18. That Funny Feeling   73
19. The Dancing Snake   77
20. The Graveyard   85
21. The Mystery Deepens   90
22. The Strange Call   94
23. The Sleeping Bat   101
24. Ancestors   106
25. A Family Likeness   112
26. The Swinging Eyes   116
27. Creatures of the Lake   124
28. The Phantom Gardener   130

29.	Intruders	137
30.	The Banana Burglar	140
31.	The Invisible Audience	144
32.	Thieves on the Beach	149
33.	The Secret of the Woodland Glade	152
34.	An Exciting Destination	158
35.	Another Strange Nest	164
36.	Mysterious Music	168
37.	A Very Weird Creature	174
38.	Stephen to the Rescue	179
39.	Primeval Forest	185
40.	Laughter	193
41.	Tig	200
42.	Slavery	207
43.	The Dastardly Captain	212
44.	Sarko and Wamiru	218
45.	Toward Disaster	225
46.	Bertie	230
47.	Death's Door	232
48.	Bugwompidae	237
49.	A Horrible Premonition	245
50.	Tragedy	248
51.	The Mighty Spirit	252
52.	The Gathering Gloom	258
53.	The Secret Valley	262
54.	The Heart of the Mystery	266
55.	The Cave	269
56.	The Three Orphans	276

Part Two

57.	A New Dawn	281
58.	Smugglers	283
59.	Drusilla	287
60.	So Near and Yet So Far	290
61.	Family Life	294
62.	Long, Sunny, Summer Days	299
63.	A Near Disaster	303
64.	Growing Worries	310
65.	Some of My Ways, Some of Yours	313
66.	Ablutions	317
67.	Mr. Shanks's Masterpiece	321
68.	Cleanliness Is Next to Godliness	324
69.	Something Very Nasty Indeed	329
70.	The Postlethwaite Tree	334
71.	B's Notes on Preparation	338
72.	Arara	341
73.	Hope	345
74.	Values	348
75.	Good-byes	354
76.	Mission Accomplished	357
77.	Such a Simple, Significant Act	363
78.	A Final Resting Place	367
	Epilogue	369
	Author's Note	371
	List of Species	373
	Select Bibliography	379
	Relevant Organizations	381

Acknowledgments

On a cold, gray January day in 1985, an eleven-year-old boy introduced his mother to a very strange animal—an example of a rare and endangered species, facing extinction because of the destruction of its forest habitat. And so began my researches into the origins of those animals, and thus my quest for the mysterious inhabitants of *The Valley of Secrets*.

My thanks must therefore go, firstly, to my son Nicholas Steele, whose very special brand of creativity triggered the idea for this book, and whose guidance in the early stages of the work pointed me in the right direction. I also owe a considerable debt of gratitude to Christopher Crump, not only for his superb illustrations, but also for his dedication to the project, his general help with the book, and for compiling the List of Species. Many thanks also go to my publisher, Hodder Headline, especially to Anne McNeil, Charles Nettleton, and Geraldine Stroud. And my heartfelt thanks to my agent, Peter Straus, and to all at Rogers, Coleridge, and White.

From the very beginning, I have been privileged and fortunate enough to have had the help of a number of people who are great experts in their own special fields. They have swung into the spirit of the book with enthusiasm, giving of their time and knowledge with great generosity and patience, encouraging me and enabling me to create a work that would not have been possible without their help. My special thanks are due to David Bradley and the late Percy Cyril Garnham, to Robin Hanbury-Tenison, Ghillean Prance, and Peter Rivière, all of whom first became involved in the late 1980s.

I also thank the following for expert help and advice given most generously to Christopher Crump and myself: Mary and Tony Atkinson, Gill and Tony Betts, Steve Braund, Jon and Kate Catleugh, Juliet Cleave, John Coles, Diarmid Cross, Jonathan Farmer, James Gray, Jim Hamill, Chris and Liz Hinks, Jo King, Angela Lee, Claire Longworth, Jenny March, Amanda Mason, Marie Minchington, Shirley Mount, Stuart Odgers, José Oliver, Annie and Graham Ovenden, Ron Trewellard, Fiona Watson, Hugo White, Mark Woodhams, and Caroline Yapp. Very special thanks to Roger Combe.

I thank the British Pharmacological Society, the pupils and staff of Callington Community College, the staff of Callington Library, Enterprise Edge, Enterprise Tamar, Falmouth College of Arts, Oxford University Public Relations Office, Southampton Central Library, together with the directors, curators, and staff of all those organizations cited in the list of relevant organizations.

In addition I would like to thank the following: Gail Arthur, Brian, Lee, James and Jack Aston, Faith Coles, Beth Cowan, Charles and Patricia Crump, Jean Horne and Thane Osborne; also Maggie and Michael Culver who, together with Bill and Nancy Kiely, have been involved from the very beginning. I am grateful to them all, as well as to my good friends Margaret and Ed Youle-Grayling and Pam Tandy, long-term supporters who never lost their faith in The Book, but who sadly died before they could see it come to fruition. I thank my husband, John, for his vital support, patience, and encouragement.

—Charmian Hussey
Cornwall, June 2004

THE VALLEY OF SECRETS

Part One

1. Old Fernley's Round

Old Fernley the postman was out and about early, making deliveries in his small red van. It was a bright and breezy March morning as he sped along the Cornish lanes, the heavenly blue of the sky above broken by scurrying, puffy, white clouds. He had been a postman on this route, man and boy, and he knew every inch of the way: the narrow lanes with their high, green banks; the dark, tree-tunneled tracks through the woods; and the freedom of long, gray, tarmac strips that crossed the wide, wild, open moor.

Fernley loved the springtime flowers. Sadly the snowdrops were over now, but the steep banks in the winding lanes were thick with yellow prim-roses. Celandines carpeted roadside verges; as he rushed along on his way, there were glimpses of tiny, purple violets.

"There's nothing quite like the pleasure you get from plants and flow-ers," he said to himself. "They certainly do cheer you up." And he sang as he drove along.

The sun climbed slowly in the sky as Fernley made his rounds: stopping

3

here and there to deliver the letters; pausing from time to time for a chat with a shepherd or farmer's wife, high up on the moor.

As the road was about to dip down at the very edge of the moor, Fernley stopped his van and stepped out onto the roadway. He always stopped at that spot every morning, and stood there gazing up into the sky—smiling up at his favorite pair of buzzards, wheeling and mewing high above. He'd been watching this pair for many years now; they always gave him the greatest pleasure. Broad, wide wings surfing the thermals. Eerie calls floating on the breeze.

The buzzards' nest would be down in the woodland. Later, as summer was drawing on, pathetic, incessant, mewing calls would echo through the valley below, announcing the presence of hungry offspring. Occasionally, Fernley would catch sight of a novice flier, flapping awkwardly about in the treetops. Then, miraculously, one late summer's day when he stopped at his usual place, he would look up into the sky high above him, and there he would see three figures soaring in perfect harmony.

Back in his van and driving down into the valley amongst the trees, on that glorious spring morning, Fernley was singing happily—until, that is, he rounded a corner and saw before him the high, stone walls that surrounded the estate of Lansbury Hall. An uncomfortable feeling settled upon him, as it always did at that point on his rounds. He stopped his singing, slowed his van, and coasted quietly along the lane—dark and wooded, past high mossy walls, the noise of his engine reverberating.

"It is the strangest of places, boy," Fernley muttered to himself. It gave him the shivers; he had to admit it.

Fernley was sure that there was something peculiar and something very mysterious beyond the great gates to Lansbury Hall. He had wondered about it for many years, but he'd never been able to solve the mystery.

2. The Copper-Brown Face

Lansbury Hall had always had a very funny reputation. The old estate had been taken over, some 250 years before by the Lansbury family—outsiders who were looked upon by the local people as foreigners, or "emmets," as the Cornish call them. As such they were not welcome.

The Lansburys had become especially unwelcome when the locals had discovered that they were the kind of snobbish foreigners who would demolish the original house—an interesting and very ancient, but certainly very old-fashioned, manor house—and would build up, in its place, something very smart and modern—modern, that was, for that time, long ago. Then, as if to add insult to injury, the newcomers had even rejected the proper Cornish name for the place. They had started calling it by the highfalutin name of Lansbury Hall.

"Lansbury Hall! 'Tisn't proper," it was said. "Who do they think they be?"

In truth, the new house was not quite as grand as the Lansbury family would have liked to believe. As if to compensate for this, they had commissioned from a local blacksmith a set of the most magnificent gates to stand at the entrance to the drive, a copy of some very elegant gates from somewhere "up-country"—gates that would show the locals just how special the Lansburys were.

"The trouble is," the locals said, "they've got more money than sense."

Yet, over the years, the local people had got used to the Lansbury family. They had come to accept them, in a cautious kind of way. One of the Lansburys had even married a local Cornish girl, and that had helped a lot.

Nevertheless, there were some strange stories about the Hall—some of them very strange indeed. Fernley didn't know which to believe. There was only one certainty: Lansbury Hall was now the home of the last surviving Lansbury, an old man called Theodore.

Fernley himself was, as they say, no spring chicken. The year was 1985; he had stayed on at his job for as long as he could, and was due for retirement the following year. But Mr. Theodore had lived on his own, in total isolation and seclusion at Lansbury Hall, since even before Fernley had been born. He must, by now, be a very old man.

Nobody knew how he managed, but manage he obviously did. For there was one place on Fernley's delivery route where he could just see the chimneytops of the Hall; only yesterday, he had seen smoke rising up from one of them.

"So, the old fellow must still be alive and kicking," he had told his wife that evening. "He'll be getting on toward a hundred years old. He must be a very tough old bird."

No one ever went into Lansbury Hall. And no one ever came out. Fernley could count on the fingers of one hand the number of times, over the years, that letters had arrived for Theodore Lansbury. When letters had arrived, he hadn't known what to do with them, for there was no way of getting in. The great gates to the Hall were always kept locked. All he could do was to slip the letters nervously through the bars of the gate onto the ground inside and hope that someone would pick them up.

In the village, there were rumors—whispered stories of strange noises echoing out from the old estate through the woodland and across the moors.

When Fernley was a boy, his parents had told him many times not to go anywhere near the place. Even in daylight it was unwise, his father had said. But, of course, he took no notice. Old people like his parents always had such stuffy ideas. Looking back now, still with discomfort, he remembered his foolishness—how unwise he had been in not heeding all the warnings. It had taken a strange experience to teach him respect for his father's advice.

It had all happened when he was ten years old. He had been given a splendid new bicycle for his birthday. Not a brand-new bicycle, of course, for times were very hard in those days, and such things as brand-new bikes were quite beyond the reach of his family. But it was a new bike to him—a hand-me-down from an older cousin.

Lovingly checked over by his father and freshly painted bright green, in the secrecy of a neighbor's garden shed, the bike was produced as a shining surprise for Fernley's tenth birthday. It became his pride and joy. During the summer holiday, that year, he went off on many, wonderful, long rides: first pushing biscuits into his pocket, then waving happily to his mother; setting off across the moor; stopping from time to time to munch biscuits and to enjoy the countryside.

Sometimes, his bicycle rides just happened to take him past the walls of the Lansbury Hall estate. Although he had been warned time and again to keep away from the place, he simply couldn't resist it. He had discovered a number of places where he could heave himself up a steep, stony bank, and peer down into the grounds below. Mostly there wasn't much to see, which was very disappointing—only thick overgrown woodland, stretching away into the distance. But in one of the places he had discovered a most enticing old orchard with some very fine greengage trees.

On one particular late summer's day—a day that he would never forget—Fernley was out enjoying a ride on his bike. It was hot and sunny up on the moor. The farther he went the hotter he became. The hotter and drier he became, the more he thought about juicy fruits: big, fat, juicy greengages, hanging on trees in the wonderful orchard. Quite soon, as if by sheer coincidence, he found himself cycling in that direction.

7

Getting over the wall had been simple, and sitting up in the branches was great: cool and comfortable and shady. The greengages were just at their best. He was sitting there, feasting on the fruit, noisily munching the juicy flesh and spitting out the stones with pleasure, when something made him stop and listen. He raised his head and looked out, up, across, and into the next tree. What he saw there gave him such a start. A face stared out from the leafy shadows—a very strange, copper-brown face.

Fernley let out a gasp of dismay. He didn't stop to look again; spluttering and almost choking, he slithered in panic down the tree, scraping his hands and legs as he went. Landing shaken at the bottom, he made a frantic dash for the bank, heaved himself over, and grabbed his bike. Then, wavering from side to side, he cycled desperately back to the village, as fast as his jellied legs would take him.

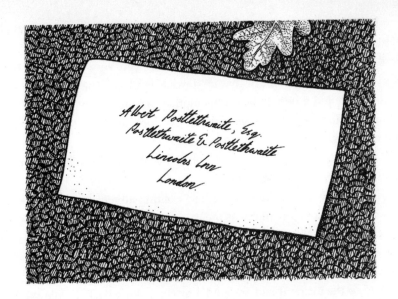

Albert Postlethwaite, Esq.
Postlethwaite & Postlethwaite
Lincolns Inn
London.

3. The Mysterious Letter

Fernley was a very sorry sight by the time he finally got back home. His hands and legs had bled quite badly. He was burning hot and wet all over, with squashed fruit mess all down his shirt. His face was a very bright shiny red.

After rushing indoors, he was promptly sick in the bathroom basin, to the great distress of his mother, but to the considerable delight of his small sister, Loveday. She always enjoyed an exciting happening, especially if it was to Fernley's disadvantage. At teatime, he had been pleased to see her sitting uncomfortably at the table, with such big, round, frightened eyes, whilst he told his colorful story—the story of the strange, brown face. He made it all as vivid as possible.

Fernley wasn't quite sure whether his parents believed the story or not. They glanced uncomfortably at each other. Then they tried to play it all down.

"Probably heat stroke and too many greengages," his mother said, with a forced little smile. "You forget all about it, m'beauty."

His father only gave him a warning glare. A sort of "I told you so" kind of glare, and he went on tucking into his pot pie.

Later Fernley realized that they had not been very impressed by his story. Perhaps they thought that he'd made it all up. The next day he was so disappointed when he heard his mother talking in the garden. She was telling the story over the fence to their next-door neighbor, Mrs. Pascoe, but she was emphasizing all the wrong bits.

"Yes! Sick as a gannet, he were," he heard his mother say. "It serves him right. He were sick as a gannet."

He had hoped that the story of his "exciting adventure"—for, now that he was fully recovered, that was the way that he liked to think of it—would have impressed Mrs. Pascoe's son, Walter, who was the same age as himself and something of a rival at school. But Walter and his skinny, sticky-faced little sister, Morwenna, had stood there in the garden laughing.

And so the incident had ended. Later on, looking back, Fernley couldn't help wondering why he had panicked and been so frightened. For he had to admit—if only to himself—that he had been badly frightened.

"I suppose it was guilt," he had said to himself. "Being somewhere where you shouldn't be."

"Trespassing and stealing fruit," P. C. Pengelly would probably call it. Fernley might even be labeled a "Thief"!

P. C. Pengelly was the local police officer, a seemingly enormous man with extremely large boots. He cycled around his beat each day, and, in some mysterious way, always knew or managed to find out who was doing what and where. He was well respected and popular with the locals, a very kindly man, as long as you did the things that you should—and none of the things that you shouldn't. But if you overstepped the mark and got into trouble with P. C. Pengelly, he was a force to be reckoned with—a force to be taken seriously.

Fernley wanted, above all things, to avoid upsetting the policeman. He had seen the effect of the man's displeasure on a number of other boys; he knew they had not enjoyed the experience. So he kept indoors for several days, hoping the whole thing would blow over; but that only meant he had more time for thinking.

The more Fernley thought about the face, the more he came to the conclusion that it had been a friendly face. A very kindly, amused, brown face. A face with very bright, dark, shining eyes.

Or had he seen a face at all? After a time, he wasn't sure. Perhaps he had imagined it.

As time went by, looking back, it all seemed rather like a dream. But it kept him away from Lansbury Hall. He had an odd feeling about the place, and he never went anywhere near it again—not for a very, very long time. Not, that is, until he left school and, taking his job as a postman, he found, somewhat to his dismay, that his regular daily delivery route took him beside the walls and right past the great gates.

In the early days, his rounds had always been made by bicycle, with the letters and packages in a big canvas bag that hung in a metal frame attached to the front of his bike. He had scuttled along beside the walls and past the gates as quickly as possible, trying not to look back.

When Fernley had finally been given his first red delivery van, it had been absolutely wonderful. He could still remember so clearly the very first time that he'd sat in the van; how he'd driven the van with such pride.

Shaking off his memories and coming back to the present, Fernley suddenly realized that he was almost level with the gates of the Hall. Over the years, from the safety of his delivery van, he had been in the habit of slowing down as he passed the gates, always hopeful that he might see something that would give him a clue to the mystery.

But he had found that looking through the gates didn't really help at all; he could only see a very short distance down the drive. The huge rhododendron bushes and trees that had once lined the drive—presumably in an orderly fashion—were now so completely overgrown that, in some places, they touched in the middle, providing a depressingly dark, dank screen— a screen of perfect privacy for whatever it was that lay beyond.

In all the years that Fernley had been driving slowly past the gates, and on the very few occasions when he had nervously slipped across the road to drop a letter through the bars, he had never seen any sign of anyone. He always looked as he drove by, but he had long since given up expecting to see anything interesting.

But on this occasion, it was different. As he came toward the gates, he caught a glimpse of some kind of movement. Then, as he slowed his van, a long, brown arm appeared through the bars, and something thin and white and rectangular was tossed out into the road ahead.

Fernley slammed his foot on the brake. The van came to a slithering halt, the engine stalling as it did so. The white rectangle, caught by the breeze, whirled then settled and lay in the road.

"Well, I be blowed!" he said in amazement. "Whatever's going on?"

He lowered his window very quietly, then sat watching and listening intently. There was silence. Complete silence, as if the trees, the birds, and whoever were all holding their breath and waiting—waiting for Fernley to do something.

Opening the door of his van very carefully, Fernley sat staring across at the gates. His left eye had started to twitch—an irritating nervous reaction. When he couldn't stand it any longer, he stepped out cautiously onto the rough tarmac.

When nothing happened, he called out, "Hello! Anyone there?"

Silence.

And then again, "Is there anybody there?"

Nothing. Pulling himself together with a grunt, he walked slowly around to the front of the van. No wind stirred the trees now. His footsteps seemed peculiarly noisy in a crunchy kind of way.

The white rectangle lay temptingly in the middle of the road. It was only a few yards away. Yet something made Fernley hesitate.

"What a ninny I am," he said, finally going boldly forward and stooping down to pick up the letter.

The envelope was clean and posh—a very good quality, heavy, white paper; Fernley was used to assessing these things. It was a superior letter, but the flap was, unfortunately, firmly stuck down. He peered closely at the address, beautifully written in an old-fashioned hand.

"Albert Postlethwaite, Esquire," he read, "Postlethwaite and Postlethwaite," and then an address somewhere in London.

"Well, I never!" he said to himself, climbing slowly back into his van.

Fernley's left eye was slowing down now into an occasional twitch that no longer troubled him. He sat studying the envelope thoughtfully. It was, indeed, a handsome envelope, but there was no stamp on it. He couldn't put it into his bag—not without a proper stamp.

Now, fortunately, Fernley was a very kind man. Some other, less caring person, might simply have thrown the letter away, probably into the nearest ditch, or chucked the letter into the van and simply forgotten all about it. But turning the envelope over in his hands, with a thoughtful look on his face, Fernley came to a quick decision. He reached inside his jacket pocket, took out his wallet, and found a stamp—a rather tired-looking stamp, from which he carefully removed fluff and hairs. Wetting it thoroughly with his tongue, he pressed it firmly onto the envelope. Then with a satisfied smile on his face, he slipped the letter into his mailbag.

Birds sang in the woodland now, and trees moved gently in the breeze, their leaves whispering overhead. Fernley drove off down the lane, singing a cheerful song out loud, feeling rather pleased with himself at having done the day's good deed.

And what a lovely day it was. Perhaps he would just have enough time to stop off at home to enjoy a cup of coffee and a chat with Morwenna.

"What a funny old world it is," he said out loud to himself as he drove. "Just to think that that skinny maid turned into such a pretty, young gal. And what a very fine wife she has made me, all these many, long years."

It is, indeed, a very strange world. But Fernley couldn't possibly have known quite how strange the world was—the world that was lurking behind the walls and the great gates of Lansbury Hall. Nor could he have imagined, ever, the wonderful chain reaction of events that he himself had set in motion by kindly picking up the letter and sending it safely on its way.

4. An Old-Fashioned Kind of Boy

Stephen sat thoughtfully in his small bed-sitting room in London. It was a very drab room, the window looking out onto the discolored brick walls and dirty chimneys of the city. Staring blankly around the room, he felt that even his favorite posters did very little to brighten the place; they only served to emphasize the dullness and the grayness of everything else around him, and especially, on that miserable morning, the dull gray thoughts that filled his mind.

Whatever was he going to do? How and where was he going to live now?

"If only I had a proper family," he said out loud to himself. "If only I had my own real family and a proper home to go to."

How many times had he said such things! But thinking and saying those things didn't help. In fact, it only made him feel worse, because it made him feel quite guilty. He'd had a very kindly upbringing in the children's home. He would always be grateful to his house parents; they'd loved him and looked after him well.

Stephen sat there thinking about them, and thinking about the past. He had so hated school; and, of course, he had never done well. He seemed to have such a lot of problems—problems with writing and spelling and math, although his reading wasn't too bad. But the problems had always made him different—teased, withdrawn, and rather shy, pretending to be one of the boys, yet sharing few of their ideas and interests. "A very old-fashioned kind of boy," the teachers said. "A loner and probably not very bright."

Stephen had never succeeded at any normal school subjects, but his interest in wildlife and botany was so great that, encouraged by his house parents, he had become knowledgeable about many aspects of the natural world. So much so, that even this went against him; it only gave the other children more ammunition for taunting him and for calling him horrible names like "The Boffin."

It had all been one long, painful battle. But his house parents had been proud of his few achievements. It was they who had arranged for him to take a special course in London: a course for pupils who had had difficulties; a course that focused on all his favorite subjects—biology, zoology, and wildlife conservation. Stephen had enjoyed it enormously, even though joining the course had meant having to leave the home, and coming to live in this small, dingy room, with his landlady, Mrs. Johnson, keeping a close eye on him.

The special course had just come to an end; Stephen was feeling at a loss. All the other students were busy packing, going back home to their families. He could go back to the children's home, but he didn't want to do that. So he couldn't help wishing all over again that he had a proper family—and a proper home to go to. Once Stephen started thinking of families, he always started feeling troubled, because he still didn't know who he was or where he had come from in the first place.

He only knew that he'd been abandoned as a small baby, left with a childminder by a pretty, well-dressed, young woman who had said that her baby's name was Stephen. But no one had ever returned to claim him. The woman, according to the childminder, had a "funny foreign accent"; but, even though she had left a surname, the authorities had never managed to

15

trace her. She had simply disappeared. What sort of mother would do such a thing? She couldn't have loved her baby. Could she?

As Stephen had grown up, he had tried hard not to wonder and worry too much about his background; tried not to care about it at all; tried to pretend that it didn't matter, which was easier said than done. If the authorities at the time hadn't been able to trace his mother, he couldn't see much point in attempting to do so himself. He had come to realize over the years that he had to make the best of things. It was just the same now—he would have to make the best of things.

All the same, he couldn't help wishing . . .

Getting up and crossing the room, Stephen opened the window and gazed out. Although it was June, the sky was dark; thick, low clouds were pressing down on a forest of sooted chimneys. The rain, falling heavily now, splashed in the blackened, oily gutters; and cars, as they rushed through the streets below, with all their noise and foul fumes, shot filthy waters onto the pavement.

All his life, Stephen had longed for space. He had dreamed of open space and freedom. He had longed to live in the countryside with clean fresh air and fields and woods. He had longed for the greenness of it all. Now he wanted it more than ever.

If he stood on tiptoe, he could just see the tops of a number of trees, standing in sad and grimy groups in a small square several streets away. You couldn't pretend they were very green, but nevertheless, it was comforting just to know that they were there. At least a small piece of the natural world was only a few steps away from his room.

During the past year, Stephen had managed to make two or three trips out into the countryside. On each occasion, he'd returned to his room with his arms full of foliage. Other passengers in the bus had not been too amused, having him sitting next to them with Old Man's Beard dangling over their heads and beech twigs sticking into their ears. But he hadn't cared. The wonderful form and color of the foliage had decorated his dowdy room; it had given him weeks of pleasure. There was nothing like plants and leaves and flowers to brighten a place and to cheer you up.

Thinking about the trees and their foliage made him think about the forests. Every time you picked up a paper or turned on the radio or even the television, there it was—the news of destruction of the world's great forests. Once it had seemed fashionable to care. But was anyone doing anything now? Or had they just got used to it?

He paced up and down the room, overwhelmed by the sickening feeling of helpless anger and frustration that always overcame him whenever he thought of chopping and burning.

He stood at last at the open window, gazing dreamily into the gloom and imagining himself, as he often did, walking through some mighty forest, the tall trees reaching high above, the green depths stretching on and on. A loud knocking at his door brought him sharply back to reality.

"There's a letter for you, Stephen," he heard Mrs. Johnson's voice.

Who on earth could this be now, with such a businesslike long, brown envelope? He sat down on the edge of the bed, turning the envelope over in his hands, surveying the postmark very closely, savoring the moment, and wondering, then slitting it carefully open at one end, noting with surprise the heading—some lawyer, somewhere in London. He read the letter slowly out loud:

> Dear Sir,
> Please come to this office at some time in the near future, when you will learn something to your advantage.
> Office hours are strictly from ten till twelve in the morning, and from two till four in the afternoon, weekdays only.
> Yours faithfully . . .

There followed a scribbled, unreadable signature.

Stephen was intrigued by the letter. He read it through carefully several times, each time feeling that, if he read it through yet again, he might find in it some vital clue as to what it was all about. There was no clue. He made a decision. He would have to go and find out about it. He would do it that very afternoon.

5. Through the Archway

After a hasty lunch and a quick look at the telephone directory, Stephen set out through the London streets with the mysterious letter tucked in his pocket. As he walked, he wondered and worried. What on earth could it mean?

Had somebody finally traced his family? Surely, it must be something like that. Though that would be much too good to be true. Yet it seemed like the only possible explanation. Why else would a lawyer write to him?

The farther Stephen went, the more excited he became. Everything seemed to be looking up. Even the weather was improving. The clouds were thinning to show small patches of blue sky. The sun would soon be breaking through.

Stephen looked anxiously down at himself, as he made his way along the streets. He knew that he wasn't properly dressed for visiting a smart lawyer's office. It made him feel uncomfortable, but he'd done the best he could.

He was of medium height, rather slightly built, with a thick thatch of straight, brown hair. His eyes were that funny sort of color people usually call "hazel." He was altogether rather ordinary looking, he supposed, and he still longed to be bigger and taller and much more dashing in appearance. And then there were the problem spots. A number of the pesky things always seemed to be in attendance, scattered across his forehead and chin, a source of continual dismay and scowls whenever he looked at himself in the mirror. He had waged a constant war against them with a whole battalion of "special preparations," guaranteed to wipe out spots, but all, alas, apparently useless.

People said that Stephen had a kind face and nice eyes. He supposed he ought be grateful for that. Somehow, it didn't seem to help. What he didn't realize was that he had a very beautiful smile—a rare smile, which, when it happened, lit up his eyes and transformed his face, making him look almost handsome.

Years of training at the children's home and the continual insistence that you must be clean and tidy had finally made some impression upon him, somewhere along the line; so before he had left home that afternoon, he had carefully washed his hands and face, and thoroughly brushed his teeth.

He had also had a go at his hair, which never behaved the way that it should. Free at last from the rules at the children's home, he had been trying to grow it longer, but there was always that difficult bit at the front, which would insist on hanging down over his forehead. He had swung it back and into place, running a hand through his hair as he did so—an old, familiar, well-tried gesture, which had become a nervous habit.

"Clothing is always such a problem," Stephen had mumbled to himself whilst preparing himself for his visit—trying to make up his mind what to wear, with a heavy frown on his face. Which of his three pairs of jeans looked the best? Which was the newest? Which was the cleanest?

His old green parka would have to do, because he didn't have anything else. And, provided he watched where he walked and avoided all the puddles, he could wear his old, black sneakers, which were the tidiest shoes that he had, but not exactly waterproof. His only pair of leather boots creaked in the most embarrassing way. He certainly couldn't face wearing those. He had recently seen and greatly fancied a splendid pair of black leather boots in a shop not far from his lodgings, but the price had put them right out of his reach, and so, as usual, he would have to make do.

Stephen was heading for Lincoln's Inn, which was right next door to the Law Courts. It was an area in which many important attorneys had their offices, or chambers, as Stephen knew they should be called. On arrival he discovered that most of the buildings were large and elegant with spacious courtyards and fine trees.

On the wall beside the entrance to each set of chambers, there was a big bank of brass plates, each plate inscribed with the name of a lawyer—smart, polished plates, and smart-sounding names. Stephen's confidence dwindled away. The lawyer's office was bound to be posh.

He wandered around feeling more and more lost, unable to find the correct address; no one seemed to have heard of the place. Having wasted so much time, he was getting very worried. If this went on, he was sure to be late. The office would close at four o'clock. He couldn't bear the horrible thought of having to wait another day before finding out about the letter.

At last, turning in through an old stone archway, he found himself in a small, cobbled yard. This had to be the right place. He'd recognized the name on the archway. But Stephen lost more valuable time scurrying around the yard, first checking two rather grand doorways, only to end up, eventually, standing in front of a scruffy, old door. The paintwork was chipped and the fittings unpolished. It was not at all what he'd expected.

Out of breath and anxious, he knocked on the door, but almost before his hand left the knocker, the door was pulled open from within; a girl came running out—a girl with a mass of dark-brown hair and friendly, smiling, blue-gray eyes.

"Hello!" she called out brightly to Stephen, as she darted quickly past. "And good-bye!" as she rushed away.

Stephen had jumped to one side, embarrassed. He wasn't very good with girls. They seemed like a different species to him.

A young man, wearing a smart pin-striped suit, appeared in the doorway.

The hallway behind him looked dark and narrow; Stephen could smell dank, musty air. It seemed the most unlikely place. He pulled the letter out of his pocket, showing it to the young man—to make quite sure he was in the right place.

"Oh, yes," said the man, glancing at the letter. "This is the place that you're looking for." He had a very broad grin on his face; he seemed to be finding something amusing.

"You'll have to go right to the top of the building." He pointed to a flight of stairs. "And the best of luck to you. You're certainly going to need it," he called out, laughing in a peculiar way, then disappearing into a side room, closing the door very firmly behind him.

If Stephen had had more time to think, he might have wondered about the man's words. As it was, he was so pleased to have found the right place, and so anxious about the time that he didn't stop to think at all, but sped as quickly as he could up the steep and winding stairs.

On the very top landing he found a door, and beside the door an old brass plate—a dull and dirty brass plate that obviously hadn't been polished for ages. Stephen stood peering at the plate, out of breath and panting hard, frowning and trying to read the inscription. Then he stood back with a smile of relief.

Yes. This was the very place that he wanted. This was the name he'd been looking for.

Postlethwaite & Postlethwaite
Solicitors

6. The One and Only Mr. Postlethwaite

Stephen stood for several moments outside the door of Postlethwaite and Postlethwaite, getting his breath back and looking anxiously at his watch. It was nearly five minutes to four.

"Phew. I'm just about in time. I hope it's going to be alright." He knocked nervously on the door.

A muffled voice came from within, so he opened the door and stepped into the room.

During the journey there, Stephen hadn't thought much about what he expected to find in the offices of Postlethwaite and Postlethwaite. But whatever he might have expected to see, he could never, ever have imagined the extraordinary sight that met his eyes. His mouth dropped open in amazement, as he stood in the doorway staring.

The Postlethwaite office was a large room. It was well lit by two deep windows and by a huge skylight, set in the roof high above. The sun, breaking through the clouds at last, shone down through the skylight and into a wilderness of greenery.

Stephen had never seen anything like it before. The walls of the room were almost completely hidden by what could only be described as rampant plant growth. The room glowed green with lush vegetation: enormous leaves with their polished surfaces shining brightly in the sun; long, pale, elegant, transparent bracts shimmering gently in the light; giant ferns with their pointing fingers poking boldly out toward him; creepers with long, gray, leathery trunks reaching up to the skylight itself, only to hang back down again in a wild profusion of tangled growth.

Along one of the walls there was something that looked as if it might be a large bookcase, but this was almost totally obscured by a writhing mass of climbing plants. These, like the rest of the plants in the room, were growing out of a series of large pots.

The warm, damp air, which engulfed Stephen and seemed to hold him transfixed, was filled with a heavy perfume. Here and there he could see strange flowers—vividly colored, exotic blooms, hanging down on long stems, peeping out from behind the foliage or thrusting out from between the leaves.

In the very middle of all this, seated at a large desk and peering out through a gap in the foliage, was a very ancient man. His long, pale face had thin, sharp features, and a wispy mass of pure-white hair stuck out around his head like a halo, spreading down and around his shoulders.

Had the old man been dressed in clothing better suited to his surroundings, the scene, as a whole, might not have struck Stephen as so odd. But the old lawyer's clothes looked quite absurd in this most unusual setting, for he was properly attired for a gentleman of his profession: black jacket—very clean and tidy—if a little shiny; a high collar and formal tie. As he tottered to his feet and leaned forward across the desk, smart, pin-striped trousers could be seen.

Stephen closed his mouth with a gulp. It was all he could do to hold back the laughter that was welling up inside him. But the smile that was creeping onto his face was very quickly wiped away by the old man's angry expression and by his words, which were far from welcoming.

"And what do you think you are doing here, walking in and disturbing my plants?" the old man asked in a menacing whisper. "No one, but no one comes in here and disturbs my plants at this time of day. I am just about to see to them all. I must ask you to leave—immediately!"

As Stephen opened his mouth to respond—to apologize for his late arrival—the old man threw up an agitated arm; pressing a long bony finger across his angry pursed-up lips, he jiggled about behind the desk, feverishly hushing Stephen down.

"Sssh! Don't speak so loudly," he hissed. "My plants aren't used to it. And they don't like it." He glared angrily at Stephen.

"There! There! My old friends. Hush now! Hush! Hush! Hush!" He was looking anxiously all around the room, making the gentle, hushing sounds.

Stephen looked slowly around at the plants, as if he expected to see some reaction. All was still and very peaceful; the only sounds were the murmur of traffic, and the steady drip, drip, drip of a tap at a sink in the corner of the room.

With a loud sigh and a heavy scowl, the old man sat back down in his chair. "Well, I suppose you had better come and tell me what it is that you want; but I certainly can't spare you much time. Close the door behind you. And do it very quietly," he added with a glare. "It's a very critical time, you know. A very critical time indeed."

Having closed the door as quietly as possible, Stephen tiptoed across the room, and came to stand nervously in front of the big desk. The old man was sitting in an almost trancelike state, staring into the foliage that overhung the desk. Following his gaze, Stephen found himself looking at a peculiar plant.

A large earthenware pot was standing beside the desk in a low trough filled with water. Quite a good-sized tree grew up from the pot, its branches reaching and fanning out well above Stephen's head. This, in itself, was unusual and interesting. But the thing that now caught Stephen's eye, and held his total attention, was the most extraordinary plant—a plant with thick, fleshy, green and scarlet leaves. It seemed to be growing out of the tree trunk. One long limb grew over the desk, and from the limb there sprouted a bud—a huge, fat, cream-colored flower bud.

"Now. What do you want with me, young man?"

The hissing voice made Stephen jump. He dragged his eyes away from the plant.

"Are you a Mr. Postlethwaite?" he asked, nervously running a hand through his hair.

The scowl on the aged, wrinkled face deepened.

"I am not merely a Mr. Postlethwaite," he retorted. "I am the one and only Mr. Postlethwaite."

The sharp, old eyes glared challengingly.

"Oh. I'm sorry. I didn't realize. Err. Umm," Stephen stammered.

"Well, will you please get on with it quickly, young man. I have already told you that I haven't any time now." He glanced hurriedly back at the flower bud. "Come along now. What is this all about?"

Stephen fumbled in his pocket, drawing out the now-crumpled letter. His hands felt odd and rather shaky, as he made an effort to flatten it out, to make it look presentable. He held it out across the desk.

"You sent me this letter," he said, as boldly as he could. "And I have come, as you asked. I am Stephen. Stephen Lansbury."

7. The Will

Mr. Albert Postlethwaite, lawyer for many, many more years than he cared to remember, propped his spectacles on the end of his nose and took a quick look at the letter. Then he took a good, long look over the top of the spectacles at the figure standing in front of him. "Yes. So you are," he said at long last. "I can see that you are, indeed, Stephen Lansbury." The old man's face relaxed a little.

"I think that you had better sit down. You may take that chair," his bony finger indicated. "But watch how you go," he added sharply.

Very gently, Stephen lifted up the long dangling arm of an exotic and colorful plant, which was hanging over the back of the chair and down across the seat. He draped it carefully along the front edge of the desk.

Mr. Postlethwaite seemed to approve. He nodded comfortably, his fierce expression softening considerably.

"You like plants then, young man?" He eyed Stephen over the top of his glasses.

"Oh, yes. Very much," Stephen answered quickly and truthfully.

"Good. Good. Good. Good . . ." The old man's voice faded away as he shuffled through a pile of soggy documents.

Stephen sank lower in his chair, waiting quietly but anxiously.

"Ah, yes! Here it is. This is your Great-Uncle Theodore's will."

Stephen shot upright in the chair.

The old man waved a large, folded document tied up with a narrow, pink ribbon. Stephen stared at him in amazement. Then he stared at the document, clutched in the old and gnarled hand.

"My what?" he gasped. "My Great-Uncle Theodore? Who on earth is he?"

"Why, Theodore Lansbury, of course, your great-uncle on your father's side." The old man was clearly exasperated.

"I didn't even know that I had an uncle. I didn't know I had any relatives." Stephen was starting to feel rather funny. A long, cold shiver shook his body—one of those shivers when people say that there's someone walking over your grave.

"Well, you have," Mr. Postlethwaite snapped back. "Or, rather, I should say that you had. He died in the spring and this is his will.

"Now, here is a copy for you," he continued, folding the will and slipping it into an extraordinarily long, brown envelope. "You must take it with you, and you must read the contents. Please make sure that you note them carefully. If you don't fulfill the conditions of the will—if you don't do what it says you should do, or if you do things that it says that you shouldn't—you will lose everything."

"Lose everything? What do you mean?" Stephen asked.

"Why, lose your inheritance, of course, boy!"

Stephen felt quite stunned and confused.

"I don't understand. Can you, please, explain. Who was Great-Uncle Theodore? And how did he know about me? And why haven't I heard of him before, and . . ."

"I am very sorry," the old man interrupted. "But I haven't got time for all that now. It's a very, very long story. All that you need to know is that under the terms of Theodore Lansbury's will, you now inherit Lansbury

27

Hall. It will be your home—to own and to look after. Provided that you do all the right things, of course." He narrowed his eyes, glaring warningly at Stephen over the top of his spectacles.

"Take the will," he added more kindly. "And here is a one-way ticket to Cornwall. You must get down there as quickly as possible, so that you can take care of things."

"Oh, please, Mr. Postlethwaite!" Stephen begged. "I don't understand. I don't understand." His mind was awhirl with dozens of questions.

But then, to Stephen's utter dismay, the old lawyer suddenly added, in a super-polite and professional voice, "Thank you very much for calling," and then he simply turned away.

It was a ludicrous situation. Stephen sat there on his chair, completely stumped and very upset. He pushed back the irritating lock of hair that had fallen as usual across his forehead, running his hands through his hair as he did so.

"Please, Mr. Postlethwaite," he begged. Panic began to rise inside him. Here was the chance that he'd always wanted—the chance to find out about his family. Yet it looked as if the interview were over. He'd hardly begun to ask any questions, let alone get any answers.

"I just don't understand," he tried again, with a note of desperation in his voice. "What do you mean—take care of things? What things?"

Mr. Postlethwaite turned back toward him, and said with a loud and impatient sigh, "I don't have time to discuss it now. You'll find out about it quite soon enough.

"Oh, yes," he added, with a sinister, knowing, little smile. "You'll find out all about it, soon. And I am sure you will cope with it—one way or another. What you must remember is—there is very little money left. You will have to manage as best you can."

He glared at Stephen. Then, after fumbling amongst the papers again, he drew out a small package. "Here is one hundred pounds for you to be going on with," he said. "I shall send you more money in due course, when everything has been sorted out. Now, I can't tell you any more. You must get down there as quickly as possible."

This was clearly the cue for Stephen to leave. The old man propped his elbow on the desk, sank his chin in his hand, and, turning his whole attention away from Stephen, sat there gazing at the flower bud.

That, so it seemed, was the end of the interview.

8. The Moonflower

Feeling stunned by all that had happened, Stephen hardly knew what to think. It didn't look as if he were going to get any more information out of Mr. Postlethwaite. During the conversation, his attitude had softened a little. But now he was looking quite unapproachable. Stephen didn't dare to ask any more questions. So he too just sat there, staring at the fascinating plant that seemed to dominate the room.

Eventually, he was roused by a quiet voice.

"Isn't it a beauty," Mr. Postlethwaite said.

Turning to look at him, Stephen was amazed to see that the old man's face, previously so sharp and angry, was now transformed by a beaming smile—a somewhat crooked, toothless smile, but a smile of pure delight.

"It is a beauty, isn't it? I have been waiting for this day for a very long time. All these years, I have been hoping that a flower bud would form. And now, here it is at last!"

"What sort of plant is it?" Stephen found the courage to ask.

"It's called *Selenicereus*." The Latin name tripped easily off the old man's tongue.

"Se-len-i-serious." Stephen experimented with the word. It certainly was a serious plant. Though he realized that the name probably wasn't spelled like that at all. "Oh! Really? How interesting!" He kept a very serious face and tried as hard as he could to look knowledgeable.

"It is also called the Moonflower," the old man continued. "The flower opens at night, do you see. It opens in the light of the moon. But it only lasts one night, sadly, closing again before dawn, never to reopen."

"It is a very beautiful plant," Stephen said carefully.

"Oh, yes. It is, indeed, most beautiful. But it is also a very sad plant, because this Moonflower you see before you, may well be the last one left in the world. Or, if it isn't the last one yet—it soon will be." The old voice was filled with anger and grief.

Stephen longed to question this. How and why had Mr. Postlethwaite come to such an extraordinary conclusion? But the old man's closed expression forbade any more questioning.

They sat sadly and quietly together, gazing at the Moonflower.

"It is a great bonus for me," Mr. Postlethwaite said, suddenly and conversationally. "I didn't know that I'd got it, do you see. I brought the tree back as a small sapling. I didn't know that I'd got the Moonflower plant until it suddenly sprouted out. My word! What an exciting day that was." The thin, gray face lit up with pleasure.

"Of course, it was only a tiny sprout to begin with," he continued. "I have waited all these years for a flower bud to form. And now at last the time has come. I believe that tonight the flower should open, as long as the moon is just right." He looked up anxiously at the skylight.

"That's why I'm so anxious." It was almost, but not quite, an apology.

"Plants are such sensitive beings," he continued. "A kind word and even a smile does them a power of good, don't you know."

They sat together smiling at the plant.

The flower bud was several inches in length, the lower section encased in a calyx of pink sepals that protected the folded petals. Only the tips of the petals protruded at the top of the sheathlike calyx, and these looked creamy white in color.

"It looks as if the petals are going to be white," Stephen ventured. "Do you think the flower might have a beautiful, bright, and colorful center?"

Now that Mr. Postlethwaite seemed so much more relaxed and kinder in manner, Stephen was gaining confidence. The question was asked, as much as anything, as a way of making conversation. Besides, he was genuinely interested; he wanted to know more about the Moonflower.

As soon as the words were out of his mouth, however, he realized that asking the question had been a mistake, although he didn't, at first, see why.

Mr. Postlethwaite turned slowly toward him, his eyes narrowing, as he glowered at him over the top of his spectacles.

"A beautiful, bright, and colorful center!" he exclaimed in a disgusted voice. "You young people today! You always seek the sensational! I have no idea what color the center of the Moonflower will be." He was obviously very offended.

"Of course," he continued, "I shall look forward to finding out, but I am not expecting anything special. Which means that I shall find it beautiful. And be more than satisfied—because I am not expecting too much. Do you see what I mean by that?"

Settling back down again, he nodded his old silver-gray head wisely; the angry expression softened slowly.

"People who expect too much are always disappointed. You would do well to remember that, my boy."

Stephen felt so uncomfortable. "I'm really very sorry," he said.

"No, no, my boy. No need to apologize." The old man was almost smiling. "Just take things as they come. And, as you go through life, find as much good as you possibly can. But never expect too much from life.

"I have always had to remember that," he added, sighing loudly and looking around the room. "All my life, I have wanted freedom, the sort of freedom that you now have, to do the things that you want to do. But I was stuck in this wretched office. Stuck behind this horrible desk. Now, I don't have anything else." His voice was bitter, so bitter.

"Of course, I have had my plants with me. All my dear, old friends, as you see." He smiled ruefully around the room.

"And there was a time, a wonderful time . . ." The voice broke and faded out. The old eyes, pale and misty, gazed unseeing across the room.

"Now go!" he suddenly snapped. "I haven't got time for all this nonsense."

Stephen rose hurriedly from the chair. He picked up the long, brown envelope and the packet of money, then backed away across to the door. There were so many questions he wanted to ask, but the old man seemed so upset. He knew that it was too late now.

He opened the door, and turned to say good-bye, his eyes irresistibly drawn back toward the big flower bud.

A frail smile was creeping across the old man's face. "It's going to be tonight, I think. Yes. I'm sure. It will be tonight." He couldn't keep the excitement out of his voice.

"All these years, I have waited and waited. And now it's going to be tonight!"

"I'm so glad for you," Stephen said. With one last smiling glance round the room, he closed the door very quietly behind him and went off down the winding stairs.

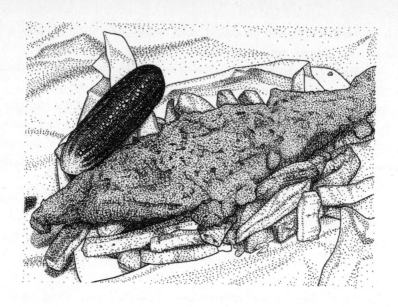

9. Fish and Chips

It was late in the evening and quite dark by the time Stephen arrived back at his bed-sitting room. He had stopped at the fish and chip shop on the corner. Fish and chips were a luxury these days because they were so expensive; but with the hundred pounds in his pocket, he was feeling more secure than usual, and he was ravenously hungry.

Fish and chips were Stephen's favorite food. He sat now, in his room, drinking a large mug of hot tea and eating the tasty food out of the paper— delicious, succulent, crunchy chips and crispy, golden battered fish, together with a long, green, juicy dill pickle. It was a scrumptious meal.

But despite the excellent food, Stephen felt exhausted. It had, after all, been the most extraordinary day. The outcome of his visit to Mr. Postlethwaite's office—the knowledge of his having apparently inherited someplace called Lansbury Hall—was overwhelming.

He kept saying to himself, "It's quite absurd! It's absolutely ridiculous! How could I possibly own a place called Lansbury Hall in Cornwall?"

And yet, he supposed, he would have to accept it. For there it was in front of him. There it was. Old Theodore Lansbury's will, in a very long, brown envelope, propped against the tomato ketchup bottle on the table.

Of course, he had no idea what the place was like. He remembered the old man's warning—about not expecting too much in life. Perhaps that was a hint to him. Perhaps, the place was no more than a tiny, scruffy cottage; although "Hall" sounded rather grand.

Having finished the fish and chips, Stephen wadded up the paper and aimed it at the rubbish bin. He cleared and wiped the table carefully, withdrew the will from its very long envelope, undid the pink ribbon, and spread the document on the table. The wording was horribly complicated; but his name was clearly there—"Stephen Lansbury, sole beneficiary." There followed a long paragraph about conditions, but Stephen was much too weary to sort all that out now.

He sat back in his chair, thinking. As far as he could see, there were only a couple of problems: to come up with a good story for Mrs. Johnson as to why and where he was going, then to send a postcard to his house parents, telling them that he would be staying with a friend for the summer. That ought to keep them happy, until he had got himself established.

The rent for his room was paid until the end of the week; but there was absolutely no reason why he should stay until then. He already had his train ticket. There was nothing to stop him from getting his few bits and pieces together the next morning, packing his rucksack, and setting off for Cornwall straightaway.

With this plan in mind, he fell into bed. Longing for sleep, he lay there tossing restlessly, the strange events of the afternoon going round and round in his head—swirling, so it seemed, in a wild profusion of foliage.

The strange atmosphere of Mr. Postlethwaite's office had made Stephen feel uncomfortable. He had taken it all very seriously at the time, but, looking back on it now with his usual sense of humor, he couldn't help finding it very amusing.

What a hoot—all that hushing and whispering, so as not to upset the plants. Suppose he had worn his old boots—the ones with the very loud squeak—that would have been a real disaster. Stephen smiled to himself in the darkness. There was something rather endearing about poor old Mr. P., despite his bitterness.

If only he hadn't been so involved with his leafy friends, Stephen might have got more information out of him. Not being able to get any proper answers to his questions had been very frustrating, although he had to admit to himself that he'd found all the wonderful plants exciting. The Postlethwaite office was like a private, miniature, tropical forest, with its lush profusion of greenery and its strange exotic flowers. His thoughts kept turning back to the Moonflower—to the great bud, pointing on its stalk, waiting patiently for the moon.

And as the moon rose that night and shone in brightly through Stephen's window, filling his room with glowing light, he lay there, gazing up at the ceiling, imagining the scene in the Postlethwaite office: the old man sitting there, quietly, devotedly, waiting expectantly with his plants; the moon stealing its silent path across the arc of the black night sky, until at last its soft, pale light shone down through the skylight—filling and flooding the room below—flooding and lighting the big, fat bud; the flower head turning toward the light; the long, cream petals opening slowly— slowly, slowly, one . . . by . . . one . . . in the mystery of the night, a sweet clear perfume filling the air.

A peaceful feeling spread over Stephen as he drifted off to sleep, watching the petals in his mind—opening, opening, one by one. Watching, waiting, and hoping to see the Moonflower's secret, hidden beauty. Looking forward to tomorrow—to the adventure yet to come.

Tomorrow would be a wonderful day.

10. Cornwall, Here We Come

Stephen slept soundly all night long. When he awoke the following morning, it was several moments before the memory of the previous day's exciting events came flooding back to him. When it did, he lay there for some time looking around his room and thinking. The whole affair of Great-Uncle Theodore still seemed quite amazing to him. It was strange to think he was leaving London, leaving people and places he knew, leaving the security of this small room, setting out into the great unknown. But it would be quite an adventure.

He gazed at the posters on his bedroom walls: pictures of endangered species; a chart that showed the relationship between the animals and plants of the Amazon forests. His greatest ambition had always been to visit those forests. That would be a real adventure! He had often pictured it in his mind. So he couldn't help wondering why it was that he now felt hesitant about a simple trip to Cornwall.

He knew he must shake himself into action. There was a great deal to be done: He would have to be very organized. First of all, he must clear and clean his room. Mrs. Johnson had been kind and helpful to him whilst he had stayed there, but she would be furious if he left the place in a state.

Then he must pack his belongings, making quite sure that he took everything with him that might be of use to him in his new life. That was going to be difficult; after all, he had no idea what he would find when he got to Lansbury Hall. Perhaps there was a housekeeper there. He hadn't thought of that before, but it was a nice idea—someone to look after him.

Getting up and dressing quickly, he had a very hurried breakfast then set about the task at hand. He packed his shoes and clothing into his rucksack. This didn't amount to much; but it would be enough to keep him going for the time being.

Most of the books that he had needed for his studies had been taken out of the library. Fortunately, he had already taken all those back; but he did have several cherished books of his own. He packed those, together with the priceless will, on top of the clothing.

Then he sorted through all the odds and ends left in his cupboard, discarding some as rubbish, but putting aside a set of billycans, a box of matches, and a flashlight, all of which might come in useful. And then there was his special mug—a mug that was beautifully decorated with a colorful design of red and blue Amazon macaws. He had recently bought it as a treat for himself from a special charity. He certainly mustn't leave that behind. His sleeping bag must go as well. That could be strapped on top, last of all.

He stripped his precious posters from the walls as carefully as possible, trying not to leave dirty marks. He would give them to Mrs. Johnson's small son, Freddy, who had made lots of hopeful hints. The posters were like old friends; but they would have a good new home and an appreciative owner. Somehow, Stephen felt that he wouldn't need them any longer.

The next important consideration was food. He cleared the small cupboard and the fridge of their contents, setting them on the table. There was half a loaf of bread; a packet with some tea bags; half a packet of sugar; a small jar of coffee; a chunk of cheese; three rashers of bacon; four tomatoes;

a carton with some margarine; and two eggs in a box. Ah, yes, and some Rich Tea biscuits—his favorites—in a tin. The tomato ketchup bottle was empty: He aimed it at the rubbish bin.

Surveying the collection on the table, Stephen decided that the most sensible thing to do would be to make a pile of sandwiches, using the cheese and two tomatoes. So he plunged in happily, using up most of the bread that way, but leaving a big thick crust, which might come in handy later. Then he packed all the food into an old carrier bag. If he bought some apples on his way to the station, a bar of chocolate perhaps, for a treat, some potato chips, and a couple of sodas, those things together with the sandwiches would see him through the day, no matter what happened.

At last, having told his story to Mrs. Johnson, and said his good-byes, he heaved the rucksack onto his back; with the carrier bag in his hand he set off for Paddington Station.

Stopping at the corner of the street, he turned for a quick look back at the house with troubled eyes and a frown on his face. Saying good-bye had not been as easy as he'd expected; Mrs. Johnson had seemed quite affected, and had mopped away a tear. He found it exciting but also disturbing to be walking off in this casual manner, not knowing the place he was going to nor who or what he might find when he got there.

Looking back, Stephen hesitated. He felt suddenly very alone: standing on the brink of the adventure, with all his worldly belongings on his back, like a disorientated snail setting off across a pavement—a wide and dry and dangerous pavement.

"Oh, well. Cornwall, here we come!" Stephen said out loud, as firmly as he could. There was just the hint of a catch in his voice, as he fought down the feelings of emptiness that rose up, threatening to engulf him.

He pushed the hair back from his face, adjusted the rucksack on his back, and strode off boldly down the street into the unknown.

11. Toward the Unknown

Stepping onto the train at Paddington Station, Stephen made up his mind that he was going to enjoy the journey. Somehow, at first, he managed to forget any worries about the future—what he might find on arriving in Cornwall. For the time being, it was quite enough to sit and watch the world go by: the wonderfully varied assortment of sights that assail those who travel by train—the contrasting scenes and the intimate details that go together to provide an intriguing display of other people's lifestyles.

There were the backs of all those long rows of dingy terraces in the suburbs: the rusty drain pipes and cracked sidewalks; scruffy collections of ramshackle sheds; dirty windows with broken blinds; the long, narrow yards with their drooping lines of colorless, tired-looking washing.

And then to outer suburbia, the houses very much smarter now: windows with widely frilled swathes of sheer curtains; houses, detached, with large gardens; dogs and children running free; ponies in their tiny paddocks—overgrazed, discolored grass and tall, intrusive clumps of nettles.

All this finally and reluctantly gave way, and proper countryside took over. The train seemed to gather impetus, as if aware of finding freedom. Fields, farms, woods, and rivers all flashed by at high speed.

Stephen sat upright and rigid, gazing out at the countryside. Real space at last. It was wonderful!

Yet from time to time, he slumped in his seat. No matter how beautiful or interesting the scenery was, there was only a certain amount that a person could take in at any one time. It was surprising how tiring the experience could be. His face and especially his jaw quite ached from so much delighted grinning at all the fascinating sights.

Despite his intention to enjoy the journey, and his determination to ignore any worries about what the future might hold, Stephen soon began to find that he couldn't keep his mind away from all the problems that seemed to surround him. His thoughts kept going back to his meeting with old Mr. Postlethwaite the day before.

As the train pounded along the tracks, he went over and over the interview in his mind, getting more and more angry with himself as he thought of all the chances he'd lost. There were all those questions that he could have asked, if only he had had the courage. How could he have been so silly? How could he have been so weak? Why hadn't he asked more questions? He could and should have insisted on answers. But he'd simply sat there like a lemon! Looking back now, it seemed ridiculous. As the train swept relentlessly on, the thoughts went round and round in his head.

The weather became better and better the farther south and west they went. The sun shone brightly on the warm-red earth and weather-sculpted cliffs of Devon. The train slowed and picked its way carefully along the coast, almost, so it seemed, on the beach. The sea lay calmly like a vast lake, its surface reflecting the afternoon sunlight; long-beaked birds probed happily on muddy flats and sandy strands.

Stephen had eaten his way through most of the sandwiches, crunched the crisps, drunk the drinks, and nibbled an apple. Now he felt very hot and dry. Yet the journey seemed to go on and on. By the time the train finally reached the River Tamar, he was feeling very weary. He craned his neck at all sorts of angles, trying to see as much as he could of the famous railway bridge that spanned the river. He remembered learning about it at school: a rather strange and massive construction, designed by Isambard Kingdom Brunel—a brilliant and famous engineer of the Victorian era.

Having crossed the Tamar River, Stephen was finally in Cornwall. There was still a long way to go, but although he wished the journey were over, in a way he dreaded arriving. He began to worry more and more about what he would find at Lansbury Hall. He hadn't liked the funny, knowing look on Mr. Postlethwaite's face when he had made it clear to Stephen that he must "take care of things."

Suddenly, he remembered the will. Surely, if he spent some time reading quietly through the will, he could find out something about the place, and maybe something about the "things." So he took the long brown envelope out of his rucksack, drew the will from its protective sheath, undid the long pink ribbon, and spread the document out carefully across his knees.

He wasn't very good at coping with all the complicated language—all those "hereinafters" and "wherefores." But he stuck at it, reading some of the passages over and over again: trying to get at the simple meaning wrapped up in the legal language; searching carefully for clues in the wording—anything that might tell him something about Lansbury Hall or something about his family.

Stephen had little success with the will. Whilst it was quite clear that he had inherited Theodore Lansbury's entire estate, there was no description of that "estate." But there were, as old Mr. P. had warned, strict conditions laid down.

As far as Stephen could work out from the complicated language that made up the conditions, it all boiled down to the fact that no alteration could be made to the property, in any way at all—not to any building or part thereof, nor to the land; that no change should be made in the way in which the property was run; that nobody, except close family, should ever be admitted to any part of the property; that the details and results of Theodore Lansbury's lifelong researches—whatever they may be, the will didn't say—were to be kept completely secret.

It all sounded very mysterious. But although Stephen read the whole thing through several times, till his head ached so much that he had to give up, he couldn't find any clues as to what he might expect to find on his arrival at Lansbury Hall. It was frustrating and rather worrying.

He folded the will and put it away.

12. A Warning

Stephen sat well back in the window seat with his head against the cushion. The worrying thoughts churned around in his mind. There must be someone looking after the house. He thought of the stories that he'd read, which included kindly housekeepers. They were characters that he could picture clearly: cozy, generally plump ladies who cooked substantial, delicious meals, setting them down lovingly on the table before the young heroes.

There would be steak and kidney puddings on cold winter evenings; roast beef with a big Yorkshire pudding, cooked in the pan beneath the meat, for all those wonderful Sunday lunches, with crunchy roast spuds and groovy gravy; scrumptious trifles, topped with fresh cream. Surely Stephen had read somewhere that Cornwall was famous for its cream. Clotted cream!

And then there'd be long, cooling drinks, probably homemade lemonade, served on balmy summer days. The very thought of it made his mouth water. Some lemonade would be great; he was hot and thirsty now. Yes, he decided to himself, he was onto a very good thing.

As the train snaked its way amongst the hills, sunlight flashed on his hot, damp face; his eyelids seemed impossibly heavy, and irritating locks of hair clung uncomfortably to his forehead. He put up his hand and swept them back; then he closed his eyes and dozed.

A slight lurch and a hissing sound woke Stephen up with a jolt. The train was standing at the station. With rising panic, he grabbed his rucksack and made a frantic dash for the door. He couldn't bear to miss the station.

The door opened easily; he stepped down onto the platform. Almost immediately a whistle blew. The train started moving away; then, quickly gathering speed, it disappeared with a dying roar, leaving Stephen standing there.

A dull, dead silence flooded back from the sunbathed hills and the looming woodland. It seemed to swamp the tiny station. Stephen stood still, looking about him. No one else had got off the train. The station, at first, appeared deserted; but as he made his way uncertainly along the platform, he saw a figure in a dark uniform standing by the exit gate. The man stood watching Stephen carefully.

"You'll not find a taxi here at this time of day, young man," the stationmaster said, holding his hand out for Stephen's ticket.

"Oh, I hadn't thought of taking a taxi," Stephen answered, handing over his ticket. "I thought I'd walk. Although, I have to admit that I don't really know the way. Perhaps you could help me?"

"I will if I can. Where are you going then?" It had been such a long and boring day; the stationmaster was only too pleased to stand and enjoy a bit of a chat. Besides, it was always interesting to find out who people were, where they were going, and what they were doing. "You tell me where you want to go, and I expect I'll be able to help," he said warmly.

"I'm looking for Lansbury Hall," said Stephen.

Surprise showed on the man's face. He peered at Stephen closely.

"Lansbury Hall?" he said, in an odd, suspicious voice. "Well, I don't know about that."

"Oh, I thought perhaps you might know where it is," said Stephen.

"Huh! I know where it is, alright," said the stationmaster. "But as for you going there, well, I wouldn't recommend it!"

"What do you mean, you wouldn't recommend it?" asked Stephen. He didn't like the man's reaction.

"Prrff," the man grunted and sucked through his teeth, in a most unpleasant way.

"'Tis a strange old place, that be. No one goes there. There be some very funny stories." He nodded his head in a knowing fashion, pursed up his lips, and squinted at Stephen with narrowing eyes.

It was not a pleasant sight and, despite the hot sunlight, Stephen felt a shiver rising.

"Oh, no! I wouldn't go there if I were you," the man continued. "If you are looking for a place to stay, you go and see my cousin, Loveday. She and her husband Walter run the village shop. They'll put you right."

"Thank you," said Stephen, "but I am definitely going to Lansbury Hall. So, could you please direct me." He took a notebook and pencil out of his pocket.

"Well, I suppose I could tell you how to get there," the stationmaster said reluctantly, "but, as I said to you before, I don't recommend it. And anyway, even if you find the place, you won't be able to get in. They gurt big gates is always locked. You mark my words, they gates'll be locked."

Stephen stood quietly, waiting.

"Well, seeing how determined you are, I suppose you'll have to learn for yourself," the man gloated. "But it's a fair long way, you know, several miles. It'll be nearly dark by the time you get there. I shouldn't fancy that," he added disconcertingly, with a grim cackle of laughter.

Stephen was beginning to wish that he hadn't talked to the stationmaster at all. He found the man and his comments disturbing; he only wanted to get on his way. It was a great relief when he finally escaped with directions scribbled down in his notebook. With a cheery "Thank you," he set off down the lane, determined not to look back.

The man stood there with a puzzled look on his face, watching the boy until he disappeared from sight.

"Well, I never!" he said out loud.

"The wife'll be intrigued by that! That'll give 'er something to natter about." He laughed happily at the thought. For he always liked a nice bit of gossip.

13. Enchanted Cornwall

The late afternoon sun shone warmly on the back of Stephen's neck as he started his walk to Lansbury Hall. Setting off down the lane with his ruck-sack on his back, he found that the uncomfortable memory of his peculiar conversation with the stationmaster was very quickly swept away by the joy that he found in his new surroundings.

As the lane plunged steeply down, he entered a long and leafy tunnel. Pale shafts of mellow sunlight fell on the tall, gray trunks of trees that grew in woodlands on either side. Their wide, spreading branches formed a leafy canopy overhead—a tracery of pale-green beech leaves, with patches of blue sky shining through.

The great tiredness that had overwhelmed Stephen as he had pounded along in the smelly old train, soon completely faded away. In contrast with the dull grayness of London and the hot stuffiness of the train, the beauty of this cool, green scene and the fragrant, scented woodland air, were like a medicine for his soul. A spring came into his weary step. Now he strode briskly down the lane, a broad smile on his face.

The lane twisted and turned on its way. Suddenly, he stopped in his tracks. He could hear the sound of running water. Pressing on hurriedly down the lane, he emerged, at last, from the end of the tunnel to find himself on an old stone bridge, spanning a wide and shallow river.

Nothing is more soothing than the constant flow and ripple of a river. Stephen lowered his rucksack to the ground, and leaned over the wide stone parapet to watch the water stream along. The cool, rough feel of the granite blocks, from which the ancient bridge was built, was comforting to his hot, damp hands; he grasped the stone with pleasure.

It was a happy, tranquil place. No one came to disturb the quiet. Stephen could have lolled there for hours, just enjoying the peaceful scene: the river running on downstream, with surface ripples over shallows, glistening in the sun; the lush, green clumps of hanging grass that clung to the mossy riverbank; thick, green, velvet-coated rocks; the ivied trunks of stooping trees that overhung the burbling water. Here and there mosquitoes hovered over deeper, darker pools. Now and again, Stephen heard the occasional plop of a jumping fish.

It was just the kind of place that he had always longed to visit. But he knew he mustn't linger. There was a long walk ahead. The sun would soon be dipping down. So he tore himself away from the river, heaved his rucksack onto his back, and started off along the lane.

Leaving the river behind, the lane wound on upward, a gentle slope at first, through woodlands of graceful birch. Stephen plodded along happily. After a time he rounded a sharp corner. The gentle slope was ended now. The road ahead ran up steeply, and he set himself to climb. The rucksack seemed much heavier now; the straps bit into his shoulders.

The lane was very narrow, enclosed on either side by high, grassy banks with many wildflowers: the shocking-pink of campion with tousled buttercups in between, glowing in the golden sun; and massing spikes of purple foxgloves. On any other occasion, Stephen would have been concentrating on the beauty of his surroundings. But he was breathless and toiling now. His damp shirt clung to his hot, wet skin; he longed and longed for a cooling drink. He wasn't really enjoying himself. This fact, when it suddenly struck him, made him feel quite miserable. For he'd so looked forward to this walk; but nothing is very much fun when you're horribly hot and uncomfortable.

He knew that he must keep pressing on; he wondered how far he still had to go. Higher and higher, hotter and hotter, the rucksack painfully weighing him down. Trees closed in on either side: stands of pine trees, tall and dark, their long, needle-covered arms reaching out and tapping Stephen as he passed quickly by.

Weary and breathless, he stopped in the lane on the edge of a small clearing. Perhaps he could rest in the shade of the pines before continuing his climb. But Stephen didn't realize that it wasn't that kind of cooling shade; he wasn't used to pine forests.

He stood hesitating at the edge of the pinewood, very close to the trees. An oppressive silence made him pause. The dense, dark canopy of branches was like a lowering roof above, and row upon row of marching pines stretched away before his eyes into an all-enveloping gloom. The air was heavy, still, and sullen, as he found himself moving quietly forward in amongst the trunks of the trees, crunching softly and sinking down into a spongy bed of needles. A thick, warm scent of pine rose up, enfolding him mysteriously, drawing him on and on and on . . .

Suddenly he stopped in dismay. What on earth did he think he was doing! He turned and retreated as fast as he could, scurrying between the trees, tripping over hidden roots, keeping his eyes on the sunny space which marked the line of the lane ahead, not wanting to look behind.

Hotter now than ever before, he set off hurriedly up the lane, with only a very quick look back, wondering to himself, as he went, if all of Cornwall would be like this—strangely enchanted, mysterious.

On and on he went. The pinewoods now were all behind him, and there was open land in front; but the high banks and hazel hedges that lined the lane on either side closed him in and shut out the view. He had no idea where he was; he so regretted not buying a map.

The rucksack now seemed extraordinarily heavy. Stephen's back and shoulders ached. His feet were hot and weary, too; yet he plodded on without a pause. Then as the road began to drop and he rounded several steep bends, he saw before him a welcoming sight.

On the side of the road at the bottom of the dip was a huge, circular granite basin. About six feet wide and twenty inches high, it nestled into the mossy bank of a shady, fern-draped dell. Gushing and falling into the basin was a clear stream of running water.

What a relief it was for Stephen to plunge his hands and arms in the water, to splash his poor, hot face and neck, to draw his fingers through his hair with wonderfully cold, wet, dripping hands. He cupped his palms and took a drink—a glorious, long, and cooling drink, only afterward noticing that he was standing ankle deep in watercress. The water, continually flowing over the wide, rounded rim of the basin, formed a pool around its base, spreading out across the road and running away as a small stream.

Stephen stood enjoying the cooling effect. Then he sat on the bank to rest. What a super place to be! But he mustn't sit there for too long. He must get on and find Lansbury Hall, before it got too late—and dark.

So he heaved his rucksack up once more and started off along the lane. At least he felt much cooler now and not as thirsty as before, though he soon discovered that wetting his shoes and feet had been a mistake, that squelching along in soggy sneakers was extremely uncomfortable. It made his feet hurt even more.

On and on he tramped. At last he came to the crossroads he sought and a wide expanse of rough, high ground with clumps of gorse and big gray boulders. He sat down on a boulder, found himself a biscuit to munch, then checked the directions in his notebook. It couldn't be so very far. He could afford to sit and rest. He would sit and enjoy the view.

It was a high, top-of-the-world sort of place, with a big view all around. "Space at last! Such wonderful space!" Stephen's voice was full of joy.

Countryside, like some giant patchwork quilt, spread out before him: a glorious, curvilinear landscape of running fields and boundary walls—a complex pattern of colors and textures that clothed the sweeping hills and valleys. It was a seemingly gentle landscape, in the mellow, evening sun-light, but with a hint of ruggedness beyond—the high tops of the craggy tors of the wide, wild, open moor.

Somewhere in that patchwork must be Lansbury Hall. Stephen sat gaz-ing out and wondering. An unpleasant thought came into his mind. Was it possible that the stationmaster had sent him on a wild goose chase? Now that he came to think of it, the man had behaved in a very strange way. He certainly hadn't been very helpful. It had almost sounded as if he were afraid.

For the first time during his walk, Stephen unwisely allowed himself to think back: to remember the stationmaster's words and the funny gleam that he'd had in his eye. It made him feel uncomfortable. He certainly didn't like the idea of arriving at Lansbury Hall after dark.

The sun was very low in the sky now. If he didn't hurry, it would be dark. Whatever would he find when he got there? He shivered and felt strangely cold, despite the warmth of the evening air.

Yet he felt reluctant to leave this place. He wished that he could stay much longer, gazing out across the view. It was so beautiful and so peace-ful. Peaceful, that is, till a cry rang out: a sudden, sad, and eerie cry that made him start up in alarm.

"What on earth was that?" he gasped.

The strange cry came again. It came from somewhere in the sky. Looking up, he saw the buzzards—a pair of buzzards, wheeling and dipping, the pale undersides of their wings catching the glow of the evening sun.

It was a great thrill for Stephen. He had never seen buzzards before in the wild, and even from this distance, their size and wingspan was impres-sive. With flight feathers widely spread, they soared above him high in the sky, hanging and drifting on warm air currents.

He stood and watched them with delight. He heard their mewing cry again, and despite his tiredness and his doubts, his spirits soared up high with the birds. He hardly noticed the pain in his shoulders, as he swung the heavy rucksack up and started off along the lane.

"It can't be far. It can't be far. I must be nearly, nearly there," Stephen chanted as he tramped—on and on then down and down, as the lane twisted and turned on its way, disappearing into woodland that seemed to fill the valley below.

The buzzards were gone now from the sky, dipping down amongst the trees and vanishing from Stephen's sight. He hurried along through the darkening woodland with a growing sense of urgency, nervously glancing from side to side. Finally, the lane divided and he saw before him high stone walls, just as the stationmaster had described. He turned to the left, as he knew he should, to follow along beside the walls that rose up on his right-hand side.

And so Stephen came at last, trudging wearily through the gloom, to stand before the great gates—the great gates of Lansbury Hall.

14. Gateway to Mystery

Stephen stood and stared in amazement. He certainly hadn't expected such grandeur. The tall, heavy, iron gates rose up high in front of him—a seemingly impassable barrier.

"You mark my words, they gates'll be locked." The stationmaster's voice came back to him. He could see in his mind the pursed-up lips, the thrust-out chin, and the gloating face. So, now, whatever should he do?

Perhaps he could climb over the gates. Looking up at the height of the gates, he knew he would never manage it, not with a heavy pack on his back; he wasn't going to leave that behind. Perhaps, if he followed along the wall, he could find a place to climb over.

Stephen stood in the middle of the road, feeling very lost and tired. It was almost dark now under the trees. He looked around him nervously. Everything seemed so strangely still. There was something watchful about the place. Something waiting for him to act.

He moved quietly toward the gates, and peered cautiously through the bars. It was not an encouraging sight. Dark, brooding masses of rhododendron seemed to be blocking the driveway, just a little way ahead. Even if he managed to get into the place, he didn't like the idea of having to push his way through those.

Just above the height of Stephen's waist, where the gates came together in the middle, there was a large lock. He could see the big keyhole clearly. He could see the large, rusty handles.

Almost in desperation, he grasped the handles, pressing down and giving them a hard push. To Stephen's surprise the lock clicked. One gate began to move. It swung slowly open in front of him, moaning and creaking noisily in the still, evening air.

"Oh dear! What a fool I am," he said out loud, stepping slowly forward.

Just inside the gate, he stopped short. He stood stock-still, his face tense, looking around him and listening carefully. When he had decided that it all seemed quiet and harmless enough, he turned to close the gate behind him. The gate was heavy and difficult to close; only after pushing and shoving did it click reluctantly back into place, in line with the other gate.

Just as he was turning to set off, a very weird noise rang out—a plaintive, somewhat musical call, echoing through the darkening treetops high above his head.

"Woomp! Woomp! Woomp!"

Stephen froze.

"What on earth was that!" he exclaimed. "Surely it couldn't be an owl."

The call had a strange, unearthly quality. He couldn't imagine what it could be. He was just beginning to relax, when suddenly from far ahead of him, came a distant, answering call:

"Womp! Womp! Womp!" The call was lower this time, but still with a strangely musical tone.

Stephen stood quite still by the gate, his eyes staring wide in alarm. But although he stood there for some time, the strange call was not repeated. At last, with an enormous sigh, he started to gather himself together. Wiping the sweat from his upper lip, and pushing the hair back from his face, he set off uncertainly, glancing around him as he went, peering up anxiously into the trees.

Forcing his way through the overgrown rhododendrons was not quite as bad as he had feared it might be. A narrow path wound its way through the sour-smelling banks of foliage, on and on through the gathering gloom.

Once or twice, Stephen stopped and looked behind him, listening intently. There was nothing to be heard. It was all peculiarly quiet—unnaturally so, he thought to himself. Not a sound or a movement anywhere. The stillness made him feel even more nervous. He shivered and carried on, moving as quickly and silently as he could, trying not to keep looking behind him.

As he burst out into the open, an impressive sight met Stephen's eyes. He stopped and stood and gazed in wonder, his face, that had been so tight and so anxious, relaxing into a big, broad smile—a smile of pure surprise and delight.

Beyond the rhododendron wilderness, it was still surprisingly light. Open grassland stretched on in front of him. He could just make out the curving line of the overgrown drive, matted over with weeds and grass.

The drive ran ahead for a short distance then swept up and around to the right. There, on the gentle slope of the hillside, in the warm evening sunlight, stood a large and elegant house, framed by a thicket of trees behind and rhododendrons on either side.

"Wow!" gasped Stephen. "What an incredible place!"

It must, he presumed, be Lansbury Hall. He simply stood and stared in amazement; then, as he stared, something struck him. Lights were shining in all the windows. There must be people there. How wonderful!

"Phew!" He let out a long, loud sigh, all anxiety fading away at such a warm and welcoming sight.

As he set off enthusiastically toward the house, a comforting picture rose up in his mind. There would be someone to meet him and greet him. Some company would be rather nice. He was feeling terribly weary. There would be drinks, proper meals, and a lovely, comfortable bed. And, above all, there would be answers—answers to all his important questions. Oh, yes. That would be brilliant!

It was not far to go now. He was nearly there and feeling pleased—pleased with the house and pleased with himself. But as he rounded the curve in the drive and made his way toward the door, an uncanny change came over the house. The lights were fading in all the windows, a cold, gray chill spreading over the walls.

Stephen stopped and stared in dismay. He watched the lights in the windows fade out. Then, whirling angrily around on his heel to look across to the far horizon, he realized his silly mistake.

There were no lights in the house, after all; it was nothing more than a trick of the light. As the last golden glow of the sunset faded, so the last reflection of that glow faded in the windows of the house.

It was a bitter blow for Stephen. He was tired, chilled, horribly hungry, and, above all, very much alone. He looked back at the cheerless house. It stood before him cold and gray, the windows dark and blank and staring.

Heavy, navy-blue clouds were building behind the house. All the warmth had gone from the air. A cold little wind whipped around the corner, rustling grasses at his feet.

Wearily and clumsily, he made his way toward the door and up the two shallow steps. There was no knocker on the door and, for a moment, he couldn't see any sign of a doorbell. Then he noticed a long, metal rod that was hanging down to one side of the door, probably an old-fashioned bellpull. He took hold of the rod and pulled. A faint, jangling noise rang out somewhere in the depths of the house.

Stephen stood hopefully on the steps. But nobody came to answer the bell. He felt so awkward standing there. How long did he have to wait before he tried the bell again?

After several minutes, when nothing had happened, he tugged again at the bellpull, harder this time than before. The forlorn jangling of the bell echoed distantly through the old house. But still nobody came to the door.

Stephen eased his arms out of the straps of the rucksack, and lowered it onto the step. He stretched his aching back and groaned. Now whatever should he do? He looked at the firmly closed door—and he wondered.

He had expected the gates to be locked. But they hadn't been locked after all. So, what about this door? Perhaps that wasn't locked either.

He put out his hand and, rather gingerly, clasped the big, round, brass doorknob. It was cold and smooth to the touch. His hand slipped as he tried to turn it.

He tightened his grip and tried again. The handle turned. He heard a soft click. The door swung silently open.

15. The Face in the Mirror

Stephen stepped quickly back from the door. He had suddenly had an uncomfortable thought. This was the right place, wasn't it? It would be so embarrassing to walk into somebody else's house—uninvited. But no, this must be the right place. Surely?

He stood rigid on the doorstep listening very carefully. There was no movement or sound from within. After a while he plucked up his courage, and stepped in quietly over the doorsill.

A pale light still lit the sky, but inside the house it was dark and gloomy. Standing just inside the door, and peering into the shadows, Stephen could make out the lines of a large airy hall. On either side of the broad space were tall doorways, their doors closed, whilst across the hall in front of him, a wide staircase with heavy, wooden banisters ran up into the darkness above.

A few slow, silent steps across the black and white marble floor brought him into the middle of the hall. He hesitated. Surely there must be somebody here. Surely you couldn't just leave a big house—with no one to look after it—and with the doors unlocked?

He was reluctant to break the silence. Yet he felt he ought to call out.

"Hullo—oh," there was a catch in his throat. His voice sounded horribly croaky.

He tried again.

"Hullo-oh. Hullo there."

Only a very slight echo. Then silence.

From his very early childhood, Stephen had been aware that every house had an atmosphere. He always sensed it as he entered. The first thing to meet him—and sometimes to hit him—was the smell. Smells were always very important. Then, in some inexplicable way, the complicated combination of sights, sounds, and smells in a house all blended together to give him a certain feeling. Even a totally empty house had its own identity and its own special atmosphere—good or bad, kindly or harsh, or just a sort of nothingness. As Stephen stood in the hallway of Lansbury Hall, the aura of the old house flowed gently and kindly around him, inviting him, and comforting him. He felt immediately warmer and better. There was a pleasing, fragrant smell and, despite the darkening shadows, a friendly feeling in the air.

A place of refuge. It gave him sudden confidence. He went back outside, picked up the heavy rucksack, and coming back inside again he closed the door quietly behind him.

The hall was much darker now, despite two large windows, one on either side of the door. The doors on either side of the large hall stood firmly closed. Stephen eyed them suspiciously. He hadn't quite got the nerve to go across and open one. A dim light at the back of the hall showed what must be a part-open doorway. He made his way slowly toward it.

A slight movement to one side made him draw up very sharply. He turned in alarm toward the movement. A tall, pale figure stood before him.

Stephen gasped and froze in horror. It took him several frightened moments to realize what he was looking at. A huge and very dusty mirror, part of an enormous piece of furniture, ran along the wall in front of him. He was looking at his own reflection. His face looked back with a feeble smile.

With a quiet "Phew!" he turned away, resuming his path along the hall.

The door at the back of the hall was ajar. Slipping through it, Stephen found himself standing next to an open doorway, leading him into a very large kitchen. There were three deep windows in the wall to his right; he could make out the shape of an old-fashioned range down at the far end of the room.

He put his rucksack down on the floor, and fumbled in it for his torch. The pale beam picked out the other main features: a long, tall breakfront with open shelves and a display of crockery stood against the wall to his left, whilst running down the middle of the room there was a very big kitchen table. Several plain wooden chairs were arranged around the table, those at either end of the table larger and with stout arms. Two easy chairs stood at the far end of the room, one on either side of the range.

Having briefly surveyed the room, Stephen searched anxiously for the light switch. The beam from his torch lit up the walls; but he couldn't see any sign of a switch.

"It must be somewhere here," he mumbled, checking the wall on either side. An unpleasant thought came into his mind. He swung the beam of the torch wildly—across the ceiling and round the walls.

"Oh, no!" he gasped in dismay. "A house without electricity!"

Stephen didn't like the idea of that. He swung the narrow beam of the torch anxiously around the room, then back into the hall behind him, then back around the kitchen again, trying to dispel his fears.

A candleholder with a tall slim candle, stood in the middle of the table. What a good thing he had his matches!

The small spurt of flame from the candle provided a friendly pool of light, but somehow it only served to make the rest of the room seem very much darker. On the table beside the candleholder, there was a small group of objects: a long, flat piece of wood, a stick, and a box full of bits and pieces. It seemed an odd collection of objects.

Despite the poor light in the kitchen, Stephen got the strong impression that the room was clean and tidy. The old, blackened range looked spotless. Beside it, against the wall, there was a pile of neatly stacked firewood and a box of kindling.

As he considered the range and the wood, an idea suddenly came to Stephen: It would be great to have a fire. There was a kettle on the stove; he could make himself a mug of tea.

So he built a fire in the open grate of the range. In no time at all, the wood was crackling, and cheerful flames licking up the chimney. A rosy glow spread through the room, together with the aroma of burning apple wood.

The heavy, black kettle was empty, but he couldn't see a sink or tap. It must, he presumed, be somewhere else, probably in the scullery. So, taking the torch and the kettle with him, he went out into the corridor, where he had noticed two closed doors.

Which one might it be? Stephen knew it was silly to be nervous. But opening doors in strange places in the dark was disturbing. He hesitated for several moments before approaching the door in front of him, cautiously grasping and turning the handle, then pushing the door open very slowly.

Cooler, damper air met Stephen, as he moved silently into the room with the torch held out in front. It was the scullery. After a quick look around the room, he hurried across to the sink. To his great relief the water ran freely.

Two doors opened out of the scullery. One of them, beside the sink, was obviously a back door leading to the outside world. Stephen pressed his face to the glazed upper section of the door, peering out into the gloom. He couldn't see very much at all, only the dark outlines of buildings that formed what looked like a large enclosed yard.

The other door, on the far side of the room, stood closed and blank. It would have to wait till tomorrow.

As Stephen left the scullery, closing the door quietly behind him, he looked at the door on his right-hand side. He wasn't feeling adventurous now—but, perhaps, he ought to investigate.

Leaving the kettle on the kitchen table, then tiptoeing silently back to the corridor, he stood there, holding his breath and listening. There was nothing to be heard. So, finally, advancing toward the door, he pushed it gently open before him, holding the torch out well in front, wondering what he was going to find next.

16. The Throne Room

It took Stephen a moment or two to realize what it was that he'd found. When he did, his exclamation, followed by a burst of laughter, echoed loudly in the room. All that stealthy creeping around had brought him to the lavatory.

But what a magnificent toilet it was! It was quite unlike anything that Stephen had ever seen before, except in books. It seemed to have been built like a splendid throne.

The bench, onto which one lowered one's rump, was a very substantial, wooden structure—an elegant sort of cabinet, smooth and dark and beautifully polished. The wood gleamed in the light from the torch. He couldn't see any chain to pull, but there was a large brass handle set into the top of the cabinet—possibly a flushing device.

"What an amazing contraption!" he muttered, lifting up the square wooden lid and exposing the polished seat beneath. He peered down into the watery depths, his torch lighting up the porcelain bowl, which was white with a pattern of large blue flowers. He shone the torch a little closer, and read the maker's mark at the back.

"Twyfords 'National' Patent," he read.

"Well, Mr. Twyford, whoever you were, you certainly did make wonderful toilets."

Stephen stood smiling to himself. It was such a splendid affair. Along the back wall, on either side of the throne, there was a polished wooden bench, on which there sat a small bowl. Stephen went closer to look inside.

"How weird!" he said out loud; for the bowl contained a number of large, freshly picked leaves. They looked as if they might be dock leaves.

Back in the kitchen, with the kettle heating up on the range, the next job was to unpack the rucksack, placing all the items of food that might be useful on the table.

"What a blessing I brought some food," Stephen murmured to himself; he was very hungry now. And what a delicious supper he cooked. He took down a pan that hung on the wall, and very soon the big kitchen was filled with the tantalizing smell of frying bacon and tomatoes.

While the food was cooking, he went out of the kitchen and across to the doorway that opened onto the hall. Stepping out very quietly and drawing the door closed behind him, he stood with his back to it, listening carefully. There was no sound from the rest of the house. After standing there for several moments, peering into the shadowy hall, he slipped back quickly into the kitchen, shutting the door very firmly behind him.

Sitting at one end of the big table, bathed in the rosy glow of the firelight, Stephen enjoyed his delicious meal: three rashers of bacon, crisp and crunchy; two juicy, fried tomatoes; a big, thick crust of fried bread; and two eggs. It was not the sort of meal recommended by modern health experts, but all the same, it was, he decided, a meal fit for a king.

"The King of Lansbury Hall," he said grandly, out loud to himself, beaming as he sat at the table, crunching the succulent, hot, fried bread. He was eating his meal from a large and very beautiful plate that he had lifted carefully down from the breakfront. Fish and chips in their paper, eaten in his bed-sitting room only the night before, now seemed like a lifetime away.

He stoked the fire, putting on the last few pieces of apple wood, then sat contentedly in one of the large chairs beside the range, drinking his tea—tea without milk, of course, but he didn't mind about that. After the hardships of the day, the tea seemed like nectar to him. He drank the warm, amber liquid gratefully, too tired to go on worrying as he lolled in the chair before the fire, staring into the glowing embers.

Stephen sat there for quite some time, until the sputtering of the candle finally roused him. He suddenly realized how stiff he felt, how much he longed to lie down and sleep.

Opening the door that led to the hallway, he stood and listened again. There was nothing to be heard. The house was sleeping peacefully. But he was too tired to face leaving the warmth and safety of the cozy room—too tired to go exploring the house, looking for a proper bed.

He closed the door again very quietly. Wherever could he sleep?

Window seats ran along below each of the large kitchen windows. On the seats were long, flat, padded cushions. Stephen laid his sleeping bag along one of the seats. It would have to do. Then he made a hasty trip to the throne room. He hadn't the courage to try the flushing device, not only because he wasn't quite sure how it worked, but also because he feared the disturbing noise it might make—though he tried to put firmly from his mind any thoughts as to who or what he might be disturbing.

Back in the kitchen, he rolled up his parka for a pillow, took off his jeans and his shoes and socks, then, rubbing his poor feet ruefully, he climbed into the makeshift bed. Comfortably installed, he sat upright in his sleeping bag, his face pressed close to the windowpane.

Bright moonlight lit the area of overgrown forecourt that swept around at that side of the house: an empty, well-lit area, ringed around by deep, dark shadows—shadows that Stephen's eyes couldn't penetrate.

In the end, he gave up trying. He lay down with a heavy sigh, stretching out in his sleeping bag and easing his tired and aching body.

He lay there gazing up through the window—only a few, scudding clouds now and one or two faint stars. With a last satisfied look around the room, and a contented smile on his face, he closed his eyes and fell asleep.

If anybody or anything approached the house that night and peered in at the sleeping boy, he was not aware of it. Stephen slept soundly all night long.

17. A Weird New Species?

Stephen woke up early the next morning, the light from the window shining painfully in his eyes. It took him several moments to remember where he was. He felt stiff and very uncomfortable. Sleeping in a sleeping bag was all very well, but he had been very cramped. There's not much room to move about, when you're lying on a narrow window seat. With his legs still inside the bag, he maneuvered himself up into a sitting position and looked about him. In the bright light of day, the room was even more attractive than he'd imagined it to be the night before. It was a quaint sort of room: The large collection of crockery on the breakfront provided a beautiful display, the patterns in a lovely shade of blue on white.

Other, more amazing plates hung on the whitewashed kitchen walls—plates whose exotic patterns and lustrous glazes added life and color to the room. An interesting collection of objects sat on high shelves around the walls: warm-brown terra-cotta jugs with wide, cream-colored rims, and pitchers with narrow yellow-glazed necks.

Sitting there, looking at the scene around him, Stephen was suddenly aware of the fact that he had a nasty taste in his mouth, that he was hungry and thirsty again. He scrambled out of the sleeping bag, dressed as quickly as he could, and set about looking for something to eat. How he longed for a hot cup of tea! Impossible without the fire.

Searching in the bottom of the rucksack, he surprised himself by finding an apple and a couple of tired-looking biscuits. Then he ran the tap in the scullery. The water tasted really good, but he didn't like to drink too much; no matter how much he ran the tap, the water was full of little bright-green bits and pieces. Rinsing out his favorite macaw mug, he propped it on the draining board.

Back in the kitchen, munching the apple and the biscuits, he set about investigating the entire room, looking in all the cupboards and drawers. There were glasses and yet more china in the cupboards at the bottom of the breakfront, and a big collection of assorted cutlery in the drawers: knives, forks, spoons, ladles—all heavy and very old-fashioned.

There were more cupboards in the scullery, full of all kinds of kitchen equipment—pots; pans; sieves; colanders; an exceptionally large and impressive rolling pin; all the parts that go together to make a large, mincing machine; and various other strange utensils, which he didn't recognize. Goodness knows what they were used for; some must be really ancient. He picked them up and examined them, one by one, putting them carefully back in their proper positions on the shelves. Everything looked so clean and tidy.

Beside the sink was a back door. There were bolts at the top and bottom of the door, but Stephen was not surprised to see that these were both drawn back. Nor was he surprised to find that, although there was a key in the lock, the door was not locked. Apparently, nothing was locked at Lansbury Hall.

He opened the door and took a quick look outside. The wide yard behind the house was enclosed by a big range of outbuildings. He would look at those properly later on. All he wanted to do now was to find something good to eat.

At the far side of the scullery, there was still one door that he hadn't yet investigated. The door stood closed and challenging. In the bright light of morning, Stephen couldn't imagine why he had been so frightened of opening doors the night before; although, even as his hand turned the handle, he couldn't help feeling rather tense, wondering what he might find this time.

Cool air met Stephen's face, as he pushed the door open. He was looking into a large, gloomy room, lit by two small open windows. The floor, like that of the kitchen and scullery, was covered with huge, gray slates, and Stephen could see that the big, wide counter, which ran around three sides of the room, was made up of thick, white slabs of marble. The surface, veined with pale gray lines, felt very smooth and cold to the touch.

In the middle of the room, there was a large and very unusual table. The top, a single, enormous slate, was supported on a whitewashed, brick-built pedestal. Large, shallow, brown earthenware bowls stood empty on the tabletop. This room must be the dairy.

At the far end of the room, he could see yet another door. He approached it warily, peering through open, vertical slots in the upper part of the door. The slots were rather like narrow windows, but so well meshed over that he couldn't see what lay beyond.

The door opened easily, and Stephen found himself in a large, walk-in larder. A small open window gave light to the room; this, like the windows in the dairy, was covered by a fine wire mesh. The air was musty, but not too bad.

Around the room there were wide, marble counters. On one of the counters there stood a row of oval, domed, wire-mesh covers—the sort of things that were used in olden days to protect the food from flies. They ranged in size from very small at one end to very large at the other. Stephen had to laugh. There was not much light in the larder; for a moment, they looked to him just like a family of peculiar creatures marching along the top of the counter.

"Some weird, new species, perhaps," he said, laughing quietly to himself. "That would be a real joke!"

On the floor, below the counters, were rows and rows of old glass bottles: some empty, some full. Stephen held one up to the light. It glowed a lovely, ruby red.

A number of large, brown, earthenware crocks with wooden lids stood on the floor. He lifted the lids, one by one, and looked inside. The first two, which were very large and oval in shape, were empty; but three were full. They seemed to contain different kinds of flour: one lot, light brown in color, looked as if it might be a coarse whole meal. But he couldn't guess at the other two: one of them was rather yellow, and the other, a grayish white, was somewhat fibrous in texture. Stephen took a small pinch and sniffed it. It smelled quite fresh and rather good, but he couldn't think what it could possibly be.

White-painted wooden shelves on the walls above the counters reached almost to the ceiling, and on these shelves were pots and jars of many different types and sizes. Some were earthenware, others glass; some were full and others empty.

Stephen walked along inspecting the pots. Many contained a firm, creamy-brown substance, which looked as if it might be honey. A few were tightly stoppered pottery jars; there was no way of guessing what they might contain. But most of the jars displayed their contents: succulent, purple plums, bottled in a syrupy liquid, stared out boldly through the glass; and wonderful, fat, black cherries too. Then further on along the shelf, there was another row of jars containing a very different fruit: plump and round, their yellow flesh burst through splits in greenish skins. Bottled greengages.

"Oh! Great!" Stephen's face lit up with pleasure. "There must be an orchard out there somewhere—an orchard with wonderful greengage trees." He had only ever eaten real greengages once before, but he had enjoyed them enormously, and they weren't easy to get.

On the floor, under the left-hand counter, there was a big wooden box. Stephen raised the lid cautiously. The box contained a large number of brown rods, about eight inches in length, each one about half an inch or so across at one end, tapering to a point at the other.

Stephen lifted one of the rods carefully out of the box and examined it. He had never seen anything quite like it before. It was waxy, yet sticky to the touch. He lifted it up to his nose and sniffed.

"Of course," he said out loud. "The honey. Where there is honey there must be bees. Where there are bees, there may be hives. And where there are hives, there is bound to be wax."

These were obviously beeswax candles. In the darkness of the kitchen the night before, he hadn't noticed the unusual character of the candle that stood on the kitchen table. If these candles were to be his only source of light in the evenings, they certainly deserved respect; so he placed the candle that he was holding carefully back in the box with its fellows, and gently closed the lid.

Then he stood and looked around the larder. It was full of all kinds of intriguing things, but nothing from which he could make a proper meal. What he needed was solid food. He would have to go out and find the village. He would have to buy what he needed there.

Back in the kitchen, Stephen cleared up the mess that was left from the night before. He took the beautiful plate that he had used for his dinner out into the scullery. There didn't appear to be any washing-up liquid, so he cleaned it gently in the sink under running water. Then, since he didn't have a towel to dry it on, he took a clean T-shirt out of his rucksack and used that instead, carefully replacing the plate in its rightful position on the breakfront.

He stood admiring the big matching set of crockery, noticing that the pieces on the upper shelves were all dull and very dusty, whilst those below were bright and clean. He loved the set of large dinner plates, each plate with a different country scene, painted in the rich blue color on a white background.

In the middle of the lowest shelf of the breakfront was propped the most magnificent plate that Stephen had ever seen: an enormous, oval dish, to be used for a very big joint of meat. Scanning the scene on the plate carefully, Stephen suddenly realized that he was looking at a picture of Lansbury Hall. At the bottom of the picture and forming part of the pattern that went right around the edge of the plate, there was a large elaborate *L. L* for Lansbury. They must have been quite a grand family in their time. His family.

"My family," he said out loud, experimenting with the idea. It was still a very strange idea. He wished and wished he could find out more. He wished that his great-uncle were still alive.

And then he remembered old Mr. Postlethwaite. He remembered about the Moonflower too. "Never expect too much from life."

What he had already gained had been beyond his wildest dreams. This wonderful house was to be his home. He mustn't expect any more than that. Though he couldn't help regretting the fact that his fantasy about the housekeeper, and about all that delicious food, had been nothing more than that—a fantasy or a wonderful dream.

The dream, so it seemed, was not to be fulfilled. Or was it? Could there be somebody else in the house?

18. That Funny Feeling

The more Stephen stopped to think about it all, the more uncomfortable he became. There was certainly something very odd about the setup at Lansbury Hall. Something very odd, indeed, with the old, empty house.

It was a bit like that ship that he'd learned about in one of his less boring lessons at school: the famous *Marie Celeste*, which had been discovered floating on the ocean, its crew and passengers having disappeared into thin air. Whilst Great-Uncle Theodore's departure was, apparently, properly explained, the silent house seemed very peculiar.

Stephen shook himself out of his daydreams. It was probably a mistake to think about it all too much. He must accept things as they were and do the best under the circumstances—strange as those circumstances might be.

He emptied the remainder of his belongings out of the rucksack and left them on the window seat. He would take the empty rucksack with him to the village shop, and bring back a good supply of food and various essential items. It was probably quite a long walk to the village; he wouldn't want to have to go there more often than necessary.

On his way out, he stopped by the kitchen table, and stood looking down with a puzzled frown—looking at the odd collection of objects that he'd found on the table when he'd arrived the night before. There was a long, straight stick, some twenty inches in length. The sides of the wooden stick were smooth; one end was worn, rounded, and blackened. Beside the stick lay another wooden object, shorter, wider and flatter than the first. Stephen picked it up and examined it. Blackened in parts, it had two, small, pitlike depressions toward the middle on one side. There was also a small, wooden box, which was filled with dry moss and wood shavings.

The objects might be important clues, but he hadn't the time or patience now to stop and try to work them out. He would have to look at them later on.

Out in the hall, with the rucksack over one shoulder, he paused in front of the enormous sideboard with its tall, elegant, mirrored back. It certainly was a magnificent piece of furniture. Stephen had never seen anything like it before: eight or nine feet long and three feet deep from front to back; warm, golden-brown wood, carved by some master craftsman, polished and smelling warmly of beeswax, and with a solid, gray, marble top.

The mirror had certainly startled him the night before. What a silly fool he was! And an untidy fool at that, which wasn't too surprising; he hadn't combed his hair since yesterday morning, and he seemed to have lost his comb.

He did what he could to tidy himself up, pushing the hair back from his face, and scowling unhappily at his reflection. Yet another maddening spot had appeared—this time in the middle of his chin. It really was too bad! He never seemed to win the battle. He must have a look in the village shop and see what they had for persistent spots. Perhaps there was a Cornish remedy.

With a last despairing glare at himself in the mirror, Stephen set off across the hall. He glanced suspiciously at the firmly closed doors on either side. He stopped to look at the grand staircase, very tempted to climb the stairs, for he longed to explore the rest of the house. But his stomach was feeling quite horrible; what he needed was solid food.

Exploration would have to wait. He would feel much better later, and probably bolder too, with some proper food inside him. Then he could enjoy exploring.

What a glorious morning! Stephen stood on the steps outside the house enjoying the sunshine. The sky was a heavenly blue, the sun was warm, and birds sang.

The lovely surroundings and the fine weather should have filled him with delight; but as he stood there on the steps, an uncomfortable feeling crept over him. At first, he wondered what it was. Then he suddenly realized. It was that funny feeling he got when he thought he was being watched.

Adjusting the rucksack on his back, sweeping the hair back from his face, Stephen stood very still on the steps, quietly considering the landscape. As his gaze traveled over the fields and the woods, a peculiar thought came into his mind. It was almost as if he were standing on a stage. Out there, somewhere, beyond and unseen, was some large, expectant audience—awaiting and watching his every move.

"What a ridiculous idea!" Stephen told himself with a scowl. He must get rid of such foolish thoughts. Nevertheless, he looked carefully around him before he finally closed the door and set off slowly across the forecourt.

He didn't stop or look behind him till he came to the edge of the rhododendron wilderness. Then he paused and turned to look back. Everything seemed very quiet and peaceful. Not a movement anywhere. As he entered the wilderness and made his way along the path between the dark-green, massing banks, a slight wind stirred the leaves of the beech trees dotted amongst the rhododendrons. Birds sang happily in the branches. Everything seemed the way it should be.

Coming at last to the great gates, Stephen stood for a while to admire them. They certainly were very splendid. At least this time he wouldn't have all that silly nonsense—thinking that they were locked, when they weren't.

He laughed to himself as he thought of it now, putting out his hand with confidence, clasping the handle and pushing it hard. But nothing happened. The gate wouldn't budge.

The gate had been heavy, of course, he remembered. He tried the handle again and again: twisting and turning, tugging and pushing, certain that the gate must open. But it was all to no avail. The gate was obviously locked.

Stephen stopped his efforts and looked around, feeling awkward and rather foolish. The smile had left his hazel eyes; he wore a very worried frown. Something strange was going on here. He couldn't imagine what it was. Someone or something was playing tricks on him, and he didn't like it at all. Some wild ideas rose up in his mind, as he stood glaring out through the bars of the gate; but he pushed them firmly back down again. It wouldn't do to get too fanciful.

His stomach rumbled noisily. There was nothing else to do but find a place to climb over. Setting off, he turned to the left and followed along inside the walls.

Eventually, he found a place where the boundary was more like a steep stone bank than a proper wall, and he was able to heave himself up. He paused for a moment on the top of the bank, surveying the empty lane below, then clambered down on the opposite side, landing with a scuffled rush on the knobbly, tarmac surface.

It wasn't exactly a gracious exit for the King of Lansbury Hall! Stephen dusted the earth off his jeans, grinning wryly to himself. Then, after one last, long, doubtful look back toward the gates, he started off along the lane in the direction that he hoped would lead him to the village.

19. The Dancing Snake

It was a very long walk to the village, longer than Stephen had expected. He tramped along happily in the sunshine. Walking with the rucksack empty was easy, but he wasn't looking forward to the return journey. As he marched along, he thought about all the things he ought to buy. He patted the money in his pocket; the list grew in his mind.

He would need plenty of bread-—and potatoes—they were heavy and would be a problem. Then tea and sugar, eggs and bacon, and butter, of course—he was fond of that. And then some sort of vegetables. Frozen peas, which were his favorite, wouldn't be practical. He wondered about dried vegetables. He didn't like the idea of those, but they might be very convenient in his present circumstances. Canned vegetables would be too heavy.

Perhaps he ought to buy some of those little bottles of long-life milk—if they had any. He didn't like the taste of it, but he did like milk in his tea and coffee, so it would be better than nothing. Stephen had never lived in a house without a fridge before. It wasn't going to be easy.

Remembering the bowl of leaves in the throne room, Stephen decided that a four- or even six-roll pack of toilet paper might be a very good idea; and then soap and toothpaste—and a new comb. And he mustn't forget more matches. Oh, yes, and batteries for his torch. There were plenty of candles in the box, so he wouldn't need to buy those. Sorting out the best way to live permanently in such a remote and primitive place, without the benefit of electricity, was going to need some careful thought.

Perhaps he ought to buy fruit—at least some apples and bananas. A box of cornflakes; packets of potato chips; some lemon and orange concentrate might be quite useful. He couldn't go lighting the fire to make tea every time he needed a drink. Plain water was very boring; and plain water with green bits in it, even though it tasted good, wasn't very encouraging. He'd have liked to get lots of fizzy drinks, but he knew he couldn't carry them—perhaps just a couple of cans.

Chocolate biscuits and rich tea biscuits; packets of soup and canned meat—perhaps corned beef; canned fish—perhaps even salmon. The list went on and on and on. He even managed to remember a couple of post-cards and stamps. At some point, he would send off a suitably vague message to the children's home, in the hope that that would keep them quiet, and help to prevent a hue and cry as to his whereabouts.

It would be a difficult journey home with such a heavy pack. Home! He was already starting to think of Lansbury Hall as home. "How extraordinary," Stephen mused as he trudged along.

Oh, boy! Was he hungry! How he would love some fish and chips. Or even just a bag of chips.

He laughed out loud when he thought of his fantasy on the train—the one about the housekeeper and all that delicious food. He dare not think about it now. His stomach was bad enough as it was—empty and grumbling noisily.

At last the tops of houses came into view and he soon found himself walking down the village street, which was lined with a surprising assortment of dwellings. There were old stone houses with gray slate roofs, attractive and simple in form and style; but in between were much newer properties, all of them very smart bungalows, with fancy fake stonework and pebble-dashed walls. It was not at all what he'd expected for an old Cornish village.

Finding the village shop was easy. It was right on the corner at the cross-roads. "W and L Pascoe." The sign above the door was old and faded.

The door of the shop was standing open. Stephen walked straight in. Two women stood with their backs to him in the middle of the shop. They were obviously deep in conversation with the shopkeeper behind the counter.

". . . and so I said to her, I said, I don't like the sound of that m'dear. I wouldn't touch it if I were you. And do you know what she had the cheek to say to me? She said . . ."

The conversation stopped abruptly midsentence, when the women noticed Stephen's presence. All three stood still and stared at him.

The woman behind the counter was the first to recover.

"Good morning, sir," she said.

Stephen moved forward slowly, looking around him as he went.

The shop was a strange combination of different styles. One section of the large room looked like a mini-supermarket, with the usual rows of packets and jars on bright, modern shelving; the usual flashy, colorful ads; the usual plastic-coated price signs. But all this was somehow out of keeping with the crooked, worn, slate slabs on the floor.

A corner of the shop was partitioned off with a high wall of security glass along the front of the counter: the Post Office section. At the very back of the shop, through an open doorway, Stephen could see a large store—a room with many shelves, loaded with an amazing assortment of items.

The shop was clearly one of those wonderful, old-style village stores, where you could buy almost anything. He was pleased to think that the apparent "face-lift" at the front of the shop, in the way of modern alterations, hadn't affected the old store behind. Some of the stock on the shelves out there looked as if it might date back to the Ark. He would have loved the chance to go out there, to have a good poke around.

"Well. Good-bye, m'dears." This came firmly from the woman behind the counter: an obvious cue for the shoppers to leave. The shopkeeper, so it would appear, wanted the newcomer all to herself. The two shoppers were not too pleased. They pursed up their lips and glanced at each other, then departed reluctantly, looking disgruntled; but not before they had both given Stephen a very good eyeing over. It made him feel uncomfortable.

But the face behind the counter looked pleasant enough. It was the face of a plump, elderly woman, with what must be very long hair—gray hair, which was plaited and coiled, snakelike, on the top of her head. The tufted end of the plaited snake had somehow escaped from the rest of the coils, and it stood up in the middle of her head in a comical sort of way. Stephen kept his face very straight, and tried not to keep looking at it.

"Now then," said the shopkeeper, with a knowing little smile, "you must be the young man from up at the Hall."

It was not at all what Stephen had expected. However did she know that? And then he remembered. Of course! Hadn't the stationmaster said that his cousin and her husband ran the village shop? News travels fast in villages. They were bound to have heard all about his arrival.

Yes. That must be it. Stephen remembered the stationmaster's words. His cousin Loveday, so he had said, was married to Walter—they ran the shop. The sign outside read "W and L Pascoe." So this must be Loveday Pascoe. What a wonderful name!

He didn't have time to answer the question, if, indeed, it was meant as a question. For Mrs. Pascoe went on quite boldly: "Well now! That is nice. I expect old Squire Lansbury was very pleased to see you, wasn't he?"

What an extraordinary thing to say! Stephen could hardly believe his ears. He couldn't have heard her correctly. Could he? But before he could make any comment, Mrs. Pascoe was off again:

"Oh yes. Poor old soul. What a tragedy! Left on his own for all those years. We've often wondered how he's managed."

There was a note of inquiry in her voice, and she looked very closely at Stephen. "Taken to the place have you? I 'spect it's an interesting spot?"

Stephen opened his mouth to reply. He was on the point of saying to her

80

that surely she knew his great-uncle was dead. Surely she would have heard about it. But something stopped him.

"Oh. Yes," he said in a rather vague voice. "A very interesting spot."

"Of course, with Squire Lansbury being such a loner, we don't know very much about him, you see," Mrs. Pascoe continued. "Never been off the place, he hasn't. Well. Not as far as I know. Not in my lifetime, anyway."

Stephen was amazed by this piece of information.

"Really?" he said disbelievingly.

"Sure enough," said Mrs. Pascoe, bobbing her head in a positive way, with the snake dancing merrily. "And no one never goes up there neither. Although I did hear tell from my cousin Petherick, over at the station that is, that a visitor did arrive there once, and he was wanting Lansbury Hall," said Mrs. Pascoe. "A gent. A smart gent with a briefcase," she added, nodding her head and smiling at Stephen. She was obviously pleased to have all the details.

"When was that then?" Stephen asked eagerly. If he could find out about a recent visitor, he might be able to find out some facts about the family, and about the Hall as well.

"Hmmm. Now, I'm not too sure," Mrs. Pascoe deliberated. "I should say it were about . . . Ooh! Let me think . . . maybe eight or nine years ago."

"Oh! Goodness! As long ago as that?" Stephen was very disappointed.

"I was only saying to Walter the other day," Mrs. Pascoe continued, "I was only saying to him, old Squire Lansbury must be well nigh on a hundred years old. Soon enough he'll be getting his telegram from the Queen, I shouldn't wonder. Although how my brother Fernley would ever deliver it, is quite another matter."

And to Stephen's dismay, she started to rock with laughter. The ample bosoms rolled and shook within the confines of a colorful, floral-patterned overall. The tufted snake's tail joggled about. Stephen stood there horrified.

"Oh dear, dear me! There now," she gasped finally, her face red with effort. "I'm forgetting m'self. You must forgive me."

She pursed her lips and recovered herself.

"There've been some grand old stories over the years, you know, about the Hall. And I don't think you would catch my brother delivering letters to the house, even if he could get through them great gates.

"Ha-aa-aa." The rolling and shaking threatened to start again.

"Over the years I've often teased poor Fernley, I have. Him and all his silly notions." Mrs. Pascoe wheezed and puffed.

"How do you mean? Grand stories? And what . . . notions? Do please tell me." Stephen was dying to know what she meant.

But Mrs. Pascoe was pulling herself together. She looked at him rather warily now.

"Family are you?" she asked.

"Mr. Lansbury . . ." Stephen hesitated; but after a moment's thought he continued, "Mr. Lansbury is my great-uncle."

He had been going to say "was my great-uncle," but somehow it didn't seem the thing to do.

"I see." Mrs. Pascoe drew herself up, her attitude brisk and businesslike now.

Stephen suspected, with regret, that he wouldn't get much more out of her now. Why did Lansbury Hall have such a peculiar effect on people? And what were these "grand stories" she'd mentioned? The stationmaster had said something similar, and he wouldn't explain himself either.

"Now, what can I be doing for you?" asked Mrs. Pascoe.

"I have a long list, but it's in my head," said Stephen. Bit by bit he gave Mrs. Pascoe a list of all the things that he needed, even remembering, in the end, the battle of the beastly spots.

"Ah!" said Mrs. Pascoe, in a conspiratorial manner, giving Stephen a knowing wink.

"I have just the thing for that. My brother Fernley's wife, Morwenna, has very special powers, you know." Mrs. Pascoe nodded wisely.

"And she's a wonder with herbal cures. All old secret family recipes. And all fresh Cornish herbs, of course."

Fumbling about under the counter, she finally pulled out a large jar, full of a pale green, creamy substance, and then proceeded to spoon out enough of the cream to fill a small carton—an old reused yogurt carton.

"I think you'll find that'll do the trick. But you must apply it twice a day. Regular as clockwork, mind!"

Stephen stood looking at it doubtfully while Mrs. Pascoe made up his order.

The pile on the counter grew very large. At last, when everything was gathered together, including, most importantly, two loaves of Mrs. Pascoe's homemade bread, Stephen paid the bill and packed all the goods into the rucksack, with the special, green cream—Morwenna's Secret Recipe—sealed in a plastic bag and fitted in carefully at the top.

He tested the weight of the rucksack, letting out a gasp of dismay. It was even heavier than he'd feared it would be. Carrying it was going to be very hard work.

What with the curious conversation and Mrs. Pascoe's surprising display, Stephen had quite forgotten his hunger. He suddenly noticed a tray of pot pies. They looked magnificent: large, golden, pastry-coated packages with plump middles.

"Made them m'self this morning," said Mrs. Pascoe, following Stephen's gaze, and noticing his hungry expression.

"And although I say it m'self, an' I shouldn', you won't find a better pot pie anywhere in these parts. The apple and jam turnovers are very good too."

She lifted the plastic cover from the plate of turnovers, and taking one of the succulent-looking pastries from the plate, carefully slit it open along one side. Stephen watched in amazement. His eyes were almost out on stalks when he realized what she was doing—taking the lid off a plastic box that was standing to one side, scooping out a great, big spoonful of the contents—a wonderful, thick, yellow, crusty cream—and pushing it with the side of one finger off the spoon and into the turnover. Then she licked her finger noisily.

Stephen's mouth was literally watering. He simply couldn't help it. Even the slicking and slurping noises of Mrs. Pascoe licking her fingers didn't seem to put him off.

Mrs. Pascoe's eyes slid up and peered over the top of her glasses, carefully noting Stephen's reaction.

"The cream is included in the price," she said temptingly.

"May I have one pot pie, please, and one turnover. Oh, yes, and a can of lemonade."

He was thirsty now as well as hungry. All he wanted to do was escape, to get his teeth into that fabulous food—to have a good meal and to have a good think. There was plenty to think about.

He suddenly had a good idea.

"May I please leave my rucksack with you? It's very heavy, and when I've had my lunch, I'd like to go and look around the village. Perhaps I might visit the church."

Mrs. Pascoe nodded amiably.

"You leave your bag here, m'dear. It'll be safe as houses with me. The church is out beyond the village," she said, pointing.

"It's an interesting place. You'll find all the old members of the Lansbury family buried up there. Always have been buried up there, since they first came to these parts."

A new idea came to Stephen. He would go and visit his great-uncle's grave. That would be the correct thing to do: to pay his respects to his Great-Uncle Theodore, though he wasn't going to say so to Mrs. Pascoe.

Stephen's stomach was rumbling even more than ever now. He paid Mrs. Pascoe, thanked her politely, and leaving the rucksack beside the counter, he turned and hurried away from the shop.

20. The Graveyard

It was past midday, the sun high in the sky, as Stephen left the shop and set off to walk up the winding lane toward the church. He could see the top of the church tower, high in the trees ahead.

As soon as he was well away from the village, he looked for a place where he could stop and eat his lunch in comfort. Just inside an open gateway he found a very large, old May tree, part of the hedgerow. He settled down on the grass inside the field, under the welcome shade of the tree.

The freshly baked meat pie was delicious. The crunchy, golden pastry-case was generously filled with a succulent mixture of meat, potato, onion, and a well-seasoned, slightly peppery mixture, very tasty and very filling. Stephen sat contentedly, munching the pie, sipping his drink, and gazing out across the hills.

Somewhere, unseen, high in the blue of the sky above, a lark sang. The seemingly endless, warbling song of the bird, the gently rolling landscape all around, the drone of the bees in the heavy pink-tinged flower heads up above, and the delicate perfume of the hawthorn wafting on the breeze—all conspired to produce a feeling of peace and tranquillity.

Stephen enjoyed his picnic very much: concentrating on the food; idly watching the activities of insects in the grass around his feet. He'd always been particularly fond of insects. The apparently infinite variety of bugs and lice, flies and ants, butterflies, moths and others never ceased to amaze him; they all lived such interesting lives. It was sad to think that so many people disliked insects—that they seemed to spend so much of their time deliberately trying to kill them off. He couldn't understand it at all.

Having finished his pot pie, he leaned back against the trunk of the tree and rested, allowing the pot pie to settle somewhat, before following it down with the bulging apple and blackberry turnover.

Looking up into the branches of the May tree, Stephen noticed a tiny, green caterpillar hanging down on its silken thread. He recognized it as the larva of the Common Marbled Carpet—a pretty, little, mottled moth that often laid its eggs on hawthorn.

Caterpillars were probably the things that fascinated Stephen most in the insect world: from the very tiniest chaps, like the one above his head, to the very biggest, meatiest beasties, with fat, segmented bodies. There was such an extraordinary range of different types: Some were so modest and beautifully camouflaged, whilst others were outrageously flashy; some looked aggressive with spikes or spines; then there were "furries," and "woollies," and "wrinklies"—all completely fascinating.

Stephen continued his peaceful meal, contemplating caterpillars. As he bit deeply into the turnover, blackberry jam and clotted cream oozed out at the side, running quickly down his chin and dripping onto the ground at his feet. It was a wonderful combination: the apple, blackberry, and clotted cream, all packed into the crunchy pastry. Stephen smacked his lips with pleasure, wiping the creamy mess off his chin, then licking the back of his hand. He wasn't going to waste a drop.

He watched with interest as, one by one, ants quickly homed in on the splotch of blackberry-rippled cream, negotiating with difficulty the long, runny, creamy paths that led to the rich, dark, sticky jam. They seemed to be enjoying their meal as much as he had enjoyed his.

But, despite his enjoyment, uncomfortable thoughts niggled away at the back of his mind. He'd been concentrating on his meal; he had managed to avoid thinking about Mrs. Pascoe's very odd comments, but now it all came back to him. Surely he must have misheard her when she'd spoken about his great-uncle. It had really sounded as if she thought that the old man was still alive.

"What nonsense!" he said out loud, getting up and setting off. He would visit Great-Uncle Theodore's grave. He would put an end to such foolish ideas.

Stephen had always found old graveyards very interesting. He wasn't silly enough to be frightened of skeletons and things like that. His house parents at the children's home had been keen on archaeology, and Stephen had been fortunate enough to go off with them on a number of occasions to help them sort out human bones from a prehistoric site. He knew from experience that old, dry bones were nothing more than they seemed to be— simply old, dry bones.

He liked churchyards. The graves themselves were, of course, impor-tant, being the final resting places for the earthly remains of people—real people just like himself. They were valuable tributes from loving relatives, who'd cared about those people in life; the gravestones were historical records.

It was always intriguing to look at the stones, to read all those funny, old names. But quite apart from that, because of the peace and quiet in a grave-yard, it was like a miniature wildlife reserve. Even in the midst of the biggest city, a churchyard could play a vital role, providing a valuable refuge for many different creatures and plants.

Stephen liked to think that, when he eventually died, he would be buried somewhere too. He'd have his own, tiny, perpetual plot: a diminu-tive haven for wildflowers and insects.

After walking along for quite some distance, contemplating such seri-ous matters, he finally turned in through a gateway; he could see the small church with its square tower ahead of him at the top of a drive, sheltered by a clump of tall trees. This was a very old church, built many hundreds of years ago from large, square blocks of granite: weathered over many ages; mottled and patterned with lichens and mosses.

It was a still and tranquil scene. Stephen walked up the drive slowly, feeling rather like an intruder; very reluctant to disturb what seemed like the peace and quiet of ages. As he let himself into the churchyard, the clanking and creaking of the old gate set off a sudden raucous chorus from a crowd of indignant rooks somewhere in the trees above.

Startled, Stephen stopped in his tracks. He stood looking anxiously around at the graves, as if he feared that his sudden intrusion, along with the loud and jarring noise, might awaken their sleeping occupants. As the noisy birds settled down in the branches, their angry chorus died away. A peaceful silence settled back.

Stephen stood still in the hot sunlight on the path, waiting. In front of him and to one side of the church door there stood an ancient stone cross. It towered above him, gaunt and gray. He wondered just how long it had stood there. He wondered about the generations—the hundreds of people, over hundreds of years, who had passed that way and had looked at the cross.

Long, long ago, some local mason had fashioned this wonderful, massive cross out of a single chunk of granite. And men had come and hauled the cross, and stood it there beside the church—a symbol of their Christian faith. Men, who might well lie there now, sleeping, at peace, in the old churchyard.

Time and the elements had taken their toll and weathered the surface of the cross. Crisp-cut edges had rounded and softened, and covering the face of the ancient stone were the spreading growths of many lichens—white and gray and palest green, and some the very brightest orange. Some were thick, and some were crumbly, others thin and powdery.

Stephen placed his hands on the cross. Its crusted surface was warm in the sunshine.

He knew there were many kinds of lichen, and that some were very long-lived. He stood there gazing up at the cross, trying to imagine what it had looked like several hundred years ago: freshly hewn from its bed of rock, then weathered by the running rain, the freezing ice, and the blanketing snow. He saw the first, tiny patch of lichen growing across the face of the stone, then many little fingers creeping: spreading and spreading over the years, till it stood before him, as it did now, wearing its ancient, encrusting coat—a witness to the passing ages, the continuity of time and growth.

Stephen turned his thoughts away. He looked around the cluttered churchyard, surveying the silent host of stones: some, very ancient and leaning at angles, discolored and weathered, their legends obscured; others, erect and clearly more recent, clean and shining with crisp-cut letters. Another example of continuity. And he was supposed to be part of it.

It was a very sobering thought. Having never had a real family, it was hard for Stephen to make himself feel that he fitted in here—somewhere, somehow. He straightened his shoulders, and sighed loudly. He would go and find his great-uncle's grave and the graves of all his Lansbury ancestors. Maybe that would really help.

21. The Mystery Deepens

Something seemed to draw Stephen on and to lead him into the little church. After the heat of the sunshine outside, the church seemed very cool and dim; but colors glowed from stained-glass windows set in the plain and whitewashed walls that rose to the curving, wooden roof. The church was silent, stark, and simple, yet it had a kind and friendly feeling as Stephen wandered happily around.

Arches ran down the aisle on one side. The columns that supported them were wonderfully basic in form and style, encouragingly solid to the touch. The carvings at the heads of the columns were rather primitive, Stephen thought, but certainly very beautiful too.

In a corner, at the back of the church, sunlight flooded through a clear-glazed window, illuminating the old stone font. It was hewn from solid blocks of granite, the harsh lines of its angular form presenting a very down-to-earth picture—a stark reminder in this House of God that He alone is immortal. Humans come. And humans go.

With a grave expression on his face, Stephen ran his fingers slowly around the curving inner rim of the font then smoothly out and down the straight-cut sides. Here Lansbury ancestors would have been baptized. His family. His people.

Yet somehow he only felt disappointed: disappointed and very empty. Where were the feelings he ought to feel? Where was the sense of family ties? Where were the wonderful, warm connections? Connections that he longed to grasp, but couldn't find in the cold of the stone.

Shaking his head and sighing again, Stephen turned away sadly. He walked as quietly as he could in the total silence of the church along the bright red carpet that led toward the altar—but not as quietly as he would have liked, for he was wearing his squeaky boots—and regretting it with every step.

He knelt down for a few moments in a pew toward the front of the church, and gazed at the cross on the simple altar. And then he sat in the pew and thought. His family must have worshiped here. Had Great-Uncle Theodore sat in this pew?

He looked around the church, and wondered. There were numerous plaques on the whitewashed walls—memorials to various people who had lived and died within that parish. The name Lansbury caught his eye, and he crossed the aisle to read the inscription:

To the Glory of God
AND IN LOVING MEMORY OF
PHILIP AND CHRISTINA LANSBURY
BELOVED PARENTS
OF THEODORE AND STEPHEN
LOST AT SEA ONBOARD RMS TITANIC
APRIL 15TH 1912

Stephen stared at the words on the plaque, reading them over and over again.

"So Theodore had a brother called Stephen!"

Seeing his own name on the plaque and realizing the family connection made him feel very odd. He tried to imagine the two boys—old-fashioned images of himself, losing their parents on that fatal night, when the mighty *Titanic* on her maiden voyage had struck an iceberg and sunk without trace. Hundreds of people had lost their lives. Mrs. Pascoe had mentioned a tragedy. This, he could only suppose, must be it.

He was turning away from the plaque sadly, when he noticed another one—the same size and shape as the first one, but a little bit further along the wall. He moved a couple of pews down the aisle to get a better look at the wording.

"Oh, no!" he gasped as he read the words.

To the Glory of God
AND IN LOVING MEMORY OF
STEPHEN LANSBURY
BELOVED BROTHER OF THEODORE
KILLED IN ACTION 1915
AGED 25 YEARS

Stephen shivered. He felt cold—suddenly very cold and lonely. With a last sad look at the two plaques, he turned and set off up the aisle, walking as quickly as he could, his boots squeaking noisily.

The brightness of the sunlight dazzled him as he emerged, with relief, from the church. The warm sunny air was welcome. Following a small paved path that ran around to the side of the building, he approached the graveyard that stretched on behind. Here and there were ancient yew trees: ominous, green-black silhouettes against the blue of the summer sky.

Stephen wandered amongst the graves. On some other occasion, in the future, when he wasn't quite so anxious, it would be well worth coming back to look at all the old tombstones: to try to find the old Lansbury ancestors. But he hadn't the time now or the patience. He needed to find his great-uncle's grave, then get back to Lansbury Hall.

At last, finding his way through a gap in the hedge, he discovered a small, enclosed field—an extension to the old graveyard. Here he found the most recent graves. He walked eagerly along the rows, reading the names on the stones as he went. All of the graves had some kind of headstone, but none of them bore the name Theodore Lansbury.

After searching carefully everywhere—up and down and double-checking, trying to keep as calm as he could, Stephen finally had to admit it. There was no grave for Theodore Lansbury.

Deep in thought, with a puzzled frown, he made his way slowly back to the village.

22. The Strange Call

Back in the village, Stephen made his way directly to the shop. There was no sign of Mrs. Pascoe. An elderly man now sat behind the counter, reading his newspaper. He nodded and smiled at Stephen—a somewhat restrained and wary smile, with the mouth switched on but the eyes merely watchful.

With some difficulty, Stephen heaved the rucksack up onto his back, thanked the man, and left the shop hastily. He didn't want any more strange conversations. He had a lot of thinking to do. There was something mysterious going on, and the reaction of the local people made him feel extremely uncomfortable.

Despite the heaviness of the rucksack, he made his way speedily out of the village. There was no one to be seen. All was quiet, apart from the distant barking of a dog; but as Stephen plodded up the street, his boots squeaking noisily, there were certainly movements behind net curtains, and eyes that watched him as he went.

Out in the country, he felt free again. He marched along, deep in thought, trying to sort it all out. He went over and over all that Mr. Postlethwaite had told him, all that he had seen at Lansbury Hall, and all that he had learned in the village that day. But, no matter which way he looked at it, nothing seemed to fit or make sense.

Some long time later, still with an anxious frown on his face, and staring down at the road ahead, he came at last, very wearily, to the great gates of the Hall. If he hadn't been so deep in thought, he'd have remembered about the gates—remembered that the gates were locked. He would probably have stopped along the lane and scrambled with difficulty over the bank.

But Stephen had his mind on other things. Without really thinking what he was doing, he put out his hand and turned the big handle. The gate swung easily open.

He was halfway through the gate before it struck him that something was wrong. The gate had been firmly locked that morning. However could it be open now?

Whose was the hand that had turned the key? Could his great-uncle still be alive? No! Surely not! After all that old Mr. Postlethwaite had said, it seemed unthinkable.

The absence of a grave was worrying, of course. But then, people were often cremated, weren't they? Though, surely, Mrs. Pascoe would have told him—and taken great pleasure in doing so. Or would she? She hadn't even seemed to know that Great-Uncle Theodore was dead.

The thoughts whirled around in Stephen's head as he stood there staring at the lock. He had never really believed in ghosts. But now he was beginning to wonder . . .

Having slowly crept in, he closed the gate quietly behind him then stood looking nervously around: easing the straps of the heavy rucksack that were biting painfully into his shoulders; sweeping aside, with the back of one hand, the irritating lock of hair that clung to his hot and sticky forehead.

The sudden, strange call made him jump in alarm.

"Woomp! Woomp! Woomp!" from high above him—just as he'd heard the night before.

He stood and waited, listening carefully. Then distantly, from somewhere ahead, came the faint and answering call:

"Womp! Womp! Womp!"

Stephen stood, fixed to the spot, peering up into the leafy canopy.

"Whatever can it be?" he wondered. It was the most peculiar call.

But there was nothing to be seen, and no more to be heard. Indeed, the trees all seemed too quiet now. An uncanny and frightening stillness reigned.

Stephen stumbled along as quickly as he could between the dark banks of rhododendron, finally bursting into the sunlight on the far side of the wilderness. He was hot and dripping but very relieved, as he looked across toward Lansbury Hall. It looked exactly as he'd left it, with no hint of any movement. He couldn't help wondering for a moment what he had hoped or feared to see.

Having made his way along the overgrown drive toward the front door, he paused to look up at the house. It certainly was the most beautiful house, not enormous, but big and elegant.

A bright splash of color caught his eye amidst the foliage of climbing plants that grew at the front of the house. There were two plants, one growing on either side of the door. Their old and twisted limbs grew up the walls, merging above the top of the doorway, and spreading out across the stonework.

Dark-green leaves—somewhat heart-shaped with serrated edges—covered the vinelike plants. Now that he came to look at them carefully, Stephen could see dozens of pale, green-sheathed flower buds. But, most exciting of all, in the warmth of the day's sunshine one of the buds had opened.

A large, bright-scarlet flower with slim petals shone amongst the green of the leaves just to one side of the door. Stephen stood admiring it. It was a strange and foreign flower.

Funny to think that you could look at a flower, and because of some obscure, exotic quality, you immediately felt that it must be foreign. Of course, the word itself, *exotic,* simply meant something that had come from abroad—something that came from foreign parts and was therefore likely to seem unusual. Stephen knew that most of England's garden plants had originally been brought from other countries, but plants such as roses and daffodils had all been here for such a long time that people thought of them as British. It intrigued him to think that his instinctive reaction to this plant made him think that it was foreign. He stood on the steps and thought about it.

Exotic things, he thought, whatever they might be, flowers or trees, sculptures or paintings—or even people, often possessed a weirdly threatening quality. But surely that was just because they were exotic. Anyone or anything from a strange country or alien culture was bound to possess characteristics that he wouldn't understand. He knew that people could feel very threatened by things that they didn't understand.

Stephen looked closely at the flower. It wasn't exactly weird or threatening, but it did have its own very peculiar and decidedly alien character.

Around the inside of the bowl of the flower, within the petals, was a ring of purple, hairlike filaments. An elongated and divided, fleshy, stalklike structure, with little green bobbles, grew right out of the middle of the flower. It was not at all what you would expect from a nicely brought up and properly behaved British flower. Stephen laughed out loud at the thought.

It looked like some kind of passionflower; but he'd never seen one that was blood-red before. It seemed a very odd thing to find here—isolated in the depths of rural Cornwall.

But whatever it was, and wherever it had come from originally, it was in its own, special way a very beautiful flower indeed, and its beauty, even if far removed from the gentle beauty of an English rose, shone there brightly beside the door to welcome him back home again.

"What brilliantly clever plants you are," Stephen said out loud with a broad smile, suddenly remembering old Mr. P.'s words.

Plants needed encouragement. He chatted happily to the flower as he took a good, close look at the vines. It was a pity that something seemed to have been eating the foliage. A couple of the branches were stripped almost bare, although the flower buds didn't seem to have been touched, and there were no signs of any pests that might be responsible for the damage.

Stephen decided that he would keep an eye on the vines in the future. It would be a great pity if something ate all the leaves and killed them off.

He stood for a while with his back to the door, looking out across the green valley. Was it just his imagination? That funny, uncomfortable feeling again. That funny feeling of being watched.

His eyes scanned the fields and the woods. Not a movement anywhere. It all looked very quiet and peaceful—and yet the feeling lingered on. Finally, he sighed and turned, and with an encouraging smile at the flower, he opened the door and went inside.

All seemed well in the kitchen. It was just as he had left it that morning, with the "odd collection," as he now called it, still lying on the table, and still meaning nothing to him.

Stephen opened up the rucksack and lifted out the priceless skin cream—Morwenna's Secret Recipe. He wondered if it would do any good. He was certainly going to give it a try. He carried it out into the hall, and stood it on the marble top of the extraordinary sideboard, in front of the big mirror. "You must apply it twice a day," Mrs. Pascoe had said very firmly. He'd have to try and remember that.

Back in the kitchen, he lifted down one of the blue and white plates from the breakfront. He took the fruit out of the rucksack and placed it carefully on the plate: seven apples and seven bananas. He was especially fond of bananas.

Stephen reckoned that, if he was careful, he could manage for a whole week on the food that he'd bought. He could just about face the idea of walking into the village once a week for stores. Why on earth had Mrs. Pascoe told him all those silly stories about his great-uncle never leaving the Hall? Obviously, he would have had to go out to buy stores. Perhaps she didn't like it because he shopped elsewhere. No one could live in a place like this without going out to buy some things, especially with no electricity.

Taking the rucksack into the larder, he unpacked all the food, and stacked it in an organized fashion on one of the marble counters. Lifting one of the wire-meshed domes from the middle of the family troop on the counter opposite, he placed it over the cheese and bacon.

He had remembered to buy a can opener, which he put away in one of the big drawers in the kitchen breakfront, along with the rest of the cutlery. Another crucial item he'd bought was a large plastic bottle of washing-up liquid. He smiled broadly to himself as he took it out into the scullery and stood it on the windowsill by the sink. Setting up home was going to be fun.

And what an amazing home it was! His next task must be to explore the rest of the house; but his stomach told him it was teatime. A mug of tea would be wonderful, but then he would have to light the range. He couldn't be bothered to do that now, and besides, he remembered from the night before, he had used up all the firewood. Having no electricity was certainly going to be a pain!

He glanced across at the old range. There, to his absolute amazement, stacked against the wall beside the range, was a big pile of firewood. He gasped in surprise. How on earth had that got there? He walked slowly across to the range, and stood there staring down at the wood.

Picking up a piece of the wood, he weighed it thoughtfully in his hand, a bemused expression on his face. He'd been tired the night before, but could he have made a mistake like that? Could he have thought that he'd used all the wood when he hadn't? It had been dark in the kitchen, of course, with only the light from the fire and the candle.

He replaced the piece of wood tidily on the top of the pile, and then he surveyed the rest of the room with a troubled look in his eyes. Nothing else seemed amiss. The remains of the burnt-out candle were still in the holder on the table.

His eyes traveled back to the wood. He must have made a mistake, of course. And yet he felt almost sure that he hadn't.

Some food might make him feel much better. Pulling himself together at last, he took a banana from the plate and made himself a big fat sandwich: freshly cut brown bread and butter, mashed banana, and a sprinkling of brown sugar. Then he hunted about for his special macaw mug. Surely he'd left it in the scullery, on the draining board by the sink. So, why wasn't it there now?

Coming back slowly into the kitchen, with a puzzled frown on his face, Stephen stopped abruptly in front of the breakfront, staring at a row of cups that hung along the front of one shelf. For there, in the middle, was the mug, hanging comfortably on a hook. It made him feel strangely cold and alarmed. He couldn't remember putting it there. And yet he supposed that he must have done it. He grunted crossly to himself as he lifted the mug down from its hook.

At last, with the sandwich in one hand and a mug of weak orange soda in the other, he wandered out through the hall and went to sit on the steps in the sun. The scarlet flower would keep him company.

"Well," he said out loud to the view, with a touch of bravado in his voice, "if there is anyone out there watching me, you can watch me enjoying my sandwich."

23. The Sleeping Bat

Stephen was anxious now to explore the rest of the house. He didn't fancy sleeping on the window seat for a second night. He hoped he might find a cozy bedroom—a bedroom with a comfortable bed—and before it got much later. The sun was getting low. He wouldn't want to be creeping around the old house at dusk.

His confusion over the firewood and the odd sensation of being watched had made him feel decidedly nervous; yet he must check out the rest of the house, though what he expected or feared to find, he didn't know. Surely there couldn't be anyone else there. He'd have seen them or heard them by now. Wouldn't he?

But, although he didn't want to admit it to himself, he needed to check and make quite sure. So, off with his old and creaking boots and on with a pair of silent sneakers. He wasn't prepared to squeak his way up and down the old, dark corridors.

The Great Exploration began in the hall. Sunlight poured in through the open front door. Stephen could see a butterfly basking in the sun on the doorstep—white spotted ends on the wings and intricate, tawny orange markings.

The house was very still. It waited patiently for his next move. Which door should he open first?

The first doorway, on the right-hand side as you entered the house from the front, seemed the biggest and the most grand. Tall, double doors faced him. Thick, heavy, warm-brown wood.

Taking a deep breath, Stephen grasped the large, round, brass handles; yet the double doors were reluctant to open. It wasn't that the doors were locked; the handles were stiff, but the catch clicked and the doors began to move. It was the hinges that were the problem. They ground and creaked and groaned mournfully—horribly loud, complaining voices in the still-ness of the house.

When the gap was just wide enough, Stephen squeezed through into the room to be met by a weird and wonderful sight. Light, from the three tall windows down one side, lit what must be the drawing room. He could see the vague form of a grand piano, and various couches, chairs, and small tables were arranged around the room.

The astonishing thing was that the room was in the most extraordinary state. Stephen had never seen anything like it in his life before. He gasped in sheer amazement.

It was not that the room was untidy or messy, in a lived-in or dirty way. Each piece of furniture stood neatly in its place. Shelves and tabletops were tidy, and ornaments on the mantelpiece all marched in proper order.

Long curtains hung at the windows, elegantly fastened back. Hanging down from the high ceiling were two, large, bulbous shapes, which surely must be chandeliers. But their true form, like that of everything else in the room, was hidden: blanketed by the dust of ages, clothed and draped by pale swathes of all-enveloping cobweb shrouds.

As Stephen moved slowly across the room, the dust billowed up around him, and then it hung in stifling clouds, illuminated in beams of light from the windows. The slight draft from the open door sent gentle ripples of swaying movement amongst the festoons of hanging cobweb that dangled up above his head. It was like a scene from a fairy story.

But the air was hot and dry and oppressive. The billowing dust made Stephen choke. He stole as carefully as he could back across the amazing room and out into the airy hall, closing the door firmly behind him, thankfully gasping drafts of fresh air.

Goodness knows how long it was since the room had last been in use. It must be a very, very long time.

"Is it possible," Stephen wondered, "that the rest of the house will be the same?"

There was only one way of finding out; so, one by one, with trepidation, he checked all the doors in the large open hallway. The second door on the same side behaved in exactly the same way as the first—creaking open reluctantly.

The room inside was somewhat smaller than the drawing room. There was an enormous billiard table in the middle of the room, and on the walls around the room a collection of mounted heads of animals—everything from deer with huge antlers, to some kind of very big cat, perhaps a tiger. But because the conditions in the room were exactly like those of the previous room—everything coated with very thick dust and draped with heavy cobweb streamers—it was impossible to tell. It all looked rather spooky to Stephen; he shivered and closed the door hastily.

On the opposite side of the hall, the door at the rear, closest to that of the kitchen, opened complainingly to reveal a big dining room. An enormously long table with rounded ends ran down the middle of the room, with chairs on either side. The surface of the table was bare, apart from a thick blanket of dust. A large piece of furniture, probably a sideboard, ran down one side of the room against the wall, along its top a row of strange and grotesque forms, their true identity shrouded by the covering of dust and webs.

Stephen went to investigate. Gingerly pulling away a handful of clinging, powdery web, he ran a finger across the surface of the largest form that stood in the middle. The object was made of smooth, black metal.

Could it possibly be silver? Tarnished beyond all recognition? And all the other objects too? The family silver, blackened by age.

"Wow!" It was an amazing thought.

The last door of all, at the front of the house, opposite the drawing room, provided a lovely surprise. The brass doorknob was bright and shiny. The door opened easily. On entering, Stephen found himself in a large and very splendid library. He gasped again, this time from pure delight at discovering such a beautiful room. It was a kindly, welcoming room with few cobwebs and little dust, a room that he could tell at a glance had been much lived-in and much loved.

The walls of the room were lined with oak shelving that reached up almost to the ceiling, and the shelves were full of books. But these were not the kind of books that you would find in a modern library. They were old books, bound in leather, their colors mostly soft and muted: russets, browns, dark maroon, and the occasional warm cream.

The room was well lit by three tall windows. The old curtains, a heavy brocade, once, perhaps, bright gold, hung down onto the floor, their color dimmed to a gentle fawn. On the floor were a number of Turkish rugs, their rich colors, though mellowed with age, glowed warmly in the room: rich scarlet and donkey brown; a rosy red, cream, gold, and blue.

It was a soothing, inviting room. Stephen wandered around happily.

A big desk stood in front of the middle window. On it were books and many papers, a blotter, pens, and an old inkwell. He sat down in the chair at the desk—Great-Uncle Theodore's chair, gazing absently out through the window; then he strolled on around the room.

On the opposite side of the room there was a long, polished table, with stacks of yet more books, and at the far end of the room, there was a rather grand stone fireplace. A big pile of firewood was stacked in the hearth and two leather armchairs were drawn up, one on either side.

Over the grand fireplace, on the only piece of wall in the whole room that wasn't covered with books, there was a large, glazed frame displaying some kind of ancient map. The lines were faded and discolored, the old-fashioned writing hard to read. Stephen stood in the hearth, peering closely, but he couldn't make it out.

In the far right-hand corner of the room, he found a small bed. It was an odd thing to find in a library, tucked in the corner beside the bookshelves. Lying on the bed was a black, walking stick. He picked it up to admire the handle—a magnificent, solid silver lion.

As he turned to leave the room, Stephen spotted something peculiar hanging on the wall at the opposite end of the room. A large, brass hook had been securely attached to the heavy oak of the bookcase, and some sort of baggy structure, made from a coarse, woven material, hung from the hook on thick cords. He couldn't begin to imagine what it was. He didn't feel like touching it. It was blackish-brown in color and reminded him of a sleeping bat—a very big bat, of course. He decided not to disturb its slumbers.

Leaving the room, he closed the door behind him and made his way across the hall. He stopped at the bottom of the staircase, and stood looking doubtfully up the stairs.

24. Ancestors

A small, dancing patch of color high above caught Stephen's eye, as he started to climb the stairs. It was the butterfly, making its way ahead of him up the staircase. He didn't expect to see butterflies in the house at that time of the year; but he was happy to see it there. At least he had some company now.

It was a very grand staircase. Stephen ran his hand up the banister, which was clean and beautifully polished—surprisingly free of dust and dirt. The dark, mellow oak was smooth and rounded by the wear of countless hands over centuries. Stephen liked the thought of that. He liked the warm and comforting feeling of the bulk and strength of the ancient wood.

At the top of the staircase, wide corridors ran off, one on either side. The doors of most of the rooms were obviously closed, for the corridors were dark and gloomy. At the far end of the left-hand corridor, a splash of light showed where doors had been left open. A tiny, flitting, colorful form flashed briefly through the beam, and then disappeared from view. The Painted Lady. He would rescue it later.

Making his way slowly along the gloomy corridor to the right, Stephen groped for the handle of the first door. Then he stopped and listened carefully. There was no sound from within the room. No sound from the house at all.

He stood there, rigid in the gloom, a cold chill creeping up his spine. With the old, familiar, nervous gesture, he pushed the hair back from his face and tried to pull himself together. He knew it was stupid to be nervous.

The door was difficult to open. Even before he could see inside, Stephen guessed what he would find—another unused and neglected room.

But this was clearly a very fine room, dominated as it was by an enormous four-poster bed. Cobwebs and the dust of ages blanketed everything; yet the room had a very special quality. Stephen could still see quite clearly the pattern of the old wallpaper: bold and wonderfully flowing designs of entwining stems and sprouting leaves in subtle shades of a bluish green; in between the flowing stems, the curving lines of large, cream lilies. On the walls near the windows, the design had sadly faded; but further back in the room, where sunlight had not affected the paper, the depth and shading of the colors gave a vigorous feeling of life and growth.

A large carpet lay on the floor. Despite the thick coating of dust, Stephen fancied that he could see there, echoed in the pile of the carpet, the curving lines of the same design.

In its time, it must have been an extremely elegant room. In fact, it was still quite lovely now. In some strange way, the dangling cobwebs added an elegance of their own. They blended in with the flowing designs. They hung in delicate, pale festoons from the frame around the top of the bed— daintily draping, gossamer curtains swaying gently in the draft.

Stephen wandered around the room, gently wiping a small, clear window in the dust of the dressing-table mirror, and smiling at his own reflection; peering through the cobweb curtain that almost entirely enclosed the bed; calmly turning to leave the room—unprepared for what he would see next.

Stephen gasped and stopped in his tracks. He was looking into a pair of eyes—a pair of smiling, hazel eyes. The eyes were staring directly back at him.

Light, flooding out from the room behind him, fell upon a colorful character. It took Stephen several startled moments to realize what he was looking at—a splendid, full-length, life-sized portrait.

The painting hung on the opposite wall of the corridor. A young man, perhaps not much older than himself, stood there in a long, white, curling wig. He was wearing a full-skirted frock-coat of scarlet velvet, with matching breeches and, under the coat, a long, dark waistcoat, the edges trimmed with wide gold braid. There were ruffles of white at his neck and wrists. With slim, pale, stocking-clad legs and very fancy buckled shoes, he stood there in a nonchalant pose—a very confident young man, with a charming, if somewhat superior smile.

Stephen relaxed and smiled back warmly. It was probably one of the Lansbury ancestors. Leaving the bedroom door wide open to give himself more light as he went, he set off along the corridor. Ahead of him, he could see the outlines of other picture frames on the walls. The opening of each door illuminated more faces—some old, some young, some pleasant, some glaring. Their eyes seemed to follow Stephen, as he made his way uncertainly, checking each room in turn.

The sun was low now in the sky. Stephen was feeling hungry again. He was getting anxious too, anxious to find a comfortable place for the night—and before it got dark.

At the end of the corridor, he turned and looked back. The light from the open doorways lit up a whole family: men, women, and children—ancestors from bygone ages. They all watched and waited in silence.

His ancestors. His family. He tried the idea out again. It didn't seem to mean much to him. Surely, he ought to have "special feelings"? Some special sense of belonging here.

Yet his face was grave; his eyes were sad. He only felt overwhelmingly lonely. Life seemed suddenly even more empty. He went back down the darkening corridor slowly, closing the doors one by one, returning all the Lansbury ancestors to their ever-slumbering gloom.

On the main landing, above the stairwell, Stephen found a very large painting. He stopped and stared at it closely. The picture showed a family group; judging by the manner of the people and by the clothing that they wore, it was a Victorian scene.

A handsome man with a bold mustache stood at the back, behind a couch, his figure held proud and erect in dark morning coat and high, winged collar. One arm was held out somewhat dramatically to the side of the couch, with the hand resting on the handle of a black walking stick. Stephen could see the silver lion's head. He grunted with pleasure, as he recognized the stick.

Seated on the couch was the upright figure of a young woman, her brown hair piled on top of her head, in the style of the 1890s. She wore an elegant, long, blue gown. The low-cut bodice was softly outlined with fine lace, exposing a curving, swanlike neck; the flared skirt fell in a silken swirl onto the ground around her feet.

Sitting on the couch beside the woman, with an air of repressed excitement, were two small boys. They were wearing matching sailor's suits; but their likeness to each other went very much further than that. They were clearly identical twins.

Stephen said the old saying out loud: "As alike as two peas in a pod."

Despite the very formal pose, the picture had a lively quality. Stephen knew instinctively that this was Philip and Christina Lansbury, with their children Stephen and Theodore.

Two, thick thatches of straight, brown hair. Two sets of shining, hazel eyes. The two boys were not only identical to each other, but, somehow, they also seemed familiar.

Stephen thought back to the village church; he remembered the two plaques on the wall. Poor old Theodore! There had certainly been a tragedy. For he must have lost, within a short spell, not only his parents, but also his brother—a very special, twin brother. That seemed to make it all much worse.

If you had never had any parents or a brother, it was difficult to imagine how you would feel if you suddenly lost them. But Stephen had plenty of imagination; he knew it would have been a terrible loss. That loss must have been the reason why Theodore shut himself away, the reason why he became a recluse. For that was what he appeared to have done, if the local stories could be believed.

He stood there gazing at the painting, wondering who had painted it. At the bottom right-hand corner there was a signature and a date. The date was easy to read—1894, but the signature was another matter. The first name looked like John. But then there were two odd squiggles, and after that what looked like *a r g e n t*. Stephen couldn't work it out.

He made his way thoughtfully along the corridor, toward two open doorways—the source of the light where he'd seen the butterfly disappear. On entering the room on the right, he could see it fluttering desperately against the windowpane. He crossed the tidy room to let it out. With the catch pushed back, the window opened easily; he watched with satisfaction as the little creature flitted away—a tiny, colorful, dancing speck, disappearing into the distance.

He closed the window, and looked around the simple room. It was spotlessly clean and tidy. The door of the large wardrobe was locked. Stephen had bravely tried to open it. When it wouldn't open, he wasn't sure whether he was sorry or relieved. There was something uncomfortable about large wardrobes with unknown contents. It could keep for another day.

The room contained a single bed. Stephen walked slowly back across the ancient rug that covered a part of the oak-boarded floor, to inspect the bed more closely: It had obviously been made with fresh linen, the covers turned back very neatly, ready for a would-be sleeper. Stephen had never seen such fine bed linen before. On one corner of the pillowcase and then again in the middle of the turned-back section of the linen top sheet, there was a large, elaborate *L*, embroidered in deep-blue silk.

A tartan rug in red, blue, and black was spread over the bed. Although it was obviously old and worn, with tattered fringes and mended patches, it looked quite clean and soft and comfortable.

Beside the bed there stood a small table. The only thing on the table was a silver-edged picture frame. Stephen picked it up; feeling rather weary now, he sat down on the bed to look at it. The photograph inside the frame, old and somewhat dimmed with age, was a muddy, sepia color. It showed a confident-looking young man with a keen and hopeful expression, wearing the uniform of a soldier of the First World War.

Stephen sat staring at the photo. If he had worked it all out correctly, this would be his grandfather, Stephen. "Killed in action 1915." He remembered the inscription clearly. War was terrible. War was wasteful.

He replaced the photo on the table; then, sighing loudly, he went out and across the corridor to look in the room opposite. It was much the same as the other room. There was a carpet on the floor, a wardrobe, and a small table.

But there was one very unusual thing about the room—it didn't have a bed. That in itself might not have seemed strange; there was, however, a very odd feature. Slung across one corner of the room, suspended at either end from very large, solid-brass hooks, each one securely attached to the wall, was a hammock: an old, dark-brown, well-worn hammock, made from coarsely woven material.

25. A Family Likeness

Stephen stood just inside the doorway of the room, considering the hammock. There was something about it that seemed familiar. When he noticed the large brass hooks from which the hammock was slung, he remembered. He remembered the hook with the "sleeping bat" in the library downstairs.

The "sleeping bat" must be a hammock. But the hammock in the library below hung folded and drooping from a single hook: a hammock in repose. He wouldn't mind betting that when he went down to look in the library later, he would find a second hook attached to the bookcase on the opposite wall, across the corner of the room.

It struck Stephen as very odd that upstairs there were only two usable bedrooms—the one opposite with the single bed, and this one with the peculiar hammock, while downstairs in the library, there was a similar situation with a single bed and a hammock. Whatever could it all mean? The mystery seemed to deepen around him.

He made a sudden and easy decision: He wasn't going to sleep upstairs.

The rooms were all so sad and lonely. Besides, he didn't like the idea of being cut off from the rest of the house, down this long and gloomy corridor.

He didn't like the uncomfortable feeling that seemed to be creeping over him. The library would be the place to sleep. It had a warm and kindly feeling. The little bed had looked quite cozy.

Returning to the bedroom opposite, Stephen collected the pillow from the bed, and the friendly tartan rug. As he turned to leave, he remembered the photo. It seemed a pity to leave Grandfather Stephen there on his own; so he picked up the silver photo frame. With the pillow under one arm and the tartan blanket across his shoulder, he made his way along the corridor and down the stairs.

The hall was dark and shadowy now. Pausing in front of the big mirror, Stephen peered closely at the dim reflection, then at the photo in his hand, then back at the mirror again. There was no doubt about it. There was a strong family likeness between the young man in the photograph and the face in the reflection. The face smiled back at him from the mirror, apparently rather pleased at the thought.

Back in the library, Stephen stood the photo in the middle of the long table at the side of the room. He picked up the walking stick from the bed and laid it reverently on the table; then he placed the tartan blanket and the pillow on the bed. He would be quite comfortable there for the night with his sleeping bag. Tomorrow he would look for some sheets and blankets, to make up a proper bed.

As he was about to leave the room, Stephen noticed something on the table—a small, worn, brown envelope lying beside the picture frame. Perhaps it had been clipped to the back, and had slipped down onto the tabletop. He picked it up thoughtfully, opened it very carefully, and slid the contents out on the table—two, narrow, folded strips of paper.

With the very greatest care, Stephen teased them gently open, pressing them flat on the tabletop. Each strip of discolored paper bore a faint pencil-written message and an official-looking stamp. He took them over close to the window, where the light was just good enough for him to make out the faint wording.

The first one was headed "Trotting Pass" and bore the following message:

Cpl. Lansbury has permission to trot mules on the level or within reason.

The second one, headed "Riding Pass," read as follows:

Cpl. Lansbury has permission to ride on the wagon.

Both were signed on behalf of the Duke of Cornwall's Light Infantry and bore the regiment's official stamp.

Stephen stood staring at the papers. Corporal Lansbury must, of course, be Grandfather Stephen. And these little slips of paper must be documents from the First World War, perhaps sent back amongst his belongings, after his death on the battlefront.

All that seemed obvious. But mules? Stephen knew that they had had horses. But what on earth were the soldiers on the battlefield in 1915 doing with mules?

It seemed incredible to him. And yet he knew that it must be so. He held the evidence in his hands.

The mules, he supposed, would have carried provisions and, of course, ammunition. Corporal Lansbury, so it seemed, had at some point been in charge of mules, and these flimsy pieces of paper were communications from a superior officer, probably carried on foot or horseback—or maybe even mule-back?

Stephen knew a little about the First World War from his lessons at school. The trenches and the front had been terrible. It must have been like the worst kind of nightmare—a nightmare that went on and on.

He folded the slips of paper along their old fold-lines, slipping them back into the envelope. It seemed a wonderful find to him—such a touching and personal find. And yet a very sad find, too. It gave him a lot to think about.

He gazed at the photo on the table, trying to imagine his Grandfather Stephen as a real, living person. A sudden nasty thought struck him.

114

Perhaps the Riding Pass had been issued when his grandfather had been wounded—perhaps the wounds from which he had died, jolting along in some awful, old wagon. Stephen could hardly bear to think of it. Grandfather Stephen suddenly seemed close.

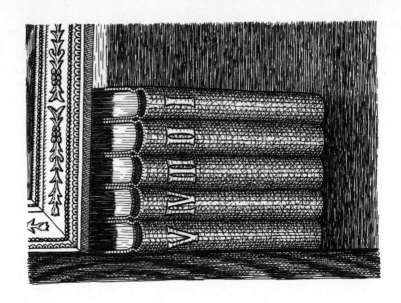

26. The Swinging Eyes

The sun was setting as Stephen sat at the kitchen table eating his cold supper. He was very hungry again, and he tackled the food with great pleasure: crunchy fresh bread with butter and cheese, cold meat and a tomato, crisps, and a rather warm can of lemonade. He was tempted to eat another banana, but he'd planned to keep one for lunch for each day, so he finished his meal off with an apple.

Having cleared everything away, he sorted out his personal belongings—bits and pieces that he'd unpacked that morning and left on the window seat. So much had happened during the day; the morning seemed like ages ago.

He stood there surveying his meager collection of belongings. It was nice to think that his few books would finally have a proper home. He gathered them up in his arms and carried them with a ceremonial air along the hall and into the library, where he stood them on the long table, standing back to admire the effect. They seemed quite out of place in their new surroundings. Stephen looked thoughtfully around the library, smiling broadly to himself at the thought of all those upper-crust books, with their elegant, leather bindings, having to tolerate the intrusion of this other motley crew—brash and modern and lower-crumb, some with flashy paper jackets.

Back in the kitchen, he assembled some tea-making equipment to take with him to the library. He hadn't bothered to light the range in the kitchen; but, as the evening grew cold, he fancied the idea of lighting the library fire, and he planned to heat water in one of his billycans to make a mug of tea. With a tray of tea-making equipment in one hand, the candleholder now with a new candle in the other hand, a box of matches in his pocket, and his sleeping bag slung over one shoulder, he made his way slowly along the dusky hall and into the library.

The front door still stood open, the cooler, damper air of evening flowing in. Having left his load in the library, Stephen went out and stood on the steps, looking around thoughtfully. The light was fading fast now, but everything seemed to be as it should be.

A bat swept low across the forecourt—the largest bat that he'd ever seen. It might be a Greater Horseshoe Bat. That would certainly be exciting; those were very rare now. Stephen was very fond of bats. He stood there peering into the gloom, hoping he'd see the bat again.

At last he turned to go inside, stopping to admire the scarlet passionflower—if passionflower it was. It glowed in the last light, against the darkening leaves of the vine. A strange perfume wafted on the evening air.

Inside the house with the door closed, he stood and listened in the hall. The house was as quiet and peaceful as ever—ready to rest for the night, so it seemed. He thought of the ancestors dozing quietly, all along the upstairs corridors. He shivered and withdrew quickly into the sanctuary of the library, closing the door firmly behind him.

The wood that was stacked beside the hearth in the library was old and dry, and Stephen soon had a warm fire going, with the billycan propped at the edge of the blaze. The old leather armchair was deep and comfortable. He sat back, enjoying the gloaming, very reluctant to light the candle, gazing into the glowing fire, and musing over the day's strange happenings.

The spluttering and fizzling of the water in the billycan brought Stephen

117

back to reality. Lighting the candle, he made his tea, and then sat looking around the room. He had been right. There was, as he'd suspected there would be, a second large brass hook, attached to the wall, across the corner from the "hanging bat." He could see it clearly from where he sat, its polished surface reflecting the firelight.

He couldn't imagine why anyone would want to hang a hammock in a library. He could only suppose that his Great-Uncle Theodore must have been a great eccentric. But, even allowing for that, it was weird.

Stephen's gaze traveled slowly around the room. With only the light from the fire and the candle, some of the room was lost in shadow; but he could see the photo frame on the table, the walking stick with the lion handle, and beside the stick his torch—just in case.

A small pile of books, stacked on the table, just behind the photo, caught his eye—a matching set of books, stacked very neatly, one on top of the other. There were no titles on the spines of the books, but even from his chair, with such poor light, Stephen could see that the books were numbered in bold Roman numerals.

As a small child, Stephen had had a great problem with books because of his learning difficulties. But his reading skills were now quite good, and he liked to think of himself as something of a bookworm. The stack of matching books on the table looked interesting; so getting up from his chair, he crossed the room, picked up the top book, which was marked number I, and took it back to the comfort of the armchair, where he could examine it by the light of the candle.

The book was obviously some kind of notebook, with pages and pages of closely written, longhand writing in faded ink. The brown, leather cover was blotched and discolored; some of the pages were badly stained. On the inside of the cover was written "Theodore Lansbury. Journal for 1911."

The first page was headed, "September 29th."

Stephen did a quick calculation. It was only a few months before the great *Titanic* disaster, when his great-uncle had lost both his parents.

The notebook was obviously a diary, with dates and a lot of writing. It suddenly seemed an important find. Was this the break he'd been looking for?

Stephen's face was alight with excitement as he stared at the book in his hands. Perhaps at last he would learn some real facts about his great-uncle and the family. That would be a big step forward—even if the facts weren't recent.

He settled down to read the faint writing:

We are off at last on our Great Adventure—my old friend B and I. Came onboard ship this morning at Liverpool—the SS Lanfranc. *Have a small but comfortable cabin. A single ticket from L to P cost nearly £27—a fortune by my standards, yet Pa and Ma coughed up happily, more than one can say for B's Pa. He has been most stingy about it, and conditions are imposed!*

Neither of us have been to sea before—at least not a proper voyage like this. After all the long months of planning, preparations, and delays—our pleasure at departure, our excitement, and our enthusiasm for the trip know no bounds.

Parents and brother S waved us off at the docks—shall greatly miss the old thing. He and I have never been parted before—not for more than a few days. But S will be happy at LH. He loves the place so dearly—farming the estate is his only ambition—strange to think that two people, so alike in so many ways, can be so very different in others. I always wanted to travel and explore—the chance of going on this trip with B too great an opportunity to miss—the one place I have longed to visit. Have both read Bates, Spruce, and Wallace—three times now at least. Can't wait to get there—to follow in their footsteps—the dream of a lifetime.

Stephen paused in his reading, staring thoughtfully into the fire. Theodore spoke of a "Great Adventure," but even allowing for modern money values, surely it can't have been very far—not for twenty-seven pounds!

His great-uncle certainly sounded very keen. But why didn't he say where he was going? Stephen found that irritating. And who was B? And what about Bates and Spruce and Wallace? Who on earth were they?

Finishing his tea and setting the empty mug down on the hearth, Stephen continued his reading—a description of the cabin and the ship on which the two friends were traveling:

This is one of Booths' most modern ships, only launched in 1907, and at 6,275 tons it is quite a sizable vessel. The Master is a rum old fellow. Tells us he's taken explorers before—that some of them never come back. But B and I are a very good team. We know we're going to be alright.

Turning the page, Stephen found the next heading:

September 30th—passing L P.

He continued to read with enthusiasm, but it was quite a battle, and slow. He had never been good at reading other people's handwriting. Great-Uncle Theodore's writing was hard to decipher, and he had sometimes used a kind of shorthand, every so often foreshortening words, and mostly using capital letters for the names of people and places.

It didn't look as if the second day of the voyage had been much fun:

B, poor fellow, most mightily sick. Well out to sea now, the ship pitching and rolling. Have to admit—don't feel too good myself . . .

The very short entry for that day seemed to speak for itself.

October 1st saw some improvement in the situation—at least for Great-Uncle Theodore:

Arrived at H. Feeling much better today—think I now have my sea legs. B still in a very bad state—worse than before—poor fellow. He is one of the strongest and soundest people. Odd to see him laid so low by such a simple malady.

Stephen sat gazing into the embers of the fire, wondering who *B* could be. *B* might stand for Brian or Bruce, but somehow that didn't seem to fit, although, he wasn't sure why. Perhaps Bartholomew or Basil? Yes. Basil sounded suitable. It was an old-fashioned-sounding name. He could well imagine his Great-Uncle Theodore having a friend called Basil. At any rate, Basil or not, *B* was obviously having a rough time.

Stephen piled more wood on the fire and continued reading very slowly, deciphering the words as best he could, but sometimes having to go back over the same passage several times to try and get the full meaning. After a while, he got better at it, and found the writing easier to read.

He was steaming along quite happily through a description of life on board ship, when a particular passage made him stop and wonder. His great-uncle had been describing a bird, which had been following the ship, then he went on to say:

The bird, circling over the ship, finally came to land on a lifeboat. I enjoyed myself by sketching him—see drawing 1.

"But what drawing?" Stephen wondered.

He flipped quickly and carefully through the remaining pages of the notebook. There were no drawings. It must mean a separate sketchbook. He got up and checked all the other notebooks in the pile on the table, skimming quickly through the pages. They were all filled from cover to cover with pages of close handwriting. There was not one sketch or drawing to be found. It was a disappointment. Drawings would have been fun. He could have had a quick look through them to see what the trip was all about.

The candle was beginning to fail. Stephen felt suddenly very tired; he decided he would go to bed. He closed the notebook, replacing it neatly on top of the pile with the others.

The bright fire had been very cheerful, but the room seemed almost too warm now. He thought he might open one of the windows. It would let in some healthy, fresh, night air.

Making his way across the room with the candleholder held high in one hand, something stopped him dead in his tracks. Outside in the garden, he could suddenly see two small lights: two, green, glowing lights that hung in a weirdly disembodied way, in the upper section of one of the windows.

Stephen's eyes stared wide in dismay. A shiver began to rise within him—his nose, his jaw, and the back of his neck tightened and tingled with alarm. He stood there frozen like a statue, clutching the candleholder tightly, trying to pull himself together, telling himself it was just an animal with the light reflected in its eyes.

Yet what sort of animal could it be? And how did it come to be hanging there? Or was it clinging to the window frame? Or was it some kind of hovering bird?

These questions were whirling through Stephen's mind when a very strange thing began to happen. The lights from the eyes began to swing. Stephen stood riveted to the spot, following the motion of the lights, with his own eyes staring wildly: across to one side, then back again; then back again a little wider; then back again yet wider still—and then across and out of sight.

The candle sputtered and went out. He stayed there frozen to the spot, staring at the blank, dark window, holding his breath and waiting anxiously. But nothing else happened or appeared.

At last, with a giant sigh of relief, he moved very slowly across to the window, and peered out cautiously into the darkness. There was nothing to be seen. There was nothing to be heard. The sky looked rather heavy and cloudy; the weather was unsettled now. The idea of opening the window seemed, somehow, to have lost its appeal. Perhaps he would leave it closed for now—just in case it rained overnight.

The "swinging eyes" had unsettled Stephen. By the flickering light of the fire, he crept across the room to the door. Opening it silently, he stood there listening carefully. The front door was still firmly closed. He couldn't hear anything moving about, only the occasional creak and sigh from the gently sleeping house.

He was suddenly much too tired to care. The kindly old house gave him confidence. Having first collected his torch, he flitted quickly along the hall to pay a quick visit to the throne room. He had worked out how to flush the toilet that morning, yet he couldn't quite pluck up enough courage to do it now: to break the silence of the sleeping house.

He'd have to leave his teeth for tonight. His enthusiasm didn't quite stretch to searching around for his toothbrush and toothpaste, dabbling about in the scullery sink, running the hissing, clanking tap, surrounded by long and jumping shadows.

Back in the library, with the door firmly closed, Stephen prepared himself for bed. Lying in his sleeping bag on the small bed, with his head on the clean white linen pillowcase—the one with the large blue embroidered L—he felt very comfortable. He stretched his tired limbs down in the bag, and relaxed with a sigh of contentment.

The old bookcases, full of their ancient books, towered above him, just visible in the last glow from the fire. He put out an arm and ran his hand along a polished oaken surface. It was comfortingly solid and reassuring.

"Yes. This is a very good place to be. A very, very good place to be," he murmured happily to himself, as he drifted off to sleep.

27. Creatures of the Lake

Stephen woke up late the following morning. From his bed in the corner of the library, he could see that the weather had taken a turn for the worse. The sky was gray, and it was drizzling; but regardless of the weather, Stephen was determined to get out to explore the Lansbury Hall estate. He wasn't going to be put off by rain.

Having dressed quickly, he rushed to the throne room, splashed his face at the scullery sink, then he made a hasty breakfast—big slabs of bread and butter and honey. He had felt bold enough to open one of the jars from the larder, which he had thought looked like honey; and indeed, honey it was—deliciously crunchy with a wonderful flavor.

Stephen washed his breakfast down with milk. On his trip to the shop the day before, he had managed to bring back a pint of milk. It wasn't possible to carry more; besides, he knew perfectly well that it wouldn't keep without a fridge. Having finished the milk, he washed the bottle in the scullery sink, saving the silver-foil top and popping it back into the bottle, which he stood down on the scullery floor. "Waste not, want not," he'd always been told.

Putting on his boots and his parka, he prepared to leave the house, first emptying his pockets of clutter and some odd loose change. He left it all on the kitchen table. He'd sort it out later on.

His eyes strayed across to the "odd collection" that lay on the tabletop. It was still a mystery to him, although he felt quite sure that if he put his mind to it, he could work out what it was doing there; but he never seemed to have the time. There were always more important things to do. He certainly wouldn't waste time now. His heart was set on exploration.

On his way out through the hall, Stephen paused in the dining room doorway. He was very interested in the large, chunky objects that he'd seen on the sideboard there. They certainly looked like old silver. If the weather was bad after lunch, he might stay in and clean them off. So he opened the door of the dining room and left it standing wide open, hoping that that would help to clear the horribly stuffy atmosphere. Then he stopped in front of the grand mirror, and applied Morwenna's Secret Recipe.

Out on the steps in front of the house, it was not an encouraging scene, quite different from the day before—a very dull and heavy scene, with the woodland in the valley below shrouded by a blanket of fine rain.

With the door closed behind him, Stephen stood hesitating on the wide top step. He was trying to decide whether or not he had that feeling of being watched. But the feeling was one of those strange, elusive things: The more he tried to decide whether or not he had it now, the more uncertain he became as to what "the feeling" was.

There had been nothing yesterday that he could put his finger on, so to speak. Today, when he came to look around, when he came to think about it carefully, there was nothing more than a heaviness—a peculiar sense of being closed in by a disconcerting dullness and stillness.

Surely he must have been potty, yesterday, with all those thoughts about an audience. He looked across the gloomy landscape. Or was it, perhaps, the simple fact that his audience didn't like the rain?

The atmosphere was depressing. If he hadn't been set on exploration,

Stephen would probably have turned around and gone straight back indoors again. There were plenty of things he could do in the house; but he'd made up his mind to explore the estate, and that was what he was going to do.

As he left the house, he was sorry to see that the flower on the vine beside the door had closed its petals and died. At the bottom of the steps, he turned to look back at the house. A new flower was blooming now on the opposite vine across the door. It was just as brilliant and just as beautiful as the first flower had been.

Stephen looked up and smiled at the vines. He noticed that just above the central window of the library, one branch was now quite bare of foliage. Whatever it was that attacked the vines, it had clearly been active overnight.

He went across to examine the leaves. Some of them looked as if something had taken a big bite out of them; sections had been chomped away and then the remainder dropped on the ground. Stephen stood frowning down at the debris, puzzled and unable to imagine what kind of beast might have done such a thing. He thought about the "swinging eyes," and he shuddered as he moved away.

In olden days, visitors, sweeping up the drive in carriages, would have drawn to a halt on an immaculately tended, wide, gravel forecourt. It was obviously a very long time since anybody had done anything in the way of maintaining or controlling the extensive grounds of Lansbury Hall. The area in front of the house was completely overgrown with weeds and grasses, so much so that it was only just possible to make out the shape of the forecourt and drive.

The lower edge of the forecourt, farthest from the house, was bounded by a long, low, stone balustrade. The balustrade opened up in the middle, then swept on down in a gentle, outward curve on either side of a flight of steps that led to the gardens and meadows below.

Two large stone figures stood, one on either side, at the top of the steps. These, like the rest of the structure, were enveloped by a mass of overgrown roses—a glorious riot of roses, with glistening leaves and gorgeous blooms, rambling on and on regardless, over steps and balustrade, their long and thorny, winding limbs reaching out in all directions.

Picking his way carefully down the crumbling steps, Stephen found himself in a forest of rampant rose growth. He had had no idea that rose-bushes could grow so big. They towered above him on all sides, originally part of a formal planting, but now completely out of control—ancient rose-bushes, run quite wild over many, many years.

The flowers that the bushes bore reminded Stephen of old-fashioned botanical prints. Some were huge, fat, cabbage-shaped blooms—deepest pink with a lovely perfume. Others were wide and strangely flat, in white or red, their multiple petals arranged in a series of rosette-like clusters around each flower head. One of the bushes bore the most deeply fragrant, dark, velvety, crimson blooms, whose branches, stems, and green parts were covered by fine, sharp bristles.

A misty drizzle still hung in the air as Stephen stood amongst the bushes, gazing closely at one of the roses. Its dark-green leaves were wet and glistening; tiny, angular troughs of water nestled amongst the pink rosettes. He bent and sniffed at the delicate fragrance, then, smiling happily, turned away and set off briskly down the meadow.

His rapid pace was soon slowed down, for the going was not to be so easy. The meadow, once sloping lawns, was now a tangled mass of grasses and wildflowers; everything was soaking wet. Stephen wished he had a poncho. In no time at all his jeans were drenched, his feet uncomfortably wet and squelching.

A large area of the lower part of the field was more like a bog than a meadow: tufted tussocks of coarse grasses in an oozing sea of smelly mud. But Stephen pressed on with enthusiasm. He could hear the sound of running water. Amongst the misty trees in the valley, he could make out the line of a small, gushing river.

He crossed the boggy terrain with difficulty, slithering and sliding from one grassy hummock to the next, till he found himself at the edge of a lake, lined by reeds and tall yellow iris. It was partly silted and overgrown; but there were still large areas of open water. Toward the middle, he could see the upturned rims of gigantic water-lily leaves. They reminded him of Kew Gardens, but they seemed quite out of place here.

Stephen crept quietly toward the lake, hoping to catch sight of some wildlife, maybe frogs or fish or newts. He was moving slowly around the edge, when a weird cry rang out. It came from the reed bed ahead of him— a ghastly, gobbling, gurgling call, which brought him to a sudden halt. The call was almost immediately answered from a number of places around the lake, the very peculiar gurgling calls echoing in the still, dank air.

Standing almost glued to the spot, Stephen stared fixedly at the reed-bed just a few feet ahead. When nothing happened, he put out a foot and started edging slowly forward. There was a rustling amongst the reeds, then, with a loud plopping noise, a large greenish-brownish body flopped quickly into the water. The creature disappeared in a flash, leaving Stephen standing there, staring down at the churning water—unpleasant, sludgy-looking water.

The rank smell of rotting vegetation rose up to Stephen's nostrils, as he stood beside the lake. Was it his imagination or could he just see some vague, pale form drifting up from the murky depths? Some shapeless creature with beady eyes—eyes like the cloudy, green-brown water.

Stephen moved cautiously forward toward the soggy edge of the lake, only too well aware of the fact that, if he weren't very careful, he might end up in the lake himself, visiting whatever it was much more closely than he'd intended.

He peered intently into the water. Whatever it was had now sunk and vanished. As he looked out across the lake, the water lay totally still and unruffled.

The heavy, misty air hung damply around Stephen as he made his way along toward the end of the lake, looking back over his shoulder from time to time, wondering what it was that he'd seen. Whatever it was, it was quite a good size—at least eighteen inches in length. Surely it couldn't be an otter. Otters liked clean running water; otters made a whistling sound. That revolting, gobbling noise certainly couldn't have come from an otter.

As an avid would-be zoologist, he knew that he ought be taking a cool and scientific approach to the creatures of the lake. Had he been one of a group of people—that might have been possible. But without support and on his own, he found that he simply couldn't do it. He couldn't help feeling quite alarmed, and he shuddered to think what the creatures might be.

28. The Phantom Gardener

Picking his way slowly along the boggy edge of the lake, Stephen watched and listened carefully for any more disturbances, with a thoughtful frown on his face.

Some very unusual-looking trees stood in a group at the end of the lake, their thick trunks fat with rotted stumps and dangling limbs. Fanning out at the tops of the trunks were huge, curving, fernlike arms. They were certainly very exotic.

Stephen wandered amongst them, intrigued. Then he stood beneath the arms, gazing up at the strange, green tracery. Droplets of water splashed in his face. He blinked and wiped the water away with the back of a wet and muddy hand.

There was something odd about the trees. He wasn't sure if he liked them or not. They were unusual, almost handsome, and yet they seemed so alien too. He looked back at them several times, as he made his way toward the path that ran along beside the river.

The source of the river—a tiny, bubbling spring—was far away, high up on the moor. By the time the stream had made its way across the moorland and down through the wooded valleys to the meadow below the house, it was some two to three yards wide: a gushing of fresh, clear, sparkling water, and a great delight to Stephen. He was so pleased with the wonderful river that he completely forgot his worries about the creatures of the lake. He turned right at the riverbank, making his way eagerly upstream, along a narrow, winding path.

Alder trees dotted the low, mossy bank on his side of the river; but the opposite bank was quite different in character, heavily wooded and falling steeply, with trees of many species and sizes growing out from the rocky bank. Here and there were ancient hollies, their smooth and sinuous silver trunks leaning out across the water, their prickly branches skimming its surface.

Stephen stopped to admire a beech tree. Thick, bulbous, muscular roots held it into its rocky bed. The broad, gray, trunk curved out from the bank, towering up to disappear in the leafy canopy high above.

A plush, green coating of many mosses crept up the trunk of the tree. It covered the tops of the lowest branches—gaunt, dead-looking, angular branches, stretching toward him like scraggy, old arms, the searching fingers pointing low and reaching out across the water. Ferns grew out of the velvety coating, and from the arms and fingers there hung long, pale wisps of gray-green lichen.

Beneath the roots of the tree, just above the surface of the water, there was a large dark hole in the bank. Stephen crouched at the edge of the river, leaning out as far as he dared, trying to see right into the hole. As he got back onto his feet, he grinned a wry grin to himself. He was almost certain—though not quite sure—that, above the noise of the running water, he'd heard another kind of sound: a very angry, gobbling noise. Perhaps there was something residing there that didn't like inquisitive eyes. He continued his way along the river, glancing back from time to time.

It was a truly magical river. The banks were draped with vegetation: ferns that glistened in the wet and hung in elegant fringing curtains; lush, green masses of broad-leafed grasses hanging over the dancing water. Ivy wandering everywhere: across the rocks and the thrusting roots, and up the curving trunks of trees; dangling down from the reaching branches and dipping into the river itself; trailing and swished by the clear, cooling water that rushed on by in the greening gloom beneath the shade of the many trees.

As Stephen pressed on upriver, the valley narrowed. Woodland closed in on his right-hand side, mostly ancient oak and holly with a few beeches in between. And wherever they could find the light, slender, spindly saplings sprouted.

The woodland was overrun with wild honeysuckle, and Stephen saw to his surprise that entwined with the honeysuckle high in the branches and dangling from the limbs of saplings were masses of blue passionflowers.

This time he knew exactly what they were, for they were more like the kind that he'd seen growing in people's gardens. The ring of purple hairlike filaments around the inside of the flower, overlaying the pale green petals, produced what looked like a blue flower. In the center of the flower was that peculiar, fleshy, branching structure. They seemed quite out of place in this Cornish woodland. Stephen couldn't imagine why they should be growing there in such profusion. They were foreign flowers. They didn't belong.

He made up his mind that, when he got home, he would read up about passionflowers in his book on botany. They might, after all, provide a clue that would help him unravel the mystery.

For as Stephen stood anxiously looking around in the gloomy, dripping woodland, he was more aware than ever of an uncanny sense of mystery. Not only was there something strange about the house, beautiful as it was, but there was something equally strange, or even more strange, about the grounds, about the plants—and about the animals. He couldn't control a nervous shiver, as he pushed the hair back from his face, and set off once again upriver.

The path was well worn, but muddy and treacherous. He slipped and slithered along the way, grasping hold of branches and saplings. Water splashed him from every angle. It ran around his wrists and into his sleeves; it trickled horribly down his neck. The cuffs of his parka and his collar had become uncomfortably soggy. From time to time he stopped on the path, and stood carefully looking around and behind him.

Yet, despite his great discomfort, the river drew him steadily on. Some stretches were very shallow, the water running between fat boulders or past wide banks of pale, fine sand. But the most exciting, mysterious places were the deeper, darker pools. Stephen crouched on the muddy bank, peering into the murky depths. The movement of the swirling water made it difficult to focus on the rocky riverbed.

He crouched there frowning and peering down. Were those two, long, dark shapes creatures? Or were they only fish? Were they moving? Or were they still? Were they only lumps of rock?

From one clear, rippling patch of worried water to another, from one deep, dark, thrilling pool to the next, the river drew him on—higher and higher up the valley toward an ever-increasing noise, an ever-growing roaring sound, which seemed to envelope and dull his senses.

The waterfall, when he came to it, was not high; nor was it one of those picture-book waterfalls with beautiful curtains of falling spray. It was a basic rushing and gushing of water cascading through narrow gaps: over massive, granite chunks; over and around boulders; the water plunging on and down into a churning, rocky pool.

Having pushed his sleeves up high, with one foot braced against a rock, Stephen dangled his hot clammy hands into a spurting arm of the water. But he didn't stop there very long, for he found that the loud noise troubled him. It filled his head and worried him because he couldn't hear properly—because he wouldn't be able to hear if someone or something crept up on him. Wiping his arms down the side of his jeans, he walked away as quickly as possible.

Above and beyond the waterfall, away from the noise of the rushing water, a wide pool opened out. The water, running over a bed of large, flat, gray rocks, had a slightly turquoise tinge. Standing toward the back of the pool, Stephen was surprised to discover a tall, slim, primitive-looking statue of roughly human form. The curving face of the bank behind formed a cozy, green-lined grotto, the cool and ever-seeping water feeding the thick and spongy growths that grew across its rocky face.

133

Stephen stood quietly, surveying the scene. On either side of the grotto, there were more large holes in the bank, their dark mouths fringed with ferns. But there was nothing to be seen or heard. If there were any "gobblers" in residence, they were keeping very quiet.

The rain was falling heavily now. Stephen decided he'd had enough. He'd been in some very wet places before, but this was getting beyond a joke. Everything everywhere was running with water, everything including himself.

It was time to go home and change his clothes; besides, surely, it must be lunchtime. He pulled up a soggy cuff to check the time. Then he remembered about his watch—he'd left it on the kitchen table.

Just at that point, a small and convenient pathway led up away from the river. He decided to take the path. With any luck, it would take him up through the woodland and bring him out somewhere above the house.

As he ducked beneath the branches, dodging the dripping hanging vines, water showered down on Stephen, splashing on his head and face, running in rivulets down his neck. His old parka was no protection. It was soaked right through and worse than useless.

He found himself getting very hot as he struggled up the muddy slope. He would have been better off without clothing; he laughed at the thought of himself battling his way through the drenching woodland, dressed only in his skin and wearing his heavy boots. He looked down at the poor, old boots. Oozing water and covered in mud, they too had succumbed to the Cornish wet. They had even lost their squeak!

At last he emerged at the top of the wood and found himself on an overgrown track. The track led up and away to the left toward the moor. Down below him, to the right, he could see the old house.

Although the rain was easing now, Stephen had had more than enough of exploration. He made his way as quickly as he could down the track. He could see the courtyard behind the house, the outbuildings ranged around the yard. To the left of all that, sheltered by the slope of the hill, there was a large, walled area, which must be the old kitchen garden.

He stopped in amazement on the track, staring at the big walled garden.

Like the rest of the Lansbury Hall estate, it was wildly overgrown, except, that is, for one large strip. Even from a distance, Stephen could see the big patch of well-dug soil, and the orderly rows of vegetables. After a moment's quiet thought, he started down the track again, making his way toward the garden.

Around the side of the house, just opposite the entrance to the big courtyard, there was a doorway in the garden wall. The old door, rotting and swollen, had long since dropped off its rusted hinges. It now stood to one side, useless and propped against the wall. Stephen walked straight in.

He made his way along a path toward the top end of the garden, then wandered thoughtfully along the edge of the vegetable patch, admiring the rows of vegetables—onions, carrots, peas, parsley, sweet corn—all in their early stages, but all looking very healthy. And then a mass of shrublike plants that he didn't recognize. The long stems were topped with wide-spreading, palmate leaves, each one composed of seven pointed leaflets opening out from the top of the stem rather like an umbrella. He couldn't think what they could be.

Beyond the strange, shrubby plants, there was a big patch of something that looked like wheat or barley, and then at the end of the garden, row upon row of potato plants, neatly banked and marching in orderly fashion up and down the plot—a whole regiment of healthy-looking spuds, the symmetry of their ranks spoiled only by the fact that one of the plants, in the row nearest to the path, was missing. A garden fork stood in the gap, with its prongs plunged firmly into the ground, and on the path beside the gap was a heap of freshly dug potatoes. They lay there on a piece of sacking—apparently waiting to be collected.

Stephen stopped abruptly in his tracks. He stood there with his mouth open, staring down at the potatoes. Then he looked quickly and nervously around. Someone had obviously been there recently—within the last hour or two. Someone, whose solid human hands were capable of digging potatoes. Ghostly hands didn't do such things. Stephen was almost sure of that.

The rain was falling heavily now. Water dripped off his nose and chin; his hair was plastered to his forehead in a most unpleasant way. But he stood for a while in the pouring rain, anxiously looking around the garden, scanning the hillside behind the house, a thoughtful, worried look in his eyes.

Finally convinced that there was nobody about, Stephen set off toward the house.

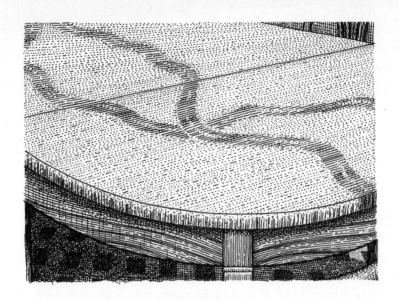

29. Intruders

Stepping in through the doorway of Lansbury Hall, Stephen felt a great sense of relief. But almost as soon as he entered the hallway, he knew that something was wrong. The door of the dining room, which he had left open on purpose that morning, was now closed—and so was the door to the kitchen. There was no draft to blow them shut. They certainly couldn't have closed on their own.

Stephen felt suddenly very nervous—and suddenly very chilled. He stood alert in the middle of the hallway, hesitating and listening intently, sweeping the dripping hair from his face.

Was that a voice he could hear somewhere? Or was it his imagination? He strained his ears to catch any sound. Perhaps there was someone there in the house—the kind of someone who dug potatoes.

Maybe he ought to call out, just in case.

"Hullo-oh. Hullo there." A shivery voice.

Total silence followed the call. And then a single, distant thud, perhaps the sound of a closing door. Then nothing else at all.

Water was dripping from Stephen's clothing. It was seeping from his muddy boots and forming a pool on the marble floor. How he longed for some clean, dry clothing. He felt pretty silly just standing there.

Bracing himself, he crossed the hall to go and open the dining room door. Much of the room looked exactly as he had left it that morning. But something unusual seemed to have happened on top of the dining room table. The thick coating of dust had been disturbed, disturbed in a very strange way; for the top of the table seemed to be covered in the most peculiar tracks.

There were tracks along the floor as well. Something had been scurrying up and down the room on the floor around the table, up and over all the chairs, then skidding through the thick bed of dust that covered the surface of the table. Clouds of dust still hung in the air. Whatever it was that had done all that, had been doing it very recently.

Stephen began to wonder what on earth he might find in the kitchen. He held his breath as he opened the door at the rear of the hall then edged his way across the corridor into the room. It all looked surprisingly normal, exactly as he'd left it that morning. Well, almost exactly as he had left it.

The milk bottle that he had washed earlier and stood in the scullery, now lay on its side just in front of him on the kitchen floor. He stooped to pick it up. The silver-foil top that he'd folded up and popped inside the bottle had gone. It must have dropped out on the floor somewhere.

"But how did the bottle get there?" he wondered.

As he placed the bottle on the kitchen table, he noticed a very strange thing. The "odd collection," as he called it, still sat in its usual position in the middle of the table, but his own collection of odds and ends—the things that he'd taken out of his pockets that morning and had left in a heap at one end—were now spread wide across the table. Some of the oddments-two elastic bands and a crumpled paper bag—had been tossed off the edge of the table, and now lay on the floor.

Stephen walked slowly down the room, looking thoughtfully at the table.

Some of the things that he knew he'd left there that morning were now missing. There had been several of those little, shiny, metal tabs that you pulled off the tops of canned drinks. For some odd reason those were gone.

Several coins still lay on the table—dull, brown, two-pence pieces, but all the silver coins were gone. Worst of all, his watch was missing. That was a really bad blow for Stephen. He would be lost without his watch—an inexpensive, basic watch, but still a precious thing to him.

The crumpled five-pound note still lay there. He stretched it flat on the tabletop, pressing the creases out with a wet and muddy hand, scowling thoughtfully as he did so. It was horrible to think that someone had entered the house and taken his belongings.

Could it be someone from the village? Some lad with nothing better to do? Could there, after all, be a housekeeper? Coming and going from the village? But no, that didn't fit at all. Why should anyone, doing such a job, want to do it like that—in secret? The questions went round and round in Stephen's head. The more he worried about the mystery, the more unpleasant the questions became. Was someone using Lansbury Hall? Squatting there without any rights? Or a criminal on the run? Or was it simply a passing burglar, taking advantage of an empty house?

But what sort of burglar would have taken the metal flip-top tabs? And what sort of burglar would have taken several coins and his watch—and left behind a five-pound note? None of it made any sense.

His eyes traveled back down the room and across the corridor to the closed scullery door. Had he closed the door that morning? Or had he left it open? Could there be someone still lurking out there?

Reluctantly and very quietly, Stephen crept across the room, stopping at the door to listen. He could hear the sound of running water coming from the room beyond. A ludicrous thought came into his mind: Perhaps the burglar liked to be clean, and was washing his hands in the scullery sink.

He turned the handle slowly and quietly, and then on a sudden angry impulse, pushed the door wide open fast, stepping smartly into the room, only to come to a very sharp halt, his mouth dropping open in amazement at the sight that met his eyes. "Oh, no!" he cried.

30. The Banana Burglar

The scullery was in a frightful state. The tap was still running in the sink, and someone or something had been indulging in water sports. The large bottle of washing-up liquid had played a major part in the games.

The bottle now lay, in a very depressed state, in the middle of the floor. Most of its contents had been used to create a truly massive mountain of foam that spread from the sink, across the draining board, and over a very large part of the floor. A long, wet, foamy trail led across to the closed back door.

After the initial shock and surprise, which had stopped him in his tracks, Stephen sprang quickly into action, grabbing the first likely weapon that came to hand—an old, wooden rolling pin that he had seen in one of the cupboards. He skidded across the foamy floor, and flinging the back door open wide, he stepped out briskly into the courtyard, wielding the heavy rolling pin.

How dare anyone enter his home and make such a stupid, horrible mess! He stood there angrily in the rain. His eyes searched wildly for the culprit.

But there was no one to be seen. No sign of any movement. Whoever it was had apparently vanished.

The pouring rain discouraged pursuit. It quickly washed his anger away. Stephen suddenly felt very foolish.

He lowered the rolling pin to his side, remembering the many times when he had tried to defend himself. For Stephen had often been bullied at school. But he'd never struck anyone before with a blunt instrument; he certainly didn't want to start now. His feelings of relief were tinged with shame, as he retreated to the scullery to return the long, wooden, would-be weapon to its rightful place in the cupboard.

Back in the safety of the scullery with the door firmly closed, Stephen removed his muddy boots, and hung his dripping parka on a hook. Then he stripped off every stitch of clothing, and dumped it in the sink of foam, turning off the running tap. He knew he would have to do something about clearing up the whole mess later on. The clothing would have to wait till then.

Nipping speedily across the cold slate floor into the kitchen, he grabbed, as he passed, his old brown towel that hung across the back of a chair. Then he toweled himself down briskly all over, ignoring the fact that what he badly needed was a good bath, and that when it came to his legs and feet, he was pushing a lot of dirt around.

By rummaging through the pile of things on the window seat, he was able to find himself a fresh set of clothing. He wriggled his damp limbs awkwardly into the garments, hopping from one foot to the other. When he had dressed, he felt much better. Nothing matched and the socks were odd, but he didn't care about that. At least he was dry and comfortable again; that was all that mattered now.

"Exploration is all very well, but explorers need their creature comforts," Stephen said out loud to himself.

Outside the weather was improving. The sky was brighter; the clouds were thinning. There were one or two small patches of blue. It might be sunny after lunch.

The most important thing now was food. Stephen had no idea what the time was, but he knew it was time to eat. It was a big relief to discover that

141

no one had raided the larder. He'd been afraid of what he might find there, but a quick look around had reassured him.

He decided to make himself a big cheese and pickle sandwich, but when he put out his hand for the cheese, it wasn't there! He distinctly remembered leaving the cheese on the right-hand marble counter, and covering it with one of the wire-meshed domes, which he'd taken from the counter opposite.

He glanced across the room at the trooping "family" of covers. They all looked just the way they should—proceeding in perfect order across the top of the counter in the dim light of the larder. And then it suddenly struck him. Of course! The very fact that they were in perfect order, meant that they weren't the way that he'd left them.

Somebody had taken the cover away—the one that he'd removed from the troop—and had put it back in its rightful position in the family line of covers. They had also taken the cheese and bacon, and had placed them safely under the cover. Stephen stood staring down at the covers. What a very odd thing to do!

When at last he finally sat down at the kitchen table, with his cheese sandwich in front of him, Stephen felt quite confused and exhausted. He sat there munching the sandwich and thinking. There were so many weird things about Lansbury Hall; so much had happened since he'd arrived, but he simply didn't know where to begin in trying to make some sense of it all, in trying to find some reasonable pattern.

He reached out his hand for his daily banana.

"Oh, no! I don't believe it!" he gasped. "That really is too bad!"

Only three bananas now lay on the plate in the middle of the table. All the apples seemed to be there. But three bananas had completely vanished.

This was getting ridiculous. How could he possibly believe in a banana eating burglar—someone who collected flip-top tabs, rolled milk bottles around the floor, frolicked on dining room tables, and wrestled with bottles of washing-up liquid in sinks of running water?

It was too ludicrous for words. Stephen felt that he had to laugh. At least the burglar must be fair-minded, for he had only taken three of the six bananas. But as he ate his way down through one of the remaining bananas, the smile began to fade from his face, to be replaced by a worried frown. He couldn't help feeling very uncomfortable. He couldn't help wondering all the time: Whatever was going to happen next?

31. The Invisible Audience

Having finished his lunch, Stephen filled his macaw mug with orange soda, and wandered along to the library. He sat down in one of the big armchairs with his *Illustrated Dictionary of Botany*.

"H, I, J, K"—he'd never been good at sequencing letters. "L, M, N, O, P. *P* for passionflower."

"A genus of five hundred species," he read out loud. "The majority coming from South America."

Further down on the same page, there was a description of the shape of the flowers and, in particular, the peculiar, branching arrangement in the middle of each flower.

"Missionaries in South America saw the flowers as symbolic of Christ on the cross."

Apparently the pistil of the flower—that odd, divided middle section—reminded them of the cross on which Christ was crucified; the stigma—those bobbly bits—reminded them of the nails; and the corona—the frilly ring of filaments—reminded them of the crown of thorns. Hence the name, passionflower.

Stephen remembered the old, old story of Jesus—the story of all the things that happened in the days before he was crucified: how his disciples deserted him; how Judas had betrayed him; how he finally suffered and died on the cross—the story of the Passion of Jesus Christ.

"What an extraordinary thing!" he exclaimed. "Missionaries in South America. Could that possibly mean the Amazon? The greatest of rivers in the whole, wide world. And the greatest of forests too."

Stephen sat daydreaming about the Amazon. Then, putting down the book, he went to look at the map on the wall above the fireplace. He'd been meaning to examine it properly; now that he came to look at it carefully, he could see that it appeared to be a map of the Lansbury Hall estate.

The old-fashioned writing was faint and difficult to read, but he could see the house quite clearly, the edge of the woodland, the line of the river. As he followed the river's course downstream across the map, he discovered to his great delight that it seemed to run out into the sea. A small bay with rocky headlands was shown—all part of the Lansbury estate.

A trip to the beach would be marvelous. Stephen didn't feel tired anymore. The weather was looking so much better.

With a last despairing look at the scullery, and final, regretful thoughts of his watch, he set off across the open forecourt toward the meadows below. His feet were dry and comfortable now, wearing his old, black sneakers. He hadn't been able to face putting his feet back inside the wet, muddy boots, despite the fact that he realized that his feet were bound to get soaked again, tramping through the long, wet grasses. But it didn't seem to matter much. His sneakers would soon dry out in the sunshine.

He crossed the meadow, and, keeping well over to the left-hand side, away from the bog and the lake, he soon came to the bank of the river. Everything looked so different now. The whole character of the river seemed to have changed, with sunlight streaming through the trees reflected on the running water. Beside the river at that point, there was a smooth, wide bank of fine grass—a perfect place for picnics on the summer days ahead.

Stephen felt completely relaxed and happy as he took the path beside the river and made his way downstream. It was a long time since he'd seen the sea. He was going to enjoy his trip to the beach. He was certainly not going to be upset by any unusual sights or sounds that he might encounter along the way.

Downstream, the river ran wide and shallow over a glistening gravel bed: no more sinister holes in the bank, and no more deep, mysterious pools; but thick stands of sprouting bracken amongst the thinning trees on the banks.

Stephen stopped on several occasions, standing still and looking about him. Those scuffling noises in the undergrowth could be due to the activities of any one of a number of normal, harmless creatures. Each time he stopped on the path and listened, the noises all stopped too; but on one occasion, he thought he heard a kind of chattering, giggling call. Squirrels make a chattering noise, but not quite like that.

Stephen decided to ignore the rustlings. A tiny wren hopped ahead of him as he made his way along the path. He would concentrate on the birds instead. After all, he had never had such a wonderful opportunity for bird-watching before.

He stood for some time observing a dipper. It bobbed up and down in an entertaining way on a small stone at the edge of the river; then it dived and disappeared from sight beneath the surface of the water, only to reappear at last in a different and unexpected place. Stephen amused himself by playing a kind of guessing game—guessing where it would pop up next. But the dipper always won.

On one of the bends in the river, he disturbed a tall and stately heron, fishing the river's shallows. He had never seen a heron before. He edged slowly and quietly forward. The bird stood frozen like a statue, with its handsome, crested head held high on long, slim, rigid neck. They eyed each other for a moment. Then, to Stephen's great regret, it rose in the air with a cry of alarm, with a great deal of flapping of big, gray wings, and with lanky legs dangling down.

It was a long walk down the valley to the place where the river ran out to the sea. The path stretched on between the trees. It seemed odd to Stephen that there was no feeling of being anywhere near the sea—no sound of the sea, no sound of gulls, nor any sense of seaside things. Could he, perhaps, have misread the map?

The valley had been steadily widening, with wooded banks on either side. It was quite a surprise and a sudden delight, when Stephen at last emerged from the woodland, and saw the shimmering line of the sea. The rolling, sloping land on his left was open and covered with grass and wildflowers. He paused to watch the butterflies. One of his favorites went dancing by—the Brimstone, with its delicately curving and neatly pointed, sulphur-yellow wings. A splash of blue with a hint of brown freckle flitted across the grassy slopes. Could it have been the rare Large Blue? It might just be possible. This was such an unspoiled place.

On Stephen's right, the slope was steeper, and woodland continued along the top of a low, rocky headland. Ahead of him, the river ran into a large lake, the water dammed by a bar of shingle along the back of the beach. Some time, long ago, Man had assisted in the creation of the lake, lining its rim with a rocky wall; but this was now quite overgrown, and the lake was largely silted up.

Stephen trudged on through the long grasses, past bank after bank of tall yellow iris that grew in the silt around the edge of the lake. He stood at last at the back of the beach. Water, escaping from the lake, ran through a gap in the wall at the end, brimming over the bar of pebbles, cascading down a slope of boulders, and out onto the beach below. Rocky headlands framed the bay, black shadowed in the bright sunlight, their craggy extremities dipping down, submerging in a tranquil sea.

"Wow!" said Stephen. "What a wonderful beach!"

A wide crescent of yellow sand lay gleaming there before him. Water from the river, running and spreading across the beach, formed a glinting pathway in the sun: a pathway stretching down to the sea, the sand washed and scoured and sculptured by the river water's flow.

The tide was low. Stephen could hear the gentle murmur of waves running softly up the beach, the whooshing sound of their curling and breaking.

He could see the foaming rims of the waves, spreading and rippling on the sand, rippling and sparkling in the sun.

After the long walk he was feeling very hot and sticky. The sea looked so inviting. He could hardly wait to get down on the beach: to take off his shoes and socks; to walk across that wonderful sand; to feel it firm and cool and wet beneath his hot, bare, tired feet.

Just in front of where Stephen stood, and stretching in a wide band right accross the back of the beach, there was a thick bed of seaweed. If he wanted to get down onto the beach, he would have to wade across that. It was not an attractive prospect. The foul reek of the rotting weed rose up to greet him, filling his nostrils; his ears were assailed by a loud sound—the ecstatic humming of countless flies.

The stinking banks of revolting weed lay there stewing in the sun, soft and oozing underfoot, as Stephen floundered and staggered across. He tried to avoid the deepest banks; but it wasn't always possible. His feet sank down in the squelching mass, his arms flailed wildly above his head, trying to fend off the hordes of flies; they had risen in an angry swarm, then followed him down and onto the beach.

As he stamped about on the sand, swatting madly at the flies, a curious chorus started up—an excited, chattering, giggling noise. It came from the bracken on the low headland that curved around at the back of the beach.

Stephen stopped his swatting abruptly. He turned sharply to stare at the bracken. The giggling stopped abruptly too.

With his fists planted firmly on his hips and a deep scowl across his forehead, he scanned the slopes at the back of the beach. Nothing stirred. There were no more giggles. The audience, if there was one, must be holding its breath and waiting.

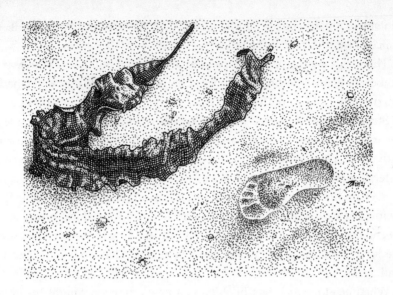

32. Thieves on the Beach

Pulling off his shoes and socks as quickly as he could, and clutching them in his hands, Stephen set off across the beach toward the shining pathway of water that ran down to join the sea.

The water felt wonderfully cool and soothing. He hopped and danced amongst the waves that ran to greet him on the beach, then wandered lazily through the water along the curving line of the shore. After all those years of town life, after all the flurry and all the grime, after all the times that he'd longed for freedom—to find himself on this tranquil beach was such a joy!

He stopped at the edge of the waves, looking out to sea, wriggling his toes and rocking his heels, sinking slowly down to his ankles in a granular soup of fluid sand. It was a satisfying feeling; yet he still looked longingly at the deep water.

"Why didn't I think of bringing my trunks and a towel?" he wondered. But the water was irresistible; he decided he would manage without them. Any spectators, who might be offended by the bright patterns of the

149

Flintstones on his boxer shorts, would just have to put up with it; he glanced briefly across at the bracken.

There was a large patch of dry sand and several boulders at the rear of the beach, below the bracken-covered slopes. The biggest boulder had a flat, dry top. It was a perfect place for leaving his shoes and clothing.

Stephen enjoyed himself immensely. Filled with a great sense of pleasure and well-being, he swam and splashed happily in the sea, wallowing in the cold, clear water. And as he swam and splashed around, he completely forgot about the audience.

Back on the beach he spied and picked up a fine example of sea kelp—a wide, flat strip with crinkled edges attached to a long, thick, meaty stalk. Up and down he ran in the sunshine, joyfully holding the seaweed on high. The long, green ribbon flew out like a banner as Stephen sped across the sand.

When he stopped to get his breath, a new attraction caught his eye: a big, wide, curving bank of sand, freshly washed and superbly smooth, on the far side of the bay—an untouched virgin territory, which he knew he had to visit. Crossing the beach, he hunted for shells, collecting some very fine stones on the way: a beautiful and perfectly round, flat, black pebble and a number of chunks of a milky-white rock—probably quartz, he thought to himself, but inset with veins of a shiny mineral that glinted brightly in the sun.

On reaching the opposite far side of the bay and the smooth expanse of pristine sand, Stephen took the greatest delight in walking boldly straight across it, noting the satisfactory line of his own crisp footprints in the sand, feeling quite pleased at the thought of himself as some modern-day Man Friday. Then leaving his precious collection of stones in a little heap on the bank, and pushing the hair back from his face with a salty, sandy hand, he set off down the beach to the headland to explore the pools at the base of the cliff.

Very few things in life are as satisfying as the exploration of rock pools. Each indentation in the rocks and every sea-filled crevice is a unique and tiny kingdom, ruled, so it seems, by tyrannical crabs that hide in cavities under the rocks or lurk behind curtains of weed. Each pool is a prison for shrimps and fish, whose camouflaged colors may save their lives—captives until, with the turn of the tide, the waves rush back and set them free, stirring the sand and disturbing the calm, as the sea reclaims the pool as her own.

Stephen wandered slowly back along the rocky base of the cliff, trying to avoid the dangerous stretches: the barnacle-encrusted rocks; the slippery, squelching patches of weed. He investigated all the pools, crouching motionless on the rocks, gazing into the calm, clear water.

Some of the pools had intriguing sea anemones. Some had brightly colored weeds. Others appeared to be quite empty; it was only after patient waiting that tiny creatures emerged to be seen.

He was so absorbed in examining the pools that he hadn't noticed how late it was: how the sun was dipping down; how the headland opposite cast long shadows across the bay. He had quite forgotten about the tide.

When he finally stopped and stood up, stretching stiffly and looking around, he was very surprised to discover that the sea was covering most of the beach. There was no sign now of the sandy bank and his precious collection of stones.

He stood on the ridge of rocks that ran along the side of the beach, feeling suddenly very cold. He didn't like the idea of stepping off the edge of the rocks into the deep water; he was much too chilled to want to get wet again. So he worked his way along the ledge and up onto the beach that way.

The rocks, where Stephen had left all his clothing, stood in a shadowy huddle below the headland opposite. He trotted across the back of the beach toward them. The sooner he could get some clothing on the better; then back to the house as quickly as possible for something good to eat.

When he came to the place where he'd left his things, he stopped and stared in sheer disbelief. Two scruffy sneakers still sat on the rock. But all his clothing had disappeared.

33. The Secret of the Woodland Glade

Stephen stood miserably on the beach beside the rock, considering his old sneakers. He was cold and covered with goose pimples. He hugged his arms around his body and shivered.

Even the Flintstones looked cold now. In the deep shadows of the rocky slopes, their colors seemed drab and faded. Suddenly, for Stephen too, all of the color and the pleasure had sadly faded from the day.

It really was too bad! He needed warm clothing and food. Funny that he hadn't noticed, whilst examining the rock pools, how cold and empty he'd become. Nor had he noticed the tide. If he'd gone on any longer, he might have got into real danger—without even noticing it.

The thought of that made him shiver more. He could, he supposed, put on his shoes and jog back through the woods as he was; but it was all very annoying. He had so little clothing to his name, he couldn't afford to lose any of it.

He looked at the bracken-covered slopes—silent now and seemingly innocent; then he studied the ground round his feet. An indistinct and blurry trail led off across the sand, then disappeared between the boulders. Stephen followed it warily, letting out a shout of triumph when he finally spotted his clothing. Someone or something had apparently dragged everything across the sand, and had dumped it in between two rocks.

Stephen approached cautiously. The clothing had been arranged to form a kind of nest. In the middle of the nest there was a group of stones—stones similar to those that he'd been collecting himself—the attractive, white ones with the bright and shining, silver streaks.

It was such an extraordinary thing to find. He simply stood there staring and shivering. Then he crouched down beside the nest and examined it very carefully. It looked as if some creature or creatures had been curled up in the nest, on top of the pile of stones: furry creatures, with golden-yellow and black hair. A number of hairs still stuck to the clothing.

Stephen quite forgot his discomfort. He collected the hairs and looked at them closely. With his interest in zoology, he ought to be able to identify them.

But the more closely he looked at the hairs, the more mystified he became, for they didn't seem right for any creature that he'd expect to find in Cornwall. In fact, he couldn't think of any animal—anywhere in the world—that made nests out of people's clothing and indulged in collecting glittering stones. It was certainly quite a puzzle!

He grunted loudly to himself, a helpless, frustrated kind of grunt, then he looked around for more clues. But there was little else to be seen: only a line of blurry tracks leading up away from the rocks and disappearing in the bracken—unrecognizable tracks.

Stephen felt quite mystified. It was yet another peculiar clue, a piece of the very strange jigsaw puzzle, that he was struggling to fit together to make up the picture of Lansbury Hall. A slowly emerging, intriguing picture, but also a very uncomfortable picture, that worried Stephen quite a lot.

Cold and discomfort took over again. Putting the glittering stones aside, he shook his clothing thoroughly and dressed himself as quickly as possible. Then, with the stones stuffed into his pockets, he started back across the beach, carrying his shoes and socks, making a detour up through the river water and along the beach bar, in order to avoid the sickening seaweed.

Instead of working his way back toward the woods along the side of the silted lake, he cut up across the grassy slopes to the right, soon finding himself on an overgrown path, which ran along the side of the slope, disappearing into the woodland.

Stephen had lost all track of time, but he knew it must be getting late; he was ravenously hungry, and the sun was getting low. Once he was up on the grassy slopes and able to move along more briskly, he soon warmed up and, despite his hunger, he started to feel considerably better. From time to time, he stopped on the slope and stood looking thoughtfully back at the beach.

The woodland seemed very quiet and peaceful; only occasional chirps of birds broke the heavy, sylvan silence. The early-evening sun shone down through widely spaced, mature trees, falling on spreading banks of ferns and beds of lush, green, bluebell leaves. The flowers, it seemed, were now all spent, but the stalks bore healthy, fat, green seedpods.

The path was very overgrown. Stephen walked as quickly and quietly as he could, between the banks of arching bracken. He was anxious not to disturb his surroundings—the tranquil evening hush of the woodland—and any creatures lurking there.

A sudden warning call rang out—a single, raucous, giggling that shattered the silence of the woods. Stephen jumped and stopped abruptly. The noise had come from the undergrowth, just a few feet from where he stood. It was answered from somewhere up ahead. He started forward, quickening his pace, thrusting the ferns aside with his arms, emerging unexpectedly into a large and sunlit clearing.

A flash of movement on the opposite side of the clearing caught his eye—a speedy flash of yellow and black, a vague impression of bold stripes, as something scurried quickly away. Stephen fixed his eye on the spot where the creature had disappeared. He watched and he waited. But nothing happened. Whatever it was had vanished now. It had gone and left him standing there, feeling reluctant to move and investigate.

Tall trees surrounded the clearing, and around the edges beneath the trees were big banks of brambles and bracken; they lined and enclosed the open space, which was covered with grass and wildflowers. Along to Stephen's right, a well-worn pathway could be seen leading off amongst the trees. The woodland glade was dominated by the most magnificent tree—a mighty beech that grew at the edge of the clearing, its giant trunk supporting a huge head of spreading foliage.

The silence of the hushed woods and the golden light of the evening sun seemed to be enveloping Stephen, soothing and lulling his worried senses. He walked forward into the glade, his feet reluctantly crushing campion and sweeping aside the buttercups. Pink and yellow petals scattering all around him in the grass.

Something seemed to be leading him on; he moved in a dazed and dreamlike state. Suddenly he caught his breath. Directly opposite him, close to the edge of the clearing, slanting shafts of mellow sunlight fell upon a wooden cross: a simple but strangely carved cross that stood at the head of a long, low mound—the mound being just about two yards long and about a yard wide.

In an instant, Stephen knew what it was. It was his Great-Uncle Theodore's grave. He didn't know how or why he knew. Some instinct must have told him, for he didn't have to stop and think, but went straight over and said out aloud, "So that's where they've buried you, Theodore." Although he couldn't for the life of him imagine who or what he meant by "they."

Stephen stood for several minutes, smiling happily down at the grave. Then he looked around the clearing. What a wonderfully peaceful location to choose for a final resting place!

There were several odd features about the grave; the more Stephen looked at it the more puzzled he became. At the foot of the mound, there was a smooth bare patch of earth—a flattened area where the grass seemed to have been worn away. Judging by marks in the grass to one side of the mound, someone or something was in the habit of coming and going regularly from the bare, earthen patch. A trail led away from the grave, crossing to the very place where Stephen had seen the creature disappear.

That in itself seemed strange enough; but there was something far more unusual about the grave. Someone had built a weird structure over it. Four tall uprights had been set in the ground—probably alder, Stephen thought, judging by the long straight lengths and the smooth bark of the unprepared wood. At about his shoulder height, the uprights supported the framework for a small, pitched roof, which had been carefully thatched with reeds. The grave was sheltered by the roof, which overlapped it well on all sides.

It seemed such a funny thing to find. It added a curious, exotic quality to Great-Uncle Theodore's simple grave. Stephen was putting out his hand to touch the wooden framework, when something stopped him. He didn't know why it was, but the idea came into his head that the little "house" was sacred. Perhaps he shouldn't touch it at all.

Stepping back away from the grave, Stephen felt suddenly tired and empty—not just empty of stomach from hunger, but empty of heart from being alone. Long shadows were reaching out across the floor of the woodland glade. They seemed to be reaching out toward him, threatening to catch him and then to hold him in their all-enveloping gloom. He knew he must get away and get home.

With the great love that he felt for trees, Stephen couldn't possibly leave without crossing to talk to the beech. Delicately veined, pale leaves whispered in the spreading branches. As he moved through the greening shade, his feet rustled softly through leaf mold, across a deep bed of beech mast.

He could sense the powerful presence—the mighty being that towered above him. His eyes followed the line of the trunk: massive and silver, up and up, dividing and twisting, on and on, the thick, gray branches reaching and curving—rising with cathedral-like splendor to the leafy roof above.

Shyly Stephen put out his hand, searching and feeling for the force of life that must pulse through this giant tree. The saddest of thoughts came into his mind—thoughts of the great destruction of trees—the daily devastation of forests.

"How could they bear to do it?" he wondered. "How could they bear to chop down and to kill a wonderful, great, living being like this?"

Some lines of a poem came into his mind.

Oh please God stay the hands that wield the axes and the fire,
Oh please God stay those killing hands . . .

Stephen leaned against the tree, his forehead pressed against the bark, his eyes closed tight in pain. He could see in his mind the chop of the axe, the sweating trunks of the dying trees, the horrible, acrid, smoke-filled air.

Even a mighty being like this was powerless and completely helpless when faced by ruthless Man. He pushed himself back, away from the tree, wiping his eyes with the back of his hand, patting the trunk in a kindly way.

"Don't you worry, old fellow," he said. "You'll be alright. I promise you. No one shall harm a leaf of your head. There'll be no axes and no fire here."

He smiled across at his great-uncle's grave.

"You can rest easy, Great-Uncle Theodore. I promise you that I'll do my best to protect and look after Lansbury Hall. I shall care for the trees. I shall care for the plants. And I'll care for all the creatures too—whatever they may be," he added, somewhat as an afterthought.

Then he turned and left the woodland glade.

34. An Exciting Destination

Stephen made his way wearily through the woods back to Lansbury Hall. The sun had slipped below the horizon; the evening air felt cool and damp as he approached the darkening house. Cautiously crossing the overgrown forecourt, he glanced around him and up at the house, wondering what he might find this time.

He was almost too tired and too hungry to care; yet he opened the front door slowly and warily, and stood stock-still just inside the hall, listening very carefully. The warm, peaceful house was inviting; so, closing the door quietly behind him, he glided quickly across to the kitchen. It was such a relief to discover that everything seemed just the way he had left it.

His priority now was food and drink; so he lit the fire in the library, he collected a stock of candles and wood, and retreated there to cook his evening meal. He knew that it wasn't really the right thing to do. The sizzling sound from the big, black pan and the delicious smell of frying bacon were quite out of keeping in this room with the rows and rows of learned books. Probably no one had ever dreamt of cooking anything there before—not even boiling water in a kettle.

Stephen mumbled his apologies around the room as he installed himself in one of the chairs to feast on an appetizing mass—eggs and bacon, heaped up high on thick and crunchy fried brown bread. Then he brewed a mug of tea, pulled the opposite chair across for his feet, and rested in front of the fire.

He lolled there comfortably for some time, mulling over in his mind the very strange events of the day, trying to make them fit into some sort of sensible pattern—without success. He was surrounded by so many mysteries. If he could only solve one or two of them, perhaps the others would fall into place.

It was evident now that his Great-Uncle Theodore had lived a totally reclusive life, shut off and alone in Lansbury Hall for goodness knows how many years. It even began to look as if the last time that he'd ventured out might well have been the trip described in the old notebooks.

Stephen turned his head and looked at the stack of books on the table. Well, of course! That must be it! The answer to it all lay there—there in those old and tattered notebooks.

He made up the fire, lit a candle, took up the notebook he'd started to read, and then sat down with a purposeful air. He would read through every one of the books. He would find the answer to the riddle.

It took him a little while to get used to the antiquated writing again. Whatever the destination of the two young men traveling on board the SS *Lanfranc* might be, it was clearly a very long voyage. For the writing went on and on and on—descriptions of weather conditions and ports, and dated headings for each of the sections, but always the irritating lack of proper names, as places were only identified by capital letters.

> *October 4th—passing U.*
> *October 5th—sailing from V to L.*
> *October 6th—arriving L and sailing for P.*
> *October 8th—arriving L.*
> *October 9th—sailing from L to M.*

October 11th—arriving M and sailing for P.
October 20th—here at last!

But where was "here"? It must, he presumed, begin with P. Stephen became more and more frustrated.

Poring over an ancient atlas that he found on one of the shelves didn't seem to help at all. Perhaps the notebooks just went on with capital letters for all the places and no proper names for anything. He might never discover where they'd been.

But then, at last—there it was! Great-Uncle Theodore had been so carried away with the excitement of finally reaching his destination that his system of capital letters had collapsed. The bold statement rose up at Stephen:

> *November 1st.*
> *B and I have finally made it. We are sailing up the River*
> *Amazon!*

Stephen stopped his reading abruptly.

"We are sailing up the River Amazon," he repeated the sentence out loud in amazement.

"Oh! Wow! The lucky devils!"

It was the place that he longed to visit. His eyes swept quickly back to the notebook, hungry for details of the adventure:

> *I hardly know where to begin in trying to describe our first impressions of this magnificent, mighty river. We had looked at the maps. We had read the books. But the reality of such a vast expanse of flowing water is overwhelming. The volume and the thrust of the water, flowing out into the Atlantic Ocean, is so great that they say that, even a hundred miles out to sea, you can lean over the side of a boat and scoop up fresh water.*
> *The mouth of the river is enormously wide and partly filled by*

*an island—but an island the size of Switzerland! Yet, the water
flowing past the island on this side is so wide that we can hardly
see the opposite shore.*

*The local people tell us that the current of the river is even
stronger in the rainy season. But now that we see the great volume
of water that is carried by this noble river, we cannot imagine
where it all comes from. Of course, we know about the size of the
forest that stretches on before us. But, even so, it is hard to imagine
the continuous production of enough rainwater to feed this
ceaseless flow.*

Stephen paused to take a quick sip of his tea, trying to imagine the size
of the river, trying to see in his mind's eye this "ceaseless flow" of swirling
water:

*It took us time and some hard bargaining to persuade the
captain of this boat to take us upriver as far as Iquitos. He is
carrying a cargo of miserable-looking, cheap trinkets, which he
plans to barter for rubber. It will be an enormously long journey—
2,300 miles—and it will take us several weeks. I only wish that I
liked the man better.*

*The only other passengers are two young men. They are forest
Indians. The captain tells us that they are supposed to be traveling
with us as far as Tefé.*

*We have spent the whole day on the deck of the boat. There is a
cabin down below, but it is hot and unpleasant there, with the
captain always smoking tobacco. We prefer to be out in the open air.
One section of the deck is enclosed and roofed over with palm leaves
to form a kind of shelter. Here we have hung our hammocks and
thereby hangs a story. . . .*

*Throughout the day, the two forest Indians had watched us
suspiciously with solemn faces. We didn't quite know what to make
of them. The captain, who is a surly character, warned us that we*

should have nothing to do with them. They were savages, he told
us, and, as such, they were not to be trusted.

B and I had smiled at them once or twice, but without getting
any response. In the end, it seemed easier to ignore them and
pretend that they didn't exist.

Stephen didn't like the sound of the Indians. He didn't like solemn, suspicious people and the captain might be right. They might be savages, after all.

As the afternoon wore on, we decided that we had better arrange
our gear for the night—that meant hanging the hammocks. Neither
of us had ever dealt with hammocks before, and we couldn't work
out the best way to attach them to the frame of the palm-leaf shelter.
We had more or less forgotten the Indians. They had been sitting on
the deck, watching us but keeping quiet.

B and I were standing there, glaring at the offending hammocks,
feeling pretty foolish by then, when we heard a laugh behind us. We
both spun around in anger. Two, brown, deadpan faces just stared
back at us. But then to our very great surprise, the two Indians
came across and, almost brushing us aside, took over the job for us.

They worked quietly and efficiently, whilst B and I stood to one
side, feeling completely useless, of course. When they had finished,
we tried to thank them, but we didn't get much response. They
simply returned to their place on the deck and sat there watching
our every move.

They really are peculiar fellows, although quite impressive to look
at—tall, well made, and quite handsome, with brown skins and long
black hair, that falls below their shoulders. They wear very tattered,
old clothing, which doesn't fit them properly and is certainly out of
keeping with the brightly colored, turquoise-blue and red feathers that
they wear in their ears.

Both Indians have long hunting bows and bundles of arrows,
which they keep close at hand. They are obviously not prepared to

162

be friendly. They are certainly not the kind of chaps one would
choose for companions on a trip like this. Indeed, we don't know
what to make of them.

Stephen paused in his reading. It was all so exciting. He needed to get up and move about.

He paced up and down the library in the glow from the firelight. Then he went over to the darkened corner and felt the coarse fabric of the "hanging bat."

"So that was how it all began," Stephen smiled to himself, "the long relationship with hammocks."

He laughed out loud in the still of the library—to think of Great-Uncle Theodore and B struggling and thrashing about.

The Indians, so it seemed, had been helpful. Yet Stephen didn't think that he'd trust them. He knew nothing about forest Indians; he wasn't especially interested in them. His real interest was the forest—its trees, its plants, and its animals. The Indians sounded rather alarming.

35. Another Strange Nest

Back in the comfortable chair beside the fire, Stephen continued his reading:

> *When we tied up for the night, the two Indians were surprisingly helpful. With great speed and expertise, they caught a number of large fish and cooked them over a fire in a small clearing on the riverbank, inviting us to join them in their meal.*
>
> *After the excellent fish, we ate fresh bananas, picked from a tree at the edge of the clearing. B and I enjoyed our food, though the captain and his crew showed little sign of appreciation. They don't treat the Indians very well.*
>
> *Later, we made a short trip into the forest—B enraptured by "things botanical," and I, admittedly, quite excited by the prospect of interesting fauna. But we were too tired to go very far, and we had an uncomfortable feeling that the two Indians had followed us.*

164

When we returned to the clearing later, they too emerged from the
forest—just a short way behind us.

As I lie in my hammock—not that comfortably, I have to admit,
for this hammock has a will of its own and I can't get used to it—
the inky black of the Amazon night has closed down all around us.
We hear the weird sounds of the forest—noisier at night than
during the day. The chorus of frogs is amazingly loud, composed of
a most surprising range of sounds—bellows and roars, clucks and
squeaks. From time to time we also hear the strange, haunting calls
of hunting beasts, the occasional strangled cry of the hunted.

We have only the light of one small lamp and that is attracting
too many insects. Of course, for me they are fascinating, but B is
complaining, as he always does, about my dedication to insects.
"Oh, you and your bugs!" he's always saying, and no matter how
many times I tell him that insects should not be referred to as
"bugs," he continues to do so—just in order to annoy me, no
doubt.

But we're having a great time. Everything seems
straightforward now. It's going to be a ripping adventure! I can feel
it in my bones.

We lie now in a row—all four of us in our hammocks under the
palm-leaf shelter—B and I at one end, the two Indians at the other.
They are not asleep. I can see their eyes—shining and watchful in
the light from the lamp.

The fire in the library was very low, and the candle had almost burned
out. Stephen stopped reading and glanced around him. He could do without the "inky black" of the Amazon night, here in the library. For although
he was very tired, he was determined to read on as far as he could. So, he
built up the fire, replaced the spent candle, and sat back down again to
read.

The two explorers were obviously having a wonderful time. He was very
envious of their travels, and dying to know what happened next. But as he

read on, he began to realize that the trip was not going to be quite as simple or as easy as they or he had expected. The Amazon River obviously had a few tricks up her watery sleeve:

November 2nd.

A truly terrible night last night! I had been sleeping soundly for quite some time, when something woke me up. I lay there listening in the dark. The forest appeared to be totally silent, which didn't seem right at all. A sudden, blinding flash of lightning lit up our small, pathetic shelter, showing me that B and the Indians were all wide awake as well, lying quietly, listening and waiting—for the storm that was on its way.

After a while the boat began to rock—gently at first and then quite violently, as the waves of the river, whipped up by a tempestuous squall, tossed it roughly from side to side. We heard the first few splashes of raindrops, falling on the palm-leaf roof. Then, without any further warning, the heavens opened up on our heads, pouring down upon us such torrents of water—quite impossible to imagine unless you have experienced such rain.

Great bolts of lightning flashed and crashed around our boat. The palm-leaf roof gave little shelter. Most of its leaves were ripped away by the power and fury of the elements. The rain was almost horizontal. B and I and both of the Indians clutched the rail at the edge of the deck—trying to save ourselves and our gear—poor old B desperately trying to protect his beloved camera as best he could.

The frantic forces of wind and rain lashed the forest trees without mercy. All around us, in the riotous blackness of the storm, we could hear a terrifying sound—the creaking and crashing of mighty trees. All we could do was to cling on tightly, to hope that our mooring rope would hold, and to pray that none of the trees fell on us.

At last the storm subsided, but I cannot describe the misery, the wetness, and the foul discomfort of the remainder of the night.

Stephen sat staring into the fire. He could hardly keep his eyes open. The writing was difficult to decipher, and his reading very slow. Living through the storm seemed to have exhausted him. He shivered despite the warmth from the fire, closed the notebook, and prepared for bed, very relieved to think that he had a proper bed to go to—not just a rocking hammock.

The mess on his bed was rather shameful. For years, he had been strictly disciplined to leave everything in good order. It should come naturally to him by now; but here at Lansbury Hall things were different. With no one to check up on him, he could do just what he liked; making his bed every morning could not be counted as something he liked.

He smiled to himself as he bent forward to straighten the bedding. There was a lot to be said for freedom. But then he paused and stood there, staring.

Things were, indeed, different at Lansbury Hall. Something had been burrowing around on his bed. The tartan blanket had been formed into a rough nest, and there, grouped together in the middle of the nest, was an unusual assortment of shiny objects: five silver coins, one milk bottle top, two metal flip-top tabs, and, most surprisingly, Stephen's precious watch.

36. Mysterious Music

It was not surprising that Stephen slept late the following morning. Having recovered his watch the night before, he'd been amazed to find that it was well after midnight; but although he had felt so very tired, he couldn't get to sleep. The sudden and unexpected reappearance of his watch was bewildering. The ever-watchful presence of someone or something—always just beyond his vision or grasp—continued to trouble him.

Lying there in the library, with only the comforting glow of the last embers of the fire for company, he had found it very hard to relax. He had lain there rigid, listening carefully, his eyes probing the dark corners. Such tension didn't allow for sleep.

There was also, of course, his great-uncle's journal—the tantalizing glimpse that it gave him of Theodore Lansbury's exciting adventures. When sleep had finally come to him, it had not been a sound or peaceful sleep. He had tossed and turned in the little bed, unable to clear his mind of the pictures—the vivid pictures of lashing rain and flashing storm on the Amazon River.

In the bright, sunny light of another new day, Great-Uncle Theodore's Amazon adventure seemed more like science fiction; it was so very far removed from the quiet of the Lansbury library, with its soft light and warm, glowing colors. And yet, as Stephen mused to himself, lying comfortably in his bed, it was all out there, somewhere—the amazing river and the forests. It was out there at this very moment; though he hated to think of all the change that had taken place since his great-uncle's trip—the total destruction of vast areas of the wonderful forests of the Amazon.

The unusual assortment of shiny oddments that Stephen had discovered the night before, in the "nest" on his bed, now lay on the table in front of the photo of Grandfather Stephen: such a youthful, smiling, confident figure. The photo continued to fascinate Stephen. The face was so much like his own face.

He lay dozing in bed for quite some time, only finally driven out by his need for food and drink. After breakfast, he started on some housework. He felt better when he'd cleared up the mess in the scullery and washed some of his clothing. It hung in the yard behind the house.

Stephen had a healthy appetite. When, after lunch, he came to check his stock of food, he found that he'd eaten up more than he'd expected. He could always raid the kitchen garden, but that wouldn't provide him with the vital basics—bread, butter, eggs, meat, fruit. Having no proper fridge or freezer was going to be a great disadvantage. How he longed for a fish and chip shop!

It looked as if he would only be able to hold out for another couple of days. After that he would be forced to return to the village shop for fresh supplies, forced to face up to Mrs. Pascoe, with her heaving bosoms and dancing snake. It was not an encouraging prospect. She made him feel uncomfortable. He didn't know how to answer her questions; he couldn't keep his eyes off the snake.

Sitting on the front doorstep in the warm sun, Stephen wondered how he might spend his afternoon. He looked up, smiling at the vines that grew across the front of the house, feasting his eyes on the day's new batch of passionflowers glowing there brightly amongst the foliage. He felt rested now. The weather was much too good to stay indoors.

After some thought, he decided that it would be a perfect day for exploring the track that ran up away from the house, past the vegetable garden—the one that he'd come down in the rain the day before. He felt sure it would lead to the open moor.

On this trip, however, he was determined not to be caught miles away from home without any food and drink. So he packed a small picnic: opening his one can of salmon for a treat, and making some thick, soggy sandwiches. Sadly, the bread seemed past its prime. It even smelled slightly moldy, perhaps because of the musty larder.

Setting out from the house with a very determined air, Stephen closed the door behind him, pushed the hair back from his face, and started out across the courtyard toward the track beyond. Making a quick diversion, he looked in through the gateway to the walled garden, just to make sure there was no one there.

He would raid the garden later on, only in a small way, of course—just a few carrots, if they were big enough, maybe some spinach and some spuds. He knew he would feel uncomfortable doing it. But, after all, he owned the place; it seemed ridiculous to be worrying about his food supply, and not to use the food that was already there.

With a wonderful vegetable garden like that, he ought never to be short of food. At least he wouldn't be short of vegetables. Although, of course, the "phantom gardener" might have other ideas about that.

Doing his best to push such troubling thoughts from his mind, yet keeping a good lookout around him, Stephen walked briskly up the track in the sunshine, passing in due course, on his left-hand side, the opening to a pathway leading off down into the woodland—the place where he'd emerged from the woods on the previous day.

The wide track on which he was walking had been formed long ago by the passage of farm carts. It followed along the top of the woodland. On his right-hand side were open fields, sloping up toward more woodland that clothed the hills beyond. The fields themselves were all wildly overgrown, almost completely taken over by masses and masses of bracken and brambles.

Stephen stopped at an open gateway and stood looking into one of the fields. The gate had long since dropped off its hinges; it was propped up now, to one side, a trellis for wild honeysuckle. On the far side of the field, he could see a number of beehives—the source of the delicious honey in the pots on the shelves in the larder—and the source of wax for the candles.

Farther on up the track, the trees closed in on either side, their branches meeting and overlapping in a curving arch above his head. Stephen had already admired the long, green, leafy "tunnels" of some of the narrow Cornish lanes. But he'd never seen anything quite like this.

A small stream of clear water ran trickling down toward him, meandering across the old green lane, exposing a bed of pale, glistening pebbles. The tunnel, roofed over with leafy branches, was filled with a strange, green light. Here and there, bright shafts of sunlight streamed down through the gaps in the foliage, illuminating hanging vines.

As he came to the mouth of the tunnel, Stephen's eyes lit up with pleasure. The vines grew up on either side, their long, slim, sinuous limbs snaking up the trunks of trees and writhing along the spreading branches, reaching out through the canopy, cascading back down through the roof of the tunnel to hang in the green-lit space beneath.

A curious perfume hung in the air as Stephen wended his way along, trying to avoid the dangling arms; anxious not to disturb the vines or to harm the flowers that were hanging there—trumpet-shaped flowers, some bright yellow, and others a very delicate violet, and in between, the pale-blues and subtle purples of passionflowers.

Long, pale, curling tendrils were reaching out from the hanging vines. Exploring space and seeking contact, they tickled Stephen's face and ears. They caught at his sleeve as he walked by. He released himself from their clingy caresses as gently as he possibly could.

In the middle of the tunnel, he paused and stood—looking slowly and quietly around him, his eyes wide and anxious now. He had that funny

171

feeling again—the funny feeling of being watched. But there was nothing to be seen, and very little to be heard: only the trickling sound of the water that ran along beneath his feet; only the gentle, rustling whisper of vines that hung around his head. He sighed deeply and moved on.

Coming out of the tunnel at last, he found that the track ahead forked: one arm curving up to the moor; the other one leading down to the valley—a very inviting track. After a long, thoughtful look around, he followed the track down to the left, till he saw below him, to his surprise, a small, delightful, open meadow that ran along beside the river—a wilderness of grasses and wildflowers.

As he stood on the path looking down at the meadow, Stephen noticed something strange—an unusual pattern of tracks in the grass—a large circle, some ten or twelve yards across. In the middle of the circle, there was a flattened, bare area and, from the middle, small tracks ran out to join up with the outer circle. It was rather like looking down on an impression of a giant cartwheel. The bare central area was like the hub of the wheel; the tracks, radiating out from the center, were like the spokes; the outer circle was like the rim.

Stephen stood looking down and frowning, wondering what on earth it could mean, very puzzled yet again. It looked as if someone or something had been stamping around in the grass to form this curious pattern. He shook his head and sighed again, then deep in thought, he returned to the upper track, making his way as quickly as possible up toward the open moor.

Up on the high moor, with wide views all around him, Stephen felt wonderfully free. He walked on and on, up and up, toward a high, rocky tor. At some time in the distant past, the lower slopes had been claimed as fields. He crossed a number of large enclosures, wild now and overgrown, with humpy tussocks of coarse, brown grass and spreading thickets of prickly gorse.

The fields were enclosed by rugged walls, built long ago from the many big boulders, collected from the rocky land when the slopes had first been cleared. He stopped to admire these chunky walls, their boulders fitted with skill and cunning, like megalithic jigsaw puzzles.

When he was almost at the top of the tor, Stephen turned to enjoy the view, looking out across the Lansbury estate and far beyond, in one direction to the glinting line of the sea, in the other to an intricate patchwork of fields.

His eye was caught by a distant field: a tiny, bright-green, moss-green field that shone in the sunlight and drew his eye. There was something uncanny about the Cornish countryside. The light seemed somehow brighter here than anywhere else that he'd been before; the colors were more vibrant too.

Stephen lolled on the slope with his eyes half closed, enjoying the air and the feeling of space. He could hear the hum of bees in the gorse. He could hear the trickling sound of a stream. And suddenly, somewhere, another sound—a faint but distinctly musical sound—the distant, trilling notes of a pipe, rising and falling on the air.

He sat bolt upright, listening intently, staring down into the valley below. Where could such music be coming from? Exotic, lilting music like that. Could it be coming from Lansbury Hall?

A slight breeze stirred. The sound was gone, leaving Stephen mystified—mystified and very intrigued, but also very uncomfortable.

Had he imagined it? Surely not!

37. A Very Weird Creature

There was quite a surprise awaiting Stephen when he reached the top of the slope. The tor was surmounted by stony outcrops, but in between the outcrops of rock, there was a wide, flat saddle of land—an area covered by short, fine grass.

Standing there quietly before him, their feet planted deeply in black, peaty soil, their craggy heads held high to the sky, were a number of tall and ancient stones. From where he stood, Stephen could see that they formed a large, uneven circle—uneven only because some of the members had long since fallen and lay at odd angles, partly embedded in smooth, green turf.

The sun shone down, as it had before. The sky remained the clearest blue, and yet the air seemed heavy and still, as Stephen drifted dreamily forward into the mysterious circle—irresistibly drawn to its center by the tall, gray figure standing there.

When he reached the stone, he hesitated, aware of the weight of total silence pressing heavily down around him. Then very slowly he stretched out his arms and placed his hands on the rough, weathered surface: spreading his fingers wide and flat; feeling and smoothing the ancient rock. Could it be that the stone that reared above him had a life and force of its own? He found it suddenly hard to focus; the wide, blue dome of the sky above seemed to reel in an arc before his eyes.

Stephen stood as if transfixed, surrounded by tall, gray, stony figures—encircled and held in a timeless zone, where the only thing that mattered now was his feeling of oneness with the stone. The unity of Man and earth. The unity of earth and sky.

Were these the feelings of ancient Man who had set these stones so long ago? Reluctantly, he withdrew his hands. Then he wandered around the circle, greeting each of the stones in turn, talking as if to a group of friends, and not forgetting the fallen few.

There was a happy spring in Stephen's step as he made his way down and across the opposite slope of the tor, heading for the glittering line of a small stream that he could see in the distance. He was hungry and very thirsty now. It would be great to have his picnic sitting beside the running water.

He came at last, quite hot and tired, to a small bridge that crossed the stream—a most unusual and ancient bridge, formed from four thick granite slabs, each one nearly ten feet long. Laid down, side by side, they spanned the running water. In the crevices between the stones were tiny rock plants—pink and fleshy amongst the yellow-green moss and lichen.

Above this bridge, the stream ran wide and shallow, dawdling over banks of fine gravel, skirting the edges of small, sandy islands. Rafting plants bordered the stream, floating on the water's surface, with small, lobed leaves and little white flower heads. Clumps of milky, blue-mauve violets sprouted from the boggy edge, with masses of long-stalked, heart-shaped leaves.

A very old tree grew out of the bank—a willow of some kind, Stephen thought. Dwarfed by the harshness of life on the moor, it hung out across the stream, swept and deformed in a permanent stoop by countless years of bending and yielding before the force of the wild, west wind. Long, pale skeins of gray-green lichen hung from its old and gnarled limbs.

Below the bridge, the stream was changed in character. Only a yard or so in width, it swirled along, cutting more deeply, with banks of thick, hanging grasses and wildflowers. Beside the stream was a flat, grassy area—a perfect place for Stephen's picnic.

He sat there happily in the sun, eating his salmon sandwiches. Even if there was, perhaps, a slightly moldy taste to the bread, it didn't put him off. He munched his way contentedly through nearly all the sandwiches, flipping little bits of food into the stream from time to time in the hope of attracting fish. The bits were washed away by the current; but, something or someone further downstream would be bound to enjoy them, so he thought.

The only trouble was that Stephen hadn't bargained for the kind of "something" or "someone" that might be lurking downstream—the kind of "something" or "someone" who might come wandering upstream, looking for more.

He sat oblivious in the sunshine: enjoying the stream; mesmerized by the swaying movement of long, green, ribbonlike weeds, as they swung in the current of cool, clear water—swinging free in the middle of the stream, but pushed aside like thick bunches of hair where the water gushed through at a narrow point.

When he had eaten all that he wanted, he pushed the rest of the food aside and lay down on the bank to rest, gazing up into the sky above, trying to spot the little lark, which he knew from its song must be hovering there.

The sky was the most incredible color—the brightest blue you could ever imagine. If he turned his head just a little bit more, he could look across at the golden gorse; the contrast of the colors was stunning—the clearest blue and the brightest yellow. If you painted a picture with just those colors, no one would ever accept it, he thought.

The warm sun was soporific. Stephen closed his eyes and dozed, lulled by the song of the swirling water—the ceaseless washing and the ceaseless whirling of the long, green, wavering tresses of the ever-flowing stream.

He wouldn't have heard the approach of the creature, making its way up the channel of water, quietly and carefully easing along beneath the shelter of the bank. He couldn't have seen the wrinkly face, which rose above the edge of the bank, just a few feet from where he lay—or the pale, beady eyes that watched him closely.

Stephen slept peacefully in the sunshine. The watching creature made no move. With its head held high and mouth aquiver, it seemed to be testing the air, glancing at the last salmon sandwich that lay on the paper, a few feet away.

Very slowly and very warily, the animal heaved itself onto the bank. The long, wet body, with its curious wrinkles, glistened in the sun. The sides of the body heaved gently as water ran off the short, fine coat—a murky, greenish-brown coat that blended so well with the bogs and the swamps in which the animal liked to live.

The small, cunning eyes, alert and suspicious, never wavered from Stephen's face as the creature moved slowly forward and started to feed on the salmon sandwich. But there seemed to be something about the sandwich that the animal didn't like. Having taken a mouthful and chewed for a while, it contorted its face in a horrible way, spitting it all back out again. After that, it kept to the sandwich filling, eating every morsel of salmon, but completely avoiding the bread.

When the creature had finished eating, it lay quite still on the bank in the sun, twitching its drying, wrinkled skin—apparently watching and considering, not only Stephen, but also the bread. First it looked toward Stephen, and then it looked back at the bread, and then back at Stephen again.

At last it appeared to make up its mind. With a somewhat devilish gleam in its eye, it picked up one of the pieces of bread and withdrew carefully into the water. There, it hung patiently in the current, controlling and watching the large piece of bread until it became just a soft, soggy mass. Then, with a very odd look on its face—a mixture of glee and unpleasant disgust—it took a large mouthful of water and bread.

Stephen lay peacefully, dozing still, a smile of contentment on his face. He was blissfully unaware of the creature, of the nasty trick it was going to play.

The animal had a remarkably accurate aim, as if it had practiced such shots before. The full force of the sickening mouthful hit poor Stephen full in the face. With one gurgling, gobbling shriek of delight, the creature submerged—and was gone.

38. Stephen to the Rescue

Stephen had been lying contentedly on the bank, almost asleep, basking in the late afternoon sun, his mind dwelling on the Wonders of Nature—the sun and the sky, the woods and the rivers, and all the marvelous wildlife too. He was full of kind thoughts for all the creatures that probably needed his care and protection.

He couldn't have known that, as he lay there, he might be in need of protection himself. He certainly couldn't have been prepared for the spurting gush of slimy pulp that was spewed forth from the dear creature's mouth.

The disgusting mouthful made a direct hit, splattering Stephen's face and hair. He scrambled to his feet in alarm, frantically wiping off the mess with the back of his hands and the sleeves of his shirt. Ugh! It was absolutely revolting!

He stood looking angrily about him, even right up into the sky, trying to spot the fiendish culprit. Then he remembered the gurgling call. Whilst enjoying the sunny hillside, he had quite forgotten the ghastly gobblers that seemed to dwell in the valley below. Now he remembered them vividly—or at least he remembered their horrible calls.

He looked closely at the sticky mess on his hands, trying to work out what it could be. When he noticed the empty sandwich paper, a rough idea of what must have happened began to form in his mind. Though what sort of creature could it be that would play such a dirty trick on him?

Everything around him now looked just the way it had been before the incident. The lark still sang, somewhere on high. The stream, apparently undisturbed, still burbled on its way. There was no sign of any creature.

Stephen was furious with himself to think he'd missed the opportunity of observing whatever it was. Impatiently, he began to pick all the nasty bits out of his hair. But, try as he might, he couldn't get rid of the horrible, smelly slime. So, in the end, he knelt down beside the stream and dipped his head warily into the water, keeping a lookout for any movement that might suggest some lurking beast.

When he was finally satisfied that all the slimy bits and pieces were gone, as well as most of the boggy smell, he took off his shoes and socks and paddled. After a while he wished he hadn't; for he was wrecking the bed of the stream. He had even torn off the long, green tresses. He watched with regret as the broken strands, twisting and twirling like thin, pale streamers, were carried away by the current of water.

He should have gone farther up the stream, where the bed was wide and shallow. He could have paddled there to his heart's content, between the banks of sand and gravel, without doing too much damage. Stephen felt suddenly angry—angry with the wretched creature that had disturbed his afternoon, and very angry with himself.

The afternoon had turned sour. Freedom, it seemed, was all very well; but on his own, without any company, surrounded by so many puzzling worries, he couldn't pretend he was having fun. As he started back down the track toward Lansbury Hall, he felt alone and quite depressed. His wet and still slimy hair clung to his skin in a horrible way; no amount of pushing it back made it feel any better. He plodded along feeling thoroughly miserable.

A sudden, strange, and eerie cry, from somewhere in the valley below, brought him sharply to a halt. It was a lonely mewing cry that echoed Stephen's own sad feelings. A cry that somehow seemed familiar.

Then there he was! The buzzard! Flapping up into the evening sun. He must have been perched at the edge of the wood. The sad and haunting cry had been his. But, now, there he was, wheeling and turning, gaining height above the valley, round and round and up and up.

As the bird rose higher in the sky, Stephen's spirits rose up too, just as they had when he'd watched the buzzards before. There was something stirring about these birds, so large and handsome and soaring on high. It must be great to be a bird—to wheel and soar in the sky like that.

As Stephen moved on down the track toward the woodland, he kept an eye on the bird above. It was wonderful to see him there—to watch his movements in the air. It looked as if he had spotted some prey, somewhere down on the ground ahead—some prey that would make him a very fine dinner. Stephen watched in admiration, waiting to see what would happen next.

The bird was cruising lower now, ready to drop on some doomed animal: some unsuspecting little creature that was about to meet its end.

"Oh well," he muttered, "that's nature's way. Animals have to die to feed others. It's one of those things that you have to accept," and he watched as the buzzard dropped to earth on the open ground at the edge of the wood.

A cry rang out as the bird found its target: a single cry of terror and pain—one, long, giggling, chattering scream.

"Oh, no!" cried Stephen. "It can't be that," and he started to run as fast as he could, not stopping to wonder what he was doing or what he hoped to achieve when he got there. But he ran and ran on down the hill, leaping boulders and tussocks of grass—a headlong dash, a frantic dash to the place where he'd seen the bird alight.

And as he ran, he shouted and yelled, waving his arms above his head. "Get away, you horrible bird! Get away!"

Not far to go. He could see the bird, grappling with some little creature—a golden-yellow and black striped creature. When he was almost on top of the bird, he waved his arms and yelled again as the bird began to lift from the ground with the striped animal held in its talons. At the very last moment, the buzzard faltered. It dropped its load and swept away, leaving its victim lying there—dusty, disheveled, and sadly maimed.

Stephen went quickly and quietly over, kneeling down on the grass at its side. The creature was about twelve inches in length: a long, plump shape, with a pointed tail at one end and a wide head at the other. It didn't seem to have any legs, as such, but it looked a bit like a very large, fat, furry caterpillar.

Stephen was amazed by the sight. He couldn't imagine what it could be. Its colorful coat was most surprising: a short, fine, silky-looking fur, with yellow and black tiger-like markings. But the coat was now in a horrible mess, very dirty and bedraggled, after the battle with the buzzard.

The animal lay in a desperate state. It was obviously badly wounded, its coat torn in several places by the sharp talons and beak of the bird. At first glance, Stephen wondered if in fact it might be dead; but as he knelt there gazing at it, he saw the body begin to stir.

One eye opened very slowly: a large, bright green, baleful eye, which turned to stare at Stephen sadly. He stretched his hand out toward the creature. It whimpered miserably, and started to tremble.

"Poor little fellow," Stephen said gently. "Come along now. You poor old chap." And he turned and glared up at the buzzard, cruising high in the sky above him.

"You hateful bird! You horrible bird! How could you do such a terrible thing?"

He stood looking down at the shaking mass. If he could get it back to the house, and tend to its wounds, it might recover—given plenty of time and good care. Very, very carefully, with both hands supporting the weight of the body, he lifted the animal off the ground. It made no move to resist him, but closed its eyes and lay quite still.

Stephen didn't want to clasp or handle the animal more than necessary, in case he hurt it even more; so he slipped it gently inside the open front of his shirt. It lay there quite calmly, supported by the material, without being squashed too much.

Stephen started off down the track toward the house, moving as steadily and evenly as he could, so as not to jolt the animal. Quite apart from the nasty injuries, it must be suffering from shock. Quiet and gentle handling was essential.

The furry body felt strange against his skin, but the violent trembling was easing a little. When he took a peep inside his shirt, two large, sad, eyes gazed trustingly up at him.

Back in the kitchen at Lansbury Hall, Stephen found a small basin, added a teaspoonful of salt, and then half-filled the basin with water, stirring the contents with a spoon. Then he spread a towel on the table, and, laying the animal on the towel, he thoroughly cleaned and bathed its injuries as gently as he possibly could—talking quietly as he worked.

The animal lay quite still on the towel, only flinching occasionally, and only whimpering once or twice when Stephen tackled the nastiest places. A couple of them could have done with some stitches, he thought; but he couldn't see how he could possibly get the poor thing to a vet, at least not without causing it a great deal more distress and discomfort. Any more alarm and upset might do it more harm than its wounds. None of the lacerations looked too deep. He would have to hope that they'd pull together and heal of their own accord.

He wondered if the creature might need food or drink. Fluid, he knew was very important; he offered it water in a saucer. At first, it seemed too shy or too weak to bother; but, after a little patience on Stephen's part, he was delighted to see it drinking thirstily and noisily. When it had finished, it flopped back down again onto the towel and closed its eyes.

Stephen dried the wet mouth and furry chin carefully, then stood looking down at the animal, wondering what to do with it next. The poor little thing was clearly exhausted. What it needed most of all was rest; yet he didn't want to leave it on its own. Since it had seemed so calm and comfortable inside the front of his shirt, he decided that that would probably be the best place for it.

As he lifted it gently up from the table, the animal opened both eyes and blinked at Stephen. It certainly had extraordinary eyes. It was, in fact, a very strange creature, but an attractive, appealing creature.

He tried to place it in the zoological scheme of things, but it didn't fit into any category of animals he had ever read about. It was warm and furry like a mammal, and it uttered strange sounds, but it had a most peculiar body. It must be something very rare.

Stephen so hoped that it would survive. But he wasn't too sure of its chances.

39. Primeval Forest

The small, striped animal soon settled down quietly again. Stephen was very conscious of its presence, lodged inside his shirt. The furry body tickled his chest. He puttered around as quietly as possible, carrying out his normal tasks; though when he went to visit the throne room, he didn't dare to flush the loo, for it made the most awful, gushing sound, and he thought it might frighten the creature to death.

As it was now well after seven o'clock, he decided to make himself some supper and to get things organized for the night; for what he wanted to do now, most of all, was to carry on reading Great-Uncle Theodore's journal.

With the discovery of the animal, he was even more anxious than before to learn about his great-uncle's travels. A very strange theory was forming in his mind—a theory about the possible origin of the weird, little creature. He was more convinced than ever now that the only way he would get at the truth was to work his way carefully right through the notebooks.

In the library, Stephen was only too aware of the stale smell of eggs and bacon, the result of his cooking activities there the night before. He vowed that he'd never cook there again. Perhaps he could heat water for tea, but nothing else. It simply wasn't right. He opened the windows and left the front door wide open to air the room as much as possible.

Back in the kitchen, cooking seemed out of the question now. Quite apart from the problem of the animal tucked inside his shirt, he was too tired to bother. So he prepared a plate of cold food: bread, cheese, tomato, and cucumber. With wistful thoughts of hot, steamy packages of fish and chips, he retired to the library.

It had been another long, tiring day. Stephen sat down in the big leather armchair with a loud sigh, smiling around at the comfortable room, taking a quick peep inside his shirt. The animal slept with its eyes tightly closed; but the breathing still seemed uneven and jerky, and every so often the small body was seized by a fit of violent trembling.

Stephen found that worrying; but at least the creature appeared to gain comfort from being close to him. It didn't seem at all disturbed by his moving around. It was almost as if it was used to being in such a position—tucked in the front of someone's shirt. That seemed rather odd.

When Stephen had rested and eaten some of his food, he collected the journal from the table and started to read again:

> After the terrifying storm of the night, all is now calmness and sunny heat. We steam steadily on upriver, along a relatively narrow channel, the dense walls of the mighty forest looming high on either side.
>
> There are countless different kinds of trees—B says many thousands. It is, of course, difficult to recognize them, as we sail on by. But B is busy spotting as many as he can. Even I was able to recognize an enormous Jacaranda tree, with its masses of pale, purple-blue flower heads. There are many different kinds of palms and what look like giant ferns. Everywhere amongst the trees are countless species of climbing plants, writhing and twisting toward the light.

186

*We have spent most of the day leaning against the railings of
the deck, trying to record as many different species as possible. For
hour after hour we steamed along, close to the thick, tall wall of
trees, through a heavy, brooding silence, with little sign or sound of
life. Indeed there is an eerie silence about the forest, which is very
surprising to us. The only sound as we move along is the chug of
the boat's engine.*

Stephen put the journal down and took a quick look inside his shirt. The
creature's eyes were still tightly closed.

*But the forest isn't all dark and gloomy. It has some wonderfully
colorful treats in store for the patient observer. Today we caught
glimpses of several fine orchids—all well out of B's reach—very
frustrating for the poor fellow. I have laughed heartily to see him
dancing about on the deck, as the boat has chugged relentlessly on,
past some amazing plant that he longed to examine closely. "Oh
you and your plants," I say to him. Since he is always getting on
me and getting on my so-called "bugs," it's good to be able to tease
him for a change.*

*A great excitement for me this afternoon—a flock of
magnificent red and turquoise-blue macaws, flapping up with
raucous screams as the boat passed by. The two Indians seemed to
forget themselves for a moment, when they saw my excitement.
"Arara!" they called out to us, pointing at the birds. And then
again, "Arara!" pointing this time at the feathers in their ears.
We thought that perhaps we were making some progress—perhaps
they might even turn out to be friendly; but they soon lapsed back
into a watchful silence, and wouldn't be drawn out again. They
are the most extraordinary fellows. Why should they be so wary
of us?*

*The wall of trees is so thick and dense that, as we sail by, we
cannot see into the depths of the forest. We look forward to stopping*

187

*soon for the night. This time, we fully intend to make a proper trip
into the forest.*

*Hanging from some of the trees are vines with wonderfully
colorful, trumpet-shaped flowers. Some are yellow and some are
violet. B says that they are members of the family Bignoniaceae. He
is determined to take some back home, as he thinks they might grow
at Lansbury Hall. I wonder if they would.*

Stephen paused in his reading. He thought he knew the answer to that.
He remembered the wonderful long, green tunnel with the hanging vines
and their trumpet-shaped flowers.

With damp, evening air spreading into the house, it seemed quite cold
in the library now. He got up to close the windows and doors. A cozy fire
would be just the thing.

Out on the front doorstep, Stephen stood looking up into the sky.
Clouds were building in the west. It looked as if rain were on the way.

He shivered slightly. The little animal stirred and murmured inside his
shirt. It might well need to relieve itself before the night. He lifted it out
from the front of his shirt and, carrying it carefully down the steps, he laid
it on the grassy forecourt, stepping back to give it some space; watching to
see what it would do.

The animal lay there for a few moments. It looked so sad and pathetic
that he almost went straight back to pick it up again. But then, very
slowly and painfully, it dragged itself off a few yards away amongst the
grasses.

Stephen could just see the small, striped body in the dusky light. After
a few minutes, it seemed to have finished whatever it was doing; he heard
a small, chattering whimper. So he went across to where it lay, picked it up
gently, and carried it tenderly back into the house, closing the door firmly
behind him.

Back in the library, the animal lay very still and quiet in the big armchair,
whilst Stephen lit the fire and a candle. At first, he was worried, in case it
was frightened of the fire. But it showed no sign of fear; it lay there calmly,

the large, sorrowful eyes glowing in the light from the fire, watching his every move.

It worried Stephen to think that the little creature hadn't eaten anything for several hours. Surely it must need more fluids. He was delighted when he managed to persuade it to drink another saucer of water.

Of course, he hadn't the slightest idea what it would normally eat. He tried giving it a few bits and pieces left over from his supper. But it seemed too weak to bother; it just lay flopped on the chair with its eyes closed.

Stephen made himself some tea, slipped the animal gently back inside the front of his shirt, then sat down in the big armchair, with his macaw mug in his hand. He smiled at the beautiful birds on the mug, murmuring to himself, "Arara."

Then he returned to his great-uncle's journal: reading on and on and on, enthralled by the stories of his adventures—stories of how, when the boat stopped each evening, Theodore and B set off into the forest to explore:

> *November 9th.*
>
> *On our evening walks in the forest, we are accompanied by the two Indians—well, not precisely accompanied, yet they are never quite out of sight and clearly keeping an eye on us. They seem intrigued by our perambulations, and they have been kind and helpful on several occasions. But we still don't know how far we can trust them. They are certainly helpful—but helpful in a rather strange way.*
>
> *As we make our way through the forest, we have to traverse the most difficult terrain, often, when crossing rivers and streams, edging our way along slippery tree trunks, sometimes partly submerged in the water. On a number of occasions in the past few days, when we have come to some perilous crossing, the two Indians have firmly insisted on taking our bags, carrying them carefully across.*
>
> *They have obviously realized how important our equipment is to us—how B sets such store by his camera, and how much I care*

about my notebooks. Their action in carrying the bags for us is
clearly an act of kindness; and yet, whatever the hazard may be,
they don't come back to help us across, but stand on the opposite
side, watching our stumbling progress with interest. Indeed B and I
have a sneaking suspicion that they are watching with
anticipation—waiting to see us make some blunder. You can be
quite sure that we are taking the greatest care, being determined not
to let the side down.

Stephen took a big swig of his tea and sat there thinking about the Indians. He didn't know what to make of them. Could they be planning something unpleasant?

B and I are continually amazed by the huge volume of water
that must flow down this mighty river. The A here is several miles
wide. Our walk this evening took us deep into the forest. Although
we had read all the books that we could get our hands on, being
here and seeing the reality of this place is both amazing and
surprising.

The forest where we walked this evening was very dark and
gloomy. The trees rose up close on every side, and the canopy high
above, which is formed by their branches and leaves, was so thick
that very little light came through; so the forest floor was almost
bare; for no undergrowth could possibly survive in the dark, green
shadow below.

The forest, as a whole, is nothing like anything that we have
ever seen before. Certainly one cannot compare it with the forests
that we have back home in England. For one thing, the seasons are
very different here. Back home, we are used to cold, wet winters and
warmer, drier summers. Many of our trees are deciduous. Because
they lose their leaves in winter, we are used to seeing large areas of
woodland with bare, leafless branches. Here the growth of
vegetation is controlled by the alternation of wet and dry seasons;

190

but the temperature never falls very low, so that few of the plants or trees lose all of their leaves at any one time.

Also, here there are countless different kinds of trees—not just a small number as we have in our forests at home, but literally thousands of species, and the odd thing is that they are dotted around in an unexpected way. You might recognize one type of tree, then not see another one like it for a farther mile or more.

Stephen drained the last of his tea and put the mug back down on the hearth. The movement jolted the little animal, which made a distressing hiccupping noise. He settled quickly back to read:

The trees themselves are quite astounding. They rise to enormous heights, towering above us, their trunks stretching on and up into a haze of greenery. Climbing the trunks of the trees are many different kinds of liana, their long, twisting, ropelike stems clinging and pushing ever upward to disappear in the canopy.

Some of the trees have strange, buttressed roots—very large, wide, wing-like structures that stand out around at the base of the tree—some as much as ten to twelve feet high. Others have roots like thick, winding cables that hardly seem to go down into the ground at all, but run along on the forest floor, twisting and turning and tripping us up. Yet the Indians move amazingly quickly and quietly amongst the trees—we do our best to keep up with them.

Today, as we followed their shadowy, flitting figures through the gloom—walking, perhaps, where no man had ever walked before, and where trees have ruled for millions of years—B and I felt as if we had been transported far, far back in time—back to the great primeval forest, long before Man appeared.

For there is a wonderfully timeless feeling about the ancient forests—a feeling of brooding strength and power that makes one aware of one's own puny size. We stood together in deep shadow,

*with giant trees rising up on all sides, like the columns of some
huge cathedral, infinite in size and sway, as we listened to the eerie
sounds—the strange, haunting calls of countless creatures, high
above and out of sight.*

*Whatever the outcome of this trip may be—even if the forest
claims us as her own—we thank God for such vast, wild places—
too big for Man to spoil or destroy.*

Stephen stopped reading, He sat back in the chair with a very sad smile on
his face, as he pondered the wording in the old notebook. His great-uncle's
journal had been written long before the development of the powerful modern machinery that was now being used to wreck the forests. He had reckoned without those developments. He had reckoned without modern Man.

Stephen couldn't help wondering: "Whatever would Great-Uncle
Theodore say if he could see the Amazon now?"

The candlelight dipped. The flame sputtered and died.

40. Laughter

Stephen sat quietly in the firelight, thinking about the Amazon forests. Just the thought of what was happening there made him feel quite sick with frustration. What could he do to stop the destruction? He always found it so upsetting.

The little animal seemed very restless inside his shirt. He knew, of course, that it must be in pain, but it was almost as if it had sensed his distress and was now, itself, even more upset. He got up, lit a fresh candle, and then sat back down in the armchair, hoping that if he sat reading quietly, the animal would settle again:

> *November 10th.*
> *For several days now, B and I have had the feeling that the two Indians have been watching and waiting for one or other of us to do something silly. When B finally obliged them this evening, by providing an entertaining show, they certainly enjoyed it.*

B had insisted, against my advice, that it was absolutely essential for us to cross a small river, to try and reach some extraordinary plant that could be seen hanging from a branch on the opposite bank. We managed to find an old fallen tree, partly submerged, but spanning the river. The two Indians, as is their habit now, insisted on carrying our paraphernalia safely across the river. They then stood on the opposite bank, where they had a good view of our progress.

B elected to go first. He was doing rather well until he got to the very middle, and then he started to wobble. First, I thought he was going to fall. And then I thought that he wasn't. And then, again, it seemed that he must. He was wavering backward and forward, rather like a clown on a tightrope, his arms wildly milling the air in a vain attempt to regain his balance.

It was quite an impressive performance. I caught a glimpse of two, brown, faces—gleeful, on the opposite bank—just before the mighty splash. And I have to confess, I was laughing too. But not so, B, poor fellow! The two Indians, laughing hilariously, pulled him spluttering out of the river—spluttering, not because of the water, but furious with the Indians' laughter. Yet by the time I had made my own way across the perilous tree trunk, B was apparently laughing too, and we all ended up with aching sides.

And so we feel we have gained two friends. For one cannot remain detached from people with whom one has laughed so much. Their names are Chico and Pedro. They are brothers, so we learn, only a year or so apart and around about our own age. They tell us they are the eldest sons of the leader of their people—a tribe that is called the Taluma.

We lie now in a row—all four of us in our hammocks under the palm-leaf shelter. It is a great blessing that B and I worked so hard at our Portuguese, for both of our new friends can speak that language. Thus we are able to converse with them, although only slowly, with difficulty and with a lot of acting and gestures. B was

always good at charades, and I am not so bad myself. We have told
them of our plans to study the trees, plants, and creatures—
especially the insects—of the forest. They speak of their home with
love and respect. Both seem eager to help with our work.

They seem great chaps to us—quietly spoken and rather shy, but
certainly kind and courteous. It is clearly quite wrong to say that
they are savages—which is what the captain says—but then we have
noticed that he and his crew are very scornful of all Indians, and
that they treat them badly too. Quite frankly, if someone treated me
like that, I should feel—and probably become—exceedingly savage
myself, and yet they seem very quiet and gentle. If other white
people here behave as badly toward the Indians as the captain and
his crew, then we begin to understand why C and P were so wary
of us.

Stephen paused in his reading. He was beginning to like the idea of
Great-Uncle Theodore and B becoming friends with the Indians, now
referred to as C and P.

"Chico and Pedro." Stephen tried out the names. Somehow, they didn't
sound quite right for forest Indians. Perhaps they were Portuguese names.

In the past, it had been the forest and especially the animals that had
interested Stephen. He had known nothing about Indians; they hadn't particularly interested him. But now he was becoming intrigued. The Indians
sounded rather fun. They might come up with all kinds of information
about the forest—about the plants and creatures. He was looking forward to
that.

November 14th.
During our walks I have hoped to see a whole variety of
creatures that I know must live here somewhere. But I am
somewhat disappointed to have seen surprisingly few. Most of the
activity seems to be high above us, in the canopy of the trees. I have,
however, made one most important find—a large and curious

beetle—a species that I'm sure has not been discovered before. Quite
a thrilling thing to happen!

A loud chorus of howler monkeys startled us on our walk this
evening. They make a weird and alarming sound. We stood quite
still in the dark-green gloom of the forest floor, looking up and
hoping to catch a glimpse of them as they moved through the
branches high above.

All kinds of extraordinary plants grow up there, many of them
actually growing on or out of the branches of the trees. It seems that's
how the forest works—everything feeding off everything else. Poor
old B was quite beside himself with excitement and wonder—seeing
so many interesting things, and almost all of them out of reach.

We also caught sight of an exceedingly large and splendid
butterfly—a member of the group called morphos, *quite six inches*
across—a dazzling flash of iridescent blue as it flapped its way across
an opening in the canopy high above our heads—well out of my reach.

I had been hoping to see tapirs. I managed, with a complicated
mix of charade and sketches, to explain this wish to C and P. But
they only laughed, telling me that I shall have to learn to move
much more quietly if I want to do that; for tapirs are very timid
beasts. I am therefore determined to do just that, since I'm
determined to see my tapir.

The Indians are wonderfully knowledgeable about the forest.
There are so many different species of plants. B and I find it very
difficult even to tell the trees apart. But C and P are very wise; they
point out different species and tell us their Indian names.

Stephen could hardly contain his excitement. He had been right about
the Indians. Great-Uncle Theodore and B were going to learn a lot from
them—and so was he. He read on quickly:

After we had been out walking this evening for an hour or so, B
and I felt completely lost. The two Indians suggested that we

196

should lead them back to the boat—just to tease us, I believe—for
they fell about with laughter when they saw our sad attempts,
setting off in what we soon learned was completely the wrong
direction. They gave us an admirable demonstration of how to find
our way back, although we are not quite sure how they did it.

At first we both thought that they had some special and
uncanny sense of direction. But B says that there's much more to it
than that. He is certain that they had left some kind of trail: a torn
leaf here, a broken twig there. But, however they did it, it was very
impressive. If it had been left to B and myself, goodness knows
where we should all be by now. It was, I dare say, a lesson for us
both. For we see that the forest commands respect.

At this point it is impossible for me not to mention the
mosquitoes—the most ferocious and hungry mosquitoes that I have
ever met. As we emerged from the trees, we were surrounded by a
huge swarm of the confounded things, every one of them looking for
its evening meal. And then there are the pium flies!

It is a great relief to be back on the boat. The captain ties the
boat up to the bank each night, but allows enough rope for the boat
to swing out and away from the bank, into the river's current,
where mosquitoes and other biting insects seldom follow.

Even the exciting appearance of fireflies in the clearing on the
riverbank cannot lure me back on shore tonight. Each beetle has two
light-producing spots, one on either side of the thorax, which glow
brightly as the beetle flies. We see the lights of the beetles dancing
in the forest clearing—a truly amazing and delightful sight as
darkness falls and we lie in our hammocks.

Stephen closed the notebook, and sat thinking for a while. He was glad that the giant, blue, morpho butterfly had been well out of his uncle's reach; glad that it hadn't ended up as a pathetic, dry, dead thing in some dusty butterfly collection. With so many species endangered now, he hated the thought of losing even one individual.

In Great-Uncle Theodore's day, things had been very different. Nobody, Stephen supposed, could have guessed at the way in which so many species would become in danger of extinction, through Man's misuse of his world. In olden days, naturalists didn't have the wonderful means that they have today of researching and recording creatures without killing too many of them. It was common practice for people to collect either living or dead examples of the plants and the creatures they studied, without a thought for conservation—a practice no longer acceptable. Yet, even today, there are greedy people—very thoughtless, selfish people who aren't content with observing creatures in their natural habitats, but who have to have them and to own them, and, in doing so, destroy them.

Stephen made his usual, late-night, fleeting trip to the throne room. As he stood beside the thronelike structure in which the toilet itself was installed, the rich, dark, beautifully polished wood from which the cabinet was made glowed in the light from the flickering candle.

Stephen smiled grimly to himself. Mahogany! What a lovely wood! In a way, it was just like the butterfly. No one in his great-uncle's day could have guessed that the fashion for using such wood could lead to the wholesale destruction of forests. Stephen sighed sadly and loudly as he turned to leave the room.

Having worked out how to flush the toilet, he did so, when necessary, during the daytime. But he didn't yet feel bold enough to use the flush in the dead of night. That might disturb the sleeping house.

It was not that the flow of water to the toilet was particularly large or noisy, for it wasn't. Sometimes, in fact, it was necessary to use extra water out of a bucket to flush the toilet thoroughly. But the pipes made a very disconcerting, clanking noise, which he found alarming in the dark silence of the night. Besides he had a good excuse—the noise would frighten the little animal.

After a very quick splash in the scullery sink, Stephen paused in front of the big mirror in the hall. He shot a quick look at his scruffy reflection and applied a few blobs of Morwenna's Secret Recipe, as was his habit now, night and morning.

Having moved quietly along the hall, he stood beside the door to the library, listening carefully. He felt a little less anxious than usual. The warm, furry body, tucked inside his shirtfront, was comforting; though he feared that the loud noise of his own heartbeat might upset the poor little beast.

Within the safe confines of the library, with the door firmly closed behind him, Stephen prepared himself for bed. It was obvious that he couldn't possibly sleep all night long with the animal tucked inside his shirt, so he made a cozy nest for it on the bed, out of the folds of the tartan blanket. Then he lowered the wounded animal carefully into the nest, which was lodged against the bookshelves on one side and his body on the other, so that, should it move about, it wouldn't fall off onto the floor.

Lying very still in bed, Stephen watched the animal in the glow of light from the dying fire. It shifted painfully around, and then was seized yet again by a bad fit of violent trembling. He stroked its furry head very gently, talking to it reassuringly—telling it that it would be alright.

But, in truth, he wasn't too hopeful of the animal's chances. It seemed so very weak. He wasn't even sure it would last the night.

41. Tig

Stephen spent an uncomfortable night. He had never been able to sleep well lying on his back; but he didn't like to move around too much, in case he should hurt or disturb the animal. After waking and sleeping, waking and sleeping, on and off all night—at last, just as dawn was breaking, he fell into a deep sleep.

When he finally awoke, it was much later than he'd intended. He lay still, wondering what was wrong, for there was something about his bed that morning that was quite out of the ordinary. He was suddenly aware of a furry presence on the pillow beside his head—a furry presence that was tickling his neck and breathing into his ear.

With the very greatest of care, he lifted up his head and shoulders and took a look at the striped creature sleeping on the pillow beside him. As he moved and sat up, it opened one eye and looked up at him. Stephen smiled with delight.

"Hello, old fellow," he said. "I'm glad to see you looking a bit brighter."

In fact, he was amazed and delighted to find that the animal was still alive. It had managed to move away from the nest, which seemed like a very good sign. It must be a tough, courageous, little beast.

The animal opened its other eye, and then it made its extraordinary noise. It had a most peculiar voice, sounding like something somewhere between a row of hiccups and a giggle. Every so often, as Stephen chatted to it, it seemed to answer him back.

"Well, now. Let's see," Stephen said. "We'd better get ourselves properly organized. I expect you'll need some fresh air and something nice to eat." He dressed himself as quickly as he could.

Out on the grassy forecourt, the animal did exactly what it had done the night before. When it had finished, it called to Stephen. He went across, picked it up, and then carried it back indoors.

In the kitchen, it lay quietly on the window seat, watching him putter around. First he prepared a plate of food for himself—some stale bread with honey, an apple, a banana, and a drink of lemonade. Then he wondered what he could give the animal to eat and drink.

It might, he thought, like some evaporated milk. Lots of animals seem to enjoy milk. By now it must badly need nourishment—the sort of nourishment that milk would provide. He had not been able to get any long-life milk from the shop, so he opened a can of milk, mixed some with a little water in a saucer, and placed the saucer on the kitchen table. Then he spread a towel on the table close to the saucer, and having lifted the animal onto the towel, he sat down himself and started to eat.

As he ate his breakfast, Stephen looked at the animal closely. Although still obviously weak, it certainly seemed brighter this morning. The wounds looked clean and tidy. There was no sign of any infection; the terrible trembling seemed to have stopped. He was already getting rather fond of the strange little creature; he was thrilled to think that it stood a good chance of recovery—if only he could get it to eat and drink.

The animal lay on the towel watching him, glancing suspiciously from time to time at the saucer of milk. Stephen was beginning to feel anxious. It didn't look as if it was going to drink at all. Maybe it needed firmer handling.

He stroked the furry head; then with a few encouraging words, he pushed the saucer forward, very close to the animal's mouth.

After a last, long, trusting look at Stephen, it put its head down into the saucer and started to drink. But the smile of success and satisfaction that was spreading over Stephen's face was very quickly wiped away. With a horrible, spluttering, hiccupping cry, the animal suddenly reeled back, spitting milk in all directions, a look of great disgust and distress on its little crumpled face.

Stephen was appalled. The poor thing lay gasping on the towel, looking very pathetic. He cleaned as much of the milk from its mouth and fur as he possibly could; but it looked worse now than it had before. The violent trembling had started again; the large, sad, green eyes were staring up at him full of reproach.

Stephen felt dreadfully guilty, as if he had done something brutal to the poor, trusting creature. He picked it up and, cradling it in his arms, he walked up and down the kitchen, talking to it quietly and kindly until the horrible trembling ceased. Then he tucked it inside the front of his shirt, and sat back down at the table again to finish his breakfast.

By the time he got around to eating his banana, the animal seemed to be perking up a bit. As he cut the neck of the banana and started to unzip the skin, somewhat to his surprise, it emerged from the front of his shirt. It appeared to be watching what he was doing. Then, staring up into his face, it made its funny, chattering noise.

"Banana! Of course!" Stephen exclaimed. "Banana would be the very thing."

If the theory that was forming in his mind about the creature was correct, it might well eat banana; anyway, banana was nourishing and sustaining. It couldn't do the animal any harm; it was certainly worth a try—but perhaps a somewhat less pushy try than his last attempt.

So he cut off the small pointed end of the banana and offered it to the animal on the very tip of his finger, without pushing it too close. Then he held his breath and waited. The animal seemed to be scenting the air, its top lip, quivering, stretched out toward his hand. Then rather warily it opened its mouth, took the banana between its lips, moved it back slowly into its mouth, and started to chew.

Stephen felt jubilant. At last, it was eating. But he hardly dared to breath or move, in case he put it off. He sat quietly with the animal on his lap, as slowly but surely, piece by piece, the creature munched its way through almost half of the banana. Then it drank some water out of a saucer, closed its eyes, and lay peacefully on Stephen's lap, apparently sound asleep.

What an achievement! Stephen sat there for a while, flushed with success, smiling happily down at the animal.

"But what next?" he wondered to himself. It was not a day for outdoor exploration; it looked as if it were going to rain. A few household chores seemed the obvious thing, then straight back to his great-uncle's notebooks—as quickly as possible.

He placed the animal, still sleeping, on a pile of clothing on the window seat, whilst he set about washing the dishes and carrying out other essential chores—washing some clothing and cleaning the throne room.

Standing, surveying the magnificent toilet, Stephen suddenly noticed something that he hadn't noticed before. He had very much admired the white porcelain bowl of the lavatory, with its fine pattern of blue flowers. Now that he came to look at the flowers more closely, he was surprised and delighted to find that they were passionflowers—passionflowers entwined with corn.

As he tidied up and cleaned the lavatory, he couldn't help wondering to himself. Perhaps this pattern of passionflowers had inspired Theodore as a child—had started him on his quest for the Amazon. It was a fanciful idea, but Stephen liked it anyway.

Having completed his chores, he collected up the little animal, retiring with it to the library, where he sat reading his great-uncle's journal, with the animal sleeping on his lap.

Now that he was more used to Great-Uncle Theodore's writing, Stephen was able to read on more quickly. The boat on which the two explorers were traveling was making its way gradually upriver. It was heading, apparently, for the town of Manaus, which Stephen learned was one thousand miles from the mouth of the river, and yet, amazingly, less than halfway along the river toward their final destination of Iquitos.

Obviously, it was not only a very long journey to Manaus, but it was also a very slow journey, with the boat stopping whenever they passed settlements to allow the captain to renew old friendships. They tied up early each night at some suitable place on the riverbank; this gave the young explorers plenty of opportunities to investigate the forest, along with their forest Indian friends.

As he read on, it became increasingly clear to Stephen that the Amazon forest was not all like the part that his great-uncle had described earlier. It was, in fact, very varied. There were so many tributaries to the river and so many islands.

At one time, the travelers would find themselves passing through complex, narrow channels of water; but then, later on, they'd find themselves crossing vast expanses of open water, so wide that they couldn't see the banks. In some places, there didn't seem to be any solid bank to the river at all—just huge areas of flooded forest and swamp. It all sounded very exciting to Stephen.

One evening, their walk had taken them to a series of small lakes. Great flocks of water birds had flown up when they approached: snowy egret, large striped heron, and various kinds of stork. There was a good description of B's excitement on discovering his first example of the giant Victoria water lily:

> C and P were delighted to be able to show the giant water lily to B. Its huge leaves with their upturned edges are a yard or even two yards across. The two Indians sometimes tease B, but they certainly also respect him, and they are, undoubtedly, impressed by his stature, his strength, and his courage. He was always much bigger and stronger than me and, of course, he got his Blue for rowing; although, as I sometimes enjoy reminding him, on the occasion when he rowed for Oxford, we actually lost the Boat Race.
>
> Fortunately, he is a stout fellow, and he takes it all in good part.

He has been amusing C and P with fabulous stories about the Boat Race.

Stephen stopped reading for a few moments and sat thinking. He would dearly have liked to know more about "B." Without his proper name, it was somehow difficult to picture him as a person, although he knew that was rather silly.

The fact was that Stephen felt irritated by not knowing who "B" really was. All he knew about him was that he was obviously an old friend of Theodore's, probably a college friend, and that he sounded pretty tough. He was clearly something of an unusual character, too; for Stephen had learned that B wore a monocle! This was an extraordinary idea to him; it amused him as much as it had apparently amused Chico and Pedro.

The more Stephen read on, the more he realized how little he had known about the wealth and variety of life on the Amazon. He learned some astounding facts. The sheer variety of species and the numbers involved were quite amazing. Just amongst the fishes, for example, there were hundreds and hundreds of different kinds, each one so cleverly adapted to its own particular habitat.

He particularly liked the description of the fruit-eating fish that lurked beneath the trees of the flooded forest, waiting for fruit to fall into the water. But he wasn't too keen on the sound of the stingray, which was in the habit of lying partially covered on the riverbed. The barbed spine could inflict a most painful and dangerous wound. That sounded really nasty!

And then there were electric eels, sharks—and a giant catfish, some three yards in length and weighing over two hundred pounds. But most surprising of all to Stephen—he learned that there were freshwater dolphins! And when he had recovered from his excitement over those, he read about the giant otters—nearly five feet long, apparently, and that was without the three-foot-long tail!

With all the modern disruption and the pollution of the river, Stephen couldn't help wondering if there were any dolphins or otters still left in the Amazon. He only hoped and prayed that there were.

Some sections of the journal were badly stained and discolored, with the writing faint and difficult to read. The morning's reading had proved very slow and tiring. Finally, he closed the book. His stomach told him that it was lunchtime.

The small striped animal had been sleeping peacefully whilst he was reading, but it was now awake and getting restless. He chatted away to it as he carried it outside. It was certainly looking much better now. As it lay in his arms, gazing up into his face, its eyes looked even bigger and brighter than before.

"You're going to be a very handsome beast when we get you back into shape," Stephen told the animal—smoothing the bedraggled fur, but carefully avoiding the wounds.

The animal chattered back to him.

"You have the most beautiful tigerlike markings.

"In fact," he added thoughtfully, "I think I'm going to call you Tig. Now then, what do you think of that?"

The animal didn't seem to mind. It answered Stephen back, in its usual peculiar voice.

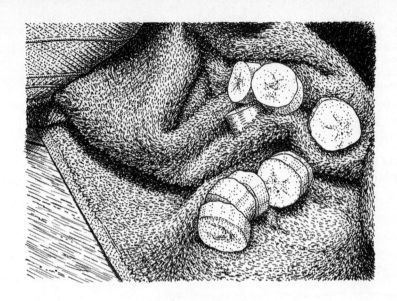

42. Slavery

Tig lay quietly on the window seat in the kitchen, watching Stephen prepare lunch. He was certainly looking much better, and his appetite had improved. For when he was lifted onto his towel on the table, he ate his way slowly but surely through the remaining part of the banana, which had been cut up into small pieces for him.

Stephen sat at the table close beside him, eating his own food, watching Tig's progress with pleasure. He knew that it was early yet, that it was by no means certain that the animal would survive. But now that Tig was eating so well, he couldn't help feeling optimistic.

He didn't even want to consider the idea of losing his newfound friend. He had quite forgotten about being lonely. There wasn't time for loneliness when looking after a fellow like Tig.

There was, however, another matter that was beginning to trouble Stephen. He was getting very fed up with the same old, boring, cold food and no proper, hot meals. It was the same old bread—even more stale today than it had been yesterday, the same old tomatoes, cucumber and cheese, with the occasional can of something or other.

He thought back—remembering the meals at the children's home, and the meals that Mrs. Johnson had cooked him over the past year. He even thought back wistfully to his much-despised school meals! Perhaps, after all, they hadn't been quite so bad as he'd thought at the time.

There was, it seemed, a lot to be said for having a hot meal put down in front of you—even if it were far from perfect and not precisely what you wanted. When you had to plan it all and cook it for yourself, it was quite a different matter—especially if it meant cleaning and lighting a cooking range first.

Stephen remembered his idea of raiding the vegetable garden. He would probably do that another day. But if he wanted hot food, he would have to prepare and cook the things; and, most annoyingly, he didn't have very much left in the way of meat products.

He wondered about the fish in the river. Fishing had never appealed to him, and the river seemed a doubtful area. He certainly wouldn't fish the lake.

As Stephen continued his meal, he offered one or two tidbits to Tig, who was lying watchfully on his towel. The animal obviously enjoyed the pieces of tomato and cucumber; but a small chunk of cheese that Stephen offered him was not a success. After a brief moment or two of perfunctory munching, the cheese was spat smartly back onto Stephen's plate. It was not quite what he was expecting; but at least, it showed that the animal was growing stronger. One must, Stephen felt, be grateful for small mercies or certainly grateful that it hadn't been spat back into his face.

After the usual routine trip outside, to ensure that Tig would be comfortable for the afternoon, the two friends sat down together in the library: Stephen with his great-uncle's notebook opened in front of him yet again, and Tig with his eyes closed, apparently contented and sleeping soundly on Stephen's lap. Despite the improvement in his condition, it was obvious that the animal was still frail. Even the small effort involved in eating seemed to have exhausted him.

Stephen continued reading the journal with enthusiasm. He still felt sure that the solution to the mystery of Lansbury Hall lay there somewhere in its pages. Each time he turned over and started a new page, he did so in the expectation that this might be the all-important page—the one that held the vital clue. So he read on as quickly as possible, but he still found it hard going:

> *November 30th.*
>
> *At last we have reached the city of Manaus, which stands to the north of the main river at the mouth of the River Negro—one of the biggest tributaries of the Amazon. The clear, dark water of that river is almost black, totally different in every way from the water of the main river, which is muddier and lighter in color.*
>
> *The meeting of the River Negro with the Amazon is a most extraordinary sight. The waters of the two rivers do not mix together as one might think they would. They flow along side by side, downriver, for many miles, the black water running along quite separately from the light-colored water, with a strangely clear-cut line between the two; so that, long before we came to the junction of the two rivers, B and I were aware of two totally separate streams of different-colored water within the one great river—an unusual and unexpected sight.*

The description of this extraordinary phenomenon made a big impression on Stephen. He tried to visualize the river, completely overcome as usual by an overwhelming desire to go and see the place for himself—to see it before it was all too late.

> *After sailing up this mighty river for hundreds and hundreds of miles and only seeing the occasional small settlement, one cannot help but be amazed by the very sight of Manaus. For it is, indeed, most surprising to find such a splendid, modern city, situated in the middle of nowhere. It owes its presence and its success to one thing, and to one thing only—the all-important*

rubber industry. The trees, whose sap is collected for making rubber, are abundant in the Amazon forest. With so many new tires required for all our modern bicycles and motorcars, rubber is now in great demand.

B and I had read about Manaus. We knew that it must be quite a big city. But we hadn't expected to find such riches, nor had we expected to find such impressive architecture.

The town and many of its people have certainly grown rich and fat on the profits from the rubber. They say it is the richest city in the world. Judging by the large and splendid Opera House, with its magnificent golden dome, and the long streets of elegant houses, we can well believe this claim.

As we approached Manaus, we noticed for the very first time on this trip that C and P seemed not only nervous, but, we thought, even frightened. We couldn't understand why. We tried to persuade them to come into town with us, to share our hotel room, but they prefer to camp in the forest.

The captain set them down on the riverbank well outside the town, and after a brief wave of hands they disappeared quickly into the forest. We shall meet again in a few days' time, when the boat continues its journey upriver to Iquitos. The captain has promised to pick them up; but B and I have a feeling that we are going to have to keep him to his promise. He has a shifty look about him and he seems to despise the Indians.

We have met an interesting fellow here in our hotel, who has been involved in some way in an investigation into the rubber trade. He has told us some terrible stories of the way in which forest Indians are being used and misused by the "rubber barons," as they are called—the rich men who manipulate others to do all the dirty, hard work, and then sit back and take all the profits.

Whole tribes of Indians are being wiped out, and the missionaries aren't helping either; for in trying to contact isolated tribes to convert them to Christianity, they are introducing death

210

and disaster, so it is said. The stories seem far-fetched to us. We find them very hard to believe.

There is talk of slavery as well. B thinks the fellow is probably potty. After all, we know that slavery ended years ago, and as B said to me today, we have always known that missionaries do so much good wherever they go.

Stephen stopped reading. He closed the journal, rising stiffly from the chair. Then he walked slowly up and down, thinking, with Tig still sleeping in his arms.

He was beginning to feel worried for the Indians. Having read so much about them, he'd come to think of them as friends. Something must be very wrong for them to be afraid like that.

He had pictured them as strong and kindly with a good sense of humor—men who would be fearless warriors, if the need arose. So why had they seemed so nervous? Why should they be afraid?

And would the captain pick them up? He sounded like a nasty character. Stephen had a horrible feeling that Great-Uncle Theodore and B might have lost their Indian friends—for good.

43. The Dastardly Captain

Out in the kitchen, Stephen prepared an early supper for Tig and himself. He was longing for a proper meal; but he also wanted to get back to the journal as quickly as possible. He needed to know what happened next.

Tig lay in his usual place on the window seat, while Stephen lit the range to cook eggs—and the remainder of the bacon, which wasn't looking very healthy. The animal lay there with a peculiarly folded-up expression on his face. He seemed to have the ability to draw his head back within a wide fold of the skin of his neck, which gave him a very odd look—a look which, on this occasion, clearly spelled out his distaste for the smell of frying food: eggs, bacon, tomatoes, and bread.

Back on his towel on the table, Tig edged away from Stephen's plate. Obviously, there was no point in offering him any of the cooked food. Stephen didn't want to risk being showered with half-chewed egg and bacon.

But he was pleased when Tig accepted pieces of raw tomato and apple, together with a few small chunks of bread and a saucer-full of water. His movements seemed stronger now. When he'd finished eating, he chattered noisily to Stephen, making it quite clear that it was time for a trip outside.

It was a rather hasty trip. The sky was very overcast; rain fell steadily. But they were soon settled down again in the library, Stephen absentmindedly stroking the top of Tig's furry head as he continued reading—the second of his great-uncle's notebooks. He could tell that Theodore and B had enjoyed their time in Manaus:

> *We have come across some very interesting people here in Manaus and B has been especially pleased to meet up with a man called Witt; although I am sorry to say that the wretched fellow has fired B with a new enthusiasm, by telling him some romantic stories about a very curious cactus—some recently discovered "wonder" of the botanical world.*

Stephen wondered about the cactus. He had always thought that cacti only grew in desert conditions. Apparently, he was wrong.

Having spent some five days in Manaus, Theodore and B had set off once more on board the same boat with the same captain. It turned out that they had been right about the captain and his promise to the two Indians. He'd been paid in full, up front, for the cost of their passage; but he didn't care about them at all; indeed, he joked openly with the crew about the way that he would trick them.

It had quickly become apparent that he had no intention whatsoever of stopping off to pick them up. Soon after the boat left Manaus, Chico and Pedro could be seen in the distance, waiting patiently at the appointed place on the riverbank. But the captain set his course away from them:

> *I have never seen B so angry before. He towered threateningly above the captain, ordering him to change course and to pick up our friends as he had promised. He glared at the man through his monocle in an exceedingly savage way. It was not a pretty sight— but it certainly had the desired effect.*

Reluctantly, the man did as requested, muttering sourly under his breath. We were happily reunited with our friends, despite resentful and scornful glances from the captain and his crew. I always knew B was a stout fellow.

Stephen felt very relieved. C and P would be alright. He read on much more happily now: colorful descriptions of flora and fauna—trees, flowers, insects, and birds—the birds sounded wonderful. Here again, so it seemed, the Amazon was rich in a magnificent variety of different species: from the tiniest and most brilliant of hummingbirds, hovering and sipping nectar from the most exotic flowers, to huge Ornate Hawk Eagles that prey on all manner of smaller creatures—everything feeding off everything else—just as Theodore said, and yet maintaining a precious balance—such a variety and richness of life, it was hard to imagine it all.

In the middle of a long section that dealt with a detailed description of several most intriguing creatures, Stephen found a disturbing account of a serious illness that had suddenly overcome one of the Indians:

Quite suddenly last night, C became extremely ill. B had mentioned the day before that he thought the poor chap looked unwell, but we were not prepared for the sudden deterioration in his condition. During the night, we heard him moaning. On lighting the lamp, we found him in a sorry state—shivering and shaking in his hammock. By our standards, the night seemed hot; but no matter what we did, we didn't seem able to get him warm.

P told us that both he and his brother had had this kind of illness before. The shivering, he told us, would later turn to a fever. From the description that he gave us, B and I are almost certain that C is suffering from malaria. We thank God that we have our quinine tablets.

B began to administer the quinine to C as soon as we felt sure that the problem was malaria. But it hasn't prevented the development of the second stage of the illness—a raging fever,

*which is quite alarming to witness. The poor fellow has been
delirious today: first burning hot and dry this morning, and now
this evening, running with sweat.*

*We have done all we can to try to help him—giving him plenty
to drink and continuing to administer the quinine tablets—though
getting them down him isn't easy. B has been such a brick—
crushing the tablets up in boiled water and somehow getting it
down C's throat. He has a wonderful way with him—an especially
good bedside manner or, as I joked with him today to try to lighten
the mood a little and to spur him on in his task, a most excellent
hammock-side manner.*

*Trying to treat such a very sick man on board this boat is
something of a nightmare. The captain has behaved in a dastardly
manner, saying that he won't have sick people on board his boat,
even pulling into the bank and trying to insist that we abandon C
there. B and I are standing guard over our patient, making sure that
one or other of us is there with him all the time.*

Stephen read on anxiously, learning a lot as he went along about malaria, which sounded like a horrible disease. It was, so he learned, the result of infection with a tiny parasite that was passed from one person to another by mosquitoes when they bit people.

"Thank goodness our British mosquitoes don't carry it—at least I don't think they do," Stephen mumbled to himself.

The quinine that the two explorers had taken from England in the first-aid kit sounded like a wonderful drug. Stephen was delighted to read that Chico responded to the treatment. Being young and strong and fit, he had made a fairly rapid recovery; although, it was clear from Theodore's comments that the fever had left him very weak. He needed careful nursing; it would be quite some time before he was back to normal again:

*Quinine is a wonderful drug. It is such a blessing that we have
it; for, quite apart from treating our friends, B and I know that*

we're both at risk. We know we may well catch it ourselves. We
also know that once you have malaria, the miserable attacks, such
as C has just experienced, keep coming back over many years—
often recurring from time to time over a very long period—perhaps
for the rest of a person's life.

It all sounded very unpleasant to Stephen. He was greatly relieved when the illness had apparently been overcome and his great-uncle's account of their adventures returned to much more pleasant matters.

The journal included amusing accounts of the various adventures in which the four friends were involved, as the boat traveled slowly on, farther and farther upstream. Stephen particularly enjoyed the story about the three-toed sloth. He knew that sloths were excessively slow and hesitant beasts that hung upside down by their hooked toes from the branches of trees. Their diet was leaves, and because of their upside-down existence, their long, gray fur grew down from their stomachs toward their backs, instead of the other way around—as with most animals.

It seemed that Theodore, despite the advice of the others, had insisted on crawling along a branch that overhung the river, in order to examine more closely an extremely handsome-looking sloth that hung at the end of the branch. He had, so he'd said, always been led to believe that some sort of plants or algae actually grew in the animal's fur. He had wished to inspect the fur more closely.

The sloth itself hadn't seemed too bothered; at any rate, it had not been galvanized into speedy action. It had merely hung there watching and waiting as Theodore edged his way along. Then suddenly, just as he was getting close enough to inspect the creature properly, the branch had broken, throwing them both down into the river.

The sloth, an excellent swimmer, had last been seen making its slow, deliberate way through the water toward the opposite bank. The two Indians had been convulsed with laughter at their friend's extraordinary antics. It had been left to good old B to fish poor Theo out.

The incident seemed to have shaken him quite badly:

I don't know when I was ever happier to be back on dry land. Only this morning, the captain had warned us about the caiman in the river—a kind of alligator, which can grow very large— especially if it's well fed! C and P insist that they are unlikely to bother us, unless provoked. But, as I was floundering about in the water, I remembered the stories of other explorers who had met their ends in a similar way; and besides, one can't help feeling that falling in on top of the creature, together with a large branch and a sloth, might well be regarded by any self-respecting caiman as very definite provocation.

A little farther down the page, Great-Uncle Theodore, having recovered, had added, almost with an air of defiance:

The three-toed sloth certainly does have extremely interesting fur.

Stephen couldn't help laughing out loud.

44. Sarko and Wamiru

Stephen sat stroking Tig's silky head and smiling to himself. He was enjoying the notebooks so much; but he was disappointed by the fact that he'd still not managed to find his great-uncle's sketchbook. Every so often, throughout the text, there were references to the sketches. It would have been such a help to him if he'd been able to look at the drawings. He longed to know what the two Indians really looked like—so when he came to the statement, See sketches of C and P, he couldn't help feeling extremely frustrated.

From time to time, Stephen left his chair and paced up and down the library, scowling and mumbling to himself. Tig seemed to take all this in good spirits, although he clearly didn't care to be jostled about too much. The woebegone expression on his funny, wrinkled face soon brought a look of concern and a smile to Stephen's eyes, which inevitably helped to restore his good temper.

By the time the Amazon travelers had reached the small town of Tefé—

the place where the famous naturalist Henry Bates had spent a lot of time in the middle of the previous century—Theodore and B had become such firm friends with Chico and Pedro that they had decided to abandon their original plan to travel as far as Iquitos, and they had accepted an invitation to go back home with the two Indians, to stay with their people for a while.

According to Theodore's journal, it was mid-December when they finally bade a not-too-fond farewell to the captain of the boat and disembarked at Tefé. The place seemed very busy, and they hadn't liked the atmosphere; so, having bought stores and two good canoes, they had left as quickly as they could. Stephen had understood from the journal that they would soon be taking a north bank tributary—the Rio Japurá:

> *December 18th.*
>
> *Leaving the boat and setting forth in our two canoes has brought us a great sense of freedom. Now, we can stop wherever we wish, to study the flora and the fauna. B is still rattling on about his beloved cactus. The sooner he finds the confounded thing, the better it will be for us all!*
>
> *We have good stocks of food that should last us for some time and, as we are traveling with C and P, we shall be quite alright. We look forward to visiting their tribe, the Taluma—to staying with their family and friends—and we know that they, in their turn, are looking forward to showing us all the interesting plants and animals that live in the forest around their home. B and I have managed to learn just a little of their language, so we shall be able to communicate with their people—if only in a small way.*
>
> *Once we were free of the captain and crew, C and P seemed much more relaxed. They told us that, if we liked, we could use the Indian names by which they had originally been known, rather than the Portuguese names by which they had become known. We learned that among some tribes an Indian's own personal name is kept a secret from other people, and that even within his family he is known only by a nickname. It seems a strange system to us, but*

219

*we are very happy to go along with using their original
nicknames—Sarko and Wamiru. It will take us time to get used to
the change, but they obviously prefer those names.*

*After the names were sorted out, they asked us, rather shyly, if
we would mind if they got rid of their trousers and shirts and lived
the way that they used to live. We told them that, of course, we
didn't mind; that we preferred them to live in whatever way was
right for them—an answer that seemed to surprise them. They are
now not only happier, but also somewhat changed in manner. In
their old tattered clothing, they always looked poor and bedraggled.
Now, without their Western-style clothing, they seem proud and
much more imposing.*

*At first we wondered why they should think that we would
object; for, as far as we understand, none of the forest Indian tribes
in South America traditionally wore much clothing. They explained
by telling us that when they were younger, out hunting together,
they had been enticed away from their tribe—taken by people who
had taught them that going without clothing was wicked. They had
been told that no decent, civilized person should go around
uncovered, that God would punish them if they did. B and I were
appalled by the story.*

Stephen was appalled too. Just fancy using God's name like that!

*We understand that after a couple of years of living with the
missionaries, they were handed over to traders as part of some deal.
They have only recently managed to escape, and they obviously
believe that all white people think that nakedness is wicked. We
assured them that this is not the case, and to show them that we
meant it, B and I stripped as well and we all went for a swim in the
river, to celebrate our freedom. Even I plunged into the water,
completely forgetting my fears about caiman and the various other
unsociable creatures that, I know, inhabit these waters.*

I am glad to be able to report that C—no! I must remember to call him Sarko—now seems to be fully restored to good health. He and B challenged Wamiru and myself to a canoe race. I had been finding it difficult to learn to handle our canoe, and even B with all his experience of boats and rowing, has found it somewhat tricky.

Of course, one cannot expect primitive, handmade boats like these—each one hewn from a single tree trunk, using only simple tools—to be perfect in form and balance. Each boat has its own, peculiar characteristic; one has to paddle the thing accordingly— to compensate for warping and so forth. Obviously, our friends are experts at handling this sort of craft, but I've heard B grumbling and mumbling away—claiming their boat has a will of its own.

Yet despite all that, I hardly need say who won the race. I couldn't help teasing B—telling him that it seemed such a pity that none of his pretty lady friends could see him as crew of a winning boat—at last! Although, come to think of it, perhaps it was fortunate that they couldn't, as neither of us bothered to put back our proper clothing till much later on. I suspect that dear Miss Cicely Stanwycke-Forbes and the ravishing Miss Drusilla Higginbotham—two young ladies of B's acquaintance—might well have been horribly shocked by the sight.

"Drusilla Higginbotham! What a dreadful name." Stephen stopped reading and enjoyed a good laugh. "B, whoever he was, must have been quite a character. Fancy having girlfriends with names like those!"

Stephen's exclamations and laughter had woken Tig, who gazed up at him in dismay, very unhappy, so it seemed, to have his sleep so rudely interrupted; though after just a moment or two, he made his funny, giggling sound, almost as if he were joining in.

Outside the house, Stephen stood in the gloom on the forecourt, waiting for Tig. He looked down at the darkly spreading woodland that clothed the valley below. It had long since struck him that, where you would find one small Tig, you were likely to find many more. He remembered the day that he'd spent on the beach and the peculiar, chattering chorus. Finding a whole group of such animals would certainly, in itself, be amazing.

Yet, somehow, Stephen felt quite sure—there was much more to the mystery of Lansbury Hall than a big collection of Tig-like creatures—however extraordinary that might be. Somehow he knew that the dark, dank valley, cool and wet in the evening rain, held a much bigger secret than that. The idea made him very uneasy. He shivered as he stood waiting for Tig.

Back indoors, Stephen collected some tea-making equipment from the kitchen. Then he returned to the library, where he lit the fire and a candle. Tig lay on the seat of one of the large armchairs, watching his progress.

When the tea was made, Stephen lifted him down onto the hearth rug and offered him a saucer of weak tea—just warm with a little sugar, no milk. The animal seemed to enjoy it, and the two of them sat companionably together in front of the fire drinking their tea. When they had both finished, Stephen lifted Tig back up onto his knee and resumed his reading.

The two explorers were obviously having a wonderful time in the forests. B was happier than he had ever been before, collecting and recording a wide range of colorful and fascinating plants, including strangely beautiful orchids—one of them, apparently, a very bright blue.

The vegetation of the forest was exciting and varied. They had discovered some extraordinary trees—trees that grew on top of other trees. B had explained to Theodore how that happens, when a seed—often a fig seed—becomes lodged high up among the branches of a tall tree, probably carried there by a bird. When the fig seed germinates, it puts out long, thin, aerial roots, which grow on down the trunk of the tree, finally reaching into the ground to suck up water and nutrients for the fig tree, which eventually strangles the original tree. Everything living off everything else.

Theodore, fascinated by this strange phenomenon, had described it in some detail, whilst at the same time describing the long, ropelike aerial roots of other plants that dangled down around them in the forest. These were the lianas, mostly harmless ropelike structures; but it seemed that you had to watch out for one particularly unpleasant species that was covered with sharp spines and hooks.

As he read on through the journal, it was clear to Stephen that Theodore was enjoying himself as much as B. He could sense in his great-uncle's writing his delight and excitement on discovering and collecting a wide variety of strange insects. Some were wonderfully camouflaged, being very cleverly shaped and colored almost exactly like leaves. Others were boldly and brightly patterned in order to warn any would-be predators that they tasted horrible. And then there were others yet again, that were in fact harmless and tasteless, but mimicked the "nasties" in color and form in order to gain protection for themselves.

Stephen beamed with delight, when he read that Great-Uncle Theodore had, eventually, seen his tapir. Indeed, he had seen two tapirs!

It was thrilling to see the mother and baby "anta"—the name that our friends use for the tapir. We watched them for several minutes before they became aware of our presence and made a hasty getaway—sliding off down the muddy riverbank on their bottoms, swimming quickly away downstream.

Shortly after that, we saw another denizen of the forest that I'd been hoping to see for some time—the "sucuri," as the Indians call him—the anaconda, not especially feared by the Indians but much respected by them as a powerful spirit of the forest. A fine example of this magnificent snake was sleeping, wrapped around a long branch that overhung the river. I wanted to get really close to the beast. But now, it was my turn to be teased.

Wamiru suggested that I should crawl along the branch to see the snake more closely, with Sarko adding that the snake had a very interesting skin. And even B had to add his bit: "Yes. Go on old chap," he said. "It would be quite an experience, don't you know,

*and if by chance you should fall in, I'll do my best to fish you out
before the caiman have you for dinner."*

Stephen enjoyed all the stories. It sounded as if the Indians had a great sense of humor. He would love to see an anaconda—the mighty sucuri—and he felt envious. They were having such a grand time. The lucky devils! The trip was obviously going so well.

But there were problems ahead for the "lucky devils." Their luck would soon be running out.

45. Toward Disaster

Luck had started to run out for the two explorers and their Indian friends early in January. The "lucky devils" were soon in trouble—and very serious trouble, too. As far as Stephen could make out, things had started to go wrong on account of B's dogged determination to find the wretched cactus:

January 7th.

Our trip has turned into a wild goose chase—or rather, I should say, a wild plant chase, with B utterly determined to obtain an example of the accursed botanical wonder. He certainly has a bee in his bonnet.

So far, we have only found fragments of the plant, broken off and lying on the forest floor; although, back on the main river, B saw a fine example of the cactus attached to an uprooted tree, which floated past our boat. So near and yet so far! The rains have started in earnest now. Everything seems to be on the move.

The days are flying by, and S and W are keen to get back to their tribe. It seems that we are not far away now from the place where they hope to find their people. But they both admire B so much—especially since B did his magnificent doctor act when S had malaria—they're anxious to help him in his quest.

Earlier today, we met a small hunting party of five Indians. They seemed to know all about the plant. They assured us that we would find some examples of it by making a small detour.

I am uncertain of the wisdom of this detour, but once B gets an idea like this into his head, it's impossible to stop him.

Stephen sat stroking Tig's head, wondering about the cactus, wondering about B. He had always seemed like such a sensible fellow. But B was a dedicated botanist. He was clearly obsessed by his search for the cactus.

Stephen was getting a horrible feeling that the search was leading the four friends toward some kind of disaster—some kind of dangerous situation, the disadvantages of which would far outweigh the value of finding and collecting a cactus—no matter how rare or exciting.

As he read on, his fears were confirmed. Nothing seemed to be going right now for the four companions:

January 10th.

Nothing but rain now, for days and days. We have never seen such a downpour before. The rain goes on and on and on. Everything soaking and dripping and running. There is constant and foul discomfort, for we can never get properly dry. We lie in our hammocks at night feeling damp, and we wake next morning, steamy and wet.

We have been badly bitten by pium flies; each bite comes up in a lump—the irritation is quite appalling, and the misery of this constant wetness day after day is indescribable. It is finally getting us down. Even B seems to be suffering. Yet still we press on— hunting for his blessed plant. For he will not give it up.

226

It all sounded extremely unpleasant to Stephen. He sat in his warm, dry, comfortable chair with Tig, trying to imagine it. Being so disgustingly wet and uncomfortable, day after day like that, must have been horrible, and the bites and the irritation dreadful.

He felt quite ashamed of himself when he remembered his own feelings of suffering and great discomfort—and all after only one brief, wet morning of exploration in the valley. He remembered the relief that he'd felt when he'd thrown off his dripping-wet clothes in the scullery, toweled himself down, and put on dry clothing. Worst of all, he remembered his naïve thoughts at the time. He remembered standing in the kitchen and saying out loud to himself, "Explorers need their creature comforts."

Out in the real world of exploration, it obviously wasn't like that at all. Stephen couldn't help wondering how he would have coped—if he'd been a member of Theodore's party. Even B seemed to be failing. So how on earth were they going to manage?

He read on as quickly as he could:

January 14th.

One of our greatest problems has been food. We have traveled on and on, day after day, without any proper, regular meals. S and W have fared much better than us.

It seems that forest Indians have a completely different pattern of eating from our own. We are used to three square meals a day. We quickly begin to feel low if we do not get them.

The Indians are used to eating when food is available. They manage amazingly well on very little nourishment, and they can go for many hours without any food at all. Then, after a successful hunting party, when they have caught and cooked something tasty, they can eat a surprisingly large amount—far more than we could ever manage—as if they were stocking up for the lean times.

This pattern of eating has played havoc with our digestions. B and I have both lost a great deal of weight. Neither of us is feeling well. We are both alarmingly weak.

We still have stocks of beijú—a useful staple food that Indians carry with them on long journeys. It is a hard, dry bread, which is made from manioc flour. It has been baked so long and so well that it would last forever, they say—provided that you keep it dry. Ours is moldy now and most unappetizing. We force it in between our lips and swallow it down as best we can. S and W don't seem to mind it.

We have with us a stock of canned food that we bought in the store at the settlement; but we are uncertain as to whether we should eat it or not, lest it be bad. When canned food goes bad, gases tend to build up inside the can, making the top of the can bulge out. All our cans look alright.

But S and W have begged us not to eat the stuff. They tell us that when the evil merchants in the towns can see that they have faulty cans, they engage special workers to puncture the cans, in order to let the gases out. Then, they reseal the tops of the cans with solder to hide the telltale signs, selling the cans to Indians and others, many of whom have died as a result.

It seems a far-fetched story to us. The poor fellows do appear to think that everyone is against them. We have opened a can of meat, which looks quite alright to us.

Stephen stopped reading. He sat there quietly, thinking about the various horrors and discomforts of Theodore's trip. He felt very ashamed of himself. How could he have been so pathetic? Grumbling away so stupidly about his own simple diet! He vowed that in future, as long as he had some kind of food on his plate at reasonably regular intervals, he would never complain again.

He read on quickly with mounting anxiety. His great-uncle's writing was deteriorating rapidly. The paper was badly stained; the writing wandered around the page. It was clear that Theodore was ill and scarcely able to write at all.

The final entry read:

228

B and I desperately ill . . . too weak to stir from hammocks . . .
S and W gone. . . . We believed in our friends. . . . We trusted
them. . . . How could they leave us here like this?

The search for B's confounded Moonflower . . . will probably be
the death of us . . .

And the writing faded out.

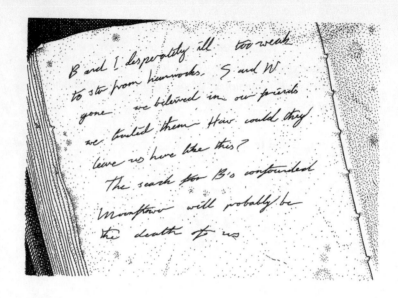

46. Bertie

Stephen sat staring in amazement at the scrawling writing. He shuffled quickly through the remaining pages of the book. They were all badly marked and stained. There was no more writing.

He read his great-uncle's last sentence out loud:

"The search for B's confounded Moonflower . . . will probably be the death of us . . .

"B's confounded Moonflower," he repeated.

"The Moonflower! Of course! The Moonflower!"

Stephen sat gazing into the dying embers of the fire—remembering. Remembering the big, fat flower bud. Now that he had finally come to recognize B's true identity, he simply couldn't imagine why he hadn't realized before.

Why hadn't he realized? Now it all seemed obvious. Although, come to think of it, it wasn't too surprising that he'd not identified the strong, dashing, young explorer, so full of fun and enthusiasm, with the frail, embittered old man that he had eventually become—Mr. Albert Postlethwaite! Or Bertie, as his friends would have called him—the nutty-looking, old lawyer with the amazing collection of plants—plants that must have been brought from the Amazon—all those years ago. Mr. Bertie Postlethwaite, who was certainly far from nutty, and who had finally found his Moonflower.

Smiling thoughtfully to himself, Stephen set the book aside. At last, a few of the awkward pieces were beginning to fit the jigsaw puzzle. At last, he seemed to be getting somewhere.

Lolling back, he yawned loudly: pressing his tired eyes with the palms of his hands; sweeping back the hair from his forehead; stretching and easing his stiff limbs in the depths of the leather armchair, with one hand supporting Tig to prevent him from slipping onto the floor. The little animal grumbled noisily at the disruption.

Having heaved himself out of the chair, Stephen walked up and down the library, with Tig cuddled close to his chest. He smiled down at the animal encouragingly. He talked to him gently to calm him down.

The reading of the journal and the exciting discovery had left Stephen feeling exhausted. He was too tired to read any more, though he was dying to know exactly what had happened to the explorers. After checking the first few pages of the next notebook on the pile—just to reassure himself that the journal did, in fact, continue—he and Tig made their final preparations for the night, and retired to bed.

47. Death's Door

The two friends slept late the following morning. Stephen eventually woke up, feeling heavy headed. Tig was still sleeping comfortably, curled up on the pillow beside him.

There was a considerable improvement in the animal's condition. He moved much more easily now, and the wounds were healing well. Stephen watched him with delight as he made an experimental tour of the bed, looking brightly all around him, and at one point looking as if he might even flop off onto the floor. He had a very odd way of moving along: a flopping, crawling, sliding kind of motion, which was very strange to watch.

It was a damp and cloudy day again, so after the usual morning routine, Stephen and Tig set off along the hall to the library. When they got to the amazing sideboard, Stephen tucked Tig inside his shirt in order to have his hands free for the early morning application of Morwenna's Secret Recipe. He stared at his reflection in the large mirror, peering closely and mumbling to himself.

Was it his imagination, or were the spots beginning to fade? Morwenna must be very clever!

He mustn't forget to keep using the cream, although he was feeling rather guilty. His previously spotless pillowcase—the one with the big embroidered L—now had nasty green marks on it. Even Tig's fur was blotched and stained.

With Tig dozing on his lap, Stephen settled down in the library once more, determined to find out what had happened to Great-Uncle Theodore, by reading the next notebook:

> *Some time mid- to late February 1912.*
>
> *At last, after many, many days of great sickness, I feel strong enough to continue my journal.*
>
> *We have no idea how many days have passed since we first became so ill. It may be several weeks. For much of that time, so it seems, B and I have lain at death's door—unconscious or delirious. We owe our lives entirely to Sarko and Wamiru. How could we ever have doubted our friends?*
>
> *As far as we can understand, having eaten the fatal can of meat, B and I both became rapidly and exceedingly ill. S and W were quite sure that the only person who might be able to cure us was their father, who is the shaman of their people. They knew that they had to act very quickly, so they took the risk of leaving us, each setting out at high speed in slightly different directions—as they were uncertain of the exact position of their tribe—yet both felt sure that it was close.*
>
> *It is fortunate for us that they can move through the forest at such an extraordinary speed. Having found their people quite quickly, and having been reunited with them—a wonderfully joyous but hasty affair—they returned for us with helpers, carrying us back in our hammocks to their home, which must have been quite a struggle. Here we have been tended with great love and care: treated with various herbal brews, which are made from special plants of the forest; almost willed to return to life by the shaman, a great healer.*

Stephen was thrilled and relieved to discover that Sarko and Wamiru had turned out to be good people after all. He had come to think of them both as great friends, and he had been very upset and so disappointed to learn that they had apparently abandoned the two sick men.

He read on contentedly through the morning, gradually learning more and more about the lives of forest Indians; for, as it turned out, B and Theodore had ended up living with the Taluma, in their long communal house, for a very long time. They had found that the Indians, far from being the vicious savages that people had made them out to be, were a gentle people, living in harmony with each other and with their strange, green, forest world— not aggressive, unless provoked:

> *These are a very kindly people, tending their gardens and cultivating their crops, collecting the fruits of the forest and hunting. They live in great harmony with one another, sharing everything equally amongst the group. When one man has success at hunting, catching something good to eat, he shares it with everyone else. We do not see the petty jealousies that we find in our own society back home in England.*
>
> *The Indians cut down trees to make clearings for their crops: but the clearings are only small; after a time, if and when the group moves on to another area or opens up a fresh clearing, the forest soon grows back.*
>
> *Life is good for these gentle people. They work when they need to, hunt when they need to, and enjoy an important social life. And for the Indians, as for every living thing in this vast forested world, it is the balance of life that is vital.*
>
> *Although, overall, the forest seems so rich in plants, fruits, game, and fish, it would be the easiest thing in the world to starve here. For the game and the fruits are widely dispersed. If the people became sick, or if for some other reason they were unable to forage far and wide, when they needed to, the group could quickly starve to death.*

This was extraordinary news to Stephen. He had always imagined that the forest was a place so lush and fruitful that self-sufficiency would be easy. He had apparently been wrong.

The Indians are deeply religious, believing in the spirits of the forest and the spirits of the animals all around them. In this way, they live nearly as one with their forest home—for they have a special respect for the forest, because of their special beliefs.

The group that we are living with have no knowledge of our religion—Christianity. It seems that S and W were the only two members of this tribe to be taken away by missionaries. Since that time, these people have managed to remain hidden deep in the forest, avoiding any more contact. But, as I said to B, only this morning, the Taluma seem to be far more kind to each other, and far more what one might call "Christian" in their behavior, than many of our churchgoing friends back in England.

The Taluma don't wear anything that we would call proper clothing. This seems a good idea to us, for clothes are a very great problem out here, in such a hot and sticky climate. One has to keep washing them all the time, or they soon become disgustingly stale and unpleasant and, as such, extremely unhealthy.

The Indians are at a great advantage, having little or no clothing to bother about. They wash much more frequently than many of our society friends back home. They are in and out of the river several times a day, and they often shampoo their hair, using the leaves of a special vine.

B has suggested that a number of his college friends could learn a thing or two about regular washing from the Indians. I couldn't resist reminding him of poor Drusilla Higginbotham's dreadful brother, Charlie. I always made a point of keeping well away from him.

Stephen enjoyed a good laugh, disturbing Tig in the process. He gave Stephen a baleful look, then closed his eyes very tightly, as if beseeching peace and quiet. Stephen read on with enthusiasm:

> *Our Taluma friends paint their bodies and their faces with beautiful, curving patterns, using very special paints that are made from colorful vegetable dyes. The results are most impressive. On special ceremonial occasions, B and I are included in this decorative procedure. How I wish Drusilla could see him then!*
>
> *We are more than happy living here in this peaceful place. I have quite lost track of the days and weeks, though I write in my journal whenever I can. We have been greatly honored by the Taluma people, who have accepted us as brothers in their tribe. We feel privileged to call this place our home.*
>
> *Several people in our family here play wonderful music on panpipes. B is a clever old stick in many ways, but he doesn't pretend to be musical. I, on the other hand, have twiddled around with a number of musical instruments in my time, and am happy to say that I am becoming quite proficient on the panpipes. One of the elders in the group has made me a very fine set of my own. I while away the hours with music, lying contentedly in my hammock.*

Stephen sat gazing into the fire. The piping he'd heard on the moor that day—it certainly could have been panpipes. It had drifted up from the valley below—drifted eerily up through the woodland.

There was something uncanny about that woodland—something uncanny about that valley. Could it have been his great-uncle's spirit playing the panpipes in that grotto? Stephen could almost believe that it could. The very thought of it made him shiver. He looked up nervously around the room, holding Tig more firmly than usual, his furry body a comforting presence.

236

48. Bugwompidae

Great-Uncle Theodore's journal was packed with fascinating facts about the lives of forest Indians. After a brief spell to stretch his legs and to get some air for Tig and himself, whilst trying to rid his mind of what he knew must be foolish thoughts, Stephen came back in and sat down again. He had just started book III. He pushed the hair back firmly from his eyes and read on with interest:

> A great many skills are required to live successfully in the
> forest. Time and again, we have cause to admire our T brothers'
> expertise. B and I are gradually learning, improving our skills as
> the days go by. With much kind help and a lot of encouragement,
> we have both become quite passable hunters—moving more quietly
> through the forest, and using our bows when necessary, though our
> friends still laugh at our silly mistakes.
>
> Indeed, there is a great deal of laughter here—much joking and

*teasing as life goes along. In between hunting and collecting, we spend
a lot of time lying in our hammocks and resting, talking and laughing
with our friends. We can now speak their language tolerably well.*

*Another useful skill we have learned is how to make fire the
Indian way, using very simple equipment. Only two objects are
required, and a small amount of tinder. One of the objects, which is
a flat piece of wood with small, pitlike depressions, is laid on the
ground and held firmly in place by the feet. The other, a stick—
long, smooth, and rounded—is held in an upright position in
contact with the wooden piece on the ground, then twirled between
the palms of the hands.*

*The friction of the two fire sticks grinding together causes a lot
of heat, and the tinder—dried grass or dried leaves—eventually
catches fire. But it's not a thing one would wish to do every time
one lights a fire, so the Indians habitually carry fire around with
them—in the form of live coals, which can be quickly blown into
life when required. Should those coals go out or be lost, then the fire
sticks come into use.*

Stephen stopped in his reading and sat there grinning broadly to himself. Of course! That was it! The "odd collection" on the kitchen table. It must have been left there especially for him—to enable him to light the range. But the big question was—who could possibly have left it there?

He sat there, thinking for a while, with a very faraway look on his face. Then he continued reading the journal:

*The group of T Indians with whom we are living is made up
of 46 people, men and women of various ages and quite a
number of children too. B is a great favorite with the children.
They are intrigued by his monocle, which he uses to great effect.
And he plays such wonderful games with them, always full of
new ideas for some sort of occupation to keep them busy and
entertained.*

S and W's little brother, the youngest son of the leader of the
tribe, is a boy called Murra-yari. The name is pronounced as if it
were two words: Murra followed by Yari—at least that's how we
hear the name. The boy is a little imp of a child, perhaps some five
or six years old. Naked, brown, and very handsome, with large,
dark, shining eyes and an extremely impudent grin, he's the leader
of the little gang that always follows B around.

They have wonderful games of hide-and-seek. Murra-yari has
a favorite tree, some way away from our clearing—one of those
mighty forest giants with huge, wide, buttressed roots—ideal as a
hiding place. It took B quite some time to realize that this is his
special, secret place—the place where we can always find him,
though, of course, we have to pretend that we can't.

B and I are both very fit again now. Our collections are
increasing daily, with MY scaling tall trees to obtain some exciting
specimens for B, and the children, as a group, helping to tend the
garden where he is growing a wide variety of plants that he hopes
to take back to England with him—eventually. He has never
mentioned the Moonflower again.

"Poor old Bertie!" Stephen groaned. "He must have ended up feeling
dreadful about his obsessive 'wild plant chase'—and disappointed too."

We have discovered that the Indians are superb pharmacologists.
Their knowledge is an ancient and growing knowledge, handed
down from one generation to the next, probably over thousands of
years. B has become a close friend of S and W and MY's father. He
is our shaman and, as such, someone with special knowledge and
powers, in contact with the spirit world, much respected by our
people—someone to whom they can turn for guidance and support
in times of trouble.

It is not surprising that these two have become such firm
friends. They share a great interest in the medicinal properties of

plants. This has led to an amazing discovery—a very well-timed discovery too, as I shall explain.

We have been living here for well over a year. During that time, S and W and several other members of the tribe have had attacks of malaria. Such attacks were, apparently, completely unknown years ago, because of the remoteness of our group. But now they are becoming more common.

On the occasion of each attack, B has treated the victim with quinine. Each one has made a good recovery, at least for the time being. But we suddenly found, to our dismay, that we'd used up all our stock of quinine.

B and I were very disturbed when we first realized the gravity of the situation; he has already had one attack of malaria several months ago, and although I haven't succumbed as yet, there is a very good chance that I shall. We both felt very alarmed to think that, if and when an attack should come, whether it be our friends or ourselves, we should have no proper treatment for it. Then, quite unexpectedly, a few days later one of the children was suddenly taken ill with an extremely bad attack.

To cut a very long story short, thanks to B's friendship with the shaman, and thanks to the man's very special knowledge, it seems that we have discovered a completely new treatment for malaria. The plant extract, which is the basis for the treatment comes, like quinine, from the bark of a tree—a hitherto unknown species to us, but something the Indians have known about for a very long time. B has promised to write out a description of the preparation of the bark for me, so that I may include it here in my journal.

He swears that his new brew is more efficacious than quinine. He already has two saplings of the special tree growing in his garden collection. I have nicknamed it Plesiocinchona postlethwaitei—a total fabrication of my own, and I enjoy teasing B, assuring him that, in the future, both he and his tree will

doubtless be famous, that the tree itself will be known quite simply
as the Postlethwaite Tree.

As Stephen turned the next page of the journal, an old and discolored sheet of paper covered with handwriting floated out from between the pages, dropping onto the floor at his feet. He leaned forward to pick it up, trying not to disturb Tig, then sat back comfortably in the chair, intending to read it.

The heading, "B's Notes on Preparation," in Theodore's hand, was easy enough to decipher. But the rest of the notes, presumably in Bertie's hand, seemed impossible to read. After struggling unsuccessfully with the first couple of lines, Stephen gave up with a grunt, content to think that since he couldn't read the notes, it was fortunate that he wouldn't need them.

He settled back to continue the journal:

> *B's discovery may prove important, but I, for my part, am much more excited to have made my own most thrilling discovery! It is all due to Murra-yari, who recently rescued a small, wounded animal in the forest. Like many forest Indians, he seems to have a special way with animals. He is keeping this one now as a pet. It is hard to describe the creature itself, but I have made some careful drawings.*
>
> *At first glance, I suppose one could say that the creature looks rather like some giant caterpillar, the body appearing to be segmented, the rear end curved first up and then down in such a way that the animal looks similar in form to some of our large British hawk moth larvae. But there, the likeness ends, for the creature has soft, fine fur—fawn in color—large, round eyes and a wide, expressive mouth.*
>
> *The creature is capable of producing a long, silklike thread, from which, so MY tells us, it hangs and swings from the branches of trees. When he first brought it back to the house, it was only about six inches long; but it has already grown to around a foot in length, and we understand that they grow somewhat larger.*

"What an extraordinary creature!" Stephen mumbled. "Whatever could it be?" He read on quickly, completely intrigued:

> I have never seen anything remotely like it in my life before. Indeed, I am quite nonplussed, and uncertain as to how I should name it. It is most certainly a great discovery—a completely new type of animal, as yet unknown to the modern, scientific world.
>
> B, in his usual joking way, says it reminds him of one of my bugs, and since it has an unusual woomping, womping call, he insists on referring to the creature as a Bugwomp—a name which, alas, seems to have stuck. He has even had the cheek to suggest that it belongs to the family Bugwompidae—a total fabrication of his own, and not a very accurate one, since these creatures may well constitute a new order. Certainly, if I were to introduce them with this absurd name on our return to England, I should become the laughingstock of the entire scientific world.
>
> Murra-yari is devoted to the Bugwomp. It seems remarkably friendly and spends a good deal of its time with the child. When I looked in at him last night, as he slept in his hammock, I could see the creature sleeping comfortably, draped across his chest.
>
> We understand that there are places in the forest where more of these creatures can be found. From the description that we have been given, we are sure that there must be several different species. One of them, so it seems, is especially adapted to living in swamps and wet places; another sounds extremely impressive, being boldly striped in black and orange.

Stephen shot upright in his chair, jolting poor Tig into unwilling consciousness. "So that's what you are, my friend," he exclaimed, holding the sleepy creature out in front of him.

"A Bugwomp! A very handsome, tiger-marked, special Bugwomp, of course. But a Bugwomp all the same." He laughed out loud at the ludicrous name, and he laughed out loud at Tig as well, giving him a beaming smile.

"What a ridiculous name! Just trust old B to think up something like that."

Tig blinked at him sleepily and made a pathetic little noise. He didn't like having his sleep disturbed so rudely. He closed his eyes firmly and was very relieved when Stephen calmed down enough to return to his chair to continue reading. A Bugwomp—especially a sickly Bugwomp—needed peace and quiet and rest.

Stephen read on for another hour or so, feeling quite jubilant at his discovery—enjoying stories of the many interesting things that had happened during the long and happy time that Theodore and B had spent with their Taluma family.

But at the end of the notebook, he found a very worrying paragraph:

We have had visitors here today—two young men from another Indian group, lower down the river. They are trying to spread alarm, so it seems, by telling some extraordinary stories—stories of white men, who they claim are traveling around and catching young Indians, taking them away by force, to work as slaves in the rubber trade.

We took all this with a pinch of salt. It must be a great exaggeration. We can't believe that the government would allow such a terrible thing to happen. The people must have got it wrong. We don't believe that our friends are in danger, and besides, our group is so remote. We are sure that our people are quite safe here.

Tomorrow, S, W, B, and I are leaving for a trip into the forest—to improve and increase our collections. MY has begged us to take him with us, and if B had his way, we will probably take him. But, as I said to B today, the child is too young for such a long trip. He will be much safer here with his family.

I am going to leave my sketchbook with him. I know that he will take great care of it, and it will give him something to do—a special project while we're away—I will leave some pencils for him too. B has been teaching him to draw, so perhaps he will sketch the Bugwomp for me, and other interesting creatures as well.

We shall be away for several weeks. I'm looking forward to the trip and to the prospect of finding new species. But it is also going to be quite a wrenching experience—leaving our large family, to whom we have become so attached. Much as we shall enjoy the trip, it will be wonderful coming back home.

49. A Horrible Premonition

Stephen and Tig sat down together for a frugal lunch. Almost all the food had now run out. Stephen knew that he couldn't last much longer without making the dreaded trip to the village.

Even if he raided the vegetable garden as planned, and tried his hand at making bread with some of the curious flour in the larder, he would still need other basic things: eggs, bacon, and cans of meat. He didn't see how he could manage without those.

In the past, he had always rather fancied the idea of living entirely off the land; but when it came to having to do it, the idea wasn't quite so appealing. Had he been in a group of people, it might have all seemed good fun. On his own and surrounded by problems—ghastly gobblers and phantom panpipers—it wasn't an attractive option.

The long and the short of it was this: If he wanted to eat reasonable meals, he would have to go to the village within the next day or so, although he couldn't work out what he would do with Tig. He certainly didn't want to take him into the village shop, to expose him to Mrs. Pascoe's charms. He might get eaten by the snake!

In the meantime, Stephen had just enough food to manage comfortably for today. He opened his very last can, scowling and grunting angrily when he read the label—Brazilian Corned Beef. He certainly wouldn't buy that again. He felt reluctant to eat the stuff.

This was not because he was afraid of food poisoning—modern canning techniques were too good for him to worry about that—but because he knew that today's barons of the Amazon forest were beef barons—and not just Brazil, of course, but all the countries with Amazonian territory. Vast areas of wonderful forest were being cut down and burned off in order to run huge herds of cattle.

Tig's unpleasantly screwed-up expression registered his own personal disapproval of the meat. Since Stephen didn't fancy being showered with half-chewed corned beef, he didn't offer him any. He plied him instead with a few pieces of cucumber and the remains of the final apple.

The little animal was eating well now. Going into the village again to buy proper food was just as important for Tig as for him. The animal would need building up.

After lunch, they toured the grassy forecourt together. Stephen was amazed to see how much better and more active Tig appeared to be. He should, perhaps, have realized then that it wouldn't be long before Tig might be setting off—leaving Stephen on his own and going back to where he belonged. But the idea of Tig leaving him had never entered Stephen's mind. They were, after all, good companions.

When Tig had finished what he was doing, he didn't call out for Stephen as usual, but he set off toward the track that led up past the woodland. Stephen was so distracted by the story of his great-uncle's adventures, and so keen to get back to the notebooks, that this didn't strike him as unusual. He simply ran after Tig, and, scooping him up carefully, took him back inside the house, closing the front door behind him.

If Tig seemed rather restless back in the library, Stephen didn't notice. He was far too interested in reading the exciting account of the long trip that Theodore and B had taken—well away from the Taluma settlement, with their two "brothers," Sarko and Wamiru.

Eventually, Tig settled down and slept. Stephen read on and on, pausing occasionally for a break. Then, late in the afternoon, he went out into the kitchen and made a meal for Tig and himself from the last remaining scraps of food.

The weather had improved, and the early evening sun now shone in a clear, pale-blue sky; but apart from opening the front door to let in the warm fresh air, Stephen took no notice. With Tig on his lap, he was too engrossed in the final pages of the third notebook.

When he had first started reading the notebooks, he had realized that Theodore had been in the habit of writing in his journal at the end of each day. After he and B had come to live with the Indians, he had usually worked on his notebook as he lolled in his hammock, provided that he had enough light, or sometimes even crouched beside the fire.

Stephen was now reading the notes that Theodore had written in his journal whilst sitting by the campfire—on the last night of their trip, as he and B, Sarko, and Wamiru were making their way back home to their family. He could tell that the trip had been most successful; Theodore sounded so contented.

Stephen could sense, not only his great-uncle's delight at the prospect of returning home next day, but also the warmth of his feelings for the people there. He and B had been truly adopted. They loved their big Taluma family.

So, why was it? Stephen wondered. Why was it that, as he read the journal, he had a horrible premonition—a sense of some impending disaster? The travelers were nearly home. Surely, they would be quite safe now?

50. Tragedy

Everything had seemed to be going so well for the four friends. But as Stephen started reading Theodore's entry for the following day, suddenly there it was—disaster! The tone of the notes had completely changed. Stephen read on with increasing horror—increasing horror and dismay:

> *This day has been the most terrible day of our lives. I hardly know where to begin in describing the dreadful events that have come to pass. Indeed, I could not describe them in detail. I can only just bear to write down here the rough outline of what has happened.*
>
> *The four of us were traveling home through the forest this afternoon, returning happily to our people. We were laughing and joking—pleased to think of the wonderful greeting that we knew we would get from our family and friends, planning the party for the evening, rehearsing the stories we had to tell, and joking about the*

funny response that we knew we would get from our family.

Suddenly S and W stopped dead in front of us, hushing us to be quiet. We all stood still and listened carefully, riveted to the forest floor as the horrible sounds drifted toward us—the shouting and screaming and banging of guns. Then silence. Total silence.

We looked at each other in fear and dismay; then, dropping all our packs and our gear, and taking only our weapons with us, we dashed off through the forest. Long before we got to the clearing, we could smell the sickening smell of smoke. In desperation we raced through the trees—panting and gasping and tripping and skidding, till we all came at last to the edge of the clearing and saw before us the horrible scene. Our beautiful house was burning down. All around was death and destruction.

We all stood frozen to the spot. Frozen in horror and frozen in fear. Then all four of us rushed forward—to see if anyone could be saved.

B was hunting madly around in the burning and the wreckage, shouting out in a desperate voice: "Murra-yari! Murra-yari! Where are you? Murra-yari!"

But no answer came from the wreckage. There was no movement, no sign of life—only the crackling sound of burning, the hideous stench of the swirling smoke.

Suddenly B gave a shout and ran off unexpectedly—out of the clearing and into the forest. For a moment I thought that he'd gone berserk. But then I remembered and realized. Of course. The Tree! The special tree. The very special hiding place.

I was just about to rush off after him, when the three of us, left in the clearing, suddenly heard more terrible sounds—shouts and screams from down near the river. S and W snatched up their bows and, checking their arrows, they started off. I snatched up my bow as well. I would have followed. I could have helped. But they ordered me to remain in the clearing. They ordered me to go on searching. They begged me, please, to do what I could to help their

people. To my greatest regret, I did as they asked, and they
disappeared amongst the trees.

Stephen could feel his eyes filling up. He gritted his teeth and carried on:

As I approached the great, buttressed tree, I couldn't see any
sign of B. But I could hear the sound of his voice, which came from
around the back of the tree. Creeping around toward him there, I
found a most pathetic sight.

The child was huddled at the base of the tree, in a fork between
tall, winglike roots. His body shook with silent sobs. Tears were
streaming down his face—dripping onto the beloved Bugwomp,
which was cradled against his chest. Obviously, the creature was
wounded and in a very sorry state.

B was crouching in front of the child, talking very quietly to
him, trying to entice him out. But the child was much too
frightened to move. He remained exactly where he was, wedged
between the roots of the tree.

As I stood well back and watched this sad scene, I suddenly
noticed the strangest thing—Murra-yari was wearing clothes. A
pathetically large, long, ragged shirt enveloped and covered his
small, brown body.

Just at that moment, sounds of fresh gunfire came from the
direction of the river. The child flinched, staring up at us, with
enormous, terror-filled eyes.

I hardly know how to describe my feelings. My feelings of
absolute desperation, my frantic efforts to reach the river, as I
tripped and stumbled along the way. My feeling of total impotence.
My terrible anger. And my despair!

When I came at last to the riverbank, it was just as I'd feared it
would be—too late! I could hear the distant sound of an engine. I
could see the ripples from the wash of a boat. But I couldn't see the
boat at all. It had disappeared around a bend in the river.

Our people's canoes had been sunk or destroyed. There was nothing that I could do but shout. So I shouted and yelled. And I yelled and I shouted. But all, alas, to no avail.

The only things left on the riverbank were the bows that belonged to our Indian brothers—two, long, hunting bows, lying broken at my feet.

51. The Mighty Spirit

The tears ran freely down Stephen's face, dripping onto poor Tig's silky fur. The animal knew that something was wrong, but he couldn't understand what it was. So he nudged Stephen's hand with his furry head, then lay quivering on his lap, making a very sad, sniveling noise. Stephen hugged him close.

Great-Uncle Theodore's journal had been continued on the evening of the following day:

> We have retreated a little way away from the clearing into the forest, and have built ourselves a temporary shelter, exactly the way we were taught by our brothers. It is close to Murra-yari's tree—he seems to feel much safer there—yet close enough to hear movement in the clearing, if anybody should return.
>
> Yesterday evening was an absolute nightmare. At first Murra-yari clung to B. At first he seemed too stunned to talk.

We do not know how much he witnessed of the terrible scenes of destruction and killing that overran this once-peaceful place. But having retreated to hide by his tree, we think that he must have gone back at some point—not only to rescue the wounded Bugwomp, but also to search for my precious sketchbook, which has gone missing in the furor. The poor child is devastated, not just by the terrible events, but also because he has lost my book. He feels he has betrayed my trust, which, of course, is not the case.

"The sketchbook! Yes, of course, the sketchbook. So that was what happened to it!" Stephen gulped and sighed heavily, returning to the tragic text:

I, for my part, no longer care about the sketchbook. I only care for the loss of our people. I only care for this poor, wounded child— not, apparently, wounded in body, but certainly wounded in heart and soul.

Fortunately, over the past two years, B has learned a very great deal from our wise and knowledgeable Indian brothers about the special, medicinal properties of certain forest plants. Thus, he was able to treat the Bugwomp, applying a special poultice, which he says will heal the wounds. Treating the animal has helped the child, as I am sure B knew that it would.

All three of us made a quick trip back into the forest to collect our packs and our gear that we had dropped and left in our panic. By the time we were finally settled in our hammocks for the night, MY seemed much calmer. Thank goodness that we've worked so hard and can speak the Indians' language well now. Haltingly, very slowly, he told us the whole, sad, dreadful story.

Within a few days of our leaving home, some men had come and discovered our group, brought there by two young Indians—people who had been employed by the men to go out into the forest with them—to help them to find and then to control isolated Indian groups.

253

Our family had made the travelers welcome, and in no time at all
the men had established themselves in our settlement, cleverly
manipulating all of our people, teaching them about a mighty
spirit—far more important and far more powerful, so it was said,
than any of their own forest spirits. A spirit who commanded total
obedience.

Stephen stopped his reading. He sat quite still, thinking and wondering. Could these men have been missionaries? Could they be speaking of God or Jesus? If so, they must be potty. It sounded as if they were drunk with power:

The newcomers taught our people about sin and wickedness,
and they taught them about punishment too—all completely new
ideas to our Indian friends, whose own special beliefs and way of
life did not encompass such things.

Having brought with them a stock of clothing, they insisted that
our people cover themselves, telling them nakedness was wicked.
Murra-yari so fears the punishment of the Mighty Spirit that he
refuses to take off the filthy shirt. He is much too frightened now to
remove it. He was told he would burn in eternal fires if he sinned in
such a way.

B and I are both firm believers, but we cannot understand how
people can behave so badly—and all in the name of their faith. How
can people be so cruel? And all in the name of the God of Love! As
B said to me this morning—How could people imagine that Jesus,
being such a gentle person, would want them to frighten a child
like that?

But I'm afraid there's worse to come. To try to make them feel
ashamed, the visitors even told our people that it was all their fault
that the son of the Mighty Spirit died a horrible, painful death—
that they were to blame for his suffering—that the only way to
atone for their sins was to do exactly as they were told.

We can hardly bear the pain of it all. Do people anywhere in the world have the right to force their beliefs on others? Why can't people be more tolerant? Why can't all the different faiths live in decent harmony?

It was the newcomers' interference here that led, albeit unwittingly, to the total destruction of our home—the destruction of our family and friends. For it seems that just a few days ago one of them brought a visitor here—a friend who deals in rubber. It was this man who came back yesterday, along with some of his other "friends."

Murra-yari told us: "When my father saw there was danger, he called me over and whispered to me: 'Run away quickly, my son. Run into the forest and hide.' I did as he asked, for his face was grave. The other children did the same—their parents quietly sending them out.

"We all ran off and away to hide. But I had my special, secret place. I had my very special tree. As you know from all our games—the other children's hiding places were never as good as mine, were they? They were always easier to find than me . . . so much easier to find."

And the poor child's sobbing started anew.

Stephen sat in the chair appalled. He'd faced some problems himself in the past—but none of them as horrifying as this. The poor little boy! How would he manage?

This morning Murra-yari seemed quite calm, full of a kind of dignity, almost as if he realized that, as the only member of his family left alive here, it was up to him to shoulder the responsibility—the burden of doing what had to be done. A very brave little boy indeed!

The three of us worked together—burying the dead. Normally the Taluma would bury their dead under the floor of their

255

communal house. But since our house was completely destroyed, this was obviously not possible. So we have built a simple structure over the graves—a symbolic house, which will shelter them properly from the elements. The Indians sometimes do this themselves if someone dies away from home.

Murra-yari, young as he is, was able to remember the correct procedure for burying his people: gathering up, wherever possible, the long hunting bows that belonged to the men; then breaking the bows, as is the custom, and placing them in the graves with the men. For their hunting days are over now. He was also able to remember some of the appropriate songs and chants. B and I joined in with him as best we could.

As we have gone about our sad task, we have realized that all the young men and women and the older children are missing— torn away from their peaceful home. Dragged away to become slaves! We shall probably never know their fate. The people that we knew and loved. We can hardly bear the thought.

B and I were so naïve. We didn't believe the stories we had heard. Coming from our sheltered homes and our small well-ordered country, we couldn't believe the stories we had heard. We didn't see the danger in time. We shall never forgive ourselves for that.

It is very difficult now to know what is best to do. We are torn between dashing off to try to track down our friends—if we can salvage a canoe—and staying here, lest some return and need our help, and we must take care of Murra-yari.

As the child slept in his hammock this evening, with the BW at his side, B and I discussed the matter. Whatever happens, we cannot leave him alone in the forest, and we will not hand him over to anyone—unless we can find his family or perhaps another Taluma group, but we are not too hopeful of that.

B says that if we cannot leave MY safely with his own people, we must take him home with us to England. It is hard to know what is *best for the boy; but I feel inclined to agree with B. The very last thing that Sarko and Wamiru said to me was: "Please do what you can for our people." It was the only thing that they ever asked of me. I intend to honor my brothers' request.*

As Stephen turned the next page of the notebook, he found himself staring at an old, faded photo. The sun had set, and the light was failing in the library. He got up from his chair, and putting Tig gently down on the seat, he took the photo across to the window.

Tig watched him from his place on the chair. Then he made an anxious, chattering noise. He didn't like the sad atmosphere. He didn't want to be left on the chair. But Stephen was far too absorbed by the photo to take any notice of poor old Tig.

The little animal lay on the chair, gazing about him around the room, the large, green, melancholy eyes turning this way and that, till they stopped and focused on the open door. Slowly and quietly, Tig slithered down from the seat of the chair and made his way toward the door, his body moving silently across the Turkish rugs.

In the library doorway, he paused for a moment, with only a very quick look back. Then he crossed the hallway, went out through the front door, descended the steps . . . and was gone.

52. The Gathering Gloom

It was late in the evening. Stephen stood close to the big library window where the light was still quite good. He wiped his wet eyes and face on the sleeve of his shirt, pushed the hair back from his forehead, and peered closely at the old photograph.

It was a good-sized photo: 6½ inches by 4¼ inches—the old-fashioned half-plate size, seldom used by modern photographers. But despite its age, the quality of the picture was still very good, presumably because it had been stored inside the notebook, well away from light.

The photograph was of two young men, standing together, full length: the one, white skinned with a thick thatch of light-colored hair, wearing an open-necked shirt, breeches, and knee-length boots—the young English explorer; the other, dark-skinned, with flowing, black hair and strong, bare limbs—the forest Indian. Both faces smiled at Stephen in a cheeky, gleeful way—two very confident young men with a strong sense of friendship and liking for whomever it was who was taking the photo. As Stephen stared at the picture closely, he felt as if he, too, were included in some kind of happy joke.

He turned the picture over. "Theo Lansbury with his Taluma brother Wamiru" was written across the back.

As a special kind of brother to Theodore, Wamiru would have been a special kind of great-uncle to Stephen. The family that he'd always longed for seemed to be growing all the time. Yet each time he found another new member, that person was swiftly taken from him.

Stephen stared at the Indian's smiling eyes. He was overwhelmed by a sense of sadness, a sense of grief for poor old Theodore, who'd lost this good and valiant friend—a sense of grief for the world as a whole. To think that people could do such things!

He wondered about Sarko and Wamiru's fate. They probably wouldn't have lasted for long at the hands of those rubber barons. And what about all the other Indians? This obviously wasn't an isolated incident. Many must have lost their lives in the same kind of way.

Stephen took the photograph back across the room, and propped it carefully against the pile of notebooks, so that it stood beside the picture of Grandfather Stephen, the one in the silver frame. He considered the photos side by side. Three pairs of smiling eyes: two pairs sadly, long since closed, far away in foreign lands; one pair resting now in the woodland, not so far from where he stood.

Why did life have to be so complicated! Why did it have to be so sad! Why couldn't Man live in harmony, and enjoy this wonderful planet in peace? Why did he have to use and abuse? Stephen supposed that it all boiled down to greed.

Animals weren't as greedy as Man. Stephen could cope with animals better than people. He smiled a sorrowful smile to himself, as he turned toward the big armchair. Tig was a perfect example of this. Tig was a gentle friend and companion. He had grown to rely on Tig.

But the chair was empty. Tig had left. Stephen looked quickly around the room, and then he noticed the open door.

"Oh, no!" he cried. "Oh, Tig! Where are you?" He raced across the room and out into the hall.

"Tig! Tig! Please don't go!"

He'd completely forgotten his great-uncle's loss, being all too quickly engulfed by his own. A great chasm of loneliness seemed to open up before him. The animal was obviously well enough to return to its own kind. It didn't need Stephen anymore. It had left now, leaving him on his own. More tears threatened to spring to his eyes. He rubbed his face in an angry gesture.

Despite the lateness of the hour, it was still surprisingly light outside. Stephen stood poised at the top of the steps, looking anxiously around. Where was the audience now, he wondered? Where were all those watchful eyes? For the landscape seemed remarkably empty and he felt completely alone—completely, utterly, and miserably alone.

On either side of him, the old vines that grew against the wall of the house now bore quite a number of scarlet flowers; their strange perfume wafted on the still evening air, as Stephen stood in the dusky light, peering anxiously around him. Suddenly his body stiffened; his eye had caught some tiny movement on the track above the house.

Without any thought as to what he would do, he set out briskly across the forecourt, hurrying now toward the track. Yes. He was sure. It was definitely Tig. He could see the small striped body clearly, as the creature moved along the track, pausing every so often to rest.

But Stephen didn't call out to Tig, and he moved as quietly as he could. For he'd made a decision to follow the animal, to find out exactly where it went. Surely there couldn't be any harm in that?

By the time he came to the place on the track where the small pathway led off to his left, down into the woodland, Stephen had quite lost sight of Tig. There was no sign of him on the track ahead that led up to the moor, so he must have taken the path to the woods. Stephen turned and took the path.

It was very gloomy beneath the trees. He moved as stealthily as he could—ducking and weaving along the way to avoid the dangling arms of the honeysuckle, the grasping hands of the prickly brambles, the prying fingers of various vines.

The smell of the woodland was delicious in the cool, damp, evening air—the scent of flowers and crushed leaf mold. Stephen slipped silently, wraithlike, between the trees in the gathering gloom: ever aware that he must keep his distance and not alert the creature ahead; ever aware that he might well lose him if he let him get too far in front.

A weird noise echoed through the treetops, jolting Stephen to a stop. It was only an owl, thank goodness! But as he pressed on steadily, he couldn't help worrying about the animal moving along in the dusk ahead. Tig could fall prey to another large bird.

The path dropped down. The rushing sound of the river below grew ever louder in Stephen's ears. It filled his head. It surrounded him. It made him feel extremely nervous. He stared about him as he walked, looking back across his shoulder, peering in amongst the trees.

At the water's edge, he glanced downstream. A ghostly figure stood in the river. Stephen stopped and froze with fear, his arms rigid by his sides, his eyes wide and fixed on the figure.

Was it still? Or was it moving? Was it coming slowly toward him?

53. The Secret Valley

Frozen on the riverbank, Stephen couldn't move or think, and several startled moments passed before he remembered and recognized the primitive
statue that stood by the grotto. With a gasping grunt of relief, he relaxed his
rigid body, then stood shakily in the shadows, breathing very heavily. At
least he now knew where he was.

Stephen grinned nervously, looking back at the dark figure; then pushing his hair back yet again with a hot and sweating hand, he turned away
to hurry upstream, desperate not to lose his quarry. He couldn't see Tig
anywhere now; but when at last he came to a place where a fallen tree
spanned the water, he was just in time to catch sight of him—sliding off the
fallen trunk, disappearing amongst tall ferns on the opposite bank of the
river.

Crossing the river in the murky light was not as easy as it looked, for the
trunk was wet and coated with moss. Stephen slipped and slithered along,
clutching onto convenient branches, the water swirling loudly below, as it

rushed and gushed between large boulders—a very dangerous place if he fell.

On the other side of the river, the path ran on beneath the trees, up and away from the running water. Stephen followed as quickly as possible; he was afraid that he might have lost Tig. The noise of the river gradually died down. The silence of the woods enclosed him.

Finally, to his surprise, the pathway came to a dead end, and he found himself in a clearing bordered by dense undergrowth. A stream, trickling at his feet, ran past him to join the river. A high cliff rose up in front, partially shrouded by many creepers. There was no sign of Tig.

Stephen stood beside the stream, wondering what to do next. Then he noticed something odd: The stream of water appeared to be flowing out of the base of the wall of rock—emerging from behind the creepers. He walked along in the stream to investigate, with a mixture of pleasure and repugnance, as the water seeped through his canvas shoes, wetting his socks and his feet. But any discomfort was quickly forgotten; on pulling back the curtain of creepers, he found the entrance to a tunnel.

Ankle deep in the running water, and faced by the large, black hole in the rock, Stephen hesitated. There was, of course, no going back. He knew he had to enter the tunnel. He had to find out where it led.

But his feet seemed reluctant to move. It should have been an exciting adventure; but something made him uncomfortably hesitant. Was it some sense of impending discovery? A loss of confidence in himself? Did he have the right to intrude upon whatever it was that lay beyond? A number of thoughts rose up in his troubled mind—all good excuses for not going on. He stood uncertainly in the stream, squelching his toes up and down in his shoes.

At last Stephen made a move, leaning forward into the darkness, craning his neck and straining his eyes. It couldn't be such a very long tunnel; he could see the dim arch of light at the end.

"Oh, well! Here goes," he said, as he slid behind the curtain of greenery into the blackness of the tunnel.

The rocky roof was just above his head; he had to move slowly, stooping

263

cautiously. He didn't want to bang his head. If only he had brought his torch!

A dry ledge, a yard or so in width, ran along one side of the tunnel well above the water's surface; but he couldn't walk along the ledge because of the curve of the roof. So he stuck to the middle of the channel. The water rose up to his knees, dragging his jeans against his legs in a most unpleasant way.

About halfway along, he stopped and looked back nervously. Then he listened carefully. But there was little to be heard: only the gentle swilling of water; the occasional splash of drips from the roof; and the beat, beat, beat, of his own heart, unnaturally loud in the dark of the tunnel. He gritted his teeth and continued along, his eyes fixed on the pale arch of light.

When Stephen emerged at last from the dark to stand in the gentle evening twilight, he was met by a wall of soft, warm air—behind him the gaping mouth of the tunnel, before him a narrow, winding valley, the steep walls on either side enclosing a secret, enchanted world.

The waters of the stream, dammed up, had formed a small and shallow lake that stretched along the valley floor. On either side, lush vegetation, arching ferns, and hanging grasses clothed and draped the rocky walls. Stephen didn't stop to think, but set off boldly up the path that ran along one side of the valley.

At the end of the lake, the walls closed in. Sheer and dark, they towered above him, their rocky faces greenly coated with crunchy masses of fleshy growths that fed upon the seeping water. He hurried through the narrow cleft, till the valley widened out again. Big bats skimmed the valley floor. They were definitely Greater Horseshoe Bats. Stephen was thrilled to see them there; they seemed to be coming from the end of the valley.

As he scurried along on his way, he suddenly came to the edge of a pool—a pool that was just a few feet across. A pool of the strangest, bluest water—the clearest, deepest, most magical pool, which froze him spellbound on its brink.

Nothing ruffled the water's surface. It lay uncannily still and glassy. A very weird feeling came over Stephen, as he stood there gazing into the depths. Like the odd sensation of someone on high, who feels he must jump off into space, so Stephen felt that he must plunge in. He moved toward the rim of the pool, his eyes searching deep in the beautiful blue, as it drew him down and down and down . . .

A sudden cry brought him back to his senses—a peculiarly low and croaking call that cut the stillness of the valley. Prowk! Prowk! It came again, from somewhere high on the cliff, a sound that somehow lacked aggression, and yet was filled with unearthly warning.

Stephen stared up anxiously. He couldn't see what had made the call, but there must be something up there somewhere. Probably some kind of bird. Probably warning him away from its nest. Or perhaps it was warning him away from the pool. He shuddered visibly. Then, with a wary glance at the water, he turned his back and slipped away.

The last light of evening was fading from the summer sky, as Stephen moved on up the path. He paused to look back at the moon, oozing over the horizon—a strangely golden moon, three-quarters full, whose light began to flood the valley. It shone upon his pallid face. It illuminated his moving form. His thoughts and even his actions now had taken on a dreamlike quality.

Silently flitting with gathering speed, he fled along the winding path, as if propelled by some mystic force: past twisted trunks of moss-cloaked trees, whose long, slim arms reached up to the moon, whose long, slim arms were draped and hung with the palest skeins of wisping lichen; past waterfalls, whose pearly drops splashed against his face and neck; past sweeping ferns and writhing vines, all lit by the gentle, silken light—pale spirits of the secret valley, leading him ever on and on.

And as he went, there came to his ears the gentle, musical sound of pipes, the haunting, lilting music of panpipes, echoing through the moonlit valley.

He came to a halt at the end of the path. He stood there, breathless, looking up. A wall of rock rose up ahead, yet the music seemed to draw him on.

He could see the open mouth of a cave, and within the cave . . . a glow of light.

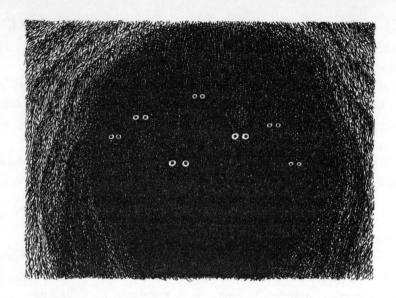

54. The Heart of the Mystery

A slope led up from the floor of the valley toward the open mouth of the cave. As Stephen stopped at the base of the slope, breathing very heavily, the music stopped abruptly too. Sweat ran glistening down his face. His shirt clung to his sticky body; but he was far too excited and far too absorbed even to notice any of that.

A stream of water ran down from the cave, the rock so thickly furred with moss that the water ran in a curious way: seeping deeply into the moss, yet falling and curving in sinuous lines across its dark and velvety surface—a strangely sensuous, swirling flow, in the light from the golden moon.

Stephen stared as if mesmerized. His eyes seemed rooted to the flow. At last, he forced his gaze away. Standing frozen like a statue in the moonlight on the slope, he lifted up his stressed, tense face, and fixed his eyes on the mouth of the cave, wide and yawning up above—straining his ears to catch any sound that would give him a clue as to what lay ahead. There was no sound except the water—and the pounding of his heart. A bat skimmed low above his head, emerging from the mouth of the cave.

His excitement was suddenly tinged with fear—a brief and fleeting, prickly fear. But despite his feelings of apprehension, in some inexplicable way, a positive feeling of warmth and kindness seemed to overcome the fear, seemed to draw him on again. And he certainly wasn't afraid of bats. Yet it needed every ounce of Stephen's courage to take the first few hesitant steps that would lead him toward whatever it was that awaited him in the cave above.

His hand crept up to the hair on his forehead. He took a number of slow, deep breaths. Then he started slowly forward—up the path at the side of the slope toward the lighted cave.

As Stephen struggled up the slope, he had no thought as to what he might find. He only knew that this was It. That he'd come at last to the heart of the mystery. That here he would find the answers he sought.

He could never have imagined the kind of scene that opened up before his eyes as he came to stand in the mouth of the cave. A lantern hung from the rocky roof. A small fire burned in the middle of the floor, and light from the flickering, orange flames was running and dancing on the walls, adding magic to the scene.

The stream that flowed outside the cave ran along inside the cave in a gully in the right-hand wall, and disporting themselves on a ledge at its side, were several of the most extraordinary creatures. Stephen couldn't see them clearly, but he had an impression of long, wrinkled bodies: some very tiny, but some quite large, maybe twenty inches in length, dark in color and silky in texture; small, cunning eyes that gleamed in the light; wrinkled faces and gaping mouths. Whatever they were, they didn't seem pleased to see him; for they made a revolting gobbling noise, and, sucking up water out of the stream, they spat at him.

On the floor of the cave, around the fire, were other very different beasts. Stephen's first impression was that they resembled gigantic maggots, with long, pale, segmented bodies. Bulgy, baggy, and softly furred, they swung their heads and chomped their jaws, hissing in an ominous way.

A wide bench ran along the left-hand side of the cave, and on the bench were various blankets and pillows. Amongst the blankets and draped on the pillows were a large number of tiger-marked creatures, all very much like Tig to look at, but varying greatly in age and size. Some were tiny—just a few inches long, whilst others were much bigger than Tig. On seeing Stephen, they rose into action—rearing up and huddling together, chattering in fear and anger, a chorus of great dismay and complaint.

This chorus was quickly taken up by something else at the rear of the cave. A Woomp! Woomp! Woomping! started up, adding greatly to the din. The only thing that Stephen could see, on peering into the inky depths, were several sets of gently swinging, disembodied, glowing eyes.

He stood in the entrance as if transfixed, his mouth drooping open in total amazement, his eyes staring wide in disbelief. At last the noise began to fade. Slowly, Stephen became aware of another presence in the cave. Beyond the fire, a little to one side, a hammock was slung from the roof of the cave. Lying in the hammock was a long, dark form.

55. The Cave

The dark form rose up in the hammock. "Please come in. You are welcome, Stephen. Far more welcome than these rude creatures would have you believe.

"Hush now! Hush now, all you fellows! Please be quiet and behave yourselves, and welcome our guest in a proper way."

The voice was not raised—it was quiet, but firm, and all the animals settled down.

Stephen shuffled nervously forward. A long, slim arm emerged from the hammock, indicating a seat for Stephen, a little way beyond the fire and a short distance from the hammock. The dark form settled back again.

"We heard the raven's warning call. We knew you must be on your way. But, even so, it's a shock for these beasts; for they've not been used to strangers, do you see. It will take them some time to get used to you, but I know they'll accept you in the end."

Stephen wasn't so sure of that. He looked very slowly around the cave, aware of the tension in the air, aware of all the watchful eyes. Then he looked at the man in the hammock.

The Indian must be very old—well over eighty, by Stephen's reckoning. Yet the face looked remarkably calm and unlined, the eyes amazingly youthful and bright. He was wearing a simple shirt and trousers. His brown skin shone in the light from the fire, and long black hair with a few spangled strands fell loosely about his shoulders. Stephen didn't like to stare; but there was something compelling about the face.

"You must be Murra-yari," he said.

The Indian smiled.

"I see you've been reading your great-uncle's journal. I'm very glad to think that you have, for it will help you to understand."

The voice, which was low and gentle, was a very English voice; not at all what Stephen had expected. He had to jolt himself to remember that, although this man was an Amazon Indian, he'd been brought up here at Lansbury Hall—brought up here by Great-Uncle Theodore, so that his speech and pronunciation were bound to be much like Theodore's—very well spoken and correct English, if a little old-fashioned.

Stephen noticed that, of all the animals that he could see in the cave, it was the maggoty beasts beside the fire who appeared to settle down first. They seemed to be far more interested in their food than in him, and after a short display of aggressive hissing, they soon returned to their munching and chomping.

"If you have read Theo's journal with care, I expect you will have realized that all these animals are various species of Bugwomp," Murra-yari said. "When your great-uncle brought me back to England, he also brought back with him quite a collection of these creatures." He noticed Stephen's gaze. "Those that you're looking at around the fire, are Maggotwomps. A Maggotwomp's greatest concern is his stomach." The Indian smiled broadly.

Stephen sat quietly, intrigued by the Maggotwomps, watching their odd behavior. One of them, very much larger than the rest, seemed to dominate all the others.

"In any group of Maggotwomps there's always one very large, dominant female." Murra-yari said. "Generally speaking, over the years, we have never given the Bugwomps individual, personal names; but your great-uncle always liked to refer to the senior female Maggotwomp as The Boss."

Stephen smiled as he watched the creatures. The Boss was a very large lady indeed, apparently a most superior animal. A number of smaller Maggotwomps—males, according to Murra-yari—gave her a wide berth and kowtowed to her. With a swing of her head and a loud hiss, she was able to drive the others away and then to take any food that she wanted. But, despite this very bossy behavior, they all seemed to be doing rather well for themselves, feeding greedily and noisily, taking no further notice of Stephen.

The wet beasts on the rocky ledge were quite another matter. Stephen noticed that Murra-yari kept a watchful eye on them. They lay around quietly for a time, gobbling gently to each other, apparently totally unconcerned. Then, surreptitiously, one by one, they started sucking up mouthfuls of water. When Stephen looked back a few moments later, they were all lying very still, staring at him in a peculiar way. But Murra-yari was used to their tricks. He turned and gave them a warning look.

"Come along now, all you Swampwomps! Will you please behave yourselves."

The firm voice had an immediate effect on the creatures. They turned away with soulful faces, then made a great show of swallowing the water; making a very odd gargling sound; presenting an apparently innocent front, as if that was all they'd intended to do. Stephen turned back to Murra-yari, grinning. He was just about to tell him of his unpleasant experience up on the moor, when he noticed something moving around inside Murra-yari's shirt. A small, striped head appeared, and two large, shining eyes. Tig.

"Oh, Tig!" cried Stephen. "I'd almost forgotten about you. I'm so glad to see that you're safe."

The little animal answered back.

"So that's what you've called him." The Indian smiled. "I was pleased to see him, too. I was very much afraid that we'd lost him for good this time." He tickled the animal's furry chin.

"He seems to have been rather badly wounded, but I can tell that you've taken good care of him. Poor little chap!" He smiled at Tig and stroked his head.

"He was orphaned as a baby, don't you know. I've had to bring him up myself. His mother was killed by a buzzard up on the moor. None of the other Tigerwomps will have anything to do with him."

"Tigerwomp! What a wonderful name! And what an extraordinary coincidence," said Stephen. "I only just managed to save him in time from exactly the same, sad fate." He told Murra-yari how he had rescued Tig.

"What a silly little creature you are," said Murra-yari. "The times that I've warned you not to stray. I have a special place in my heart for orphans, after what happened to me as a child. I have done my best to care for him; but he's at an awkward age, do you see, inclined to be rather too adventurous, without the wisdom or the experience to know how to cope with the dangers of life."

Murra-yari made a fuss over Tig, before continuing with his story:

"Some years before his death, I promised Theodore that, should anything happen to him, I would write and inform Bertie. So when he died, I wrote as promised. I realized that you would probably come. Recently, I started wandering down to the gate each morning, unlocking it, in case you should arrive that day, then locking it up again at night—we don't like to leave the gate unlocked.

"Since your arrival, all of the Bugwomps have been restless. They were rather nervous about you; not too pleased to have an intruder, yet at the same time quite intrigued, wanting to find out what you were. So, I'm afraid that they've been stalking you, watching your movements very closely, and causing trouble along the way."

Stephen laughed. He told Murra-yari about some of the ridiculous things that had happened. Looking back now, they seemed quite amusing, though they hadn't been funny at the time: his feeling of always being watched; the disappearance of his clothes; the nasty experience beside the stream; the shock he had got from the swinging eyes.

The thoughts of swinging eyes reminded him. When he had first arrived, he'd noticed several sets of eyes, glowing in the darkness at the rear of the cave, reflecting the light from the lantern and fire. But where were they now, he wondered?

He looked all around the cave in vain, till he noticed Murra-yari's eyes—watching something above his head. A group of long, pale forms, some very tiny, but some quite large, seemed to be hanging by silken threads from the rocky roof above his head. It gave him quite a start.

"You needn't worry about the Silkwomps," Murra-yari said. "They are the friendliest and the most gentle of all the different species of Bugwomp. They are not threatening you. They are only curious to see what you are, but they're much too shy to approach you directly; so they've grouped together and are hanging there quietly, observing you from a safe distance.

"Of course, I know that one shouldn't have favorites, but they are the most endearing creatures. You needn't fear any nasty tricks of the kind that those impudent Swampwomps play. I'm afraid they made a terrible mess one day in the scullery up at the house. I knew that you were out that day, so it seemed a good time to slip into the house—to make quite sure that all was well, and to see if you had enough firewood and food.

"Over the years, Theodore and I have been in the habit of allowing some of the better-behaved Bugwomps into the house; in fact, they were often there, but only under strict supervision. They're rather inclined to get carried away, and although they don't mean to do any damage, they can cause the most awful chaos.

"I suppose I must have left the back door open that day by mistake. Anyway, a whole troop of very irresponsible Tigerwomps slipped in without my noticing, and thoroughly enjoyed themselves, capering about in the dust in the dining room. And then, to make matters even worse, the Swampwomps got into the scullery, undoubtedly led by that big chap there."

Murra-yari nodded toward the largest of the Swampwomps. He lay well apart from the rest of the group, his beady eyes not quite closed. Stephen had the feeling that the animal knew they were talking about him.

"He is the oldest and the largest, and he is the dominant male," Murra-yari continued. "You would think that, by now, he'd have learned some sense. But I'm afraid he's up to all sorts of tricks, always leading the youngsters astray.

"When I caught them that day in the scullery, they had all been having a wonderful time. You would be surprised how strong they are and how clever at using their mouths. I hadn't realized before that they knew how to turn on the water tap. Though I suppose I should have guessed. For that big fellow over there has been in the sink once or twice before—when he has been in some kind of scrap and needed treatment for his wounds.

"By the time I'd discovered what they were up to, they'd all begun to itch and to wriggle. Whatever that green liquid was in the bottle, it must have irritated their skins. So I took them all out into the yard, and without a lot of ceremony, I washed them off at the water pump.

"They didn't think much of that, I can tell you," Murra-yari laughed at the memory. He turned and smiled across at the Swampwomps. Cunning, beady eyes looked back.

"I was just returning to the scullery, to clear up all the mess that they'd made, when I heard you enter at the front door. We all panicked and left in a hurry. It was a foolish way to behave. But the time didn't seem right for our meeting, and I have to admit that I felt afraid."

"Afraid?" asked Stephen. "Whatever for?"

"I was afraid of what your reaction would be—your reaction to me and to all this crew." Murra-yari waved an arm to indicate all the Bugwomps.

"Looking back now, I suppose it would have been much better if I'd remained in the house all along. I should have been there to welcome you when you arrived. But I didn't feel I could face you then.

"I discovered this special secret valley when I was a child. It was always a wonderful place of refuge if I'd overstepped the mark and found myself in trouble with Theo, or just a peaceful place to be when I wanted solitude. It seemed the obvious place to retreat to—when I knew that you would be coming here."

Murra-yari smiled at Stephen. But his eyes looked sad and filled with doubt.

"I felt just as nervous as the Bugwomps did about facing somebody new. Can you understand that? Lansbury Hall has been my home for a very, very long time. But now, of course, it belongs to you."

"Oh, no!" Stephen cried. "Don't talk like that. You probably have more right to it than I do. I didn't even know that I had any family. I certainly never, ever expected that I'd own a place like this."

He put out a hand toward Murra-yari.

"No! Please!" he begged, with a choke in his voice. "I hope you will live on happily here. I want us to share this wonderful place."

"I was an orphan too, as you know," Murra-yari added quietly. "Your Great-Uncle Theodore gave me a marvelous home here. He treated me just like a son, don't you know. So I found my family here with him—and with all these, dear, old creatures—they have been my family.

"But we are not used to strangers." He turned away, looking very upset.

56. The Three Orphans

Murra-yari and Stephen sat together in total silence. At length, Murra-yari said, rather carefully, "Why don't we share both the home and the family? What do you think of that idea?"

For Stephen, it was a huge relief. He'd been sitting there feeling so worried, not knowing how to find the right words. "It sounds like a great idea to me. I've always wanted a family."

Stephen was quite overcome. He beamed delightedly back at Murra-yari, then smiled around at all of the Bugwomps, wiping his eyes with the back of his hand. A murmur rose up in the cave. It was almost as if they understood.

During the conversation, Tig had emerged from his sanctuary. He lay now along the edge of the hammock, apparently reluctant to leave Murra-yari, yet seemingly glad to be close to Stephen.

Stephen was pleased and quite flattered to find that Tig took notice of him. He put out his hand and stroked the animal. Tig giggled back at him in a most satisfactory way.

The three orphans sat companionably together, feeling very contented in the midst of their special family.

After a while Murra-yari said, "How about something to eat and drink?"

It was a long time since Stephen had thought about eating and drinking, but now that he came to think about it, he realized how hungry and thirsty he was. He also felt quite tired and cold, and suddenly rather shivery too.

Murra-yari rose from the hammock, and, moving softly about the cave, he heated water over the fire then poured it carefully into a bowl together with some kind of mashed fruit. The resulting drink was delicious. Stephen sat happily beside the fire with a blanket across his shoulders, enjoying his drink and eating some unusual, flat cakes that Murra-yari offered him from a basket; they tasted as if they were freshly baked.

It was very peaceful now in the cave. All of the animals seemed quite calm. The Maggotwomps were curled up, sleeping around the hearth, their hunger finally satisfied. The Silkwomps hung over Stephen's head, perfectly still with all eyes closed. The Tigerwomps slept on the bench at the side. Even the Swampwomps seemed at peace, although every so often an eyelid moved, exposing the glint of a watchful eye.

Sleep came easily to Stephen later, as he lay on the bench at the side of the cave. Most of the Tigerwomps had moved over quite happily to give him space. Only one or two had seemed offended; but they all lay peacefully now around him. He could smell their pleasant, furry smell.

Murra-yari slept in his hammock with Tig tucked comfortably inside his shirt. The embers of the fire died down.

A large, pale form with a segmented body moved along the wall of the cave, just a few feet from Stephen's face. It was like some gigantic caterpillar.

But the animal didn't disturb him at all; it paused for a while, scaled the wall, and came to hang above his head. He found it difficult to focus on the gently swinging body. His eyelids closed and he felt himself drifting into a comfortable, happy sleep.

Tomorrow he could ask all the questions.

Tomorrow would be a wonderful day.

Part Two

57. A New Dawn

Bright sunlight, shining in through the mouth of the cave, woke Stephen up on the following morning. He lay half-conscious on the bench. Something seemed to be weighing him down.

A long, furry body was lying across his chest. He ran his hand tentatively along its length. The body didn't seem to mind. It let out a deep, contented sigh, and then lay completely still.

The memory of yesterday's amazing events came slowly flooding back to Stephen; but on looking around the cave, he found that the place was strangely deserted. No Silkwomps hung from the roof above. No Swampwomps lay in the stream on the ledge. No Maggotwamps munched around the hearth.

The only other occupant of the cave, apart from himself, seemed to be one huge Tigerwomp, draped and sleeping across his chest. But the fire was alight in the middle of the cave, and something was sizzling over the flames. A delicious aroma filled the air.

Stephen lay still for some time, uncertain as to what he should do with the Tigerwomp. The animal was quite a size. He smiled down and talked to it. It answered back in a deep, gruff voice, then it lay there staring at him. He felt quite relieved when Murra-yari finally appeared at the mouth of the cave, laughing at Stephen's predicament.

"All the other Bugwomps have gone off to hunt and feed," he said. "I'm not quite sure why that big fellow stayed behind; nor am I sure whether he's lying there to pin you down, in order to keep you under control, or whether he's simply warm and comfortable, and thus extremely reluctant to move. Tigerwomps do demand comfort, don't you know," he added with a laugh.

"Normally, he would be out with the troop, keeping an eye on all the others. But, perhaps, he felt it was more important to stay and keep an eye on you.

"If I were you," Murra-yari continued, "I would simply lift him gently to one side, then come and have some breakfast."

Stephen did as Murra-yari suggested. The Tigerwomp didn't seem to take offense; although Stephen noticed that, when he put it down on the bed, it rolled around amongst the blankets, and wriggled its skin in a rather odd way, as if its fur were out of place. Then with one, last, long look at Stephen, it slipped away out of the cave and disappeared down the valley.

Stephen sat with Murra-yari in the early morning sunshine at the entrance to the cave, eating a splendid breakfast of grilled trout, freshly baked flatbread, and a warm drink, similar to the one he'd had the night before.

They sat very happily together, looking down the secret valley, enjoying the warmth of the early sun: the old forest Indian seeming remarkably young, with his slow, sure movements and quick, shining eyes; the boy feeling very mature, experienced now, and much more secure.

58. Smugglers

Having tidied up the cave, and Murra-yari having gathered up his few bits and pieces, he and Stephen moved slowly back up to the house together. Murra-yari was pleased to be back in his old bedroom, and it was at his suggestion that Stephen established himself in what had been his Great-Uncle Theodore's room, just across the corridor. Apparently, during the last few months of his great-uncle's life, when Theodore could no longer manage the stairs, both he and Murra-yari had slept downstairs—hence the bed and the hammock in the library.

Stephen carried the photograph in the silver frame back upstairs again, together with the photo that he had found in his great-uncle's journal—the picture of Theodore with his Taluma brother Wamiru—Murra-yari's eldest brother. A special frame must be found for that; for the time being, it was propped against the silver frame on the small table beside his bed.

That evening, after supper, as they sat together in the library, it seemed a suitable moment for Stephen to ask Murra-yari some questions. He was dying to ask him what he knew about Stephen's own family; but he felt it was only polite to ask Murra-yari first about himself—how he had coped with coming to live at Lansbury Hall.

"There were, of course, so many things that I found very strange about life in England, when I first arrived here," Murra-yari said, in answer to Stephen's question.

"Towns, houses, and motorcars. And then the vegetation too—whole woodlands of naked trees, and peculiar plants as well. They all seemed very strange to me, all except the bracken, that is. The bracken was extremely important to me, for it is the only shared species, found in much of the Amazon forest as well as the grounds of Lansbury Hall. I used to go out into the woods, and wander about amongst the bracken. It helped me feel much more at home.

"Coming to live at Lansbury Hall was a very exciting time for me, but it was also a painful time—a very painful time for us all. Bertie had always looked after me, very much as a big brother would. When we arrived in England, he wanted to be the one to give me a proper home."

He smiled sadly.

"But, alas, that was not to be. His father had paid for the cost of his trip to the Amazon strictly on the understanding that when Bertie returned to England he would join the family firm."   .

Murra-yari sighed heavily.

"His father was exceedingly strict, don't you know. Once Bertie was back home in London, there was to be no more frivolity in his life. No more wearing of his monocle. No more fun and larking about. And, above all, it was very clear, there could be no possible place in his life for a small, brown, Amazon Indian boy—a boy who was an illegal immigrant.

"Even after all this time, I wonder at the way in which Theo and Bertie managed to hide us—bringing us all back to England in total secrecy. Bertie's large plant collection could be safely and openly stowed on board ship in special cases, called Wardian cases. But all of the Bugwomps and I had to be secretly smuggled on board in cabin trunks. We spent the whole trip in our suite of cabins, very carefully hidden from view. Just the fact of having to feed us, having to keep us clean and tidy, then keeping the Swampwomps wet, to boot—and trying to stop their noisy gobbling, must have posed enormous problems.

"It must all have been a tremendous struggle for Bertie and Theo. For me it was a great adventure, though I do remember some alarming moments when we were very nearly caught. But I also remember a lot of laughter at one or another of Bertie's tricks—or at some clever piece of subterfuge."

Murra-yari laughed at the memory. Stephen urged him on again.

"You have to remember that Bertie and Theo were driven by great determination—and by great anxiety too. Theo, on one hand, was very much afraid that, if his newly discovered creatures were exposed too early to the public gaze, he would find that he'd lose control of them, that he wouldn't be able to continue his studies in peace, and that the animals would suffer.

"Bertie, on the other hand, was equally worried and very anxious—but all on my account, so it seems. For he feared that if the authorities found me, they would put me into an orphanage, or even worse, send me back. Neither he nor Theo was prepared to allow that to happen. They had taken responsibility for me. Both were certainly honorable men—despite all their larking and fooling about.

"I can only suppose that, at the time, smuggling an Amazon Indian child into England along with all the Bugwomps, had not only seemed an essential act, but also something of a jape—an irresistible challenge, I suspect—both for Theo and for Bertie.

"Probably neither of them had intended to keep the secret for the rest of their lives. Neither had looked very far ahead. But they soon began to realize the enormity of what they'd done. With Bertie becoming a lawyer, any kind of illicit adventure would surely have destroyed his career, and brought shame on the family firm.

"So I was quickly brought down here, together with all the Bugwomps and some of Bertie's plants and trees—and here we remained."

Murra-yari sat gazing into the distance—remembering.

"It was to be a very sad homecoming for your great-uncle. He had already learned of the loss of his parents from letters sent out to Manaus, which we had visited on our way back downriver. The news had distressed him so much.

"He had also learned of the start of the war. But—to arrive back home and find nobody here—only a letter from Stephen, his beloved twin brother, telling him that he had joined the army the previous August, and had already left England for the battlefront . . . Well! That was quite a shock for Theo. Then, to make it all much worse, Theo later found out that he'd only just missed Stephen.

"We had traveled back to England on the very same ship that Theo and Bertie had traveled out on—the SS *Lanfranc*. She docked in Liverpool on May 7, 1915. But with all the complications—the plants, the Bugwomps, and me—there were quite a few delays. Eventually, when it was too late, Theodore discovered that Stephen had embarked for Boulogne on May 15—never to be seen again."

Murra-yari sat grim faced, remembering the times that followed.

"I don't think Theo ever forgave himself. He felt so guilty and so ashamed—to think he'd been off enjoying himself, whilst Stephen had stayed and done his duty; he hadn't even wanted a commission. He only wanted to fight for his country.

"Poor Theo. It must have been very hard on him. He felt a great weight of responsibility—for me and for all the Bugwomps too. But for that, I have no doubt, he too would have gone to die in the war.

"And then there was another tragedy—although not quite so close to home. Bertie and Theo had become quite good friends with the master of the SS *Lanfranc*. But when the war came, the ship was requisitioned as a hospital ship for soldiers. She was torpedoed in 1917. We never heard what happened to the master and his crew," Murra-yari added sadly.

"But to come back to the story of your father."

Stephen wriggled in his seat.

"None of us, at the time," he continued, "had any idea that, shortly before he embarked for Boulogne, Stephen had fathered a child. It took a long time to unearth all the facts. The story that I can tell you now was only gradually revealed over a period of many years."

Stephen sat rigid in his chair. Now he would finally hear the truth. Now, at last, he would finally know.

59. Drusilla

Murra-yari continued his story. "Theodore and Stephen had studied together at Oxford, along with Bertie. They had many friends in common, amongst them Drusilla Higginbotham—a young and extremely pretty girl who was, so it seems, very smitten with Bertie. He cut an extremely dashing figure, in those days, don't you know."

Stephen remembered the reference to the "ravishing Drusilla" in his great-uncle's journal. He grinned broadly at Murra-yari. "Please go on," he begged.

"It seems that, after Bertie and Theo had left on their trip to the Amazon, and in the two years after his parents' death, Stephen became much better acquainted with Drusilla. In time they fell in love. There was, apparently, considerable opposition to the match from Drusilla's parents—pretentious people, it would seem, with very much higher hopes for their daughter than the younger son of a Cornish landowner. Younger, so I understand, by ten minutes.

"However, despite the opposition, Stephen and Drusilla planned to marry in secret, assuming that once the knot had been tied, her parents would have to accept the situation. But with the outbreak of the Great War, Stephen, goaded on by his friends, decided to enlist immediately. The young couple spent their last few hours together, the night before he left for Boulogne. Then, devastated at losing Stephen, Drusilla waved good-bye to him at the station."

Murra-yari shook his head sadly.

"All these facts, you understand, were gleaned much later on," he said. "From a close friend of Drusilla's—a young lady called Cicely."

Stephen nodded to urge him on.

"Some weeks after Stephen had left, Drusilla's parents were shocked to learn that she was expecting Stephen's child. She was shipped off very quickly and quietly, in disgrace to America, where she stayed with a distant cousin until after the baby was born.

"Poor Drusilla! I fear that it must have broken her heart. Despite all her sobbing and and all her pleading, the baby was taken away from her and handed over for adoption-to a wealthy industrialist and his wife—a child-less couple called Markovitz, who lived in the city of New York. They named the baby David.

"One can only suppose that, at the time, it seemed a safe and suitable home for the baby. Perhaps the Higginbothams didn't care, or perhaps with their very superior ways, they had planned to bring Drusilla back—planned to find a suitable match for her, pretending, I can only suppose, that nothing had happened. We cannot know. But what we do know is that with the Great Depression in America, the Markovitz family fell on hard times, both parents finally dying in poverty. It seems that, as the mother lay dying, she told her young son about his adoption, and she must have given him certain details about his family background.

"The young man, David, had an extremely difficult life. It was only after many years of hard work and endeavor that he finally found success in business. He married rather late in life—married a very young wife, we believe, who produced a fine baby boy."

Murra-yari paused and smiled at Stephen.

"I can see that you have guessed what I am going to tell you now. Yes. They named the baby Stephen."

Stephen sighed a giant sigh, and he said in a very quiet, hoarse voice, "Please go on, Murra-yari."

"When you were a year old, your father and mother brought you with them on a trip to England. It seems that whilst they were over here, they adopted the name of Lansbury. We shall never know exactly how it came about; but after what his mother had told him about the adoption, it could be that your father had been toying with the idea of changing his name for quite some time.

"David probably felt, understandably, that he had a right to the name of Lansbury, and it may well be that here in England it suddenly seemed more fitting and comfortable. Whatever the truth of the matter may be, it is certain that whilst they were here in England, they introduced themselves to people using the name of Lansbury—though no official change was made.

"During their visit to London, your mother left you overnight with a childminder, telling the woman that your name was Stephen. It seems that she explained at the time that you were poorly with teething troubles. She and her husband were off on a trip because they had family business to see to. She wanted you kept warm and quiet. She would come back for you two days later.

"That was the last that anyone ever saw of either of your parents."

60. So Near and Yet So Far

Stephen sat frowning at Murra-yari. "But what on earth had happened to my parents? Why didn't they come back for me? I'd always assumed that I'd been abandoned because they simply didn't want me. But the people that you've described to me now don't fit that sort of picture at all."

Murra-yari smiled kindly at Stephen.

"It took us a very long time to work it out, and I don't think it can ever be proved, but I believe we know what happened to your parents.

"Around the time that you were left in London, a very serious accident took place between two motorcars on a major roadway not far from here. Four people died in one of the cars—a man and his wife, whose identity could be traced through the ownership of the car, and two other people—two passengers, a man and woman who were never identified. A fierce fire had ensued at the time, destroying all hopes of identification.

"Bertie finally became convinced that the two passengers in the car were your parents, although, of course, we could never be sure. He believed that they'd traced the family home and were coming here to pay us a visit, brought, perhaps, by some kindly acquaintances."

Stephen gasped.

"What a dreadful thing to happen," he said. "So near and yet so far!" He relapsed into a thoughtful silence.

After a time Murra-yari continued.

"Back in London, there was nothing to link you in any way with the two people who'd died in the accident here. The woman with whom you had been left really knew nothing about you, except for the fact that your name was Stephen, and that your mother who'd left you there, had said that her name was Lansbury. The only other clue was that the childminder did say that the woman had a 'funny accent.' But I understand that Americans do speak in a rather strange way," Murra-yari added wisely.

"And so you were placed in a children's home, not even free for adoption, it seems, since no one could find out who you were. Perhaps at the time, no one tried very hard. Perhaps there were many abandoned babies."

Stephen and Murra-yari sat quietly together, thinking it over.

"How on earth did you piece together such an amazing story?" Stephen finally asked.

"Ah! Well! That was all due to good old Bertie," Murra-yari replied. "Though it took years of persistent inquiry.

"When he first got back to London, Bertie did all that he possibly could to find out what had become of Drusilla. He had been so fond of her, do you see, and Cicely was very distressed because Drusilla had disappeared.

"After the news of Stephen's death, I am sure that Bertie made an even greater effort to trace Drusilla's whereabouts, for there'd been a vague rumor about a baby. But Bertie was working for his father. He wasn't free to do as he wished—to carry out proper investigations. Cicely married some bright, young spark. I believe he became a diplomat and they went to live in India. And so the matter was dropped for years.

"Theodore pushed any thoughts of the possibility of Stephen's child right to the very back of his mind. We lived our lives peacefully here. The Bugwomps were our chief concern, with Theo devoting most of his spare time

291

to making a detailed study of the different species and their behavior patterns.

"But as time went by, he became increasingly anxious about the future welfare of this place—and of the Bugwomps and of me. He became more and more determined to find out if there had been a child, and, if so, to trace that child no matter what. So he asked Bertie to do all he could, to make the fullest investigation, regardless of cost.

"For a long time, there were no results; but then, at last, Bertie had an amazing piece of luck. He was walking down some famous street in London—called Piccadilly, I believe—when, quite unexpectedly, he bumped into Cicely. She and her husband, now retired, had returned to live in England. Over lunch and later tea, in the Hyde Park Hotel, so we gathered—they talked about old times together. It was then that Bertie learned about the letter—the letter about Drusilla's death.

"It seems that after the birth of your father, poor Drusilla had been pressed into marriage with a very rich, but elderly landowner, from one of the southern states of America. Powerless to contact her friends in England, not knowing the whereabouts of her child, and unaware of Stephen's fate, her health had rapidly declined. She'd struggled on as best she could, remaining loyal to her husband, but she died at a very young age, following some nasty fever.

"Drusilla had had a devoted maid. Following the death of her mistress, and carrying out her last request, she had managed to send a letter to Cicely. It was little more than a scrappy note, without even a proper address. The maid's writing was very basic, and some of the spelling inaccurate, but Cicely did receive the letter.

"Apart from grieving for her friend, she had taken no further action. But she'd kept the letter all those years. It gave good, old Bertie the clue that he needed. By hiring detectives to follow it up, the whole, long story gradually unfolded."

Murra-yari beamed at Stephen.

"By the time we had finally discovered your whereabouts, you were nearly eight years old—about the same age as I had been when Theo and Bertie had rescued me."

"But why didn't Theodore contact me?" Stephen asked in a voice of despair.

"I am sure that, at first, he intended to do so. But he never quite got around to it, do you see. He was so excited at finding you, yet quite unable, I think, at his age, to face up to the responsibilities of having a child in his life again. I expect he remembered, only too well, all the problems of looking after a very adventurous eight-year-old boy."

Murra-yari grinned at the thought, remembering some of his childhood tricks—the very naughty tricks that he'd played on a kindly but unsuspecting Theodore.

"He cared about you, I'm sure of that, and he took great comfort in knowing you were there. He commissioned Bertie to keep a secret eye on you; not to make any contact with you, but to make sure that you were alright.

"Then when you were older, and he learned through Bertie's investigations how much you cared about animals, he decided to make his will in your favor. He knew he was taking a very great risk. But you were his only hope for the future—the future of Lansbury Hall that is, and the future of the Bugwomps too.

"Bertie came down to stay for a few days. We all had a rare old time together. But we had some serious talks as well. It was agreed that, should Theo die before me, I would write to inform Bertie, then he would act accordingly. And, as you see, it has all come about—exactly according to our plans. Theodore would be delighted."

The day after this suprising conversation with Murra-yari, Stephen made a pilgrimage cross country to the place on Highway A38 where the motoring accident was supposed to have happened—to the place where his parents must have died. He stood at the edge of the busy road, wondering what he ought to feel. Some sense of the past and its tragic event? Or the spirits of those who had died in that place? But, try as he might, he couldn't feel anything. There were only the fumes and the noise of the traffic.

He hurried back home, feeling quite depressed.

61. Family Life

Over the days and weeks that followed, Murra-yari and Stephen established a simple daily routine, and they soon became firm friends. They worked together. They talked together. And they laughed together—a lot.

The Bugwomps came and went about the place quite freely if the door was open, although only when there was somebody there to keep an eye on them. Generally speaking, they seemed quite content out and about, around the estate—doing what came naturally to Bugwomps, without any human intervention.

With two, doting foster parents, Tig was in his element. What he didn't get on demand from one, he could always hope to get from the other—plenty of attention and lots of tasty tidbits to eat. From time to time, he disappeared, into the woods and fields; but it was never very long before he returned, demanding more.

He still liked the sanctuary of a shirtfront, although, it was obvious to Stephen that he much preferred Murra-yari's shirtfront. Stephen supposed that was only natural. He fought down any feelings of jealousy that might have risen up within him.

It soon became apparent that Murra-yari was much better at getting up in the morning and getting breakfast organized than Stephen was. In fact, he was very much better at doing all the simple, practical things that had to be done, despite his great age. Stephen made a point of taking over the heavy jobs. He chopped and carried wood, for example; he did the cleaning and clearing up, learning how to run Lansbury Hall as he went along. For the place needed very careful management—if they were to be self-sufficient and to live in reasonable comfort.

Murra-yari was a quiet, kind, but very firm teacher. Stephen quickly developed a great respect for him. He made a beautiful set of panpipes for Stephen, and then he taught him how to play them.

He taught him other new skills as well: how to make fire with the two fire sticks; how to grind the corn and maize; how to make and how to bake the delicious flatbread that Stephen enjoyed; and, perhaps most important of all, how to hunt for the meat that they needed.

He made a splendid bow for Stephen, and a beautiful set of arrows. With practice, as the weeks went by, Stephen became quite a skillful hunter. But he only killed what they needed for food, and he knew that no matter how much he practiced, he would never, ever learn to move as smoothly and silently as Murra-yari.

On some days, when the weather was bad and Stephen decided to stay indoors, he spent his time exploring the house: probing about in the attics and bedrooms; opening cupboards and looking in drawers. One of the things that intrigued him most was the wonderful clothing in some of the wardrobes.

Over the years, Theodore and Murra-yari had helped themselves to whatever they needed from the stock of clothing in the house. Theirs had been a simple life. It hadn't mattered how they'd looked; if some of the clothing was too large, they'd held it up or together with string. Their only consideration had been keeping comfortably warm and clean.

Between them, they had used up most of Theodore's clothing, and the only item that Stephen found in the wardrobe in his great-uncle's room was an old and battered panama hat, very worn and badly stained, a relic of the Amazon trip. He lifted it down from the top of the wardrobe, handling it with care and respect.

What a priceless thing to find! He placed it reverently on his head, turning to survey his reflection in the mirror inside the wardrobe door. He presented, so he fondly imagined, a rather dashing sight, gazing sternly back at himself, posing with a grave countenance.

As Stephen turned his head to one side to admire the apparently handsome profile, he suddenly remembered about his spots. He'd quite forgotten all about them, though he'd gone on, out of habit, applying Morwenna's Secret Recipe. Stooping close to the mirror to admire his amazingly almost spot-free face, his appearance suddenly struck him as comical, and he collapsed in helpless laughter.

He ended up feeling quite ashamed of making fun of Theodore's headgear. Magnificent, long-lived, and undoubtedly loyal, it surely warranted his respect. He replaced it with due ceremony, on the shelf in the top of the wardrobe, closing the door gently upon it with a suitably serious expression, though having to bite his lip to do so.

When Grandfather Stephen had gone to fight in the Great War, he must have left most of his things behind. A large collection of his clothing still hung in a wardrobe in the bedroom next to Theodore's, exactly as he'd left it all those years ago.

A musty smell greeted Stephen's nose when he opened the wardrobe door. Yet the clothes were all in such good order. At first he didn't like to disturb them. Clothing was so personal.

He ran his hand slowly along the brass rail, parting the hangers one by one, admiring each of the garments in turn. Murra-yari had come in to look, and had told him the proper names for the garments. There was a dark-gray morning coat, together with elegant, narrow, striped trousers; and a rather long, double-breasted jacket called a reefer, made of fine herringbone tweed, with matching trousers, very wide at the thighs and knees, but quite narrow at the turn-ups—a strange fashion, Stephen thought.

There were Norfolk jackets in heavy tweed with matching knickerbock-ers; riding breeches with flaring wings; and the garment that Stephen cov-eted most—a navy-blue, velvet smoking jacket with elegant, quilted lapels and cuffs. He ran his hand down the silk-smooth sleeve.

Some fascinating clothing hung in the wardrobe in the main bedroom—the room Stephen now called the Lily Room. The musty air inside the wardrobe was perfumed still with the faintest trace of lavender; he noticed the little muslin bags that hung from the rail in between the hangers. The clothing in this wardrobe must have belonged to his great-grandmother—Christina.

She was bound to have taken her best things with her on her voyage across the Atlantic; but, even so, there was plenty left. He slid the hangers along the rail, inspecting each of the garments in turn. Some were sadly stained and spoiled, but others amazingly bright and fresh.

There were long, trailing, chiffon skirts with delicate pleating around the hems; a lacy tea gown in rose pink; soft, satin blouses with high, boned collars in creamy oyster and pale apricot; a wonderful black-and-white-striped petticoat, the surface looking like watered silk, stiffened, and trimmed with black velvet ribbon. There was very practical clothing too—country tweeds with long, thick skirts, and a riding habit of black felted wool, the voluminous skirt looking heavy and clumsy. It can't have been comfortable riding in that!

Stephen stared at a long, blue gown—a swirl of silk that was trimmed with lace. Somehow, it seemed familiar to him. Then he remembered the group in the painting.

He felt quite certain that this was the dress. Christina had kept it all those years, like some old and trusted friend. He smoothed the pale-blue, lustered silk, amazingly soft beneath his hand. He sighed as he closed the wardrobe door.

Across the corridor from the Lily Room there was a simple, plain room with a small bed and a very large wardrobe. This had apparently been designed as a gentleman's dressing room. It had been used by his Great-Grandfather Philip.

In the wardrobe, Stephen found a wonderful collection of clothing: smart frock coats and narrow trousers; evening dress—tails and all; shoes, spats, and some fabulous hats, amongst them a simply brilliant topper. He lifted it carefully down from the shelf, and polished it tenderly on his sleeve. It fitted him well.

Some of the garments were in a poor state, having been ravaged by moths and mold; but others were still amazingly sound. Considerably emboldened by now, Stephen became quite carried away, and he had a truly splendid time trying on various suits and hats, standing in front of the ancient mirror, smiling back at himself and posing.

Later, to Murra-yari's amusement, when it was finally suppertime, Stephen appeared at the top of the stairs most elegantly "dressed for dinner." He descended with an air of panache, and drifted along the hall to the kitchen—wearing the coveted smoking jacket.

62. Long, Sunny, Summer Days

The long, sunny, summer days often found Stephen and Murra-yari lazing on the grassy bank beside the river. It was such a peaceful place, and a perfect place for a picnic.

Tall stands of Indian Balsam lined the riverbank, its delicate, pale, mauve flowers somewhat orchidlike in form. Stephen looked it up in his book of botany. Originally brought from the Himalayas, it was quite common now in some parts of Britain. Nevertheless, it still seemed exotic, and it appeared to be taking over.

Whilst Stephen basked in the sunshine on the grassy bank, Murra-yari dozed in the shade beside the river, lulled by the gentle song of the water. Watching him, Stephen marveled at the way that he blended in with his surroundings: his slim, dark shape relaxed against the green, mossed trunk of a tree; his long hair hanging entwined with the ivy. It was not just his physical appearance or the way in which he moved, nor his gentle but practical approach to the natural world, nor even his firm but kindly manner with the animals that impressed Stephen so much. There was something very special about him that went far deeper than that.

The forest Indian's calm acceptance of the world around him, his ability to get on with things and manage whatever had to be done, his apparent lack of need for possessions or for power over those around him—these were things that Stephen had never seen before, all combined in any one person. If only people generally were more like Murra-yari, he mused, Man could live in harmony—not only with the natural world, but also with his fellow Man.

But Stephen realized, of course, that this could never, ever be. There were too many greedy people out there, people who did seek possessions and power. The very fact that Murra-yari and his people were not like that meant that they and others like them were often the ones to be used and abused.

On the many peaceful summer afternoons that the two friends spent together, Stephen thought deeply about such matters, whilst Murra-yari dozed in the shade.

If the Bugwomps got wind of their presence, the peace and quiet was generally shattered, for they loved to be part of a gathering. The Silkwomps swung and sang from the trees beside the river. The Tigerwomps made themselves comfortable as usual, making the most of the blanket that was laid on the grass and of any discarded clothing or pillows, always somehow, much to Stephen's amusement, finding a cozy place to be.

The Maggotwomps chomped their jaws hopefully around the perimeter of the group, and the Swampwomps cruised around in the river, or wriggled about in the mud at its edge. Stephen noticed that they didn't seem to like remaining clean for very long. Having emerged from the river with sparkling coats, they would often go and wallow in the nearest patch of oozing mud. They certainly were obstreperous beasts, but he couldn't help liking them, despite their awful misdeeds.

One day, Tig was playing too close to the water's edge. Stephen had called to him several times, but he took no notice at all; nobody was very surprised when he fell in with a splash. Almost immediately, one of the

Swampwomps rose to the surface at his side and, grabbing him in its mouth, swam off quickly downriver, gurgling with glee.

Stephen sprang swiftly into the river, splashing wildly around, almost up to his waist in water, desperately trying to rescue Tig, whilst Murra-yari sat on the bank, laughing heartily at the spectacle.

"Silly little creature," he said, as he rubbed Tig briskly down with a towel.

"It's a good thing your Uncle Stephen was there, or you might have come to a sticky end," he added, trying not to laugh too much at the gasping, soggy mass of fur and the large, pathetic, round, green eyes.

The weeks passed quickly. They were wonderfully happy and joyful times. In the early days, Stephen never stopped to wonder if it might all be too good to last. Such negative thoughts never entered his mind.

The whole of the Lansbury Hall estate seemed to be full of life and color. Butterflies flitted along the tracks. Dragonflies hovered over the lake. A kingfisher darted along the river. Swallows swept through the blue, high above, or swooped and skimmed the flower-filled meadows.

Rows of foxgloves lined the paths: stately spikes of tier upon tier of long, pink-purple, curvaceous flowers with their weirdly spotted, out-turned lips. They were a constant source of delight to Stephen, who loved to watch the bees creep in—alighting, at first, on the hairy, curving lower lip, then climbing up inside the flower, bizzing and buzzing and zizzing with pleasure. He sat and watched them in the sun, playing his panpipes on the bank, or picking and eating the tiny, wild strawberries.

Sometimes, Stephen and Murra-yari strolled along to the woodland glade together to visit Theodore's grave. Stephen was surprised to discover that one or other of the adult Bugwomps was always lying at the foot of the grave.

"All the Bugwomps were so devoted to Theodore, do you see," Murra-yari explained. "When he died they grieved for him. Since that day, one or another of them has kept a vigil at the grave. Just to keep him company. Only the adults do it, of course. It's not something that they would allow the frivolous youngsters to do." He smiled.

"As you can see, there is a completely bare patch of earth at the foot of the grave—a patch worn smooth by the constant presence of one of the Bugwomps lying there."

After Murra-yari had checked the roof of the "house," they would sit together talking, in the shade of the mighty beech.

"Your Great-Uncle Theodore was a splendid person, don't you know," Murra-yari told Stephen one day, as they sat together, resting, with their backs against the trunk.

"He and Bertie were only twenty-one years old when they set out on their travels. From all that he told me, and we spoke of it often, I know that the lengthy period of time that he and Bertie had spent with my people— more than two years in all—had made a great impression on them. It had changed the way that they looked at life.

"They had both been brought up as Christians, and I know that your great-uncle kept his faith till the end of his days." He smiled at the grave with its cross and its house.

"But he always encouraged me to keep my own faith and my own beliefs. Theo always used to say that, regardless of race and regardless of creed, it was the goodness within the person that mattered—the goodness that the person shared." He sighed deeply and very sadly.

"I feel his spirit around us here, now. It is a good and kindly spirit."

Often on these occasions, Stephen would go and leave Murra-yari resting peacefully beneath the tree, communing with the spirits. He would speed off along the path that led to the beach. It was such a wonderful place to be. A sense of freedom filled his soul as he ran about on the smooth, yellow strand, and splashed happily in the waves.

Returning later, brown and salty, he would meet Murra-yari in the glade, and they would stroll back to the house together. On those occasions, Tig would make a great fuss over Stephen, and after supper he would sit on his lap, surreptitiously licking his salty arms.

63. A Near Disaster

The days were speeding by happily. But a darkly brooding and worrying shadow seemed to be hovering over Stephen, very often disturbing his nights. A question kept coming back to him: How was he going to keep Lansbury Hall running?

Over the years, the Lansbury finances had been managed by Bertie, who had made sure that all the bills were paid on time. In that way, Theodore had managed to avoid any legal problems, and had staved off the possibility of visiting officials.

Theodore had been certain that nobody, apart from himself and Bertie, knew anything about Murra-yari or the Bugwomps. He'd wanted to keep it that way; for he was sure that, once the public came to hear of them, their peaceful existence would be destroyed. People would come and try to exploit them.

After all the years that he'd spent caring for them and trying to protect them, Theodore certainly wasn't going to stand for that; and, although there was no actual mention in the will of Murra-yari or of the Bugwomps, certain clauses were included that made his feelings very clear regarding the secrecy that must be maintained.

Stephen felt sure that Theodore had been right. If any of the local people should find out what was going on at Lansbury Hall, avoiding publicity would be impossible. He was determined to honor his great-uncle's wishes; but, as the days and weeks went by, he became increasingly anxious—not only anxious about money problems, but also anxious about security, following a most unfortunate incident.

Above all things, Stephen hated writing letters. But he had disciplined himself to write a number of short notes to Bertie to let the old man know how he was getting on, and to try to get more information from him about his late great-uncle's affairs. He had also sent a couple of vaguely worded postcards to the children's home—both sent in carefully sealed envelopes to avoid the postman's eagle eye—just to keep his house parents happy.

Stephen had placed a large, square biscuit tin for letters just outside the great gates. He had developed a habit of borrowing the big key from Murra-yari and wandering down across the estate on most weekdays to inspect the tin. He did this around about midmorning, by which time the postman would have passed the Hall on his rounds.

On one of these occasions, Stephen had an uncomfortable experience that nearly gave the whole game away—as far as the Bugwomps were concerned. It all happened when he set out one morning, as usual, on his regular trip to check the post tin.

It was a damp, cloudy, very Cornish sort of morning. Before he left the house, Stephen swept up his old, green parka from a chair in the hall, and flung it on around his shoulders. As he crossed the forecourt in front of the house, Tig appeared, emerging from the rose wilderness onto the forecourt, and calling out in his usual, friendly, chattering way.

Making his way toward the gates, Stephen did his best to shoo the animal back toward the house. He certainly didn't want any of the Bugwomps anywhere near the great gates, where someone passing by might see them. He had been relieved to notice that they seemed to keep well away from the lane; that no matter where the Bugwomps were on the estate, the

304

distant sound of occasional passing traffic in the lane always seemed to make them stop in their tracks.

On this occasion, however, it was quite clear that Tig was determined to be part of the expedition to the gate, and no amount of shooing, on Stephen's part, would drive him back. His pathetic, whimpering, hiccupping calls, as he lolloped along behind, desperately trying to keep up with Stephen's intentionally very brisk pace, finally affected Stephen. With an air of kindly irritation, he paused to allow Tig to catch up with him.

"Oh, Tig! You are a nuisance!" Stephen said in a mock-scolding voice, as he scooped the animal off the ground, tucking him firmly inside his shirt-front. There was something irresistible about Tig; Stephen never failed to feel flattered by any attention or affection that the animal showed toward him.

He continued on his way, a smile of pleasure on his face, talking quietly as he went. Tig giggled and chattered his appreciation, poking his head out through the gap at the front of Stephen's shirtfront. The large eyes stared up at Stephen, in apparent adoration.

It was not until Stephen had unlocked the gate with the big iron key and was stepping out into the lane beyond that he realized his mistake. A small, red, postman's van was parked a few yards down the road from the gate, and in the van was the postman himself, apparently enjoying his midmorning snack. Stephen could see a large, plastic thermos cup in the man's hand, and he was close enough to see that the man's jaws were munching rhythmically.

A cheery hand, holding what looked like the remains of a large, half-eaten pot pie, was waved at Stephen, who realized, to his dismay, that it was too late to duck back inside. But what on earth should he do with Tig? If the man came up close, he was almost certain to notice the animal. And then the "cat would be out of the bag," as the old saying goes—or, more likely, knowing Tig, the Bugwomp would be out of the shirtfront!

Stephen hissed loudly at Tig. He pushed him quickly and roughly back inside his shirt, pulling the parka more closely around his body. In such a situation as this, most of the Bugwomps would have been too alarmed to emerge in front of a stranger.

But Stephen knew that Tig was different. He was not only young and silly,

305

but, having lived so much with humans, he was much bolder than the others. It was, Stephen felt quite sure, only a matter of time before the little golden-and-black-striped head, with its wonderful, bulging, bright-green eyes, would appear through the gap in his shirtfront to give the postman a merry greeting.

Stephen was alarmed at the thought. He was also furious with himself for being so careless. He stood rooted to the spot, angrily clenching his teeth, wishing he could turn and run, but aware that such unfriendly behavior would be suspicious and a mistake.

From the elderly postman's "Good morning, young sir," and the way in which he stepped nimbly out of his van and made his way hastily across to Stephen, it was obvious that there was to be no quick escape from the man. He was clearly keen to chat at length: to tell Stephen how his wife, Morwenna, had made him a special treat that morning—a very fine pie and a thermos of coffee. For it seemed that she had, that very day, gone on a trip all the way to Truro. There, as Stephen was soon to learn, various delights awaited her, including a tour around the cathedral and, most important, shopping for a special outfit, suitable for attending the postman's eldest granddaughter's wedding—a pretty maid called Karensa.

As the man chatted away, Stephen could feel that Tig, who had at first gone quiet and still, was beginning to wriggle inside his shirt. If it hadn't been for the old, green parka, his peculiar movements would certainly have attracted attention. But, thankfully, the man chattered on, blissfully ignorant of the fact that, at any moment now, Tig's head would come popping out.

Almost at the last moment, inspiration came to Stephen. He had noticed from his observations of Tigerwomp behavior patterns that they had their own peculiar alarm call, which consisted of three loud clicking sounds, one after another. Stephen had experimented in trying to copy the sound, and had discovered that, by clicking his tongue very hard against the roof of his mouth, he could produce a tolerable impression of the call.

The clicking sound clearly upset the Tigerwomps. On hearing it, they would freeze and remain motionless until they were sure that any danger had passed. Stephen being thoughtful and kind, knowing that the sound frightened them, had seldom used his newfound skill against them; but now, the memory of it came suddenly and fortunately back to him.

Completely ignoring the flow of chatter from the postman, Stephen let out three loud clicks. The strange noise had an immediate effect—not only on poor Tig, who, to Stephen's considerable relief, froze instantly inside his shirt, but also on the postman, who stopped in midsentence and stared at Stephen. After a moment, he looked away in an embarrassed sort of manner; then, when nothing further occurred, he resumed his relentless chatter, but with a doubtful look on his face.

When Stephen thought about the incident later on, he couldn't imagine how he had managed to keep a straight face. Yet none of it had seemed remotely funny at the time. Indeed, it had all seemed deadly serious.

The postman had plenty of questions to ask about Stephen's "dear old uncle," and during the awkward conversation that followed, several more loud clicks were necessary to control Tig's movements. The postman's face was a study!

Stephen just stared back at the man, as if nothing at all had happened. He was sweating profusely inside the parka, and his hair clung horribly to his forehead. But he had to put up with the discomfort, for he didn't dare to lift his hand, in case the front of the parka swung open.

On top of that, there was another problem. Tig's fur was tickling Stephen's chest. He wriggled his body inside the parka, desperately trying to overcome an overwhelming urge to scratch—an urge to which he mustn't give in, since that would have meant having to let go of the parka that he was holding firmly closed. And so he wriggled and squirmed and twitched.

The postman stopped in midsentence and gave him a penetrating look before returning to his narrative. The boy looked as if he had problems.

"Shouldn't wonder if 'tis lice or fleas," he would tell Morwenna later that day. "What he needs is some of your special, herbal louse powder, my dear."

At last, the postman seemed ready to leave. After a final, long, hard stare at Stephen, he had climbed into his van and driven very slowly away, watching carefully in his side mirror. Stephen dreaded to think what kind of story the man would now tell in the village. He could see it all in his mind's eye: Mrs. Pascoe's great delight in spreading a

307

somewhat embroidered story, the snake dancing merrily on her head.

Arriving back at the house, Stephen collapsed in a chair in the kitchen, and confessed the whole sad story to Murra-yari. Being such a kind man, he made a joke of the whole thing, and they had a good long laugh together. But Stephen could see from the bright intelligence in Murra-yari's eyes, that he fully realized the dangerous implications of too much outside interest in their affairs.

The only one who most certainly did not find any amusement in the situation was Tig. As soon as Stephen was safely back in the kitchen he had lifted the pathetic, sticky bundle out of his shirtfront. Poor Tig was a quivering mass.

The recurrent clicking had terrified him; the wriggling and writhing had made it all worse. As Murra-yari took the animal onto his lap and gently rubbed him down with a towel, he turned reproachful eyes upon Stephen, as if he simply couldn't believe that someone whom he'd thought was a friend could do such a horrible thing to him.

Stephen felt terrible. Murra-yari laughed and laughed at the thought of Stephen itching and wriggling. But poor old Tig cowered low on his lap.

The funniest thing of all happened on the following day, when Stephen crept quietly and warily down to the great gates after lunch to check the post tin. Having looked carefully through the gates, to make quite sure there was no one there, he had opened the gate cautiously and lifted the lid of the biscuit tin. Inside, he found to his surprise, a small metal container— an old, reused tobacco tin with a handwritten label on the lid: "Morwenna's Special Herbal Louse Powder. Use twice daily."

Hardly able to contain himself, Stephen carried the treasure back to the house, where he and Murra-yari enjoyed a very good laugh together. But, despite the wonderful joke, Stephen still felt bad about Tig, who seemed to be avoiding him.

"Give him time," Murra-yari said. "He's really very fond of you. He'll soon get over his nasty experience."

Stephen found that Murra-yari was right. After a few days, Tig had stopped avoiding him, though he still seemed jumpy when Stephen picked him up, and he certainly avoided his shirtfront. Yet, sad as Stephen might feel about Tig, his mind was filled with other worries—worries about the money problem that cast a shadow over him.

In the privacy of his room at night, Stephen spent long hours, by the light of a candle, poring over his great-uncle's will and various other legal documents. He had never been any good at math. He had hated the subject when at school; but even he could see from the figures that the situation was very serious.

There was no doubt about it. A small fortune had been spent on Theodore's behalf, in the search for his brother Stephen's child. Detective work cost a lot of money in England. In America, it cost even more.

Stephen sat staring blankly at the figures on the paper. The bank account was almost exhausted. They would soon find themselves in a lot of trouble; but he kept his worries all to himself, for he couldn't bear to upset Murra-yari.

It might have been alright if Stephen had been able to sell some of the family treasures. He hated the very idea of it; but if selling the silver would have solved the problem, then he knew that it would have been worth it. Or maybe the magnificent sideboard in the hall. Murra-Yari had told Stephen that it had been made by a very famous Victorian craftsman—Pugin. Stephen thought that it might be quite valuable, and although he loathed the idea of losing it, selling it would have raised much-needed money.

But he didn't have the freedom to do such a thing. There were special clauses in the will about what he could and could not do with Lansbury Hall. "None of the land, nor any part of the dwelling, nor any part of the contents thereof" could be disposed of in any way. He read the various clauses over and over again.

The will made it all quite clear. If Stephen went against his great-uncle's wishes in any way, he would lose his rights to Lansbury Hall. Goodness knows what would happen to the place. The will didn't say. But he wasn't prepared to take the risk. He loved the place so dearly now. He knew that somehow he had to save it.

So, despite the happiness of the glorious summer days, Stephen often lay restless at night, worrying and wondering about it all. Whatever was he going to do?

64. Growing Worries

As time went by, Stephen learned a great deal more about the different species of Bugwomps: about their different behavior patterns, their feeding habits, and how they bred and multiplied. He learned how Theo and good old B had invented Latin names for them: *Bugwompus tigrinus*—the Tigerwomp; *Bugwompus bombicynus*—the Silkwomp; *Bugwompus paluster*—the Swampwomp; and *Bugwompus vermiculus*—the Maggotwomp.

The names made Stephen laugh so much. He decided that during the winter, when he would spend more time indoors, he would work his way through the rest of his great-uncle's notebooks, as well as a manuscript that he had found in a desk drawer, titled *A Field Guide to the Study of Bugwomps in the Wild, Their Care and Breeding in Captivity*.

One night, Murra-yari took Stephen up along the track toward the moor to watch the Tigerwomps' mating dance. The full moon in the sky above shone down crisp and white and staring. It lit the paths and the fields all around,

310

as they made their way along the aisle between tall, ghostly foxglove spikes—their lovely colors strangely paled, their empty flowers silent now.

When they came to the tunnel of hanging vines, Stephen stopped on the path, uncertain. The place had had an uncanny feeling, even in broad daylight. Now, by the light of the clear, cold moon, it had an even stranger feeling. Murra-yari turned to him, a smile of encouragement on his face.

"Your Great-Uncle Theodore loved this place," he whispered into Stephen's ear. "His spirit will roam happily here. Come. Follow me." He turned to go. "All the spirits are kindly here," he added, slipping silently away between the hanging arms of vines, with Stephen following as best he could.

They took the pathway that led down toward the river, stopping at a place just above the long meadow, standing frozen in the shadows and watching the Tigerwomps' odd behavior. Stephen stood grinning to himself. He remembered how mystified he'd been by the curious tracks that he'd seen in the grass, on his first visit to the meadow. Now that seemed like a lifetime ago.

Two shadowy Tigerwomp figures could be seen in the meadow below, one rather larger than the other. They were moving around slowly, opposite each other—moving around in a wide circle. Every so often both of them turned and moved in toward the center, then back out again and around.

Round and round and round they went; backward and forward and backward and forward, urged on, so it seemed, by a large crowd of spectator Tigerwomps, all chattering and giggling in a peculiarly rhythmic way. When, eventually, the two dancers ended up together in the middle of the circle, the spectators drifted away.

Some weeks later, Stephen was surprised, if not entirely delighted, to discover that the female Tigerwomp had given birth to four tiny Tigerwomps in a very comfortable nest that she'd made in the blanket on his bed.

Some of the other Bugwomps had been very productive as well. The Boss had retired to a large Maggotwomp hole beneath the roots of an old tree. There, she had successfully hatched out a number of eggs. Murra-yari was very proud of the increase in their population; he referred to the large group as a multiplicity of Maggotwomps. It certainly seemed an appropriate name.

The youngsters were very comical to watch. They squirmed about around their mother, safely protected from others by her fiercesome glance. Stephen felt quite honored when she allowed him to pick one up and hold it for a few moments; though, it didn't want to stay for long. Like all Maggotwomps, it was already terribly greedy. Being held up and away from the others, it feared that it might be missing something—something in the way of nourishment.

The Silkwomps lived in small family units made up of an adult male and female and their young, the youngsters only leaving the parents when they were fully mature and able to manage on their own. One of the pairs had produced an infant—a totally adorable creature, which was very silky and cuddly. Stephen spent long hours watching the antics of the parents teaching the youngster how to behave—how to swing amongst the branches on his long, silken thread—encouraging him on with a great deal of woomping.

Despite their very bad behavior, Stephen felt sorry for the some of the Swampwomps. The young males and females romped about in their separate groups; but the adult male Swampwomps led a solitary life, only mixing with the rest of the group during the mating season. At other times, they kept their distance. They wandered up and down the river, or hovered about at the edge of the main group, which consisted of females and their young.

It seemed a very lonely life: At first, Stephen couldn't help wondering if it was boredom and loneliness that drove them on to such naughty tricks. But the more that he saw of the Swampwomps generally, the more he came to realize that they were all inclined to misbehave. The juveniles, in particular, were full of mischief.

The more that he watched and studied the Bugwomps, the more involved with them Stephen became. The more he cared about their welfare. The more he worried about their future.

65. Some of My Ways, Some of Yours

As summer drew toward its close, Murra-yari and Stephen were very busy working together—collecting and bottling the honey, harvesting the fruit and vegetables that had to be stored away for the winter.

Working side by side with Murra-yari, as they tackled the various tasks together, Stephen learned all manner of interesting facts from him.

"When Theo first brought me back to England," Murra-yari told Stephen one day, "I found the idea of all this harvesting and storing very strange; for there is no real winter in the forests of the Amazon. Fruits and vegetables, of one kind or another, are available all year round. My people lived, very much, from one day to the next—hunting and gathering most of whatever they needed, whenever they needed it; although they did grow a few crops, amongst them, bananas and manioc.

"I suppose that Theo and I lived a rather strange life, here, at Lansbury Hall—a mixture of some of my people's ways, together with some of yours—and in that way we have lived very well."

313

"I'm very surprised that you didn't keep any sheep, goats, or cows here," Stephen had ventured to Murra-yari.

"We never really needed them," Murra-yari had answered simply.

"My people in the Amazon don't keep domesticated animals for meat or milk. It's not a part of their way of life, and I'm sure that it wouldn't be practical. Besides they have no need of them. Dairy products are quite unknown, and after living without them for so long, I am sure that Theo didn't miss them."

Stephen had learned that the rather peculiar, shrubby plants that he'd found in the kitchen garden were manioc, which was also known as cassava. Theodore, so Stephen was told, had been very proud of his success with the manioc. It was one of those plants brought back by Bertie—an unlikely plant to try to grow in an English vegetable garden.

The Lansbury Hall valley seemed to have its own special, frost-free, mini-climate. Theodore and Murra-yari had found that, by taking cuttings in late summer and nursing them carefully through the winter, the cuttings could be planted the following spring, thus ensuring a continuity of the crop. Although it was not nearly as heavy a crop as would have grown in tropical conditions, they had kept the manioc going year after year, and Bertie had been very proud of them, greatly praising their success on the one occasion when he had visited.

Manioc had provided a staple food for Murra-yari's people, the Taluma. They had used it to make a variety of things, including a flatbread called beijú and a toasted flour called farinha. Manioc and its processing had played an important part in their lives, and ancient customs were involved.

At certain special planting times, they had feasted and drunk manioc beer, singing and dancing to celebrate the wonderful cycle of regrowth. It was a colorful occasion. Over the years at Lansbury Hall, Theodore and Murra-yari had themselves used manioc as one of their staple foods, along with maize and wheat.

It wasn't until after Stephen had finished helping to harvest the manioc, that he learned that the tubers were poisonous. They contained a very dangerous acid, which had to be eliminated to make the manioc safe to eat.

Ridding the manioc of the poison was a very lengthy and tedious process.

With a grave expression upon his face, Murra-yari had made it quite clear that, were he back in the Amazon, he wouldn't be doing the work at all. It was, so he said, a task for women. Yet he worked away contentedly with Stephen, in the backyard behind the house.

First, they washed the manioc tubers and left them to soak in a vat of water, which helped to leach out some of the acid. Then they peeled and grated them; and over a period of several days, they soaked and washed the pulp, finally squeezing it out as dry as they could in a sort of cylindrical, woven tube. The pulp emerged from the squeezer as a hard, dry sausage, and this could then be crumbled and passed through a sieve to make flour. Stephen learned that further drying and roasting of the flour helped to finally make it safe.

As the juice was squeezed from the soggy pulp, it was collected up in a large bowl. Murra-yari took the bowl and stood it in the old dairy, waiting for the contents to settle. The poisonous fluid could then be poured off; Stephen was very surprised to discover that the white stuff left at the bottom of the pot was apparently tapioca. It was a far cry from the tins of creamed tapioca that sat on the shelves in the Pascoes' store—but real tapioca, nevertheless.

Even the poisonous juice was used, since boiling drove off the remaining acid, and the fluid was then safe to use; it was good in stews, or brewed with peppers they'd picked from the garden, it made a very tasty sauce.

Learning to process the manioc was quite an experience for Stephen. Cushioned, most of his life by having had regular meals put before him, and spoiled by modern convenience foods that provided an almost instant meal, he had no understanding of what real, basic life was like.

The hard work involved in processing the manioc gave him a special insight into the way in which people who live off the land must plan their food and work hard for it. Eating the bread that Murra-yari baked on the griddle gave him a sense of satisfaction quite unlike any previous experience. It was a whole, wide world away from pouring boiling water onto processed noodles.

As they sat together in the evenings, resting in the comfortable library,

Murra-yari tried to remember some of his people's myths and legends concerning the origins of manioc. It seemed a very odd thing to Stephen that people had chosen a poisonous plant, which meant they must labor so long and so hard to make it finally safe to eat. It surprised him that the Indians understood the complex process.

But the more he thought about it, the more he realized that he shouldn't be surprised at all. Theodore had referred to the forest Indians as "superb pharmacologists." They were obviously very knowledgeable about the plants and trees of the forest. Knowing how to process the manioc was a small example of their great expertise.

There was a lot of fruit to be harvested at Lansbury Hall. As he clambered about in the branches of trees, harvesting the rosy apples, enjoying the warm, September sun, Stephen thought a lot about Theodore. After reading so much of his journal and living through all his adventures with him, he thought of him more as a very close friend than as an old and remote great-uncle. It saddened him that they'd never met. He wished that Theo could see him now and know of his love for Lansbury Hall, know that Stephen would somehow manage.

"But perhaps, after all," he said to himself, smiling around at the trees and the sky. "Yes, perhaps, after all, he can see me now."

He remembered the promise that he'd made to his great-uncle—when he'd found the grave in the woodland glade. It was essential to honor that promise—though he didn't yet know how he would do it.

66. Ablutions

The scope of Murra-yari's knowledge never ceased to amaze Stephen. Theodore had obviously done a splendidly patient and thorough job in educating the little Amazon Indian boy in a wide range of subjects, from the history of art in the Western world to modern science—or at any rate, to science as it was modern in 1915.

His grasp of the English language was far better than Stephen's own, and Theo had even taught him Latin. Murra-yari could quote long tracts of Virgil's *Aeneid*, both in the original Latin and in a very good translation. Stephen sat spellbound in his chair, listening to the exciting stories, and enjoying the flowing language.

Yet in many ways, Murra-yari was still very much a forest Indian, and, like so many of his people, one of the things he enjoyed very much was wallowing about in water. If Stephen looked out of his bedroom window early in the morning, he would see Murra-yari making his way across the meadow to his favorite pool in the river—to partake of his "morning ablutions"—apparently. It had been a great relief to Stephen to find that he himself was definitely discouraged from attending these cold, wet, morning jaunts, which didn't appeal to him at all. It was the one time of day when Murra-yari enjoyed being quietly on his own—communing with the elements.

After sunbathing, or when he was hot and sticky from working, Stephen enjoyed a splash in the river—always provided, of course, that there weren't any Swampwomps present. For swimming with Swampwomps could be hazardous. They could never resist playing tricks on him—some of them very unpleasant tricks.

Most of his dips in the river were, therefore, very brief. Even when Stephen found an apparently perfect time and place, without a Bugwomp of any species in sight, in no time at all Swampwomps would appear on the scene, as if by magic. They seemed to have some special, extra sense as far as "their river" was concerned, and they always turned up out of the blue, managing to make great pests of themselves; although Stephen had suspected—and indeed, had had it confirmed—that they never troubled Murra-yari.

Stephen had developed his own routine for keeping clean, which involved making the very best use of the ancient plumbing at Lansbury Hall. Whilst rooting about in the library, he had found a wonderfully useful book, *The Principles and Practices of Plumbing* by S. Stevens Hellyer, a book that had especially delighted him because it had helped him to understand and appreciate the plumbing and sanitary arrangements at Lansbury Hall—a subject that was beginning to fascinate him. The book, which was dated 1891, must have been bought around the time of the updating and modernizing of Lansbury Hall.

Some of the sanitary and lavatorial habits common amongst people in the past, and described in graphic detail by Mr. Stevens Hellyer, had amazed Stephen. He had never before stopped to consider the many and varied problems relating to toilets and such, in the days before the invention of modern sanitary fittings: the down pipes, the S bends, the ballcocks, the flushings, and all the things that went to ensure that "relieving oneself"—if that was the 'nice' way to put it—was not an unduly unpleasant or noisome experience.

Noisome! What a splendid word that was! It seemed to be a favorite of Mr. Hellyer's, who chatted on about "noisome vapors." Having looked it up in the dictionary, Stephen decided that he liked the word and that he would adopt it in future.

Not long after his discovery of the intriguing book, Stephen had been thrilled to discover a wonderful relic of the past. The outbuildings at the rear of the house were a constant source of delight to him, containing, as they did, so many fascinating objects: old, unwanted furniture; pots, pans, buckets, baskets, and a whole range of household equipment, some of it positively antique; ancient and mysterious agricultural equipment—he simply couldn't fathom the way in which some of that had been used.

There was one last door in the yard, close to the house, that Stephen had not yet investigated. There was a deep gap between the top of the door and the doorframe, but Stephen wasn't quite tall enough to look over. As the old door grumbled open, he stepped gingerly over the threshold. Thick dust and the cobwebs of many ages had blanketed the fittings in the room so well that it took him a few moments to realize what it was that he'd discovered—an old earth closet.

The newly discovered room in the yard was obviously the family privy, but clearly a palatial privy, for it included the most extraordinary arrangement that Stephen had ever seen. He gasped with laughter and delight when he realized what he'd found. A splendid, communal, six-seater toilet.

According to Murra-yari, Theodore had believed that the house had been built around 1740, a very modern and smart house for the time, but probably modest and quite simple when compared with the elaborate mansions that were being built "up-country" at that time. As Stephen considered the palatial privy, he thought it highly probable that it dated right back to 1740. Strange as it might seem to him now, it would in those days have been very modern.

Six, rounded, well-spaced holes were cut in the continuous bench that ran around three sides of the room: two sets in the bench at the back, and two in the benches on either side. Wide, square, wooden lids that could be lowered over the holes were propped back against the wall. Sections of the top of the bench, on either side nearest to the door, were very much lower and closer to the ground; the holes in those were considerably smaller.

It was probably this last fact that tickled Stephen most of all. The one on the left was close to the ground, and the hole in the top was very small. It was clearly intended for a tiny bottom.

Stephen stood there laughing out loud at the thought of the whole family sitting there: Mother, Father, Grandma, and Grandpa over the higher, larger holes; the children over the smaller ones. Yet he found it difficult to imagine the kind of social get-together that must have taken place in the privy. As he retreated from the room, convulsed in laughter at the thought, one word kept coming back to him. . . . Noisome? Yes! Most certainly noisome!

67. Mr. Shanks's Masterpiece

The modernization of the sanitation at Lansbury Hall, which had been carried out by Stephen's great-grandparents, Philip and Christina, soon after their marriage in the early 1890s, had included the installation of a thoroughly modern, luxury bathroom in one of the upstairs rooms.

There was a small, square boiler room, outside in the yard, with a big, black, bulging, cast-iron boiler that crouched against the rear wall in what Stephen felt was a threatening way. Murra-yari had instructed him in the lighting and tending of this curious and somewhat temperamental beast: a voracious beast, as Stephen quickly discovered, that needed constant feeding with wood, in order to provide enough hot water in the upstairs tank for him to have a decent, warm bath.

It seemed like a very primitive system. The clanking and rattling of the old pipes, as the heat from the boiler took effect, thoroughly alarmed Stephen. Even when the boiler wasn't alight, he felt unreasonably wary of it—lurking in its murky den.

When the boiler was alight, it reminded him of some of the mythical creatures rampaging in Virgil's stories. Had it not been for Murra-yari's calm, continued insistence that the system was safe and efficient, and his pooh-poohing of any doubts, Stephen would probably have given up his contest with the boiler. He would have gone back to the considerable discomfort—but relative safety—of heating a kettle in the kitchen for some hot water, and washing various crucial parts of himself at the scullery sink or, on really warm days, standing at the pump in the yard.

The upstairs bathroom was certainly magnificent. It contained a splendid "throne," similar to the one downstairs and with the same passionflower design, but possibly a little more grand and fitted cunningly into a corner. On one wall, there was an elegant washbasin, set into a mahogany cabinet, and beside it a primitive-looking towel rail, made from very wide copper piping, jointed with shining brass. In the far opposite corner of the room, there was the most extraordinary bath.

Boxed in on all sides with mahogany paneling, the bath had a tall, hoodlike canopy at one end, housing the shower. The front of the tall hooded section of the cabinet was framed with elaborate carving, the top central panel of which carried a bold and elegant L, entwined in curving stems and leaves. Amidst the leaves were occasional blossoms—beautifully carved passionflowers.

Set into the front support of the shower section of the cabinet was what could only be described as a truly magnificent control panel. This consisted of a very large brass plate into which were set two massive, shiny, brass tap handles, together with a heavy, bar-shaped handle—a special selecting device, which could be grasped and turned so that the attached indicator pointed to the type of water flow required: DOUCHE—PLUNGE—SPRAY—SHOWER, these words being heavily impressed in the brass, as was also the maker's name, SHANKS. Below this eye-catching panel, there was a separate brass handle, which could be pulled out or pushed back in to engage some kind of unseen plugging device for the bath.

The large and impressive panel of tap handles gave the appearance of being better suited to the operation and control of some mighty ship's boiler, rather than to a domestic bath. The Victorian inventors and engineers, responsible for the manufacture of this magnificent appliance, had clearly depended upon bold and basic design, incorporating both strength and simplicity when it came to the controls.

Stephen couldn't fault the ingenuity of those who had created the bath, although on his first introduction to its wonders, he had experimented with the waterworks with some fear and trepidation, testing the massive overhead shower, as well as the ingenious side sprays, which shot water out at him from a large number of tiny holes set in the walls of the shower cubicle. Thereafter, he had enjoyed it enormously, not least because of the other aspect of the bathroom that gave Stephen great pleasure—the glorious and colorful tiles that lined the bathroom walls.

Murra-yari had told Stephen that these tiles were the work of a famous Victorian potter and tile maker—a man called William De Morgan—a contemporary and personal friend of another Victorian, William Morris, whose elegant, lily-pattern wallpaper and large matching rug decorated the main bedroom. These men, so it seemed, had been friends of Theo's grandfather.

William De Morgan had become famous for his fabulous hand-painted pottery and tiles. As Stephen lay happily in the bath, enjoying the decorated tiles, he could readily understand why. For the tiles were not only glorious colors—mainly greens, purples, and cream on a background of bright turqoise-blue—but brilliant designs as well.

The tiles on the lower part of the wall around the room, formed a mass of interlocking stems and foliage, and along the top of the panel of foliage, edged by narrow indigo tiles, was a stunning frieze of entwining passionflowers.

On the wall opposite the bath, there was a panel of tiles with red and blue macaws. It was Murra-yari's favorite feature in the house, and on more than one occasion, Stephen had found him standing in front of the tiles murmuring to himself, "Arara."

As Stephen wallowed in the warm, comforting water, enjoying Mr. Shanks's masterpiece and Mr. De Morgan's wonderful tiles, he indulged in all manner of philosophical thoughts. But, although he tried to avoid it, his mind kept drifting back to the same, old, uncomfortable worries—how to protect Lansbury Hall, and, of course—the money problem.

68. Cleanliness Is Next to Godliness

One day, Stephen set out to visit the village again. Generally speaking, he was quite contented with their self-sufficient life. But there were one or two items of modern living without which he still felt uncomfortable. His need for those items drew him very reluctantly out.

During all his time at Lansbury Hall, Stephen had only ever made the one visit to the village and the shop. It had been fortunate that he'd been wise enough at the time to buy the big double bar of soap, the jumbo pack of his favorite toothpaste, and a big six-pack of toilet paper. He had taken care to eke out all those things for as long as possible, but when they had started running out, he couldn't decide what to do for the best. For a time, he had managed with leaves instead of toilet paper. But, although he didn't like to grumble to Murra-yari, he couldn't pretend that he found the leaves satisfactory.

This time, it was a very different-looking Stephen walking down the village street—walking with confidence and a sense of purpose. He appeared to have grown in stature. The open-air life and physical work obviously suited him very well.

His diet, which might have seemed limited to some people, lacking all convenience foods, was far more healthy than before: homemade flatbreads baked on the griddle; plenty of fresh fruit and homegrown vegetables; honey from their very own bees; the most delicious spring water from the pump in the yard behind the house; fish from the river and game from the woods.

His winter diet would be slightly different, but the larder was filled to overflowing. He and Murra-yari would certainly never go hungry. For they'd dried and bottled and saved and stored enough food, so it seemed, for an army.

There were, however, one or two things that Stephen missed in the way of food: a nice chunk of cheddar cheese, and maybe, yes, he had to admit it—a packet of steaming-hot fish and chips!

Stephen had spent a good deal of the summer wearing little more than his oldest, most ragged pair of jeans, from which he had chopped off the legs to make shorts. He was fit and bronzed, and his hair, grown long, was bleached quite fair by the sun and the sea. Murra-yari had shown him how to weave some plant fibers to make himself a band for his head. It held the hair back from his face. He'd quite grown out of his silly old habit of always having to push it back.

On leaving the house that very morning he had scrutinized his face in the Pugin mirror. Now, he felt quite jubilant. Not a single spot in sight. Hooray for Morwenna's Secret Recipe! Hooray for the wonderful Cornish herbs! Stephen wondered about her Louse Powder. That was probably useful too—if you happened to have such a problem.

Marching along with a swinging gait, Stephen made his way briskly down the village street to the shop. Several sets of hidden eyes stared out from behind net curtains. Amazed voices murmured comments. "Such a confident, swaggering boy. Such a happy-looking boy. But just look at the length of his hair!"

Stephen grinned as he strode along, noticing the twitching curtains.

None of it bothered him anymore. Even the prospect of Mrs. Pascoe, together with her rolling bosoms, held no terrors for him now.

The shop was empty when he entered, save for the proprietress herself, slumped in a chair behind the counter, apparently sleeping very soundly. Her large body heaved with the rhythm of sleep. The gobbling, gargling snorts it gave forth would have rivaled the efforts of any Swampwomp—even the largest, most dominant male! Stephen stifled a laugh at the thought; but there was one disappointment—the dancing snake was not to be seen.

"Good afternoon, Mrs. Pascoe."

The woman was jolted into action. It took her some moments to recognize Stephen. When she did, she was full of questions: "Well now, m'dear," she said. "How are you getting on at the Hall? And how's that dear, old uncle now? Doing well, I hope, is he?"

"Yes," said Stephen very firmly, trying to control his face. "He's doing very nicely, thank you."

He gave Mrs. Pascoe his list: a jumbo tube of his favorite toothpaste; a twin-bar pack of a healthy soap; a can of deodorant; two four-roll packs of a nice, soft toilet paper; and a bottle of shampoo. He nearly forgot the washing-up liquid and he couldn't resist a large piece of cheese.

Stephen stood quietly and patiently beside the counter. With so few items to collect together, it seemed that Mrs. Pascoe was doing her best to spin out the interview. Her movements appeared to get slower and slower. She seemed to be watching him rather closely.

It was almost as if she were waiting for something to happen. Of course! Stephen suddenly realized. She was waiting for the clicking noises, and, perhaps, the wriggling too.

The temptation to scratch and wriggle, to provide even a modest clicking display, which might satisfy Mrs. Pascoe's expectations, was very great indeed. Stephen's tongue made several exploratory trips across the roof of his mouth. He had to clench his jaws together to prevent himself from clicking or laughing.

Turning away to hide his face, he noticed a pile of bulging pot pies

326

under a cover along the counter. A genuine and delicious Cornish pot pie would be a new experience for Murra-yari. He would have to buy two for their tea.

"I can't resist your magnificent pot pies," he told Mrs. Pascoe, with his most charming smile. "There's no one in the whole of Cornwall who makes a better pot pie than yours.

"And, of course," he added, "those wonderful apple and blackberry turnovers. Would you have any of those, I wonder?"

His beguiling smile quite overcame the shopkeeper. "Well! Thank you, young man. Though I say it m'self, an' I shouldn', I am quite renowned in these parts for my pot pies. And, of course, for my turnovers too."

"May I have two of each, please," Stephen asked, beaming warmly. "One of each for my dear old uncle—and one of each for myself." He couldn't resist adding this extra piece of information; though he hoped he wasn't overdoing it.

The shopkeeper giggled and wobbled with delight, as she lifted two, fat, succulent pot pies into a big, brown, paper bag. Then with a somewhat coquettish, big wink, she scuttled quickly out to the back room, returning almost immediately with two crispy, golden turnovers. But, alas, there was no Cornish cream.

At last, Stephen was able to make his getaway, paying her and thanking her very politely.

"Well, now! Did you ever! What a charming young man!" Mrs. Pascoe said out loud, to nobody in particular. "A very discerning young man, I should say. And quite a handsome young man too."

"His heart and his stomach appear to be in the right places, and whatever anyone says of him, he's clearly bent on keeping clean. And, as they always say—'Cleanliness is next to godliness.' Mrs. Pascoe nodded wisely to herself.

"He certainly didn't make any strange noises. All those stories of fleas or lice! I didn't see him scratch once.

"Poor old Fernley! Seems like he's failing. Probably imagined the whole thing, he did. The sooner he retires, the better. Though what Morwenna will do with him then—round her feet all day long—I really can't imagine. Poor woman! She's going to find it very trying."

And she settled back down to resume her slumbers.

Stephen walked home quickly, laughing happily to himself. He let himself in through the gate, locking it carefully behind him. But, despite his happy trip to the village, by the time he emerged from the rhododendron wilderness and stood there gazing across at the Hall, the old money worries were creeping back.

Tomorrow he must tell Murra-yari. He couldn't keep it all to himself any longer. Tomorrow they would have to talk.

Stephen couldn't possibly have known that tomorrow they wouldn't be able to talk. That something very nasty, the next day, would drive such worries from his mind. Something very nasty indeed.

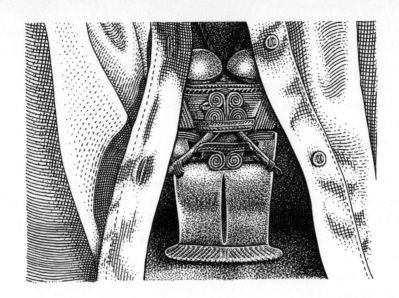

69. Something Very Nasty Indeed

Stephen woke up late the following morning. He lay there thinking how quiet it was. Murra-yari was usually up by now, and having had his dip in the river, would be down in the kitchen, preparing breakfast.

It was, of course, a very large house. Stephen didn't expect to be able to hear from his bedroom the sound of activity in the kitchen. But, even so, he couldn't help thinking that, somehow, the house seemed very quiet—too quiet, he thought—and empty.

A rather louder than usual gargling, gobbling noise, from somewhere down by the river, drifted in through Stephen's open window. Crossing the room, he looked out—down across the meadow toward the river. There in the distance, to his surprise, he could just make out what looked like Murra-yari, sitting on the riverbank. It seemed strange to see him still there. He was usually back in the house by this time.

Stephen glanced quickly at his watch. He could hardly believe his eyes. It wasn't breakfast time. It was nearly midmorning. He had badly overslept.

He stood at the window, peering down at Murra-yari. He looked rather funny. Why wasn't he sitting normally? Why was he slumped in a heap on the bank?

Stephen had never dressed so quickly in his life before. He tore across the landing, down the big staircase, across the hall and out onto the fore-court, mumbling desperately as he went, "Oh, no! No! No! What on earth can have happened to him?"

He came at last to the grassy bank, and stood there panting and gasping for breath, staring down at the crumpled figure, shocked by the horribly thin, drawn face. For a terrible moment he thought the worst! But then, as he knelt down on the grass, the figure was seized by a fit of trembling. A faint smile curved the Indian's lips as Stephen touched a trembling shoulder. His eyes fluttered open for a moment, as he tried to focus on Stephen's face.

"Oh, Stephen! I'm glad. So glad that you've come." The voice sounded weak and far away.

Stephen was suddenly very alarmed. Something was badly wrong with his friend. Even as he knelt and watched, Murra-yari was gripped again by a terrible fit of trembling and shivering.

"Oh! I'm cold! So cold!" He could barely squeeze out the words between shivers, his teeth literally rattling together.

"We must get you straight back up to the house. At least, you've got some clothing on. You must have my jumper. Hang on!"

Stephen ripped off his old, gray sweater, managing with some difficulty to get it over Murra-yari's head; wriggling it down over his body.

"Do you think you can stand and walk, if I take most of your weight?"

"Yes. I'm sure I can walk . . . a little . . . if we take it very slowly." Murra-yari's weary voice was not much more than a sighing whisper.

Just as they were about to set off, a very loud gargling, gobbling noise caught Stephen's attention. A large group of Swampwomps was huddled at the river's edge looking very agitated. As he set off with Murra-yari, a noisy chorus swelled behind them.

And as he struggled across the meadow, he remembered the story in Theodore's journal: how the forest Indian brothers had turned out to be so

loyal; how they had returned for their friends; how they must have struggled through the forest, carrying the two men in their hammocks—to save
them from a horrible death. The thought gave him extra strength—to help
him support Murra-yari.

Staggering up the steps and into the hall, Stephen felt Murra-yari's body
go limp. The bed in the library would be the best place. With a final effort,
Stephen gathered the man up in his arms, and carried him carefully across
the library. As he laid him gently down on the bed, Murra-yari stirred and
murmured.

"Oh, Stephen! I'm sorry! Where am I?"

"You're alright now," Stephen said firmly. "You fainted, I think, but
you're back in the house, and everything will be alright. I am going to take
off your cold, damp clothes. But first, I must dash upstairs to the linen cupboard, to collect some clothes, some sheets, and blankets. Will you please
stay just where you are. I'll be back in a few minutes."

Murra-yari smiled weakly. "I wasn't thinking of going anywhere," he
whispered, in between violent shivers.

When Stephen got to the library door, he found his way was completely
barred by quite the largest gathering of Bugwomps that he'd ever seen.
They must have crept in quietly, and now they almost filled the hall, pressing together and jostling noisily, wanting to find out what had happened to
Murra-yari, yet none of them apparently bold enough to come right in and
see for themselves.

"Oh, no!" Stephen gasped in dismay. It seemed like the final straw.

"I'm really sorry," he said with feeling, as he shooed them all out
through the door and down the steps in front of the house. "I simply can't
cope with you all. But I promise you I'll look after him."

He closed the front door firmly behind them, shutting out their mum-
blings and grumblings, feeling very mean about it. He knew they were all
devoted to Murra-yari; but, with so much to do, he'd go quite mad with
them round his feet. And Murra-yari must come first.

Stripping clothing off the almost helpless man, and getting him into
fresh, dry clothing was very much easier said than done; for he was so

weak, and couldn't do much to help himself. As Stephen worked, he got a shock, not just to see how thin and frail Murra-yari looked, but as he lifted the damp shirt over the old Indian's head, he made the most extraordinary discovery. Hanging against Murra-yari's chest, suspended on a long, leather thong around his neck, was the most amazing object—an enormous, chunky, gold pendant—a very exotic-looking object, quite unlike anything that Stephen had ever seen before.

Stephen gasped when he saw the pendant. He found it very hard indeed to drag his eyes away from the gold, as the pendant swung and glowed in the light. But Murra-yari was much too ill to notice Stephen's reaction. He shook and shivered alarmingly.

Trying to push all thoughts of the gold to the back of his mind, Stephen concentrated harder than ever on getting Murra-yari tucked in with clean sheets and plenty of blankets—including the old, favorite tartan blanket—the one that had belonged to Theo. At last, when that was done, he pulled the nearest armchair close to the bed, and collapsed amongst the cushions, with a deep and noisy sigh of relief.

As he sat there gazing at his patient with a worried frown upon his face and a strained and anxious look in his eyes, wondering what he ought to do next, a familiar whimpering came to his ears from somewhere underneath the bed. Stephen's tense face relaxed at the sound. Two, large, round, green eyes, were staring miserably up at him from the gap beneath the bed.

"I suppose I might have guessed," he said, bending down and pulling Tig out, swinging him up and onto his lap.

"I suppose I should have known that you'd manage to creep in somehow or other. What a bad lad you are!"

But, in truth, he was very pleased to see Tig, and he lovingly wiped the animal down: picking off all the dust and cobwebs that he'd collected on his coat, whilst hiding underneath the bed.

Murra-yari turned his head on the pillow, smiling weakly at Tig. He put out his hand and beckoned to Stephen.

"How are you feeling?" Stephen asked. "Is there anything I can get for you?"

"I'm feeling a little warmer, thank you," he whispered between trembling lips. "But the worst is probably still to come. Malaria is never fun."

"Malaria!" Stephen gasped in surprise.

He sprang up hastily out of the chair, clutching Tig tightly to his chest. The animal wriggled in alarm.

"I must go at once and fetch a doctor."

"No!" cried Murra-yari sharply, trying to rise up in the bed, and clutching hold of Stephen's hand.

"We don't want or need a doctor." The words were hissed between clenched teeth.

"What we need is the Postlethwaite Tree! There are two in the thicket behind the yard. Take your knife and collect some bark—a piece about eight square inches. It has always worked very well in the past."

"But what do I do with the bark?" asked Stephen.

"Bring it back here straightaway. . . . I will tell you how to prepare it. . . . It must be done in a special way . . . or it can be very dangerous . . ."

He slumped back down on the bed again.

"Hurry, please. . . . Oh, do hurry!" he added weakly.

70. The Postlethwaite Tree

Stephen didn't stop to argue. Dropping Tig hastily onto the bed, he set off immediately out of the library. He remembered the piece in Theo's journal—the piece about the Postlethwaite Tree. He even remembered the wording: "B has two small saplings growing in his garden collection." Bertie must have brought them back, along with the rest of his collection.

Standing breathless beneath the trees in the thicket, Stephen felt extremely anxious. How would he know which tree it was? Supposing he chose the wrong one! Extracts from bark could be very poisonous. He might end up by killing his friend. What a terrible thought that was!

With his mouth set in a grim line, and a deep scowl across his forehead, he ran from one tree to the next, forcing his way through the undergrowth with Murra-yari's last words ringing loudly in his ears—"Hurry, please. . . . Oh, do hurry!"

Finally, after what seemed like an age of scurrying about and searching wildly, Stephen stopped beside one of the trees, and took his knife out of his pocket. Then he paused, feeling uncertain. Somewhere in the undergrowth he had lost the band that held his hair back. His hair now hung around his shoulders; it clung about his sweating face. He swept it back with an angry gesture as he stared up anxiously into the branches.

"Please, tree!" he cried in a desperate voice, running his hand down the knobbly bark. "If only you could talk to me. If only you could answer me. Are you or aren't you the Postlethwaite Tree?"

It was quiet and gloomy in the thicket. A light wind rustled the yellowing leaves that whispered high above his head. Could he be sure that this was the tree? If only the whispering leaves could tell him.

He had no certain way of knowing; but only this tree stood out from the rest, its trunk marked by a series of scars. Surely they must be the telltale signs—the areas of damaged bark where pieces had been stripped in the past. It was the only clue that he had.

Precious minutes were ticking by. Stephen knew he must take the risk; but his hand shook as he lifted the knife. Slowly, carefully, he started to strip a small section of bark from the trunk.

He mustn't strip too much of the bark. He mustn't damage the trunk too much. He hated defacing the poor tree, standing tall, yet powerless before him, offering, so he hoped, salvation.

As Stephen ran thankfully back to the house, clutching the piece of bark in his hand, his face wore a determined smile, his eyes were alight with optimism. He had noticed before he left the house that the shivering fits were abating. Murra-yari seemed warmer and better. Now he felt certain that, with the bark medicine, his old friend would soon be well.

But he hadn't reckoned on the effects of malaria. When, at last, he got back to the library, a nasty shock was awaiting him. Murra-yari seemed much worse. His condition had completely changed. Now, instead of freezing and shivering, he appeared to be burning hot.

He had thrust off all the sheets and blankets. He tossed and turned in obvious pain. Tig was dancing around on the chair, clearly distressed and chattering loudly.

Stephen ran quickly across to the bed.

335

"I've got the bark," he told Murra-yari. "Look! Here it is. What should I do with it?"

But Murra-yari was too ill to answer. He pushed Stephen's hand and the bark away, groaning loudly, his voice filled with pain.

"My head! My head! My poor head!"

Stephen was suddenly very frightened. He stood there looking down aghast at the figure thrashing on the bed. Murra-yari was seriously ill. His skin felt horribly hot and dry; his behavior was alarming. It was painfully obvious to Stephen that the apparent solution to the problem—the piece of bark that he held in his hand—was going to be useless to him now; his friend was much too ill to tell him how he should prepare the bark.

"I'm hot! So hot! Get these clothes off!" Murra-yari's desperate voice galvanized Stephen into action. He took the vital piece of bark across the library to the table, and left it in a safe place there. Then he went back to help Murra-yari, stripping off his clothes with difficulty, and covering him with just a sheet.

"Feel sick! Very sick!" the frantic voice came again.

Stephen ran to the scullery for a bucket, returning only just in time. Tig lay silently on the chair with a look of terror on his face, as Stephen rushed backward and forward, doing what was necessary to try to make Murra-yari comfortable. He watched Stephen's progress anxiously as he paced up and down the room, muttering angrily to himself.

Murra-yari needed a doctor. Stephen felt savagely angry with himself for being so foolishly irresponsible—for not finding out a long time ago where a local doctor lived—just in case he needed one. But Murra-yari didn't want a doctor. And then, there was the other problem: their wonderfully peaceful life would be ruined if he brought anyone into the house. Yet, if he didn't do something quickly, he feared that he would lose his friend.

Stephen's face was grim. His hazel eyes were full of despair, as he turned and looked across the room at the poor old man, who lay tossing and moaning. How strange it was that he'd never before thought of Murra-yari as "old"!

The long, frail body frightened Stephen. Murra-yari had always been slim; but he'd always seemed so lithe and strong. Now he just looked painfully thin. It was almost as if he were dwindling away.

Stephen's heart was full of pain—full of pain and full of fear. How would he manage without Murra-yari? How would he manage without his friend? He couldn't bear to lose him now.

71. B's Notes on Preparation

Stephen slumped in the big armchair beside the bed, his elbows resting on his knees, his head sunk deeply in his hands. He felt exhausted and very upset. It was all up to him now. But he simply didn't know what to do next.

He pressed his forehead with his hands, raking his fingers through his hair then dragging his hands right down his face—massaging his tight jaw, stretching out his neck and shoulders. There must be something he could do.

It was late afternoon and almost dark now in the library. Stephen rose wearily out of the chair and, having collected candles from the scullery, he lit them in candlesticks and candleholders around the room. Tig lay along the top of the back of the armchair, looking very dejected.

Murra-yari looked even worse now than before. He was terribly dry and terribly thirsty. Stephen had dashed out to the pump to fill some jugs with fresh spring water. From time to time he propped Murra-yari up, and held the mug up to his mouth, enabling him to take cooling sips—the mug with the blue and red macaws.

After one of these occasions, when Murra-yari seemed more calm, Stephen had collected the piece of bark from the table and carried it back with him to the bed, determined to press Murra-yari about it. But the poor, old man was clearly in pain; the more Stephen questioned him, the more upset he became, pushing Stephen away and shouting, so that Stephen became even more afraid. For he didn't need a thermometer to tell him that the old Indian's temperature was already dangerously high.

Having replaced the bark on the table, Stephen picked up the photo of Theo with his "brother" Wamiru. This was now framed in an old brass frame; it stood in a place of honor in the middle of the table. Stephen stood there peering at it by the light of a flickering candle.

"Oh, Theo! Wamiru! What shall I do? If only you were here now. If only you could speak to me," Stephen said in a desperate voice, gazing into the smiling eyes of the two young men in the photograph.

And then it suddenly came to him. How could he have been so stupid! The answer was there in front of him—just a few inches away from his hand. It was there in his Great-Uncle Theo's journal.

With a gasp of excitement, he started rummaging through the books. If only he could remember which one! It was several months since he'd read the journal. Where was the paper? It had to be there! The piece of paper with scribbled writing, headed neatly in Theo's hand "B's Notes on Preparation."

Stephen felt jubilant and excited, until, that is, he found the notes. Then he remembered why it was that he hadn't read through them before. For B's writing had seemed impossible. It was rather small, spidery writing, quite the opposite of what you might expect from such a unusual, flamboyant character.

"Oh, no!" Stephen groaned, as he glared at the notes. "How am I going to decipher this?"

There was nothing to do but to sit down at the table with the candleholder at his side and go through it calmly and quietly—and yet as quickly as possible. For every time Stephen looked across at the bed, Murra-yari seemed worse. Immediate action was essential.

339

Yet everything seemed to conspire to slow him down. He could hardly bear it when, just as he had started on the notes, a faint voice came from the bed: "Going to be sick! Very sick!"

More dashing about with the bucket! Managing the situation hadn't been easy in the daylight. Darkness made it all the more difficult.

Thinking about it later on, Stephen was amazed to remember the way in which he had sat at the table—how, despite overwhelming anxiety and the very poor light, he had coolly and calmly deciphered the notes. Tig had given him great support. He seemed aware of Stephen's need to concentrate, so he lay quietly on his lap, allowing Stephen to stroke his back, whilst he wrestled with the difficult writing.

The presence of Tig's warm body and the feeling of his silky fur were a great comfort to Stephen, who needed all the support he could get. He couldn't help giving a rough, grunting laugh when he remembered one of his schoolteachers—someone who'd been very mean to him, when he'd had problems with reading and writing. Stephen had been told by the teacher that he was "completely useless"!

The very thought of the teacher's cruelty drove him coldly, relentlessly on, until at last he had before him a clear and surprisingly readable copy of the notes—a description of the simple but crucial stages involved in turning the Postlethwaite Tree bark into the wonderful medicine.

Bertie's last comment had read: "A wonderfully speedy and beneficial remedy to be used for the treatment of malaria." Stephen hoped and prayed that it was so. He cast a quick thought back to the thicket. He hoped and prayed that he'd got the right tree.

72. Arara

Now that he knew exactly how to prepare the bark, Stephen felt quite torn. It would have been so much easier to carry out the whole process in the kitchen; but he didn't like to leave Murra-yari for more than a minute or two at a time. He decided on a compromise—to do the basic preparation outside on the kitchen table, then to roast and brew the bark back in the library.

Having made his decision he sprang into action, first ripping a strip off one of the sheets to use as a headband for his head. Nothing else suitable came to hand; he needed to be at his most efficient, which didn't allow for dangling hair.

With his hair bound neatly back and his sleeves rolled firmly up, he lit a small fire on the library hearth—the smallest possible fire, so as not to heat up the room. Then, having assembled all the things that he needed for chopping and pounding the bark in the kitchen, he worked and worked away at the task: grinding and scrunching as hard as he could; every so often whizzing back along to the library to see how Murra-yari was doing, to give him regular sips of water, and to make quite sure that his dear old friend didn't think that he'd gone and left him.

Murra-yari was getting worse; but Stephen didn't dare to hurry the process. With the crushed and roasted bark finally brewing in a small saucepan over the library fire, Stephen turned his full attention back to his patient. The poor man was clearly delirious. He had frightening spells of thrashing around—raving and muttering garbled sentences, or calling out excitedly.

"Arara, Stephen!" he shouted at one point. "We have Arara in the library. A whole flock of beautiful birds!" he clutched at Stephen's hand in excitement, his eyes wildly bright and staring. "I saw them flying. Did you see them?"

It seemed important to humor him.

"Oh, yes! I saw them. Beautiful birds!" Stephen smiled encouragingly, doing his best to calm Murra-yari.

The old man sank into his pillow, muttering over and over again: "Blue and red, red and blue, blue and red, red and blue. Beautiful! Beautiful! Beautiful birds!"

Stephen found this behavior frightening. Tig was clearly very disturbed. On several occasions he'd done his best to try and comfort Murra-yari, creeping up onto the bed, and trying to get close to his friend. But he'd soon been pushed away again or bounced off by thrashing limbs.

He lay now, completely bewildered, along the arm of the big leather chair, watching nervously from a distance. Stephen felt very sorry for him, but he hadn't the time to console him. He was fully employed, doing all that he could to try to cool Murra-yari down.

He seemed to remember that in olden times, when a patient had a high temperature, it was always thought best to keep them warm. Clothes and bedding were piled on high, in the false belief that that would help the patient to "sweat it out." Stephen thought that modern experts said that that was the wrong thing to do—that high temperatures could be danger-ous; they could lead to serious complications, they could even lead to death. Fever patients must be cooled down.

342

He remembered hearing recently about a child with a high temperature being immersed in a bath of cold water. He knew he couldn't manage that; but he decided to do the next best thing. So whilst the bark brewed over the fire, he worked hard on Murra-yari, covering him with cold, wet towels, and patting his head with a cool, wet flannel.

Some of the time, he seemed quite lucid. On one occasion he turned to Stephen, his eyes, although too bright to be healthy, firmly focused on Stephen's face.

"Apart from that one time on board ship, I have never, ever slept in a bed." His voice was surprisingly calm and normal. Stephen was quite taken aback. "I much prefer my hammock," he added.

Despite his worries, Stephen smiled. But he wasn't fooled by the occasional, calm moments. If anything, Murra-yari seemed hotter. Dangerously hot and dangerously dry, and in between the calmer spells, the delirious fits were very disturbing. He struggled on with hardly a pause, doing everything that he could to try to cool Murra-yari down: backward and forward to the scullery, replenishing bowls with fresh, cold water—working away with determination.

Tig lay quietly on the armchair, watching Stephen's progress intently, only occasionally letting out a small, chattering, whimpering sound, when he couldn't contain himself any longer. The other Bugwomps were anxious too. Stephen had noticed several sets of eyes, glowing in the darkness outside the library windows.

The eyes were reflecting the light from within the room, as the animals made every effort to see what was happening to Murra-yari. Some of the eyes, presumably belonging to Silkwomps, hung in space in the middle of the windows. Others were clustered lower down, their owners huddled on windowsills.

At last, to Stephen's great relief, the bark brew appeared to be ready. It had been boiling for the correct length of time, and the fluid had been reduced to the required level. Stephen removed the pan from the fire, spreading the embers wide in the hearth, anxious to put the fire right out. It wasn't really warm in the library, but he didn't want extra heat in the room.

With the greatest possible care, Stephen drained the precious fluid off into a large jug, straining it through a piece of muslin. Then he topped it off, as directed, with a pint of cold spring water. His hands shook, as he took up a spoon and measured out the correct dose, spooning it into the special macaw mug.

The medicine was finally ready, but Stephen eyed it with suspicion. He couldn't help feeling very worried. Supposing he had got it wrong? The wrong tree and the wrong bark! The wrong reading of the notes! His face was tense and his eyes troubled as he took the mug across to the bed; raising Murra-yari up, he pressed it gently to his lips.

"Please, God!" he said very quietly, as Murra-yari sipped the fluid.

Stephen sat beside the bed, anxiously watching his patient closely—waiting and dreading some reaction, gently pressing the cold, wet flannel on Murra-yari's hot, dry forehead. Would he keep the medicine down? Stephen was afraid he might not. The bucket stood on duty, ready.

Five. Ten. Fifteen minutes. The medicine had not come back. But Murra-yari was burning hot—perhaps even hotter now than before. Stephen sprang into action again with the bowls of water and cold wet towels, every so often raising the old man up and giving him tiny sips of water, working ceaselessly on and on, but always carefully watching the time, ready to give the next dose of medicine.

Having administered the second dose, and satisfied that Murra-yari was managing to keep it down, Stephen nipped out into the kitchen. He must find himself something to eat. He'd had nothing all day except water and fruit. Tig must be hungry too—and need an outside visit!

Returning some minutes later with a loaded tray of snacks—some for him and some for Tig—Stephen was stopped in his tracks in the hall by a sudden voice from the library.

"Stephen! Stephen! Are you there?" Murra-yari's voice sounded different.

73. Hope

Stephen ran quickly into the library, still grasping the tray in his hands, terrified of what he might find. He could see, as he crossed the Turkish rugs that Tig, who had returned before him, had reared up in the armchair, hiccupping and chattering loudly, staring across toward the bed, clearly very excited by something.

Dumping the tray on Theo's desk, Stephen rushed across to the bed. Holding the candlestick high in his hand, he peered down at Murra-yari. His old friend looked different now. He was still, quite obviously, very hot, but his body was wet with perspiration; he seemed calmer than before.

Stephen was overwhelmed with relief. He stood there beaming down at his patient.

"How are you feeling?" he asked Murra-yari.

"I am a little better, thank you. But I am so hot and so wet." He managed a very weak smile for Stephen. "I'm terribly thirsty. May I have water . . . ?"

Stephen held the mug while he drank, then he hovered about, uncertain—

345

uncertain and very anxious, for he wasn't sure what he ought to do next. He knew that when someone was sweating so much, it was very important to make up the loss of fluid by giving them plenty of water to drink. But he wasn't sure about the rest.

Should he keep Murra-yari cool, and go on applying the cold, damp towels? Or should he try to dry him off? He decided to do some of both: drying the man as best he could and changing the wet sheets for dry ones, mopping his face with a cool, damp flannel, and giving him frequent sips of water.

Once he had started this new regimen, it was almost nonstop action for Stephen, who had never before in his whole life seen anyone sweat so much. No sooner had he dried Murra-yari, changed the sheets, and settled him down, than he had to start all over again; for the clean, dry sheets were soon soaking wet. A large mound of soiled bedlinen was steadily growing on the library floor. But Stephen couldn't worry about that. He was only thankful and very grateful that the big Lansbury Hall linen cupboard had such a wonderful stock of sheets.

He worked away through the long, dark night, keeping a single candle burning. He worked on and on and on, determined to pull Murra-yari through; grabbing a bite to eat when he could and giving some bits and pieces to Tig; drinking plenty of water himself; dashing out to the pump in the yard to refill the water jug; nipping quickly into the throne room; splashing his face at the scullery tap in a desperate attempt to keep alert. Then back again to the same routine.

Once or twice he had dozed in his chair with dear, old Tig lying on his lap, only to jerk awake in alarm—worried, in case he had missed the time for giving his patient the next dose of medicine. And so the long, tiring night wore on.

As the first, pale light of dawn seeped in through the library windows, Stephen stirred in the big armchair. He stretched and yawned loudly, easing his aching back and legs, adjusting the band around his head.

The room seemed very peaceful now. Murra-yari was sleeping quietly. His breathing sounded even and strong, his skin felt cool to Stephen's touch. Tig had crept up onto the bed. He lay curled up beside his friend, with his eyes firmly closed.

Stephen smiled wearily, heaving himself out of the chair. He wandered across the room to a window to stand and gaze out at the view. Most of the Bugwomps had drifted away, somehow aware that the crisis was over.

Stephen grinned broadly to himself. There was not one Maggotwomp in sight. He didn't doubt their concern for their friend, but their stomachs had doubtless called them away and they'd left at the earliest possible moment. Life, which for any self-respecting Maggotwomp meant Feeding, must go on regardless.

"Stephen." A quiet voice from the bed drew him back across the room.

Although Murra-yari looked so much better—cool now and perfectly calm, Stephen could see he was still very weak, scarcely able to raise his head.

"It's wonderful to see that you're better," Stephen told him with a smile, raising him gently up on the bed, holding the macaw mug up to his lips, so that he could sip some water.

"Isn't it strange," Murra-yari said, as he noticed the mug in Stephen's hand, and the colorful birds caught his eye. "I had a peculiar dream, don't you know. I dreamt that we had a flock of Arara living happily here in the library."

He raised a long, thin arm from the bed and traced the design with a shaking finger, then slumped back weakly onto the pillow, adding in a faint voice, "Wouldn't it be wonderful if we did! I would so love to see the Arara."

347

74. Values

Cornwall was experiencing a very delightful Indian summer, as it often does in October—a gloriously mild spell, when the warm midday sunshine allowed for sitting outside in comfort. Stephen had carried the two, large kitchen chairs from the house, and had stood them on the forecourt just outside the front door, so that he and Murra-yari might enjoy a picnic lunch, whilst taking advantage of the sun.

A warm blanket had been draped around Murra-yari's knees and tucked in behind his back, to make quite sure that he didn't get chilled.

So far, he had made an excellent recovery. If he seemed a little less upright now, and his movements somewhat slower, he was at least eating well. He'd put back some of the weight that he'd lost and the twinkle had returned to his eyes.

As usual, their picnic was well attended. A group of Silkwomps hung along the front of the house, suspended from the passionflower vines. Stephen kept his eye on them; although they were gentle, friendly creatures, they were certainly very destructive as well, quite capable of stripping all the leaves from the vines and damaging most of the shoots as well. Each time he turned his head toward them, eyeing them in a suspicious way, they started up a "Womping" chorus—melancholy, reproachful voices, as if proclaiming their innocence.

Maggotwomps were, quite naturally, present. For Maggotwomps never, ever miss picnics. The Boss was there with her entourage, swinging her head in an ominous way, hissing her minions into submission, her ever-watchful, greedy eyes noting every piece of food that was lifted up to the human mouths, awaiting any tasty morsel that might, just possibly, fall to the ground.

A big group of Tigerwomps was huddled close to Murra-yari. Determined to be as comfortable as possible, they were making the best of a section of blanket that lay on the ground around his feet. Tig was nowhere to be seen.

Occasional splashing, plopping sounds came from the lake below the meadow, accompanied by gargling, gobbling calls. Thank goodness the Swampwomps had stayed in their lake!

Stephen sat chewing silently. He had not yet spoken to Murra-yari about his worries over money, about his anxiety over the house. It had started to eat away at him, but he'd managed to keep it all to himself, satisfied that Murra-yari had no idea of the problems ahead.

After his horrible illness, it seemed unfair to worry him, and it seemed pointless too; for there was, obviously, nothing that he could do. The problem was something that Stephen must keep to himself. Yet it gnawed away at the back of his mind, like some nasty, secret shame.

Murra-yari had gone very quiet. When Stephen looked around with a start, he found that the old man was watching him closely.

"Something is worrying you, my friend. I can see it in your eyes. Indeed, I have seen it there for some time. Won't you tell me what it is? Perhaps I can help you in some way."

Stephen couldn't hold out any longer. It was such a relief to unburden his worries. Why hadn't he done it before? In a way, it had not been fair to keep the whole thing to himself; besides, the old maxim "A trouble shared is a trouble halved" seemed to be true. As soon as Stephen had explained "the problem" to Murra-yari, he felt considerably better. At last the matter could be discussed openly, and they were in total agreement—somehow, between the two of them, they would come up with a solution.

In the end, it was dear old Tig, who finally solved the problem for them. He had made great progress over the summer. His wounds were now completely healed; only a slight discoloration of the fur marked the injured areas.

He was much larger, too, almost an adult, Stephen suspected. And he was far more independent, spending almost all his time out and about in the woods and the fields. Yet it saddened Stephen to see that Tig was still not fully accepted by the other Tigerwomps.

Once they reached a certain age, the young males of the species banded together to form a group. There were occasional frolics with the young females, but, generally speaking, they kept apart. They larked about, as youngsters will, though Stephen could see that the dominant male—the leader of the Tigerwomp troop—kept them all well in their places.

Tig was often to be seen in the company of this group of youngsters. But, as often as not, he was hanging around at the edge of the group. On several occasions, Stephen had seen the rest of them baiting and teasing poor Tig, then finally chasing him away.

As Murra-yari and Stephen sat together on the forecourt, thinking quietly about "the problem," Tig appeared from out of the rose garden. He made his way across toward them, demanded a place on Murra-yari's knee, then tried to climb inside his shirt.

"Oh, come on, old chap," Murra-yari said, quite kindly but very firmly. "I think you're too big for all that now, don't you?"

He held the Tigerwomp up in front of him at arm's length. The long, striped body dangled down heavily. Tig stared back with baleful eyes.

"Dear Tig," said Stephen. "He's so devoted to you, isn't he!"

Murra-yari laughed heartily. "I dare say he is quite attached to me," he said. "But there is another reason for his constancy. I have something that he likes much more than he likes me."

Stephen looked surprised. "Whatever do you mean by that?" he asked.

"As you know, all Tigerwomps love bright and shiny objects," Murra-yari said with a smile. "I'm afraid that they simply cannot resist them."

Stephen laughed, telling Murra-yari about the nest of shiny objects on the beach and how his watch had disappeared.

"Then you'll understand," said Murra-yari, "just what this naughty chap is after."

He slipped his hand inside his shirt and withdrew the golden pendant, then, slipping the leather thong over his head, he handed it across to Stephen. The large, chunky, gold object lay heavily in his hand, shining brightly in the sunshine in the most extraordinary way. Tig reared up in great excitement, giggling and chattering loudly, accompanied by a loud chorus.

In all the excitement and crisis of Murra-yari's illness, Stephen had quite forgotten the pendant.

"Where on earth did you get it?" he asked.

"It belonged to my father and to his father before him, and probably to many other leaders of my people for centuries," said Murra-yari. "It is a piece of pre-Columbian gold, very old and very special."

"But how do you come to have it now?" asked Stephen.

"When the rubber men came to visit our home, my family offered them hospitality. Everyone sat around, eating and drinking. They seemed to be friendly, pleasant people.

"But there must have suddenly come a time when my father became afraid and suspicious, for he called me across to his side. Turning his back on the rest of the people, he slipped the pendant into my hand. Then he whispered in my ear, 'Run away quickly, my son! Run into the forest and hide.'

"He said it in such a serious way that I knew that I had to obey him—although I have sometimes wished that I'd stayed. That was the last that I saw of my father," Murra-yari added softly.

"The pendant has always hung around my neck since that terrible day, long ago. I have always kept it hidden there. It has an inscription on the back. Theodore always wondered about that. He said it was not original,

351

that the people who fashioned this wonderful gold didn't have a system of writing. He made a rubbing of the inscription on paper. It's somewhere around here—probably, I suspect, in the library."

Stephen turned the pendant over to have a look at the inscription. He couldn't make any sense of it.

"Only Theodore and Bertie knew of the pendant's existence originally," Murra-yari continued. "You must have seen it when I was ill. And, of course, Tig discovered it when he was orphaned as a baby and I tucked him inside my shirt.

"So, I'm sorry to have to tell you," Murra-yari continued with a grin, "that he doesn't come to visit me just because he likes me so much. He comes because he cannot resist this big, shining, golden object."

It was almost as if the animal knew what they were saying about him. He sat on Murra-yari's lap with a very sheepish look on his face; then he turned away slowly; slipping down onto the ground, he disappeared across the forecourt.

They sat there quietly, watching him go.

Then suddenly, Murra-yari exclaimed, "By Jove! Of course, that's it! The pendant! That's the solution to our problem. How very clever of Tig."

"Whatever do you mean?" asked Stephen. He was still thinking about poor Tig. He had looked so very dejected.

"Theo told me on several occasions that this was a very valuable object. He said that it was worth a fortune—that it would raise a lot of money, if ever it were sold. Of course, I never expected to sell it, so that didn't mean anything to me.

"But I haven't much use for it now, after all, and my greatest concern is my family. Before I go to join our spirit world, I want to know that you will be safe, that this will always be your home—and a safe home for the Bugwomps too.

"So! How about selling the golden pendant? Bertie would advise us, I'm sure. Perhaps you could take it up to London."

"Well," said Stephen doubtfully. "It certainly is quite an idea. But I don't like to think of you losing it, especially after all these years."

"There are many more important things in life than gold. I hope you will always remember that," Murra-yari added firmly.

"But all the same," said Stephen doubtfully. "Are you sure that you want to sell it? It's such a beautiful thing," he said, lovingly stroking the smooth, bright gold. "I can't blame Tig for wanting to have it. I'd rather like to have it myself," he added, somewhat wistfully, reluctantly handing the pendant back.

"I should, indeed, be delighted to sell it," Murra-yari said with a beam.

"I need very few possessions—only my pipes, my bow, and my arrows. Nothing would give me greater pleasure than to know that my one and only possession of value will be the thing to save us all."

75. Good-byes

Some three weeks later, Stephen was ready for the trip to London. As soon as he had contacted Bertie, some special arrangements had been made. The old man seemed to know "the right people."

The pendant was to be included, at rather short notice, in a major sale at Sotheby's, a very famous auction house. Bertie had been advised that such a large, important gold object would raise a considerable sum of money. If that money were properly invested, it would be a large enough sum to assure the future of all at Lansbury Hall.

Stephen still had some misgivings about selling the pendant at all. It was such a fabulous object. But Murra-yari seemed quite happy, so he said no more about it. He certainly didn't want to spoil his dear, old friend's obvious pleasure at being the one to save them all.

There was an almost festive air about the place on the day that Stephen set off. As he and Murra-yari came down the steps in front of the house, a chorus of gleeful gobbling and gargling rose up from the lake below.

Stephen grinned down across the meadow. From where he stood on the overgrown drive, he could just make out the churning water and could hear the distant plopping of bodies.

A multiplicity of Maggotwomps cavorted about their feet on the fore-court, then followed them for a short distance. But they soon gave up and dropped behind. This, so they sensed, was a trip without food.

Along the wooded section of the drive, Silkwomps swung and sang in the branches. The whole troop of Tigerwomps moved in single file through the rhododendron wilderness, escorting their two human friends with a great deal of chattering and giggling, but gradually quieting down again, the nearer they came to the gates and the road.

When they all arrived at the great gates, Murra-yari reached down into his pocket and retrieved the large key that hung from a chain attached to his belt.

Stephen turned to him. "I shall be back in three days' time," he said. "Not tomorrow or the next day, but the day after that. I shall come down on the morning train. I'll be back sometime in the afternoon. You will be alright, won't you?" he asked, with a note of concern in his voice.

Murra-yari seemed almost back to normal now—fully recovered, Stephen thought. But despite the old man's great delight at finding a solution to their financial problem, and his claim to be back to normal, he seemed to tire quickly now.

Stephen looked closely at his face. The smile was still as sweet as ever, the eyes still bright and shining. But were they perhaps a little too bright? Were there tears in Murra-yari's eyes, as Stephen clasped the lean, brown hand?

"Of course, we shall all be perfectly alright," Murra-yari answered gruffly. "We shall do very well for ourselves, thank you." He included the Tigerwomps in his smile. The Tigerwomps chattered back.

"Please take good care of yourself in London and come back home to us safely, soon. Your family will need you here. We all have the greatest faith in you," he added quietly.

He cleared his throat. "Now. Here is the pendant. You had better wear it around your neck, and hide it well inside your shirt."

He lifted the leather thong over his head and handed it across to Stephen. As the pendant spun and flashed in the sunlight, an excited chattering rose up from the group of Tigerwomps around their feet. Stephen and Murra-yari looked down; they laughed at the sea of amazed faces—at all the round, green, staring eyes.

Tig had pushed himself to the front of the group. He had reared up on his tail end, watching the transaction with obvious excitement and dismay. Stephen swept him up off the ground.

"I hope you're going to behave yourself while I'm away," he said, smoothing the Tigerwomp's silky head. "And make quite sure that you look after Murra-yari. He has spent a lot of time and energy looking after you, you know." And he handed the animal over to Murra-yari, who tucked him firmly under one arm.

Tig struggled for a moment or two, as if he wanted to follow Stephen. But Murra-yari, speaking gently, soon had him under control.

"You know perfectly well that you mustn't go out through the gate," he said very firmly to Tig. "You wouldn't last long out there on the road. So come along now. You stay with me."

With a quick handshake, Stephen went out through the gates and started off along the lane. The pendant seemed surprisingly heavy as it hung around his neck. He raised his hands to the neck of his shirt, doing up all the buttons carefully.

It wouldn't do to be seen on the train or on the London underground wearing a huge chunk of gold like that. His mission was of the greatest importance. Whatever happened, it must succeed.

A little way along the lane, he turned to wave to Murra-yari. The forest Indian waved his hand—just once in reply, then he disappeared from sight.

76. Mission Accomplished

It was a fine October morning. Stephen sat comfortably in a window seat as the train made its way back down to Cornwall. There was a rather smug grin on his face, as he sat and watched the world go by. His mission was certainly well accomplished; and as the train sped along, he considered the events of the past few days with an air of great satisfaction.

The auction had gone extremely well—even better than expected. The gold pendant had reached a record price for such an artifact. A check for a very large sum of money—many, many thousands of pounds—had been handed over to the bank. In the future the bank would handle all Stephen's financial affairs—overseen, of course, by Bertie. Security for himself and for Lansbury Hall was now assured.

On the strength of this success, Stephen had got quite carried away. He had bought two handsome, black sweatshirts from a special charity. He very much liked the idea that some of the money he'd paid for the shirts would go to help Indians in the Amazon.

357

The shirts were beautifully decorated with a bold design of macaws—turquoise-blue and red macaws, of course. One shirt was for himself and the other for Murra-yari, who would finally have his Arara. Stephen grinned with delight at the thought.

He had also bought not just one, but two new pairs of very smart sneakers. The faithful, old, black things that he'd worn for so long were in a very sorry state. Somehow he'd grown very fond of them; when it had come to throwing them away, he had found himself strangely reluctant. It might have been appropriate to have a ceremonial pyre—to have sent them off in a manner befitting their age and their status; but this had not seemed practical whilst walking along on the Thames embankment.

Finally, after some deliberation, he had propped them carefully in a prominent position on top of a rubbish bin. There was, after all, just a slim chance that they might be useful to somebody else. They might even find a new lease on life and wander along for many more miles.

Stephen had liked the idea of that; the sneakers had given him wonderful service. Their final performance, in walking him around Sotheby's auction room, had been such a laugh! For they had received some very odd looks from the smart clientele.

Stephen had thought it quite a joke that the very posh people all around him, some of them bidding so greedily for Murra-yari's magnificent pendant, had looked askance at his tatty, old shoes. They obviously thought him a very poor specimen.

"If only they knew," he had grinned to himself.

Stephen had remembered Murra-yari's words about the gold. Regardless of what money the pendant made, as long as he could keep Lansbury Hall and keep his special family, he was richer by far than any of them; though he couldn't help feeling a stab of regret when the pendant was finally whisked away to be handed over to its new owner.

As Stephen was leaving the auction house, he had had a rather strange encounter. A young girl had appeared at his elbow, obviously wanting to talk to him—a girl with a mass of dark-brown hair and friendly, smiling, blue-gray eyes. There was something vaguely familiar about her.

"Are you Stephen Lansbury?" she asked shyly.

Stephen had smiled and nodded awkwardly, his confidence suddenly draining away.

"My name's Beth Pos . . ."

But as she started to give him her name, a big crowd spilled out from the auction house onto the busy London pavement. The surge of people parted them, and she was suddenly lost from view. He'd been forced from the pavement into the road, narrowly missing a passing taxi.

By the time he had recovered himself and regained the pavement safely, the girl had completely disappeared. He couldn't see her anywhere, and in the end he had had to give up. But he couldn't help wondering who she was, and how it was that she knew his name. Had he seen her somewhere before?

Stephen had had to admit to himself that he'd rather liked the look of the girl. But if he ever did have a girlfriend—and at the moment that seemed unlikely—it could pose a big problem. The will had clearly stated that nobody, except relatives, could be brought to Lansbury Hall.

Walking back again along the embankment, some hours after leaving the old black sneakers on top of the rubbish bin, he was very pleased to see that they were gone. The bin had not been emptied yet; so they must have gone to a good, new home—a very satisfactory outcome.

Stephen's one big disappointment was that he hadn't managed to see Bertie. When he'd arrived at the Lincoln's Inn office, he had found the downstairs door wide open; but, after rushing up the stairs, his heart beating hard with anticipation, he had found to his complete dismay that Bertie's door was firmly locked. No amount of bold knocking had brought forth any response from within.

Stephen sat happily in the train, grinning down at his flashy footwear. Murra-yari would be amused. Perhaps the other pair might fit him.

He could hardly wait to get back home, to tell his dear, old friend the news. Murra-yari would be so thrilled—so proud to know that his special possession had provided the means for saving them all—just as he had hoped that it would. His eyes would light up with joy and pleasure. Stephen was looking forward to that.

And yet there was very sad news as well. Stephen's worst fears had been confirmed. He had visited an organization that defended the rights of tribal peoples, only to learn that Murra-yari's people, the Taluma, had all been wiped out long ago.

What a terrible thing to happen—to lose a whole tribe of people like that! It seemed to Stephen that Mankind was impoverished by such tragedies. For it wasn't just the people you lost, as if that weren't bad enough, but a whole body of information. The knowledge of an ancient culture—the greatest treasure in its possession—was totally lost to the world forever: songs and dances; myths and legends; a wealth of knowledge about the forest; plant lore and herbal medicine—knowledge acquired over thousands of years, all wiped out with the people themselves.

Stephen didn't know whether or not he ought to tell Murra-yari the sad news about the Taluma. Up until that time, he had managed to avoid telling his dear old friend anything about the modern destruction of the forests of the Amazon. He feared it would break Murra-yari's heart.

Sitting in the train and reading a bulletin that he had been given in London, he couldn't avoid the dreadful statistics: In the five centuries since the European conquest of the Brazilian Amazon, the Indian population had fallen by more than 90 percent. Of the originally estimated one thousand tribes, only just over two hundred remained.

Stephen hadn't realized the extent to which the forest Indians were still suffering. The instigation of their suffering took a rather different form from that experienced by Murra-yari's people. But it was quite as nasty, quite as lethal, and the end result was the same.

Another very interesting fact had emerged from his visit. He had often heard about "uncontacted" groups of Indians, and had always supposed that these were very primitive people who had never had any contact with the outside world. This, he now realized was completely wrong. There was no such thing as an "uncontacted" group in Amazonia. Some groups had, as a result of European intrusion, isolated themselves; but preconquest, most of the area had been covered by a dense network of trading routes, which was surprising news to Stephen.

A very small number of groups still remained isolated in the forest, avoiding contact. But these people, so he learned, were extremely vulnerable. They had no resistance to the diseases that were introduced by outsiders. Even the common cold could kill them.

Theodore's journal had told the story of how Sarko and Wamiru had been snatched away from their people as young boys. Having learned in London about a system called "debt slavery," Stephen began to understand how remarkable their escape had been.

Indians, so he learned, had been forced to work for the rubber barons. Having no money of their own, they had been given credit and encouraged to buy all sorts of things from the stores that were run by their bosses. Unable to earn enough to pay off what they owed, they had soon became ensnared by their debts—trapped in a form of slavery from which they could never hope to escape—and yet somehow Sarko and Wamiru had escaped.

The more he read about it, the more Stephen came to realize that it was the very governments of those countries that had allowed such things to happen, who were now, themselves, ensnared by debt—but debt on a very grand scale.

Millions of pounds had been borrowed to spend on the construction of roads—roads that often led nowhere. These, so Stephen learned, encouraged waves of settlers, who came to cultivate the land, destroying the forest to make their fields, stealing the Indians' tribal lands. But finding over and over again that the soil could not support their crops, they moved ever deeper into the forest, leaving a desert waste behind.

The statistics were there before Stephen's eyes: nearly five million acres of forest disappearing every year, much of it along corridors, thirty miles in width on either side of the roads.

Countless millions, so he read, had been spent on dams for hydroelectric power. These grand schemes destroyed more forest, flooded the Indians' tribal lands, upset the vital balance of rivers, then silted up and became useless—and all at huge financial cost, creating a truly gigantic debt.

Now, so Stephen read in the bulletin, the governments of those very same countries were using those debts as an excuse to exploit the forest and its inhabitants on a greater scale than ever. It was causing widespread despair and destruction. Unless the destruction stopped very soon, the Amazon forest would be no more.

As the train drew up at the station and he climbed down onto the platform, Stephen finally made the decision. No. He could not tell Murra-yari. But he vowed that someday, somewhere, somehow he would try to do something about it himself. He would have to find out what he could do. There must be some way of saving the forests.

In the meantime, he had a duty: to work as hard as he possibly could, along with Murra-yari, of course, to protect and to care for all the Bugwomps. For with the destruction of the Amazon, the Bugwomps that lived at Lansbury Hall might soon be the only ones left in the world.

With several other people arriving on the platform, Stephen managed to slip quickly past Petherick, the stationmaster; though he couldn't avoid the man's keen glance. The long walk from the station, the wonderful, clean, moorland air, and the sight of buzzards wheeling on high soon banished sad thoughts from Stephen's mind. The closer he came to Lansbury Hall, the more excited he became.

He strode on happily down the lanes, thinking about the wonderful greeting that he knew he would get on his arrival; planning the happy days ahead. He almost ran the last few yards. Clasping the gate handle joyfully, he pushed hard to open the gate.

Nothing happened. The gate was locked.

77. Such a Simple, Significant Act

Stephen stopped in his tracks with a jolt. He hadn't expected the gates to be locked. "Perhaps Murra-yari is resting," he thought. "He knows I can get in over the wall."

He retraced his steps back along the wall till he came to a part that he knew he could scale.

It was very quiet as Stephen made his way amongst the trees and onto the path that led along through the rhododendron wilderness—peculiarly quiet for a sunny, autumn afternoon. Everything was very still. No birds were singing.

There were no signs and no sounds of any Bugwomps either, which seemed odd to Stephen. He had fully expected a group of them to be lurking somewhere not far from the gates, awaiting his arrival. Perhaps they were planning a trick on him, and would jump out at him around the next corner.

He moved on quickly out of the wilderness, along the curving, overgrown drive and across the forecourt to the house, but still no sign of anyone. He felt a sudden sense of foreboding as he opened the front door and stepped quickly into the hall.

"Hullo-oh!" He called out anxiously. "Hullo there! Anybody home?"

There was no reply. The house seemed lonely and forlorn. Stephen ran quickly from room to room. Everything seemed in perfect order; but there was no sign of Murra-yari, and no sign of any Bugwomps.

He stood on the steps outside the house, looking across the estate and frowning. Everywhere seemed so extraordinarily empty. Stephen didn't like the feeling.

Then he gave a sudden laugh.

"Of course!" he said out loud. "They'll all be in the cave. They'll all be waiting for me there," and he set off at a rapid jog, up the track that led to the woods.

He sped along in his bright, new sneakers. It was going to be good to see them all. Down the path that led to the river and across the tree that spanned the water. They'd have a wonderful celebration. On he went through the banks of bracken, on through the tunnel and into the valley. What a good thing his new sneakers were washable!

When he came at last to the mystic pool, he paused for a moment to get his breath. The mysterious water always drew him. As he stood on its brink and sought the blue depths, he became aware of the strangest sound—a weird, unearthly, crooning noise, which seemed to come from the head of the valley—a very peculiar, musical sound, which seemed to float on the afternoon air.

Stephen ran a few steps along the path toward the cave. Then he stopped, uncertain, listening. It must be the Bugwomps making the noise. But what an extraordinary noise it was! And whatever could they be doing now? It sounded so sad. So terribly sad.

He walked on, very slowly now, listening carefully as he went.

The sorrowful chorus rose to a crescendo as Stephen appeared in the mouth of the cave. Then it dwindled and died away, as all of the Bugwomps noticed his presence.

Murra-yari lay in his hammock. His eyes were closed. He was sleeping peacefully. A gentle smile curved his lips.

Stephen stepped happily forward toward him. Then he stopped and stood there, staring. And all the happiness drained away.

He looked quickly around at the Bugwomps. The Bugwomps all stared back at him, their grief-stricken faces making it clear. It was Murra-yari's final sleep.

Stephen stood silently at the foot of the hammock, staring down at his good friend—bewildered by his disbelief, by an overwhelming sense of loss.

It was very peaceful now in the cave. All the animals lay quite still. They were watching and waiting for Stephen's next move.

At last, with the very greatest effort, Stephen pulled himself together. He knew exactly what had to be done.

"Come on, now then, all you fellows," he said rather gruffly, clearing his throat, and smiling weakly around at the Bugwomps. "There's work to be done."

And he busied himself about the cave, making a very simple sledge from the boards that formed the Tigerwomps' bench. Everyone bustled around him, helping.

The big key to the gates of Lansbury Hall was lying on top of the bench, together with its chain and clip. It must have been left there especially for him. Reluctantly, he picked it up and clipped it on to his own belt. Such a simple, significant act. Stephen had to bite his lip.

Blankets and a pillow were laid on the sledge, and Murra-yari, still in his hammock, was gently lowered into place. Stephen collected the old Indian's hunting bow, his arrows, and his panpipes, tucking them safely in beside him.

And so the cavalcade started out. It was not to be an easy trip; but the Bugwomps were a tremendous help. Steadying and tugging, pushing and pulling, they did everything that they possibly could to ease their dear old friend's last journey.

The Swampwomps were particularly helpful in all the wet places:

towing the sledge along like a raft through the channel of water inside the tunnel; rafting the sledge with its precious cargo safely across a calm stretch of the river.

The procession slowly wound its way toward the house, stopping to rest in the forecourt, whilst Stephen went through to the yard behind to collect some tools for digging, then quickly back into the house to pick up one of the carrier bags that was lying on the floor in the hall.

Then on they went again—on toward the woodland glade, where the mighty beech would welcome them. It had changed its colors, now ready for winter, and the warm, copper-brown glow of its foliage smiled down at the strange procession, halting beneath its wide-spreading arms.

There they all stopped and rested, whilst Stephen worked very hard: digging a large hole with the pick-axe, and using the long-handled Cornish shovel; preparing a final resting place for Murra-yari—a few feet from where Theodore lay.

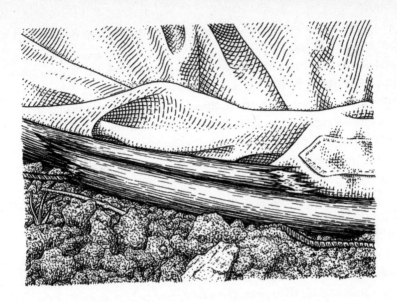

78. A Final Resting Place

It was late in the afternoon. Slanting, golden rays of mellow, autumn sunlight lit the woodland glade. The mighty beech tree, clothed in russet, overlooked the sad proceedings as Stephen laid Murra-yari to rest. Then he opened up the plastic carrier. Lifting the sweatshirt out of the bag, he laid it carefully across Murra-yari.

"I wanted you to have these Arara. I bought them especially for you," he whispered, trying to hold back the tears.

Then came the hardest task of all—the breaking of Murra-yari's bow. For his hunting days were over now.

Stephen stood, hesitating, beside the grave. He knew what he had to do. But he couldn't bear to hurt the bow. As he stroked the polished wood, the tears ran freely down his face.

Then, gritting his teeth, he broke the bow, and he laid it carefully in the grave, smiling down at the sleeping face.

"Rest comfortably, my dear old friend," he said. "I know that your spirit will always be with me." He covered Murra-yari carefully with a deep, soft blanket of woodland earth.

At last, it was finished. He stood well back. All of the Bugwomps were grouped about him, their gentle crooning filling the air. Stephen smiled down, through a mist of tears, at the sea of sad faces around his feet.

"Come along now, all of you," he said very gently but very firmly. "We shall be alright, I promise you. I shall miss him badly, too. But I still have you, my good friends. You'll always be my family, and we'll go on forever and ever."

The crooning gradually died away. A lone figure detached itself from the group, and started forward toward Murra-yari's grave. A murmuring of discontent began to rise from the rest of the Bugwomps.

The large Tigerwomp stopped in its tracks, then turned to face them all. It was Tig. He looked up at Stephen with baleful eyes—huge, green eyes, that seemed sadder than ever. Then he glared boldly around at the group.

Stephen stood still and held his breath. The murmuring faded and died away. Tig turned very slowly back then continued across to Murra-yari's grave, where he established himself at the foot of the mound.

"Oh, Tig!" Stephen said, in a choking voice. "So it wasn't just the gold pendant. You really loved him, after all."

Tig lay proudly in his place.

The Boss Maggotwomp made her way, almost humbly, to sit at the bottom of Theodore's grave. The glade was filled with kindly spirits and everybody seemed at peace.

With a final encouraging smile at Tig, Stephen turned and left the glade.

Tomorrow he would come and build the "house."

Tomorrow he would carve and erect the cross.

Tomorrow . . .

Epilogue

Stephen's days were now empty, and he felt very much alone. He saw very little of the Bugwomps, who were all out doing Bugwomp things in preparation for the winter. At such a busy time of the year, they had very little time for Stephen; although he understood why, it saddened him to see them so seldom at a time when he badly needed company.

He had tried to keep himself busy: visiting the cave with a heavy heart, and rebuilding the wooden platform—an important haven for the troop of Tigerwomps. He had also spent time in the woodland glade—building the "house" over the grave, and setting up a wooden cross that he'd fashioned with his knife.

He was getting worried about Tig, who was spending much too much of his time lying in his place at the foot of Murra-yari's grave, when he ought to be out foraging. Stephen had picked him up and tried to cuddle him; but he didn't seem to want the attention. He only wriggled and chattered loudly, demanding to be put back down so that he could resume his vigil. Stephen knew that it wasn't healthy; but there wasn't much he could do about it, except to take a few snacks for Tig on his daily pilgrimage to the glade.

A short note had been sent off to Bertie, just to tell him the sad news. In the hope of finding a reply, he wandered down to the gate each morning—late enough to avoid the postman.

On the tenth day after he had sent the letter, as he made his way through the rhododendron wilderness, Stephen was surprised to hear a car door slam out in the lane, and then a vehicle driving away. The postman must be very late.

Safe in the knowledge that the postman had left, Stephen emerged from the wilderness and set off across to the gate. He stopped abruptly in his tracks.

A figure was standing in the lane—a girl in denim jeans with a rucksack. A girl with a mass of dark-brown hair, and friendly, smiling, blue-gray eyes. He recognized her immediately. It was the girl he'd met in London—the girl outside the auction house.

Beth! Yes! That was her name. Then it suddenly came to him—where he had originally seen her—outside Bertie Postlethwaite's office, on his very first visit there. Now, it seemed like a lifetime ago.

The girl stood quietly, watching and waiting. Stephen didn't waste any time. He started forward toward the gate, a smile of welcome on his face.

"Hang on, Beth! I've got the key." He fumbled with the long chain that hung from his belt with the key attached. "Just hold on and I'll open the gate."

Author's Note

Because the research for *The Valley of Secrets* has given me so much pleasure, and I have learned so much about so many interesting subjects, I have decided to include a list of species, a select bibliography, and a list of relevant organizations. I hope that these will help any readers who find that the book has whetted their appetite for further information.

List of Species

Common/Book Name	Scientific Name	Chapter
alder tree	*Alnus glutinosa*	28, 33
algae	*Algae*	43
anaconda [sucuri]	*Eunectes murinus*	44
ants	*Formicidae*	20
apple	*Malus domestica*	10, 17, 20, 30, 49, 65
banana	*Musa acuminata*	19, 30, 35, 41, 42, 65
barley	*Hordeum vulgare*	28
barnacle	*Balanus spp.*	32
bat, greater horseshoe	*Rhinolophus ferrumequinum*	26, 53, 54
beech	*Fagus sylvatica*	4, 13, 28, 33, 62, 78
bees	*Apoidea*	17, 20, 36, 62, 68
beetle	*Coleoptera*	40
bignoniaceae [trumpet-shaped flowers]	*Bignoniaceae*	36, 39
birch	*Betula spp.*	13
bluebell	*Hyacinthoides non-scripta*	33
bracken	*Pteridium aquilinum*	31, 32, 33, 36, 58, 77
bramble or blackberry	*Rubus fruticosus agg.*	20, 33, 36, 52, 68

373

Common/Book Name	Scientific Name	Chapter
buttercup	*Ranunculus spp.*	13, 33
butterfly, brimstone	*Gonepteryx rhamni*	31
butterfly, large blue	*Maculinea arion*	31
butterfly, morpho	*Morpho spp.*	40
butterfly, painted lady	*Cynthia cardui*	23, 24
buzzard	*Buteo buteo*	1, 13, 38, 55, 76
caiman	*Caiman spp.,*	43, 44
	Melanosuchus sp. & Paleosuchus spp.	
campion, red	*Silene dioica*	13, 33
carrot	*Daucus carota*	28, 36
catfish, giant	*Piraiba Brachyplatystoma filamentosum*	41
celandine, lesser	*Ranunculus ficaria*	1
cherry [black cherries]	*Prunus cultivar*	17
cinchona tree	*Cinchona spp.*	43, 48
[source for bark from which		
quinine is produced]		
climbing plants, vines, and creepers	Numerous different	6, 28, 36, 52, 53, 64
	families, species, & genera	
crab, shore	*Carcinus maenas*	32
crowfoot, round-leaved	*Ranunculus omiophyllus*	37
[floating water plants]		
cucumber	*Cucumis sativus*	39, 42, 49
dipper	*Cinclus cinclus*	31
dock	*Rumex spp.*	16
dolphin, pink river	*Inia geoffrensis*	41
dragonfly	*Odonata*	62
eagle, ornate hawk	*Spizaetus ornatus*	43
eel, electric	*Electrophorus electricus*	41
egret, snowy	*Egretta thula*	41

Common/Book Name	Scientific Name	Chapter
ferns, giant and others	*Filices*	6, 13, 28, 33, 39, 53
fig tree [strangler]	*Ficus spp.*	44
firefly	*Phrixothrix spp.*	40
fish	*Pisces*	13, 27, 32, 41, 42, 68
flote weed [ribbonlike waterweed]	*Glyceria fluitans*	37, 38
foxglove	*Digitalis purpurea*	13, 62, 64
fruit-eating fish: pacu	*Myleus pacu*	41
gorse	*Ulex europaeus* & *Ulex gallii*	13, 36, 37
greengage tree	*Prunus domestica subsp. italica*	2, 3, 17
hazel [hedges]	*Corylus avellana*	13
heron, gray	*Ardea cinerea*	31
heron, tiger [striped heron]	*Tigrisoma lineatum*	41
holly tree	*Ilex aquifolium*	28
honeysuckle	*Lonicera periclymenum*	28, 36, 52
howler, red [howler monkey]	*Alouatta seniculus*	40
hummingbird	*Trochilidae*	43
Indian balsam	*Impatiens glandulifera*	62
iris, yellow	*Iris pseudacorus*	27, 31
ivy	*Hedera hibernica*	13, 28, 62
jacaranda tree	*Jacaranda mimosifolia*	39
kapok [giant buttressed tree]	*Ceiba pentandra*	48, 50
kelp	*Laminaria saccharina*	32
kingfisher	*Alcedo atthis*	62
lark	*Alauda arvensis*	20, 37, 38
liana		39, 44
[ropelike woody climbers, numerous species from a number of genera]		
liana, spiny: palm vine	*Desmoncus spp.*	44
lichen	*Mycophycota*	20, 53

Common/Book Name	Scientific Name	Chapter
lichen, gray-green	*Cladonia spp.*	28, 37
macaw, red and green [red & turquoise-blue macaw—arara]	*Ara chloroptera*	10, 39, 67, 71, 72, 76
mahogany	*Swietenia macrophylla*	40, 67
maize [sweet corn]	*Zea mays*	28, 61, 65
manioc [strange, shrubby plants in vegetable garden]	*Manihot esculenta*	28, 45, 65
may tree or hawthorn	*Crataegus monogyna*	20
moonflower	*Selenicereus wittii*	8, 9, 45, 46, 48
mosquito	*Culicidae*	13, 40, 43
moss	*Bryophyta*	1, 13, 20, 28, 53, 62
moth, British hawk	*Sphingidae*	48
moth, common marbled carpet	*Chloroclysta truncata*	20
nettles	*Urtica dioica*	11
oak	*Quercus robur*	23, 24, 26, 28
old-man's beard	*Clematis vitalba*	4
onions	*Allium cepa*	28
orchid	*Orchidaceae*	39, 44
otter, European	*Lutra lutra*	27
otter, giant	*Pteronura brasiliensis*	41
owl	*Tytonidae & Strigidae*	14, 52
oystercatcher [long-beaked birds]	*Haematopus ostralegus*	11
palms	*Palmaceae*	34, 35, 39, 40
parsley	*Petroselinum crispum*	28
passionflower, blue	*Passiflora caerulea*	28, 31, 36, 41, 67
passionflower, red [scarlet]	*Passiflora coccinea*	22, 26, 36, 52, 74
peas	*Pisum sativum*	19, 28

Common/Book Name	Scientific Name	Chapter
pine	*Pinus spp.*	13
pium fly	*Psaroniocompsa incrustata* (= *Simulium incrustatum*)	40, 45
plum	*Prunus domestica subsp. Domestica*	17
potatoes	*Solanum tuberosum*	19, 28, 29, 36
primrose	*Primula vulgaris*	1
raven	*Corvus corax*	53, 55
reed, common	*Phragmites australis*	27, 33
rhododendron	*Rhododendron arboreum*	3, 14, 18, 68, 75, 77
rook	*Corvus frugilegus*	20
rose	*Rosa spp.*	22, 27, 63, 74
rubber tree	*Hevea brasiliensis*	42
sea anemone	*Actinaria*	32
seaweed	*Phaeophyta, Chlorophyta, & Rhodophyta*	31, 32, 33
shampoo plant: soap rattan or chewstick	*Gouania lupuloides*	47
shark, bull	*Carcharinus leucas*	41
shrimp, common	*Crangon crangon*	32
sloth, three-toed	*Bradypus tridactylus*	43
snowdrop	*Golanthus nivalis*	1
spinach	*Spinacia oleracea*	36
stingray, freshwater	*Potamotrygon spp.*	41
stonecrop, English [tiny, pink, & fleshy rock plants]	*Sedum anglicum*	37
stork	*Ciconidae*	41
strawberries, wild	*Fragaria vesca*	62
swallow	*Hirundo rustica*	62
tapir, Brazilian [anta]	*Tapirus terrestris*	40, 44

Common/Book Name	Scientific Name	Chapter
tomato	*Lycopersicon esculentum*	10, 16, 39, 42, 43
tree ferns [unusual-looking trees]	*Dicksonia sellowiana*	28
trout	*Salmo trutta*	57
violet, bog	*Viola palustris*	37
violet, common	*Viola riviniana*	1
watercress	*Rorippa nasturtium-aquaticum*	13
water lily, Victoria [gigantic or giant water lily]	*Victoria amazonica*	27, 41
wheat [In UK "corn" = wheat]	*Triticum aestivum*	28, 41, 61, 65
willow tree	*Salix cinerea*	37
wren	*Troglodytes troglodytes*	31
yew	*Taxus baccata*	21

Select Bibliography

Some of the following books are out of print, but all should be available through good local libraries.

Anscombe, Isabelle. *Arts and Crafts Style*. New York: Rizzoli, 1991.

Beckett, Kenneth A. (comp.) *Illustrated Dictionary of Botany*. London: Triune Books, 1977.

Campbell, Alan T. *Getting to Know Waiwai: An Amazonian Ethnography*. New York: Routledge, 1995.

Davis, Shelton H. *Victims of the Miracle: Development and the Indians of Brazil*. New York: Cambridge University Press, 1977.

Descola, Philippe. *The Spears of Twilight: Life and Death in the Amazonian Jungle*. New York: New Press, 1996.

Hanbury-Tenison, Robin. *A Question of Survival for the Indians of Brazil*. New York: Scribner, 1973.

Hemming, John. *Red Gold: The Conquest of the Brazilian Indians*. Cambridge, Mass.: Harvard University Press, 1978.

Honigsbaum, Mark. *The Fever Trail: In Search of the Cure for Malaria*. New York: Farrar, Straus and Giroux, 2002.

Kricher, John. *A Neotropical Companion: An Introduction to the Animals, Plants and Ecosystems of the New World Tropics*. Princeton, N.J.: Princeton University Press, 1997.

Lambourne, Lionel. *Victorian Painting*. London: Phaidon Press, 1999.

Mackenzie, John, ed. *The Victorian Vision: Inventing New Britain*. London: V&A Publications, 2001.

McEwan, Colin, Cristiana Baretto, and Eduardo Neves, eds. *Unknown Amazon: Culture in Nature in Ancient Brazil*. British Museum Press, 2001.

Mee, Margaret. *Margaret Mee: In Search of Flowers of the Amazon Forest*. Woodbridge, England: Nonesuch Expeditions Ltd., 1988.

Naylor, Gillian. *William Morris by Himself*. Book Sales, 2000.

Prance, G. T., and T. E. Lovejoy, eds. *Key Environments: Amazonia*. Oxford, England: Pergamon Press, 1985.

Sponberg, Stephen A. *A Reunion of Trees: The Discovey of Exotic Plants and Their Introduction into North American and European Landscapes*. Cambridge, Mass.: Harvard University Press, 1990.

Wallace, Alfred R. *Infinite Tropics: An Alfred Russell Wallace Anthology*. New York: Verso, 2002.

West, David. *The Aeneid: A New Prose Translation*. London: Penguin, 2001.

Relevant Organizations

Cornish Studies Library, Redruth, TR15 2AT. www.cornwall.gov.uk

The De Morgan Centre for the Study of 19th Century Art and Society, London, SW18 1RZ. www.demorgan.org.uk

Department of Ethnography, British Museum, London, W1S 3EX. www.thebritishmuseum.ac.uk/ethno/ethhome.html

The Eden Project, Cornwall, PL24 2SG. www.edenproject.com

National Maritime Museum, Cornwall, Falmouth, TR11 3QY. www.nmmc.co.uk

National Tropical Botanic Garden, Kalaheo, HI 96741. www.ntbg.org

Natural Resources Defense Council, New York, NY 10011. www.nrdc.org

Rainforest Conservation Fund, Chicago, IL 60614. www.rainforestconservation.org

Royal Institution of Cornwall, Truro, TR1 2SJ. www.royalcornwallmuseum.org.uk

Save the Rainforest. www.savetherainforest.org

South West Tourism, Exeter, EX2 5WT. www.swtourism.co.uk

Survival International, London, EC1M 7ET. www.survival-international.org
Survival is a worldwide organization supporting tribal peoples. It stands for their
right to decide their own future and helps them protect their lives, lands, and human
rights.

United States Botanic Garden, Washington, D.C. 20024. www.usbg.gov

About the Author

CHARMIAN HUSSEY began her career modeling in London. Later she trained as an archaeologist, studying at the University of London Institute of Archaeology and working on excavations in Great Britain and the Middle East.

Through her interest in the indigenous tribal peoples of the world, she has developed an increasing concern for those peoples and for the future of the very world in which they—and we—live.

Her first book—a chronicle in verse and prose of the Iraqi conflict in 1991—was published to draw attention to the plight of Iraqis suffering under the regime of Saddam Hussein, and to raise money to help them.

Ms. Hussey's global view has long encompassed a deep concern for the welfare of the world's rain forests. *The Valley of Secrets* combines this understanding and passion with her love of the Cornish countryside, where she now lives and farms with her husband in the timeless isolation of a hidden valley.